PETER

A MATTER OF DOUBT

THE NOVEL OF CLAUDE BERNARD

Copyright © 2011 Dr Peter Wise
All rights reserved.
ISBN: 1466339896
ISBN 13: 9781466339897

ACKNOWLEDGEMENTS

Many people have helped me to draw the threads of Claude Bernard's life together. Marie-Aymée Marduel's descriptive genealogical analysis, personal records and copies of important documents were the starting point of my research. Christian Guillarme, president of the association *Les Amis du Musée Claude Bernard* in St Julien-en-Beaujolais allowed me to access Bernard's dwellings and personal belongings, and provided important additional background material.

I would also like to thank the staff of the *Collège de France, l'Institut de France*, the *bibliothèque* of the medical school of the University of Paris and the *Bibliothèque inter-universitaire de Santé* in Paris (previously BIUM) as well as the *Bibliothèque Municipale* of Lyon. Above all, my wife Irma helped in so many wonderful ways by collating information, listening patiently to my ideas and reading the text.

Additional factual elements of Bernard's life and work were obtained from newspaper archives and the wide variety of resources that I have listed in the bibliography section of my academic website www.claude-bernard.co.uk. In creating the fictitious content of letters and dialogue, I have tried to remain true to the situations and relationships obtained from existing literature, in accord with the general concept of the biographical novel.

Further themes on CB's life and work are accumulating on my blog http://tinyurl.com/BernardBlog. Reactions to the book are also welcome: either there, or on www.twitter.com@wisepeter1.

PW

CONTENTS

Prologue		*vii*
Chapter 1	First Steps	*1*
Chapter 2	A Play On Words	*15*
Chapter 3	To Paris with Hope	*33*
Chapter 4	The Awakening	*49*
Chapter 5	In New Directions	*65*
Chapter 6	Painful Decisions	*81*
Chapter 7	More Than One Revolution	*97*
Chapter 8	Arrows Find Their Mark	*113*
Chapter 9	Sweet Success, Sour Discord	*127*
Chapter 10	A Mounting Controversy	*143*
Chapter 11	Event Extraordinary	*163*
Chapter 12	No Pleasure Without Pain	*183*
Chapter 13	A New Way Of Life	*203*
Chapter 14	Most Complex Emotions	*219*
Chapter 15	Another Visit, Another Challenge	*237*
Chapter 16	To Face Reality	*257*
Chapter 17	Toward The Highest Honour	*269*
Chapter 18	Shine On The Horizon	*285*
Chapter 19	A Storm Brewing	*305*
Chapter 20	Soft Awakening, Hard Decisions	*327*
Chapter 21	More Problems, - But More Solutions	*345*
Chapter 22	A Slow Decline	*359*
Chapter 23	Disclosure	*371*
Epilogue		*381*

PROLOGUE

Hope and dreams are the stuff of youth – and for some, it stays that way. Others will try harder: striving to excel, to become rich – or simply to understand what makes the world turn. At age 18, Claude still dreamed, but he was also becoming inquisitive. With surprisingly bad results from the Jesuit college of Villefranche-sur-Saone, his parents had decided to enrol him for one more year in the college of Thoissey – hoping that this reputable institution would get him his *baccalaureate*. It was quite far from their home in the Beaujolais, so that boarding was the only option. Claude was abysmally lonely there: one good friend from Villefranche days was already working in Lyon, and two others were studying in Paris. Somehow, he could not bring himself to befriend his new classmates. Distancing himself from them only alienated him further.

Nor did his studies inspire him any more than at his previous college. He could get passionate about some of the science topics. That man Fresnel was surely a genius: his clever prismatic lenses now sat atop lighthouses that ringed the coast of France, making shipping channels so much safer. The subject of philosophy also interested Claude. 'One should always doubt', the great Descartes had written. On a couple of occasions then, he had made himself unpopular by challenging his teachers. All he achieved was a snigger from the students and disapproval from his teacher – and so he decided to keep his thoughts to himself. If he could find a quiet corner after his lessons, he just sat and read. The new *romantisme* was not much in evidence in the college library, and when writing to his friend in Lyon, he often bemoaned that fact. He really enjoyed writing. His letters had become longer and longer. They were often in verse, interposed with descriptive and highly imaginative prose.

No one in the family had trodden a literary path. Most had worked with their hands. Claude's father had acquired quite good mathematical skills, but it had not helped him much. His less-educated mother had her feet firmly planted on the ground: it was she who generally made the decisions. Their finances were not very sound, despite owning several hectares of vines – and what would they say when they discovered that he had again flunked his *bac*? He was terrified.

Sharing his coach now are two girls. Both are buxom, and their pouting lips stir his manhood – uncomfortably. Claude is quite handsome in a lanky sort of way. Yet, preoccupied as he is with yet another dismal college report in his satchel and so apprehensive about what was to come, he cannot bring himself to respond to their coquettish sidelong glances with anything more than a faint smile.

In Villefranche, he changes from his coach to a trap driven by a villager whom he knows well. As they wend their way through the rolling vine-studded hills, he enjoys the local gossip: about the unexpectedly good harvest and the new road which will shorten the access to St Julien, village of his birth. Wearily, he now climbs the hill to the tiny hamlet of Chatenay. His heart is thumping – and much more from anxiety rather than from the steepness of the track.

CHAPTER 1

FIRST STEPS

"*Merde!*" – he mumbles as he approaches the cottage. Pushing open the door, he flexes his neck to avoid striking his head on the lintel. Relieved that there is no-one about, he quietly takes the stairs to his room. Bag and satchel hit the floor as he ignores the letter on the table and slumps on his bed.

Claude really wanted only one thing from life: the freedom to express himself in fine language. His ambition was incomprehensible to his parents – and now to his college as well. In his satchel is the report: '*...he cannot accept what he is taught... dreams...lets his imagination run away with him...*' He had certainly enjoyed history: in his eyes, simply facts laced with fantasy. He had also liked dabbling in Descartes and the importance of seeking truth. Yet where *was* the truth – supported by proof – in all those facts that the college had expected him to regurgitate? The disillusioned Claude had indeed resorted to dreaming; of becoming a Eugène Scribe or a Victor Hugo: basking too in the themes and colours of Poussin and of Delacroix, whose print of *Dante and Virgil in Hell* he would never, ever part with.

While reading the damning report on the coach, Claude's anxiety had mounted at the prospect of confronting his father. He would have wanted better results: some idea of a future career, too. He would surely again hold up Ronne as an example: a committed pharmacy apprentice in Lyon – or perhaps Claude's other good friends, Lambert and Chrétien who were studying law in Paris.

The scene is exactly as expected: his father at the table opposite him, alternately venting anger and disappointment. Claude can accept the reasonableness of his complaints: yes, indolent, and so ungrateful for the opportunities presented. His mother bustles, listening carefully, yet pretending concern only for the tureen of soup on the hearth. The child in the enclosure wedged under stairs whimpers at her father's tirade:

"Why did we bother? The Jesuits in Villefranche couldn't do the right thing by you; and now this...!"

Claude shrugs while his father's attention shifts towards the sheets of paper on the table in front of him. He frowns at the comments scrawled on the report of his son's year at Thoissey; such an expensive attempt to get him his *bac*. Tall, serious, Jean-Francois is also a teacher; of necessity. Several hectares of vines plus the cottage had been his wife's dowry, but the local market for fruity Beaujolais wine had become saturated. So why not Paris?

With his friend Paul Richard, he had sent their precious commodity up to the warehouses in Bercy by way of the Saone, Marne and Seine. The wine had spoiled; the venture had failed. Each day now, a few children arrive at the large room adjoining the kitchen. For meagre fees, Bernard senior consolidates their arithmetic, reading and writing. It pleases the better-off families who want that bit more for their children than the *curé* can offer at the church school in St Julien – and Madame Bernard supplies the soup.

"Leave him now!" She interjects, almost roughly, "He did his best."

She turns to Claude; patiently.

"So what *do* you want to do now?"

Shoulders droop; head too as he fumbles in his pocket. He nervously unfolds the note that he had extracted from the envelope in his room.

"I don't really know, but Ronne has just written from Lyon. He seems to like his apprenticeship with Millet. Perhaps *I* should try pharmacy too: apparently, you don't need a *bac* for that. The pharmacy now supplies medicaments to the veterinary college, so Millet needs more help. He is offering a *stage*. I could try it, and if I liked it..."

His voice trails off as he again sees anger contorting his father's face.

"...and how much would that cost us again – just so that the two of you can go cavorting around Lyon together?"

"Go on upstairs, Claude." His mother, softly. "Your father and I will discuss it later."

He sighs and stands; tall frame unwinding from the uncomfortable chair, nodding a vague goodnight. Patting his sister gently on the head as he passes the enclosure, he wearily climbs the stairs. Shortly afterwards, he is only vaguely aware of raised voices as sleep displaces morose thoughts.

"You're very hard on the boy, François."

"Of course I am! At eighteen, I was working the vineyards – and studying as well. He's a dreamer, Jeanne – just as his report says. Believe me; he won't get anywhere that way."

"Yes, and where are *we* now? With all your study and your ideas, it's still my Saunier vines which give us our living, and ...."

" I know my plan for Paris didn't work out. That was Richard's fault, though. Anyhow, my teaching is going well enough."

"For the moment; but you know quite well that the mayor doesn't want you to teach beyond the end of the year. And your silkworms will not be much good to anyone either, if the merchants get their way and import foreign silk. It will put our silkweavers out of work."

Crestfallen at the harsh truth, he glances at his weary, even haggard face in the mirror over the dresser. Jeanne Bernard embraces him; nestles her head against his chest.

"He needs time to himself, François. He will find his way, and we can still help him if necessary. For now, let him keep himself busy with the harvest."

The toil and ritual of harvest – *le vendange* – is in full swing. Claude tolerates, half enjoys the daily task, anticipating the faint reward of evening festivities fuelled by the boisterous *montagnards*. They have descended from the hills for a season's work, and relax each night with bawdy songs, good food and wine – and with any woman prepared to submit to their passion between the tidy rows of tall vines. Claude enjoys the atmosphere, but retires early to his room to write – often in verse – to Lambert and Chrétien in Paris, and now especially to fledgling pharmacist Benoit Blanc, whom only he calls Ronne: '...*and I have this idea for a piece of vaudeville – like the one we saw during Easter in Villefranche.*'

Hands sticky with grape juice, back aching and longing for rest, he passes Lombard's elegant manor house. It completely obscures the family cottage and the rambling garden lying behind it; the leaves of two mulberry trees nurturing a probably pointless silkworm colony. A letter addressed to him in an unfamiliar hand lies on the kitchen table. He opens it, reads it and smiling broadly shows it to his mother busy folding laundry in the adjoining pantry.

"He'll take me, Maman! Millet wants me to begin a trial *stage* already in November."

Madame Bernard hugs her son; savouring the rare enjoyment of seeing him enthusiastic.

"I'm pleased, Claude, and don't worry about your father. He just wants you to have a secure future. Does Millet talk about costs?"

"He says that for my trial period, he will provide accommodation free, and even give me spending money – and at the moment there wouldn't be tuition fees. If he eventually accepts me for training, it seems that there will be charges, and I will have to register with the authorities as an apprentice."

Madame Bernard takes the letter from Claude:

"Leave this with me. I will talk to your father. He can get more detail from Monsieur Millet concerning those charges, but I'm sure that he'll agree. I only hope that you will be happy there."

As usual he is early; disappointed that the scheduled departure from Villefranche had been cancelled because the coachman was ill. Too many people are on the next coach; tempers running high because of the delay, the discomfort – and the smell. Then such hubbub as he steps off the coach in Lyon! The *canuts* – Lyon's silk weavers – are demonstrating, angry at the merchants who control their work; their future threatened by cheap silk imports from Italy, China and Japan. '*So then, Messieurs, move into the surrounding districts, where the more efficient four-metre-tall Jacquard looms can be accommodated!*' The *canuts* reject the merchants' order; happy where they are, doing what they have always done, and clamouring now for the protection of fixed working tariffs.

Angry groups are marching down from the Croix-Rousse district into the main streets of Lyon and towards the riverbanks where Claude is walking – searching for the pharmacy on the west bank of the Saone. Their fury is frightening and he is uneasy; bitterly cold too on the bleak *rue Royale* in the suburb of Vaise. He discovers Millet's pharmacy, still closed for the midday recess. He huddles under the canopy, feet wet from inadequate boots. Coaches clatter past, the horses' hoofs splashing muddy water over hunched figures disguised by winter cloaks; intent on getting quickly to their destination and as far as possible from the violent demonstrations. Millet's shop remains shuttered. An hour passes. Rain gives way to sharp gusting wind, and bright blue clearings appear between heavy clouds.

"Bernard, is it?"

The owner of the voice steps down from his carriage – slim and almost as tall as Claude; probably in his mid-thirties.

"There's trouble over there. Come inside, young man!"

Millet is dapper in dark cloak and tall shiny hat, moving slowly and purposefully as he opens shutters on the shop front. A broad shaft of afternoon sunlight illuminates long shelves lined with colourful jars and a long oak counter; bare except for a large register with an embossed leather cover. Sweet but pungent smells pervade the shop.

"Heard of the Comte des Guidi?"

"No, Monsieur."

"I've just been to his lecture at the *Hôtel Dieu* – on homeopathy. D'you know what that is?"

The look on Claude's face is sufficient answer. Millet smiles:

"Well, I'm busy now: we can talk about homeopathy another time. I received a note from Thoissey about you only yesterday – not impressive I must say, but I'll draw my own conclusions. Blanc tells me that you are enthusiastic, and the idea of two assistants who already get along with one another rather appeals..." He smiles, "...which of course is why I asked you to come."

Claude is saved from further inquisition by the doorbell. A woman enters the pharmacy; face troubled, flushed.

"Up you go, Bernard. Madame Millet will find you something hot to drink. We can talk later."

Claude climbs steep, creaking stairs. Foreign pharmacy smells give way to familiar cooking aromas and the clatter of cooking utensils. He follows his nose and ears to the end of a corridor; knocks. The kitchen is in considerable disarray. Madame Millet is young, short, smiling, and attractive. Claude contrasts her disorderly, frenetic activity with his calm and tidy mother who at that moment must surely be preparing a meal for his father and sister back in St Julien.

A young girl with attractively tousled hair and a warm smile places a bowl of soup in front of him. Madame Millet and he sit together, conversation often interrupted by her attention to the large stove, queries from the maid and her brief errands to the adjoining pantry. She coos reassuringly to her young son, sitting in the corner of the room folding pieces of newspaper into unrecognisable shapes. Claude's awe at meeting Millet eases as his wife talks of their arrival in Lyon from Valence several years ago; their adjustments to a new way of life.

The repeated distant sound of the doorbell indicates that Millet is well occupied.

"You must be so tired, young man; Sylvie will show you to your room."

Claude follows the maid up steep stairs to the attic; shapely white-stockinged legs provocative beneath flaring pink petticoats. He absorbs the room's small dimensions: Ronne's made-up iron-framed bed in one corner; a bare yet so inviting mattress on a wooden frame opposite. He smiles at her; coyly, provocatively:

"Would you...."

She blushes: "Excuse me, Monsieur, I will be up later with some linen; I must get back to the kitchen..."

He shrugs hopelessly, hungrily watching her disappearing down the stairs – and then reluctantly takes stock of his new lodgings. The window opens on to the street; in front, a rough table with tarnished brass oil lantern, books and sheets of paper. Some are blank; some bear scrawls that even Claude – Ronne's best friend – cannot decipher. A wooden chair sits forgotten in the centre of the room. Claude moves it to the table so that he can observe the street below in comfort, chin resting on clasped hands. He could be living and working here for some years – if Millet liked him; but would he like Millet and the practice of pharmacy? A sudden clatter of boots on stairs and Ronne bursts into the room excitedly, embracing his friend:

"Claude. Wonderful! You are here and I am so glad; but there is so much trouble out there. The *canuts* have gone wild; there must be thousands of troops out there!"

"Thanks, my friend. I'm happy to be here at the moment, but I do wonder about city life. I suppose I'll get used to it – especially if all the girls are as pretty as Sylvie."

Ronne smiles, wagging his index finger jokingly in Claude's direction:

"*Attention!* Hands off, Claude! Millet has made it clear that we keep our distance...and you won't have much free time anyway: one night off every two weeks if you are lucky, and plenty of study I can tell you."

Claude grimaces; doubts already.

"Easy for you: with Marianne here in Lyon."

"Not really: she doesn't get much time off from the veterinary college either. It's bloody frustrating!"

They laugh, sit, chatting away about families, happenings, ideas and dreams. A bell in the corner of the room returns them abruptly to reality. Millet had apparently recently installed the device linked to the shop below by a cord passing through a hole in the floor. They race down the stairs, where their *patron* promptly dispatches Ronne to a house nearby with some evil-looking medicine for an elderly widower, apparently stricken with severe diarrhoea:

"…our clients' commonest complaint these days…may even be cholera." Volunteers Millet.

He leads Claude up a flight of stairs to the preparation room to meet his rather plump assistant, Justin. The young man nods vigorously, causing his spectacles to slide down his rather diminutive nose. He is busy mixing a large quantity of black paste with a pestle and mortar. Can it really be a medicine? Millet sees Claude's confusion, smiling:

"Don't worry, Bernard; that's polish for patent leather boots; one of our more useful products!"

….and gesturing towards the other end of the room:

"One of your first jobs will be to keep these spirit burners full, and the balances, glass cylinders, flasks and spatulas meticulously clean…."

While Millet is talking, Claude finds himself staring at a large, highly decorated urn, standing at the end of the oak counter; an ornate copper tap emerging from one side. Millet follows his gaze:

"…and that's for *thériaque*. Galen devised his recipe to relieve snakebite many centuries ago. Now we use it for many complaints and conditions for which we don't have any other remedies."

"I look ridiculous". Claude comments to Ronne as he looks at himself in the cracked mirror attached to the back of their bedroom door. "This is just like the apron that the baker in St Julien wears; and the cap makes me look like an undertaker's assistant."

Ronne smiles tolerantly. Claude had also acquired a new pair of black boots, which he is obliged to polish to such brightness that he can see his face in it! With breeches tucked into black socks, he certainly looks awkward; already the next morning, he is the focus of heckling when a coach-load of youngsters passes by just as he is sweeping the path.

"And how about Marianne?" Claude asks abruptly. "When am I going to have the pleasure of meeting her?"

"Not so soon, Claude; I try to get the job of delivering medicaments to the veterinary college, just so that I can meet her – even briefly. As soon as you and I have time off together I'll try and arrange it. By the way, the college's director is another Claude – by the name of Bredin; he's Madame Millet's father."

The discussion drifts back to work, but Claude's fantasy is running riot as he recounts the imaginary domestic life of one of the day's more difficult clients. Ronne is laughing tears.

"So tell me Claude, how is your masterpiece coming on?"

"I'm getting there. I have a good plot up here in my head, but I need more time if I want to get it on to paper. Do you want to hear the theme?"

Ronne tries to look interested, and Claude requires no further prompting:

"It's about a rather simple girl whom I have decided to call Rose."

His friend winces.

"Come on Ronne; humour me! Imagine a gorgeous girl with long black unkempt hair and a fiery temperament; she's the daughter of a humble farmer who ekes out a living on the banks of the Rhône. After working her hands raw in the fields, she has little option but to dally amongst the local population; fending off the approaches of the coarse men of the village."

"Foolish girl!" quips Ronne.

Ignoring his comment, Claude continues:

"Rose hates this hardship: she wants a better life, and one day her beauty attracts the attention of a handsome nobleman, lodging in the village on his way from Lyon to Paris. He falls desperately in love with her. When he arrives in Paris, he fabricates the girl's origins so that he can gain his parents' approval for them to marry. They prepare for a splendid wedding. The girl arrives and her beauty overwhelms all the guests. However, catastrophe soon strikes: she simply cannot hide her simple origins, nor can she adjust to such a different way of life! She longs to be back amongst her familiar surroundings. In despair and under cover of darkness she finds her way back to her family – and a life of resigned boredom and shallow pleasure in her little village on the banks of the Rhône."

Silence. Claude looks quizzically at Ronne. He had listened attentively enough, without further interruption.

"...but it's so predictable, Claude; like all those other melodramas? Spend the effort on your studies and try and impress Millet – so that he offers you the apprenticeship?"

Claude is crestfallen and Ronne puts his arm warmly around his shoulders as if he were a lost child.

The weeks fly by. Claude cannot assemble his impressions into any sensible pattern. The work was mundane, but what otherwise at this early stage? He complains incessantly to Ronne about boringly repetitive tasks, yet he is curious about the many ingredients imported from exotic places like Honduras and the Far East: dried snake skins, ground-up eggshells, deer antlers and human skulls.

"How do you suppose those things were found to heal people, Ronne?"

"I have no idea. I suppose that people did experiments on their sick patients."

Claude cannot get answers from perusing the various books behind glass doors in the preparation room. His little demon of doubt does not leave him – and then of course Ronne – in peace.

"Instead of chasing shadows," Ronne suggests one day, "use your time learning how to disguise the evil taste and smell of medicines."

"That's not enough. If I am going to commit myself to pharmacy, I want to know how medicaments work – even if they work at all! By the way, weren't we going to go out together tomorrow and meet Marianne? I have been here now a whole month and I am also dying to see Lyon at night."

"Well, that's all off now. Marianne has to work and Justin is running a fever. I fully expect that Millet will ask me to remain on duty tomorrow night...." He smiles, "...someone around here needs to work!"

It is a marvellously clear and cold night. Hat pulled down over ears and coat buckled firm, Claude – alone – heads for the city centre. He walks briskly past the veterinary college, and along the dark river. A coach turns left to cross the Saone. He follows it. As he crosses the *pont du Change*, an icy wind whips up the scarf around his ears. He drives his hands further into his deep pockets. Turning right, the un-shuttered bookshops of the narrow *rue Mercière* are only feebly illuminated by lamps set in the street at inadequate intervals. He moves on, his rural senses offended by the urban smell of casually discarded waste.

He reaches elegant *place Bellecour;* cafés filled to capacity. Couples are coming and going, arm in arm, and so smartly dressed. Carriages pass, hesitate and move on: peace and calm everywhere. It is hard for him to imagine the violence that had filled the streets just weeks ago. In half shadow, a heavily made-up woman, cigarette glowing, winks at him. He avoids her gaze, wondering nonetheless how her body might feel; with empty pockets, even a cup of coffee now attractive. Turning back, he passes shops with interesting names; undoubtedly splendid displays hidden behind closed shutters. To his left is the bright foyer of the *Théatre des Célestins*, where he had laughed tears at the Easter vaudeville. The evening performance had ended; people descending the broad flight of steps, voices shrill with excited chatter. A billboard announces the programme for the forthcoming two weeks, amongst which he notes *la Famille de l'Apothicaire*. He smiles. Should he use his one free day in the month to see it?

Now he is walking through almost deserted streets towards the *Grand Théatre*. There is no performance here: the building in darkness, with *clochards* in bizarre protective trappings huddling under the deep arches. They rouse themselves long enough to appeal to his generosity; then express their disappointment in foul language. Will his play ever see the light of day? Yet with Ronne usually retiring to bed before him, perhaps he could spend some time on it each night. He retraces his steps; deep in thought. The coaches had gone for the night. The wind is now even colder; the sky if anything darker. By the time he arrives back at the pharmacy an hour later, his hands and nose are numb. His yearning for something hot is overwhelming, but kitchen and pantry are in darkness. He climbs the final flight of stairs to the attic, slips between the covers of his bed and as he thaws out, drifts into dreamless sleep.

December advances rapidly. One evening, the two young men return to their bitterly cold room in which the window had completely iced up. Claude feels decidedly uneasy:

"Do you think Millet is satisfied with me?"

"He would have said something by now if he wasn't,"

"Yes but I'm going back to St Julien at the end of the week; he can't leave his offer much longer!"

"How do *you* feel about it though?"

"I'm not sure I can face the idea of spending six years within four walls. You're a city man Ronne, and I already miss the hills and vines. Of course, I like the Millets – and the Society's new award of thirty-five francs a month."

"Have you seen enough to judge, Claude? If he offers you the apprenticeship, why not accept in any case. If you find that you're not happy you could always leave. It's been done before."

Claude; silent for a few moments, then:

"I appreciate your reasoning Ronne, and your company alone is worth a lot to me."

Ronne smiles; pleased at having found a solution to his friend's dilemma.

"Anyhow, what are your alternatives?"

"Well then Monsieur Claude, what about staying with us next year?"

Millet issues his offer the next evening as they are finishing the meal with an enormous dish of his favourite *bugnes* – which Claude has recently discovered is a traditional recipe of the *canuts*.

'Thank you, Monsieur. I do like working here and Madame has been very hospitable. I would be very happy to start my apprenticeship."

"That's settled then." comments Millet. "I am sorry that we have kept you so busy: you probably have not had much time to see our great city."

"Only to taste a little of its atmosphere. I'm really looking forward to seeing some theatre: plays are my passion. They're performing *la Famille de l'Apothicaire* at the *Célestins* at the moment: I definitely want to see it when I return after Christmas."

"No need to wait that long. My colleague Bruchon tells me that he is taking his family to see it on Sunday, so Madame and I will take you both as our guests. Justin can stay on duty for anything urgent. Speaking of literary matters, I've been invited to the *Hôtel Dieu* tomorrow for the unveiling of a new monument to Rabelais; he was a physician there just three hundred years ago."

"I didn't know that he was a physician." says Claude.

"Not only that, but his writing was inspired by his patients and their illnesses."

Later, the two young men are in their room.

"Did you hear what Millet said about Rabelais? Couldn't you do the same – as a pharmacist? If you must write a play, then why not about the real lives of our clients that you so often ridicule?"

Light snow had fallen overnight; by late afternoon reduced to muddy slush, and so very unkind to the boots that Claude and Ronne had carefully polished that morning. As they step out of Millet's carriage in front of the *Célestins,* a small group of children is singing Christmas carols. Inside, the theatre is full to capacity by the time they find places on uncomfortable benches. The buzz of excitement subsides only slowly, and Claude can barely hear the first sentences uttered on stage.

The story took place somewhere in the late seventeenth or early eighteenth century; in a setting that closely resembled the drawing of an ancient apothecary's office that Claude had once seen in Diderot's encyclopaedia. The theme was simple enough: the age-old competition between apothecary and physician. The apothecary strutted about on stage extravagantly costumed like one of Daumier's caricatures. In his shadow the physician, much more humbly attired but well meaning and supposedly knowledgeable, found himself outwitted and out-manoeuvred by the apothecary at every turn. The apothecary became ever more arrogant with his own success in diagnosis and healing. In the second act, the apothecary's wife suddenly becomes seriously ill.

Without a diagnosis the confused apothecary, pathetically helpless in the eyes of his distressed family is obliged to call in the physician. Eventually their combined skills succeed in curing her. Fully recovered, his wife observes that the humbled apothecary has become a so much better and more modest man. In turn, and relieved by his wife's excellent recovery he praises the physician to each and everyone. The latter's self-respect and reputation increases enormously and the play ends happily with everyone the best of friends. The dialogue is fast, and some of the humorous asides are lost in the murmurings of a restless audience. They are only quiet during the dramatic scene in which the apothecary's wife is critically ill!

Claude arrives back in St Julien for Christmas with a certain pride; his parents pleased – his father even proud – that he had found a career to which he could commit himself. Questions abound concerning Millet and his wife; the details of his work. Christmas Eve means midnight mass in their local church. Sitting on the familiar uncomfortable pews his mind typically wanders during the sermon; recalling events of his early days as a choirboy and his embarrassment at being called up to assist at Mass. What about religion and the existence of God? Descartes' writings come to mind; the immense strength of his words:

I may imagine a winged horse,
although no horse with wings exists
So I could perhaps attribute existence to God,
although no God existed"

How could Claude reconcile his belief in God with his desire for truth – and didn't Descartes regard belief as an act of will, rather than a result of reason? He had better return to reality. He was on the necessary road to his career, even though nothing would deter him from writing, even if it meant staying awake until all hours. He reflects on his visit to the *Célestins*; wonders now how he might interest someone in producing his play. Yet he knows no one in the literary or theatrical world. In any case, is it a publisher or a producer that he should be looking for?

The next few days are for sleeping and eating. Rugged up against the cold, he also wanders around the village and its surroundings, takes the local coach into Villefranche and calls at the homes of both the Chrétiens and Lamberts, disappointed to find that his friends have stayed in Paris for Christmas.

CHAPTER 2

A Play on Words

"Why do we dispense *ményanthe* so often?"
Claude had brought back some plants from the pharmacy's garden; now waiting for the water in the glass beaker to boil prior to adding the leaves.

"I suppose it's because abdominal colic and fever are two of our most common problems," Justin replies, "And we use it for other conditions too; why don't you look them up in the *Materia Medica* over there?"

He gestures vaguely towards the glass-fronted cupboard.

Later that morning Claude takes down Barbier's immense tome: confirms that *ményanthe* – buckbean – could indeed be used for gastric colic and fever. It was also recommended for irregular heartbeat, gouty arthritis and recurrent headaches. Using a mixture of leaves and seeds, it had also been used for treating scurvy.

"I don't understand how a single plant extract can benefit so many different conditions?" he asks later.

"Questions, questions! Look, it's just a matter of observation and experience," Justin replies wearily. "Many of our medicaments were used two thousand years ago in China and India. Since then, physicians report their experience in lectures or articles. People like Barbier assemble everyone else's findings in a book like that one. It's simple!"

Claude frowns; Justin's comment had not answered his question. Later in the week, well out of earshot of Justin, he challenges Millet with the same query. Millet looks at him carefully; neither annoyed, nor impatient:

"Pharmacy is not the precise science that we would all like it to be; but I'll try and find an explanation for you." He hesitates, "One major nerve called the pneumogastric is known to send major branches to both the heart and the stomach. If an extract of *ményanthe* acts as a nerve sedative, might not both organs benefit from its effects? Perhaps heart irregularities and stomach cramps are *both* due to over-activity of the nervous system."

Claude looks at him in silence for a few seconds. "But does *ményanthe* actually contain a nerve sedative?" he asks.

"I really don't know that, Monsieur Claude."

It was a terse reply, clearly intended to end the discussion; close the subject. Millet promptly leaves the room. Claude has no idea how to pursue the matter, and since both Millet and Justin are obviously becoming irritated at his many questions, he is keen not to antagonise them further. Claude shares the dilemma with Ronne that evening:

"Look Claude, there's enough work for us to memorize names and procedures – without needing to concern ourselves with *how* certain preparations work. If physicians prescribe something, is it for us to question their choice?"

One Sunday – his free day – Claude again visits the *Célestins*, this time hoping to be able to meet the director of the theatre; Jean-Marc Berliet's name is prominently displayed at the foot of the billboard advertising the theatre's forthcoming productions. Such an unhelpful receptioniste! Berliet is simply not available. Her aloofness suggests that even if he had been, the director would be much too busy and important to concern himself with a young unknown.

He sets off on his walk back to Vaise, disheartened. With time on his side, he takes a devious route along the narrow streets: ahead of him a passageway covered with a series of imaginative, elongated domes of glass simulating the passageways – the *traboules* – of the Croix-Rousse, home to the *canuts*. At its entrance is a pedestal surmounted by a small statuette of Mercury with prominent winged heels. Fascinated by its design, he walks through the arcade, past artisans' shops mostly displaying extravagant silk clothes. He hears voices in unison coming from a stairwell to his right. Curiosity leading him by the nose he climbs stairs; finds himself at the entrance to a very large room, at one end of which is an elevated platform. By the side of the door is a sign announcing *École de Drame Mercure*. Standing on the platform is a middle-aged man in fiery red shirt, surrounded by some dozen and a half young men and women in four groups. Each group in turn is chanting verses describing the seasons, accompanied by gestures and expressive body movements. Seeing Claude, the instructor points in the direction of a bench, and when the students are eventually dismissed, he introduces himself as the school's director, Ramon:

"Do you want to join our happy family?"

"*Bah!* Not with my voice, Monsieur; but I've almost finished a play that I hope to have performed one day".

"Tell me about it!"

Ramon smiles tolerantly, and in no way condescendingly, as Claude outlines the theme; enlarges on his ideas about its production and mentions his fruitless attempt at meeting Berliet. He fully expects Ramon to be dismissive; indeed to laugh at his enthusiasm and optimism.

"You know, I always need new material for my drama students. It could be your first step towards fame! Here in Lyon, there are plenty of people interested in seeing a good play. Try to finish it as soon as possible. Let me see it, although I promise you that I will be brutally honest with you; false expectations are of no help to anyone."

Claude leaves the arcade and blows a kiss to Mercury, the versatile god of commerce, of the traveller, of weights, measures and inventions – and above all of wisdom and skill. He returns to Vaise with a brisk and confident step.

He is having problems with his play. One night Ronne is woken up by Claude's loud cough, quite certain that he had been roused intentionally! His friend is bent over the desk, hands supporting his bowed and indeed rather handsome head. To the left is a small open notebook; pages blank. To his right is the text of his play, its top sheet now bearing a title, *Rose du Rhône*. Directly in front of him is a sheet of paper with only one line of writing upon it. Claude looks up at Ronne with red, watering eyes:

"Sorry. Did I wake you…?" he asks innocently. Ronne shakes his head; just as unconvincingly. "…but since you are awake, you might help me. I am at such an impasse. Rose has just burst into tears for about the fourth time; made a fool of herself at the banquet. She has spilled wine over the countess' wonderful white dress. Her lover Gilbert is at his wits' end trying to excuse her behaviour to the Count and Countess, while at the same time trying to placate Rose. Neither of his attempts is meeting with success. Where do I go from here?"

"You know that I am no good at this sort of thing: tomorrow you'll find new inspiration. Go back to bed, otherwise you'll be of no use to anyone tomorrow; me neither!"

Claude looks at him; the corners of his mouth drooping and eyes bloodshot; a pitiful sight.

"You are just trying to do too much, Claude. Why not concentrate on pharmacy and put aside your play for a while. What's your hurry? I am really worried that Millet will discover what you are up to."

"Perhaps that would be a good thing."

"I don't understand."

"Well look; this evening I asked Millet what I should do with half a dozen leftovers from our earlier preparations. 'Oh!' he said, 'Just put them in that flask of *thériaque*.'"

"Well…"

"It's dishonest! Pharmacy is supposed to be science. It is clearly not. I might as well just write my play. It might be fantasy, but at least I am not pretending that it's something else."

"*Nom de dieu*, Claude! You may have a point, but in the middle of the night…! Let's discuss it tomorrow."

Claude stands abruptly, walks to his bed, lies down and pulls the covers over his head.

"It's not looking good."

Millet looks grey and tired as they sit around the table after dinner.

"I was at the *mairie* this afternoon with Bruchon and our medical colleagues, Lamont and Duplain. They tell me that they notified six cases of cholera yesterday. We need to look at the sort of treatments that will be prescribed."

"Does any treatment work?" Asks Claude. They all look at him. Millet answers, carefully.

"The Paris doctors have given us their opinions. That illustrious physician Magendie recommends only camomile. The surgeon Dupuytren suggests treatment with incisions in the abdominal wall, removal of two to three ounces of blood followed by dry rubbing with a flannel containing an extract of poppy heads. I've just read in the *Courrier* that Hahnemann, the doyen of homeopathy advises treating all suspected cases with camphor. He warns that once the disease is established camphor will not work. It either has to be used early – or not at all."

Justin adds his comment:

"If you go to number seven, *rue des Augustins*, three francs will buy you a special chlorine mixture which can apparently prevent an attack; I've just seen that advertisement in the *Gazette*!"

Millet laughs derisively, shakes his head. "You see, Monsieur Claude: no-one really knows what works, and everyone wants to make money out of other people's misery and fear. *That's* the world we live in!"

Later that evening they are in their room when Claude confronts Ronne with a new dilemma:

"Not only does one preparation seem to benefit dozens of conditions, but now it seems that many different treatments are all effective in treating the one condition of cholera?"

Ronne too is becoming irritated by his friend's continued questioning, but Claude is not to be stopped:

"It seems so unlikely, doesn't it? If there are so many treatments, it must be possible to know which works best. Where can I find the truth? When Descartes' was writing about God and the soul he could afford to step aside from a line of doubtful reasoning and change direction. When a person is ill, one does not have that luxury; and what treatment would *I* get if *I* caught cholera? I need to look it up in Pinel!"

Candle in hand, a confused Claude descends stairs, surprised to find Millet standing in front of the bookcase in the preparation room reading Pinel's text. His face is etched with lines of concern, which soften as he sees Claude. He points at the book, shaking his head:

"As you can see, I'm as puzzled as you are."

"Monsieur, I really do need to solve this dilemma about the variety of treatments for cholera – and then what would happen if I was unlucky enough to get the illness."

"Come and join me for a *tisane*?" Millet offers, smiling. "Perhaps it will help you not to worry so much!"

They cross a passageway, through a door and into the living room; private quarters pleasantly but not extravagantly furnished. On the left a bare table with a highly polished surface of inlaid woods; in the far corner a fireplace with an ornate brass surround; logs within smouldering and hissing. A variety of chairs, two sofas and an armchair are all upholstered in blue velvet while curtains of the same material isolate the room from the blackness and cold outside. Two glasses stand on a low table close to the fire. Claude assumes that they contain a *tisane*, but he wonders about Millet's anticipation of his being there. Seeing Claude's puzzled face Millet provides the explanation.

"At ten o'clock each night Sylvie brings us *tisanes*. However, Madame is not herself tonight: I think she is worried that cholera will affect our family, too. She's gone to bed early."

Once they are sitting comfortably, he begins:

'You know Monsieur Claude; there are hardly any treatments which specifically treat a single condition. I've told you that pharmacy is not an exact science; but then again neither is the physician's process of diagnosis. Many people die carrying their hidden diagnoses to their grave. Even autopsy often fails to provide an answer. In so many other people, conditions improve by themselves. We are no wiser about their diagnoses either. I sense your disquiet about what we do and how we do it. However, both physicians and pharmacists must work with what knowledge and experience they have at their disposal. By the way, when I mentioned Hahnemann's article in the *Courrier*, did you appreciate the subtlety of his method?'

"Do you mean Hahnemann's camphor treatment, which he said would only work if given in the very earliest stages of cholera."

"Exactly," says Millet. "I can tell you that in those early stages there is little to separate cholera from other causes of vomiting and diarrhoea – which are more often simply the result of poor food hygiene. Indeed, most of such patients recover perfectly well with just a little patience! Imagine now; if doctors used Hahnemann's camphor treatment for each and every person suffering from vomiting and diarrhoea, would it not appear that a miraculous cure had been achieved in most cases? The reputation of his 'camphor cure' would be enormous, even though it had no benefit whatsoever on people genuinely suffering from cholera."

Millet pauses for a sip of his favourite bedtime drink:

"It is also not too surprising that if camphor is used in the truly ill with advanced cholera, the results will be bad. I doubt whether camphor has any benefit whatsoever, especially in the ridiculously low concentrations that he uses. Our friend Hahnemann is without doubt a clever man, but in a particular way!"

He smiles, hesitates and his face darkens a little:

"I also understand your concern about coming down with cholera yourself. The truth is that we simply do not have enough experience with any of the treatments. During the cholera epidemic in Siberia a few years ago, much seemed to depend on people's general health. If you were healthy and well nourished, you were less likely to catch the infection in the first place – and if you did contract it, more likely to survive. The malnourished and sickly were prone to get cholera – and to die from it. So keep on enjoying Madame's cooking and get some rest!"

Claude walks back to the attic; disillusioned and more confused than ever. It would be better to escape back to his creative world and complete his play. Rose had by now returned to her family's humble dwelling: ashamed of her failed ambitions and humbled by the events of the last months. He had very little to do in order to finish it; determined now to deliver it to Ramon by the end of the month. He feels both awkward and relieved that Millet does not know about it; tempted to leave him in that state of ignorance. Was it such a sin to pursue his passion for writing in his leisure time? Ronne is in no doubt though. Tell Millet now; better he should find out from Claude than from someone else.

Marianne is delightful; rosy cheeks, a generous smile and long, fair hair tied back usefully but still attractively. It is Sunday morning at the veterinary college and owners of the animals entrusted to the care of the college are everywhere. Exchanging light-hearted banter, Ronne and Claude allow themselves to be guided through corridors flanked by small animal cages; cats with mangy coats, dogs of all imaginable breeds; smells overwhelming. In paddocks and sheds are the cows, pigs and particularly horses, for whose treatment the college had received such wide acclaim. The paths between pens and paddocks are muddy with yesterday's rain, and Marianne's neat white shoes are soon covered with filth; barely noticed in all her enthusiasm.

Claude is fascinated by her vivid descriptions of the illnesses and their treatments. She shows him a strange wooden frame to which horses had to be strapped when an operation needed to be performed. They had previously to be killed when they fractured bones; the frame now allowed fractures to be treated effectively: many were later able to walk, even if not work. Time evaporates. They say goodbye to Marianne and walk back to the pharmacy, taking a small detour that allows them to sit by the river – just like old times.

"She's fantastic, Ronne; everything you told me about – and more."

"I am glad you like her. It's annoying that we can't see more of one another though. Next year should be better: her classes will allow her more time off; and if Millet gives *you* more responsibility in the pharmacy, then I might get a better deal too!"

Claude laughs; wondering now if Millet will allow him to bring medicaments to the college occasionally.

"Do you think that there is something wrong with me, Ronne?"

"In what way?"

"I mean with girls."

"You don't give yourself a chance, Claude. Your mind is always busy with something – and you are impatient. You simply expect girls to fall into your bed, breathless with gratitude. Life isn't like that!"

Claude laughs at the imagery: "Alright, you may have a point."

They sit for a while in silence until dusk dictates a return to the pharmacy where Ronne will again be 'on duty' for the night.

Only two weeks later, Claude hears form Ramon that he liked the play; wanted to produce it at the *Galerie*. He mentions in his letter that because of the cholera epidemic, the *Grand* and the *Célestins* have had to cancel some of their performances. He had therefore been lucky enough to secure the services of Mademoiselle Saint-Ys, one of Lyon's top actresses, for the part of Rose. The supporting cast would come from his drama students. With so few performances in the other theatres, *Rose du Rhone* might attract good audiences: Lyon should welcome some cheering up.

Claude is ecstatic. With enormous excitement, he writes to his parents: will they please promise to come to Lyon; he would let them know as soon as performance dates had been set. Claude knows that he must tell Millet, too. The play might be reviewed in the *Gazette*, and that would not be the way for Claude's nocturnal activities to be discovered.

Claude is assisting Millet with preparing some senna, a popular remedy for constipation that Millet assures him to be one of their more effective products! Once the correct amounts have been mixed, weighed and finally neatly folded into packets for the patient, a considerable quantity remains.

"Add that to the *thériaque*, Monsieur Claude", instructs Millet.

Claude is fully aware that senna compounds are not among the list of seventy constituents of Galen's *thériaque* published in all the formularies. Millet sees him frowning, hesitating:

"It's only a small amount in that large container: a little purgative will hurt no-one. I have to say though that I am impressed that you seem to have memorized the constituents so well. You have obviously been keeping your head well down with your studies".

Claude's confidence is boosted, and as they are leaving the preparation room, he decides to break the news of his other endeavour:

"I should probably have told you rather sooner about my hobby, Monsieur."

Millet stops abruptly on the stairs, a quizzical expression on his face.

"I am surprised that you have time for anything other than your studies."

"I have always enjoyed writing, Monsieur. Once I am up to date with my reading, I have been using a little time each evening to write a short play. I learned yesterday that it is going to be performed at a drama school here in Lyon."

Millet's face freezes into a mask of disapproval:

"This is quite a surprise: I think that you might have mentioned it to me earlier. It is not exactly what I encourage my apprentices to do. Were you by any chance prompted to do this by the play at the *Célestins?*"

"No, it has nothing to do with pharmacy at all. It is actually a modest melodrama; an idea which I had even before I began my apprenticeship with you."

They continue down the stairs in silence, Claude following at a respectful distance. Millet turns to him:

"I can't say that I am very happy about all this. I insist that anything you still have to do in connection with that play must be done within your free time: you surely can't expect to have extra for your dramatic pursuits. I expect every spare minute from now on to be committed to your pharmacy studies. Is that understood?"

Claude blushes, nods; relieved when Millet has to deal with a query raised by Justin.

The small auditorium is full. Claude is at the rear of the hall; back pressed against the wall as if he wanted to disappear into it. He is nervously biting his nails, peering at the people who had come to see his, Claude Bernard's first play. His mother is there, alone. She had written to Claude that she would stay for a few days with his father's cousin. Ronne is sitting next to her, making her laugh. Two benches behind them, Claude is astounded to see Millet and his wife – and even after that stern rebuke that he had received! For the rest, both young and old talk excitedly even as Rose takes centre stage; face radiant and fine features subtly illuminated by oil lamps across the front of the stage. Does the audience's unusual silence and stillness mean something?

Applause! Ramon had invited a juggler to entertain the young during the interval, keeping them firmly in their seats while their parents stretched their legs. Claude thanks the Millets; introduces his mother to an excited Ramon. He overhears polite, even enthusiastic comments from some of the audience – yet the second act would be the key. Now the audience is silent as Rose is confronted by all the social challenges, humorous and serious, that Claude's ingenuity could have devised. Ramon's students are marvellous and as the play ends to enthusiastic applause, Claude sheds tears of gratitude and relief. His mother is pleased and proud, and Ramon announces four more performances. Together with the Millets and Valerie, they all head for *l'Image de Lyon* for a celebratory glass of champagne – an offer from Millet that Claude swears he would never forget.

Summer is over; the *canuts* still without tariffs and uncertain of their future. Claude's father is relieved that he has now decided against involving himself in the silk trade. He remains tetchy with Claude; interested in his activities in Lyon, but strictly in connection with his pharmacy studies. Claude finds it difficult to enthuse openly about Lyon; dares not voice his thoughts about the future. He only discusses his venture into drama with his mother when his father is well out of earshot.

Cases of cholera have reduced to a trickle; the theatres of Lyon have re-opened. Valerie Saint-Ys is again the star of the *Célestins* and its rich variety of vaudeville and melodrama. All five performances of *Rose du Rhone* had been well attended, so that before Claude leaves for St Julien, Ramon unexpectedly presents him with one hundred francs. Ramon explains that since he had only modest production costs and is required to pay only Valerie Saint-Ys for her participation, he is happy to give Claude his just rewards.

On Claude's free day in August, Ramon invites him for dinner. His wife worked in one of the bookshops on the *rue Mercière*. With some feeling she pleads with Claude not to break his apprenticeship for the sake of a doubtful future in drama. Pharmacy, she assures him is such a respected and reliable profession when compared to the fragile theatrical world which she had seen at first hand. They had suffered truly hard times until Ramon had been able to establish himself in the drama school.

Claude battles with this dilemma for many days. Life at the pharmacy was enjoyable enough. Yet the way in which Millet expressed uncertainty about the effectiveness of drugs unsettles and haunts him. He decides to seek clarification from Millet's assistant:

"Tell me Justin," he asks one morning, "Don't you have any qualms about preparing a medicine for a patient in the knowledge that it often doesn't help?"

"But that's how it is!" is the cryptic answer. Justin smiles, wipes his hands in a towel. "Let me show you some quotations from my little red book."

He opens a drawer in the workbench and produces a notebook that he passes to Claude. "This is for my random thoughts and the quotations that I come across…"

Claude is fascinated. One entry read: *'Medicine kills and nature heals'.*

Another stated that: *Doctors pour drugs, of which they know little, for diseases of which they know even less, into patients – of whom they know nothing.* Both quotations were by Paracelsus.

On yet another page was a quotation by Voltaire: *The art of the physician is to amuse the patient while nature cures the illness.*

Justin takes the book back, and carefully restores it to its place in the drawer.

"Voltaire and Paracelsus were no fools." He says. "What's more, I believe that deep in their hearts, doctors and pharmacists – even members of the public – are fully aware of how limited we are in treating illness."

For Claude, the quotations had opened important philosophical issues of truth. Buried in both wisdom and wit were exactly the doubts that had been troubling him. He just could not put aside such matters of doubt.

"If Voltaire is right about nature, I would like to know how physicians decide whether to act – or just wait and hope for a condition to get better itself."

Justin smiles. "It would be nice if it was that easy, Claude. If you read the chapter in Pinel entitled '*Traitement Expectant*' you will appreciate just how difficult it is! Not only that, but Paracelsus clearly implied that drugs can sometimes delay an otherwise favourable outcome. So look carefully in those pharmacopoeias over there – when you have a moment to spare. You will see how numerous the side effects of medicaments can be; I have little doubt that they can even hasten an inevitably poor outcome."

In Justin's slim little notebook Claude had noticed yet another dictum: *He cures most in whom most are confident.*

It had been coined by Galen, the remarkable physician who had lived in the third century. It was he who had invented the *thériaque* to which Millet had introduced him on his very first day in the pharmacy. Claude puzzles over this quotation for some time. In a quiet moment he decides to ask Justin about its meaning. Justin pauses thoughtfully:

"Millet tells me that you are familiar with *thériaque.*"

Claude nods, smiling.

"And there are seventy ingredients, correct?"

Again Claude nods in agreement.

"Have you thought of comparing those ingredients with the recommended dose stated in Jourdan for each individual drug when given separately?"

Claude admits that he has not done this nor can he see its relevance, so Justin continues:

"Well, I was given that rather onerous task in one of my pharmacy classes at the hospital. Using a pharmacopoeia, I found that the amount of each drug recommended by Galen for his *thériaque* was only the tiniest fraction of the amount currently recommended for the individual use of each drug – with the possible exception of opium. I also discovered that many of the ingredients even have opposing actions on the body. Despite fourteen centuries of use, I have my doubts whether *thériaque* has any value at all."

"Do you mean that Galen knowingly devised a mixture using such low dosages that neither harm nor good could possibly come from taking it?" Claude asks.

"Exactly" says Justin. "My theory is that he simply tried to impress patients with the multitude of its constituents – a placebo, as that Englishman Hooper called it in his article a few years ago. I feel much the same about the waters and tonics we prepare. It is probably the colour, the smell – and of course the ceremony with which we present them to patients which does most of the good!

He adds wistfully: "Like so many things in life; it is not so much what you do but the way that you do it".

Claude is staggered; dishonesty, almost witchcraft so solidly entrenched in the practice of pharmacy! Disillusioned, and quite unconcerned about the consequences, he decides that he will embark on another play. During September, he had seen performances of Dumas' *Henry the Third and his Court* as well as a French translation of Shakespeare's *Hamlet*. Both had been performed in the *Grand Théâtre* by Firmin's travelling company and he had loved the language, sentiment and movement. So then, why not a historical drama? What he needed was a picturesque theme from history, which had not yet been introduced to the stage. He was familiar with the complicated thirteenth century events which culminated in King John murdering his nephew, Arthur of Brittany. He figured that the theme could provide plenty of action and the opportunity to develop interesting characters. The more he thought about it, the more confident he became about developing it into a full-length play.

This time, title came well ahead of text. Ronne hears nothing from Claude except his thoughts and ideas about *Arthur de Bretagne*. Ronne again tries to convince Claude that with his rather cynical approach to disease and its cures he might at least have chosen a more medical theme – perhaps along the lines of Molière's *la Malade Imaginaire* or *le Médecin Malgré Lui*. Indeed, both books had been recommended by Millet to help them appreciate the more bizarre elements of behaviour of the sick and suffering. However, Claude would not hear of it. His passion for *romantisme* was clearly the driving force for his creative writing and nothing would divert him from this path.

Predictably he says nothing of this new venture to Millet. He maintains his interest in pharmacy and directs question after question both to Millet and to Justin; always in a challenging, almost threatening manner. In the attic however, the scene is different. He had visited the bookshop in the *rue Mercière* where Ramon's wife worked, and had returned with a pair of historical treatises: thick tomes with deeply embossed leather covers that she had allowed him to borrow. Their contents would provide the material for the basic structure of his play.

His late night writing sessions resume, and rousing Claude each morning becomes an ever-increasing effort for Ronne. However, Claude does not budge; he almost taunts Ronne by insisting – as he had done with *Rose du Rhône* – that he listen to all manner of ideas and phrases which he is using in the play. If Ronne dares to protest, Claude sulks; the corners of his mouth turned down like that of a petulant child. It is a relief for Ronne when they are both released for a couple of days over Christmas.

The spring of '33 is outstandingly warm and peaceful, as if designed to erase the unpleasant thoughts and happenings of the previous year. With no evidence of a return of the cholera epidemic the spirits of the Lyonnais run high. Yet April is to be the month of Claude's downfall and as such, sad for everyone concerned. The crisis takes place on a busy Saturday morning on which it seems that everyone wants attention at the same time. Millet, Justin, Claude and Ronne are all behind the counter with a dozen clients waiting, all impatient to be heard.

"Monsieur Claude, please bring up the mixture that you prepared for Madame Garet yesterday" Millet requests.

Meanwhile he deals with two women simultaneously pressing him for advice on hygiene for their household pets (an article in the *Courrier* had recently drawn attention to this as a possible source of infection with cholera). Another lady with her daughter crying on her shoulder was asking for something to soothe her earache. The child is clutching her ear frantically, noise is everywhere and the elderly Madame Garet is becoming impatient for her mixture.

"Justin, Do see what is delaying Claude down in the cellar." he asks quietly.

In less than a minute Justin returns, face white as a sheet.

"He is unconscious, Monsieur!"

Ronne and Justin race back down the stairs, returning with the inert body of Claude whom they lay on the floor in the preparation room away from prying eyes. Within thirty seconds he begins to stir, eyes fluttering open, mouth agape and moaning softly. Justin announces that Claude had apparently upset a large shelf carrying at least ten bottles of charged water. They had shattered on the stone floor, releasing carbon dioxide in large quantities. Claude had presumably bent down to search for the bottle of mixture from amongst the glass fragments in the gloom of the cellar. Forgetting that carbon dioxide was heavier than air, he had suffered the earliest stages of asphyxia. Once he is fully conscious, Ronne helps him up the stairs to the attic room, out of his clothes and on to his bed.

Some two hours later the pharmacy closes for lunch, and the two young men suddenly hear footsteps on the attic stairs. There is a knock on the door and Millet enters:

"I thought that I would make sure that you were alright but ..."

Claude is sitting bolt upright in his bed, reading one of the historical texts that he had brought back from the *rue Mercière*. Millet approaches, his eyes falling on the desk. One step backwards and he pauses briefly, noting the title page of *Arthur de Bretagne* amongst a variety of sheets bearing Claude's literary scrawls. Simultaneously, he sees Virey's two manuals of pharmacy lying on the floor under the desk; undoubtedly used as convenient footrests.

"...it seems that I have little to be concerned about."

Turning on his heel, he walks out of the door. Claude is terrified; Ronne speechless.

At dinner that night, conversation is singularly sparse and impersonal. As Millet leaves the table, he addresses Claude in a voice carved in ice:

"When you have finished Monsieur Claude, kindly join me in the salon!"

They are now sitting face to face across the inlaid table in the salon:

"You may consider me to be harsh, but enough is enough! I went into the cellar following that fiasco. You had obviously arranged the bottles of charged water – which it was your duty to store properly – on shelves that were unsuitable for the purpose. Apart from this singular act of carelessness, having broken the bottles that you yourself helped to fill, you should have known about the dangers of stooping down and breathing in the gas after such a spillage. Instead of your high and mighty thoughts about the imperfections of our profession, it might have been better for you to have been studying basic pharmacy procedure with more diligence."

He pauses for breath; face dark with mounting anger:

"On top of this I come to your room only to find that you are writing yet another play for what now seems to be your chosen career. Pharmacy does not allow such diversity, and the fact that you have done this behind my back reflects poorly on your character."

Claude does not know which way to look, but Millet is not to be stopped:

"This afternoon I have written to your parents indicating that your apprenticeship will terminate at the end of July. I would have preferred you to leave more promptly, but it will unfortunately take me a number of weeks to find a new apprentice. What really saddens me is that you would have made a good pharmacist – had you acted with appropriate commitment to the profession. Good night, Monsieur Claude."

Claude is neither asked for, nor is he inclined to make a comment in his defence. It is clear to him that any argument would be unacceptable. He returns to his room and throws himself on to his bed.

His last weeks in Vaise pass all too slowly. Claude does not wait for his parents' reaction to Millet's letter. He writes them a note in which he says that he had become disillusioned with the profession of pharmacy. He promises to explain other elements of his life in Lyon once he is home. Claude does apply himself during his last few weeks, trying to anticipate the needs of Millet and the pharmacy. His manner to clients and to Madame Millet is exemplary, and he makes no further visits to the veterinary college. However, he makes no pretence of studying pharmacy books either. His evenings are spent on his play.

"Why couldn't you restrain yourself..." Ronne asks, "...even for the sake of our friendship?"

"I have to be true to myself Ronne." He responds. "When I am writing, I live in an imaginary world where the truth is irrelevant. What I cannot do is to continue the pretence of using science for the sake of humanity. If I felt that there was much factual substance in pharmacy, I probably wouldn't have strayed from it so readily. You must agree that both medicine and pharmacy are simply meddling – without real knowledge. I am sure that people would be better off if there were no pharmacists, drugs – perhaps even doctors."

"*Bah!* That's extreme; plainly stupid! Surely there's value in the reassurance and support which the healing professions provide?"

"That's not true either – in fact, the way that it is done is sometimes dishonest too: but our friendship won't be broken that easily Ronne. I want to finish my play as soon as I can and I'm taking it to Paris to have it produced. I know that I can do it and I can't look beyond that at the moment. Perhaps you will come to Paris one day, too!"

Indeed they both know that their bond will be lifelong; no matter by what distance they are separated.

Claude's return to St Julien takes place a few weeks earlier than anticipated. Millet had found another apprentice, and having made his decision he was only too happy for Claude to leave. Millet presents him with little more than a polite report on his eighteenth months of apprenticeship. It could have been worse! His arrival home is also remarkably without serious consequence. His mother is full of understanding; his father resigned to supporting Claude on his already-strained resources, at least for a short period. He is also satisfied that he had predicted to his wife that Claude would not last the distance! Claude is certainly content to be home for the summer. He offers to roll up his sleeves and keep the small garden tidy. He also takes Caroline, now almost four years old, for walks amongst the vines and manages to persuade her that she might help with the harvest this year. Work on his play dominates his evenings as well as any stray afternoon when neither parent can find any jobs for him to do. He cannot keep his project secret from his father who reacts predictably, dismissively and even angrily, even when Madame Bernard again emphasizes the success of *Rose du Rhône*. Claude had given himself a target – November – during which he wanted to take his new play to Paris in order to find a publisher or producer. What he needed now was a contact in Paris.

One morning, whilst talking with his mother about his concerns, she recalls having met a woman in Villefranche whose son lived in Paris; apparently holding high office in government. She had talked glowingly about his literary achievements. After some correspondence between the two mothers, this Madame Vatout agrees to write to her son, asking if he might receive young Claude; perhaps even provide the bright young man with guidance. Claude also receives a response from his friends Lambert and Chrétien, now in the third year of their law studies. They will at least temporarily accommodate him in their modest apartment in *rue Victor* – with a choice of sleeping on a rather short sofa or on the floor.

CHAPTER 3

TO PARIS WITH HOPE

The stagecoach bearing its ten tired passengers reaches a cold and misty Paris, wheels crunching through potholed streets. Odours of decaying food and sewage seep into the cabin, and the three women sitting opposite Claude bow their heads demurely and cover their noses delicately with lace handkerchiefs. Crossing the Seine by an unnamed bridge their conveyance grinds to a halt; its team of horses exhausted. Two of them simultaneously defecate in acknowledgement of their grubby surroundings.

Bag slung over left shoulder and scrawled address and instructions clasped firmly in his right hand, Claude tries to find the apartment, the stench in the streets unbearable. He narrowly avoids being hit by an assortment of rotting vegetables jettisoned from a window; keeps to the sides where he hopes to be less exposed to that risk – and also well away from the rivulet of filth which courses down central gutters. What seems like an age later he finds *rue Victor*, and after a dark and musty ascent of three flights of stairs he is greeted warmly in the apartment by his two smiling friends. Now in the third year of their law studies, freedom seems at a premium; demanding examinations that are regularly imposed to check progress. Yet all their talk, well into an unheated autumn night is of the lighter side of Paris; the affordable and mischievous exploits for which there was always time.

Claude takes stock of his surroundings, gradually absorbing the bare essentials of their student existence. If anything, they were more rudimentary than the attic room in Vaise: shoddy furniture, bare floors and faded curtains depressing enough without the added disorder of clothes, pots, food and books that covered every surface. The small sofa in the salon seems the best option for his much-needed sleep, the uncomfortable and noisy lodgings *en route* at Chalons and Auxerre best forgotten.

He wastes no time the next morning in finding the office of Jean Vatout. His route takes him past the *Palais Royal* and the *Théatre-Français* where *Hernani*, Hugo's exploit into *romantisme* had been staged: its premiere marred by rioting as the classicists clashed with the romanticists. Close by were two arcades awash with elegance such as he had never seen even in Lyon. The sight of rows of tall pillars, glass domes and intricate ironwork brings about a sudden rush of sentiment and purpose as he recalls that special day in the *galerie de l'Argue*, the starting point for all the complex events that had culminated in his arrival in this extraordinary city.

Just as he announces himself to Vatout's rather officious assistant the man himself emerges from his office; portly, jovial with a silk hat perched jauntily on the back of his head and a coat slung casually over one arm. How would Claude feel about joining him for some lunch at the *Café Montansier?*

"This is a crazy city, Bernard…." Vatout exclaims, almost as soon as they are seated, "…but the more I live here, the more I love it. If you stay here, you will see changes that you won't believe possible. The King has given me what amounts to a free hand and a bottomless pouch. The finest architects have been commissioned to create buildings that will be the envy of the world. People will flock to this city as never before. Paris already has the finest carpenters, and the most superb painters and plasterers come here from Piedmont each year: the *Maçons de la Creuse* have only this morning confirmed to me that they will again commit themselves to our five-year plan. Do you know, all ten thousand of them walk the 400 kilometres to Paris every autumn to construct buildings for us – and then return to their homes in the Limousin for the summer?'

Smiling broadly, he adds:

"...but it's also a long way from Villefranche and my mother tells me that I am to help you. Anything I can do for you will give her pleasure."

Claude is overwhelmed by his gracious offer and the sumptuous surroundings of the *café*. Between mouthfuls of superb food he outlines to Vatout his last eighteen months' activities, talking proudly of the success of *Rose du Rhône* and describing the theme of *Arthur de Bretagne*. Vatout listens without interruption; broad forehead creased with concentration.

"Saint-Marc Girardin is your man! He has the chair of literature at the Sorbonne; really one of our finest critics – on the *Journal des Débats*, you know. He won't beat around the bush, mind you. I'll write to him today but you should make an appointment immediately – he won't be able to see you for a couple of weeks. I would offer to look at your manuscript myself – sounds interesting enough – but there's already too much on my plate. Next time we meet I will try and remember to bring you my book of poems that Hachette has just published. You can tell me how you like them!"

Their meeting ceases all too abruptly. Vatout consults an enormous gold watch suspended over his considerable paunch and suddenly springs to his feet. He clasps Claude's right hand within both of his in that warmest of handshakes, turns on his heel and strides through the *café*; many pairs of eyes following his unnecessarily tortuous passage between the tables. With an outstretched hand, he accepts coat, scarf and hat from the attendant who had obviously seen him coming, presses an undoubtedly generous payment into the waiting palm of the cashier with the other hand and disappears through the ornate glass doors.

Paris, November 17th, 1833
Dear Ronne

What a wonderful city – and I have only been here a few days! That man Vatout to whom I had an introduction is such a flamboyant character. I could put him straight into a play! He really wants to help me. He has asked me to leave my manuscript with a critic called St Marc Girardin at the Sorbonne and I can't wait to hear from him. Chrétien and Lambert seem to enjoy life. They are allowing me to stay as long as I like; I haven't even thought of where I might go afterwards. Could Paris become my future home?

For the moment, I spend all my time in my suit and polished boots wandering along the boulevards. You can see the most elegant carriages there. My imagination goes wild; just wondering who is in them and where they are going. I would love to follow them. Everywhere the women are beautiful and elegantly dressed, some in the company of national guardsmen; so smart in their blue jackets, stretched white breeches and tall helmets. The rue de la Paix is particularly impressive. Its shops are protected by enormous awnings so that passers-by have no excuse but to admire the elegant window displays. When I get tired, I take an omnibus to its terminus for a meagre twenty-five centimes so that I can admire the most ornate buildings you can imagine, all the colourful markets and simple teeming humanity. I have discovered the galerie d'Orléans where writers meet their publishers, and where I hope one day that I will seal a contract for my play.

I hope that you are well. Please don't take too seriously all that I said about pharmacy. It is I rather than the profession that is at odds with the world. Since I can't change myself I must find something else in which to involve myself and my ideas.

Do greet the Millets for me - and then most specially Marianne. And write soon to...   Your friend, Claude

Claude certainly enjoys visiting the arcades and peering into elegant *cafés* and restaurants along the boulevards; but takes his bread and cheese in cheaper, smaller side streets where Auvergnats in traditional garb ply their trades as water and coal carriers; and where tradesmen argue. If he is lucky, the sweeter scents of a bakery or florist will, for a short time blot out the pervading smells of discarded waste. As he eats, he watches a *chiffonier* – a rag picker – at work, sifting through the filthy street debris with his hooked stick in the hope of finding some accidentally discharged trinket, carelessly dropped jewellery or even a lost coin. In the evenings he strolls only through the boulevards, forewarned by his friends of violent danger should he linger in the side streets. He passes the *Théatre des Variétés* where even *Rose du Rhone* might just be performed one day. After all, if Lyon had liked it, then why not Paris? On most evenings, he would finally collapse at Flicoteaux, Bobino's or the Café Roussel in the Latin Quarter. In one or the other he would almost certainly find Chrétien and Lambert. There he would be introduced to some of their colleagues, and end the evening modestly with a *menthe* before retiring to bed.

"It's all a question of what you are trying to achieve…."

Girardin's opening remark; quietly spoken, polite. His conduct was that of a man of position with the drama world of Paris at his feet. The manuscript is open in front of him. Claude sees extensive notes in the margins of each page; he had clearly read the play in depth. Claude is impressed; even flattered.

"…however, if I were you, I would have stayed closer to the reality of history rather than embellishing it with all those overtones of *romantisme*. Take your scene where King John orders Arthur's eyes to be burnt out; or the one where Des Roches perishes in what you refer to as 'a sea of blood'. They are overly dramatic. It would have been better to put your characters in situations that reveal more about their personalities rather than just presenting them as extremes of good or bad. It's melodrama of course, and we have quite enough of that here already."

Claude understands what he is referring to. Any argument or justification seems pointless, given the eminence of the man. Quite abruptly, Girardin switches the conversation to Claude himself; drawing him out on his family, work in the pharmacy, his Cartesian principles and even on the vineyards of the Beaujolais! Claude sees little relevance in all this, yet flattered by Girardin's interest. Just as abruptly, he reverts back to the play:

"I will be direct with you, young man; it won't get you a producer. You could re-write it, but I doubt whether you have the right spirit for it. Here in Paris you can find talented authors, playwrights, poets, composers and artists on every street corner. As you walk around our city, you may well believe that we have enough platforms for all this talent. Let me tell you that only the exceptional and highly gifted have a chance of succeeding, and even some of those might just as easily starve while they await their turn."

Claude's mouth is dry and he feels faint in the head; yet he manages to maintain an expression of polite interest as Girardin continues:

"Despite your enthusiasm I don't believe that being a playwright is your destiny. You have had a fine education and now some experience in pharmacy. You have an evident interest in human behaviour and the process of thought. You have a certain ability to express yourself but I would guess more appropriately suited to factual forms of writing. Have you perhaps considered the profession of medicine? In my view this might best suit your talents."

Claude tries not to let his shock and dismay show. He thanks Girardin for his trouble, thrusts the manuscript under his arm and escapes into the *rue de la Sorbonne* fighting back tears of bitter disappointment.

It is late evening as he retraces his steps towards the Latin Quarter and much needed refreshment at Bobino's. Chrétien and Lambert are already in position at their usual table indulging in an overcooked sausage accompanied by a rather limp salad. Another young man is with them, introduced to Claude as one Jean Viallon who is apparently a senior student of French literature.

"Well, tell us the worst."

Chrétien speaks for the group, fully aware from Claude's face about what he is about to say.

"It was awful" replies Claude. "I might as well pack my bags and go back to the Beaujolais. I suppose Girardin tried to be nice but he told me in no uncertain terms that I was not meant to be a playwright. Can you believe, he actually proposed that I should study medicine?"

Lambert interjects: "Not so fast Claude. What did he say was wrong with the play?"

"Oh! He didn't like the way I treated the subject. Of course the play is historical, but he wanted me to portray the characters literally rather then romantically. That was not what *I* wanted to do."

"Your friends here tell me that it was the illustrious Vatout who recommended Girardin." Viallon said. "I'm not sure that it was such a good choice. I sometimes attend Girardin's lectures and I can tell you that there is no firmer opponent of *romantisme*. When they performed *Hernani* a few years ago, he stood shoulder to shoulder with the classicists and absolutely slammed Hugo in the *Journal des Débats*. I am sure that he would have wanted a more *classiciste* interpretation of your theme!"

Lambert, thoughtful: "If Viallon is right, then why not ask Vatout for somebody with a less-biased view; there must be plenty to choose from in this great city?"

"Not a bad idea," agrees Claude with a sigh, "I'll do that."

Lambert tries to lighten the atmosphere by telling a joke, but Claude's mind is elsewhere. Why *had* Vatout recommended Girardin? He would surely have been aware of his literary inclination. On the other hand Vatout had not read the actual manuscript and may not have appreciated Claude's style. On his return to *rue Victor* he would write to him.

Vatout's response was sympathetic and understanding; he recommended Pierre Ligier, a highly regarded actor known to favour more romantic roles. He had taken the lead role in the one-and-only performance of Hugo's *le Roi s'amuse* at the *Comédie* – before the play was abruptly censored by the heavyweights of the July monarchy! Vatout also suggested that if Ligier provided a similar opinion to Girardin, Claude might then consider heeding the advice of two such highly respected gentlemen. Vatout had concluded that he had the feeling from his enjoyable conversation with Claude at the Montansier that indeed he might be better suited to a profession that used his '...*other excellent qualities*'.

Ligier proves to be a charming man; but takes major issue with Claude's style which he feels does not give his characters sufficient credibility. His final verdict is essentially the same as Girardin's; perhaps with even greater emphasis. Seeing Claude's crestfallen face, he offers him free tickets for a production of Racine's *Esther*, in which he was taking the role of the evil Haman.

At Bobino's the next day, Chrétien had already consumed rather more wine than was good for him and was watching other peoples' comings and goings with a glazed look in his eyes. Lambert was leafing casually through the manuscript of Claude's *Arthur de Bretagne*; twisting the document this way and that so that he could read Girardin's marginal comments. Claude looks from one to another and eventually breaks the silence:

"The problem is what to do now and I…"

"You don't have a problem, Claude." interjects Chrétien roughly, "Your writing career simply doesn't exist. You have been warned off and in my opinion you'd be a fool not to take notice of the advice. Ramon was a nice guy and wanted the best for you, but he didn't know the local Paris scene."

"There are certainly a lot of negative comments on your manuscript, Claude…."

Lambert gestures dismissively at the manuscript in his lap.

"…and it doesn't sound as if you will have much chance of success with it. Why *not* study medicine? You said that you were disillusioned with pharmacy; but if you became a doctor you could push back the frontiers by doing research into medicines and their use."

Chrétien is nodding slowly in apparent agreement.

"That's all very well my friends," Claude responds, "You have great confidence in me, but I don't even have my *bac*. The idea of restudying and then doing so many years in medical school doesn't much appeal."

"Yes, but what are your *alternatives,* Claude?"

The challenge comes from Lambert and is followed by a minute of silence during which Claude looks thoughtfully in the direction of his boots.

"It's even more complicated," he says mournfully. "I have just heard that I have to do my five years army service; I can't see how I can find two thousand francs to buy myself a substitute."

"*Zut!* That bloody lottery" quips Chrétien. "You poor chap. We've all escaped that – so far. Couldn't you ask your parents for an advance? With your brilliance, you'll rake in the money once you are an eminent physician; you'll easily be able to pay them back!"

Claude shakes his head with the hopelessness of it all.

"I'm tired," he finally says. "I'll sleep on it – but thank you both for your ideas: it's nice to have friends who care."

Relieving Lambert of the manuscript, he waves casually to his friends and disappears into the dark.

"Poor chap." Chrétien remarks, "I'm not sure that he would make such a good doctor. You know, he'd want written proof that his treatment was going to work before he ever prescribed anything for a patient...." He laughs loudly at his imagery: "...and the patient would be dead by then!"

Claude had a bad night; Lambert's stark comment about his lack of alternatives impossible to suppress. In the early hours of the morning, he writes to his parents, breaking the news about the negative critiques of his play, and asking their advice about his proposed career in medicine. He also mentions that there was apparently a list of recruits in each district who were willing to be 'bought' into army service, in order to replace him. Would his parents be prepared to advance such a large sum, knowing that supporting him for his medical studies alone would be expensive? He takes a long time to compose the letter – and he sends it enclosed in a small parcel containing two figurines – for Caroline.

While waiting for their response, he desperately tries to distract himself with visiting an exhibition of Delacroix's latest paintings and a lecture on Poussin. He walks his feet off along the Seine and lingers in street markets where he could always eat cheaply. He attends several new plays where he is able to slip past the door attendant without paying, and consumes endless cheap drinks with his friends whose lives seem so much less complicated than his. He finds the medical school and wanders through its corridors, its library and its new auditorium which could seat up to fifteen hundred students – as he is informed by a passing medical student.

"What do we have here?" comments Lambert, as Claude joins them at Flicoteaux late one evening; his face radiant.
"Just got a letter from home," he says. "They are happy for me to study medicine; and unbelievably, they have already found a chap to go into the service for me."
"Wonderful, Claude, no more worries then." Chrétien adds. "You can knuckle down to your *bac* studies now: we'll give you your own corner of the room in which you can work."
"No. You've both already been too kind to me: I'm going to find a place of my own now."

The tiny room into which he had just moved was not far from *rue Victor*. He is now gazing out of its large window – the only redeeming feature of his new and rather tawdry dwelling. An array of windows looks back at him across a narrow alleyway from which both noise and smell emanate in abundance. He draws the blind and immediately feels unbearably cloistered from the world. The blind dominates the room, and he tries to imagine the bizarre events that had created its myriad of stains. With a woollen shawl wrapped around his neck and torso, he sits on the edge of his bed. It sags terribly; but is at least more comfortable than a single rickety wooden chair only usable to deposit his clothes. On the bed next to him is the syllabus for the courses and examinations for the *bac*. He had decided to get help from some classes at the nearby *lycée Louis-le-Grand,* particularly to bring his Latin and Greek up to standard. Relearning the necessary history, philosophy and geography would be an effort too.

Six months seem to get him nowhere; his examinations at the end of his laborious six months yet another ordeal. The results of the *bac*, eventually posted on the *lycée's* notice board provide exactly the disappointment he had dreaded. He had totally failed in Latin and Greek and gained inadequate marks in the other subjects. He is offered a retake of all the examinations in the following month. However, it is made clear to him that unless he has adequate passes on that occasion, he would have to defer his entry into medical school for a further year.

To everyone's relief, he manages to pass the examinations in that crucial month of August – but only just to the level required for entry into medical school; unsurprisingly, his best results were in philosophy and history! Chrétien and Lambert with two of their other friends take him out to celebrate with dinner at Bobino's. Perhaps for the only occasion in his entire life Claude drinks himself almost into delirium. They finish their evening weaving their way down the *rue St Jacques*, yelling bawdy songs at the tops of their voices either to the amusement – or to the annoyance – of passers by.

Claude is impatient to discover the reality of his new professional studies: yet the subjects in the first year of his course – physics, biology and chemistry – seem to have no direct bearing on illness. As always, he has real difficulty in memorizing the necessary 'facts'. With pharmacy experience behind him, the practical aspects of chemistry are not a problem; its theory however is an uphill battle. He is fortunate that an instructor by the name of Théo Pelouze sympathizes with him; providing the extra tuition necessary for him to eventually pass the examination. Pelouze and his wife also take Claude 'under their wing' for the occasional meal in their cosy apartment near the medical school.

It is now the start of his second year of studies, and Claude is in front of the medical school notice board:

'*Richet, Bernard, Davaine, Lasègue*'

The names had been neatly written beneath the location '*École Pratique, Room A, table 6*'. He is delighted that the office had respected his and Casimir Davaine's request; to be part of the same dissecting group. During their first year, they had struck an immediate friendship, based on their mutual love of the theatre – and their difficulties with chemistry.

Now the four students are standing around the long, waist-high dissection table, gazing steadfastly and silently at the body – once a man.

"You will remember from yesterday's demonstration…" begins the prosector who has been allocated to them, "….that we have to open the thoracic cavity by dividing the ribs and clavicle on either side of the sternum, in order to gain access to the pericardium, heart and major vessels. Bernard, perhaps you can deal with the right side, and you, Davaine can then do the left."

Blood drains from Claude's face and his forehead glistens with sweat as he steps bravely forward. Closely copying the routine of the previous day's demonstration, he first incises the bloodless skin and then takes the shiny saw from the prosector to begin his task. After dividing each rib he glances furtively at the face of his unknown victim as if he expected him to object to his violent, even noisy actions. Davaine reluctantly takes his turn. Patiently describing his actions and findings, the prosector now completes the careful separation, freeing the intact anterior chest wall from its host. He finally places it on a small table nearby for detailed examination.

"I want you to now identify, describe and dissect out in their entire length, all the arteries, veins and nerves in this preparation." He adds.

"Lasègue, you can do the first part of the dissection, and you Richet can complete the task at tomorrow's session. Please use this as your reference."

With that comment, he places a stained and rather dishevelled anatomy atlas on a primitive lectern and moves off to another table.

By noon their dissection has advanced much more slowly than anticipated. The students cover Gaston (as they have decided to call him) demurely with a large, damp piece of towelling, and gratefully hurry from the dissecting room. With extensive notes and hastily drawn diagrams tucked under their arms, hands well washed with dilute carbolic and relief showing on their faces, they escape from the building. They join their friends around the tall columns that front the medical school, breathing in the cold but now welcome winter air; chattering about their experiences and reactions, their need for a midday meal somehow less pressing than usual.

As usual, Claude is not without criticism; and today it is the lack of explanation about the way that anatomical structures relate to one another.

"Look Casi, the radial artery runs close to the median nerve – which I presume it nourishes. I want to know whether that nerve has a reverse influence on the behaviour of the artery. That's surely a logical question; yet no-one can give me an answer."

"You can't expect an anatomy dissection to tell you that, Claude: be reasonable. Why don't you ask Bérard after his next physiology lecture?"

The forty francs that he had paid gave him access to all lectures held in the medical school, but there were additional presentations at the *Collège de France*, a short distance from the school. He learned that it had been established three centuries earlier as a centre of research in science and in the humanities. In addition, it had the function of educating not just professionals-in-training, but also the general public. Pelouze, whom he still met from time to time, tells him about François

Magendie, a leader in the physiology movement and the recently appointed professor of experimental medicine at the *Collège*. Magendie often brought one of his patients into the lecture theatre to reinforce his lectures. Sometimes he used post-mortem material like a shrunken liver of an alcoholic; then discussed its features and what they revealed to him about the life of its owner! He also experimented on animals with a view to demonstrating how organs functioned – their physiology. It is this which prompts Claude to make his first visit to the lecture theatre at the *Collège*.

François Magendie sweeps into the amphitheatre closely followed by his assistant. Both wear spotless white aprons tied firmly at the waist. The babble of voices subsides as the eminent lecturer surveys his audience. He nods with approval at the fully occupied benches rising in curved rows to the vaulted ceiling, at the apex of which is the large skylight that provides the theatre's only illumination. Placing his hands palms down on the lectern in front of him, elbows fully extended, he leans backwards impressively and begins:

"Vomiting is fundamental to survival…"

He pauses briefly and dramatically;

"…and yet despite the fact that the stomach may contain quite harmful contents, the body sometimes fails to initiate that process. Then it becomes the responsibility of physicians to induce vomiting, using drugs that we refer to as emetics. Some of what I will show you today is not new: I first demonstrated my experiments of vomiting to the Baron Cuvier and to Pinel, whom at least some of you will remember"

He hesitates again, searching the audience's faces for signs of recognition of the two famous Paris physicians whom he has named.

"However, despite my presentations to the *Académie des Sciences* there is disbelief, even amongst my colleagues at the *Hôtel-Dieu*."

Magendie now turns to a blackboard on which he draws a vertical tube representing the gullet, attached below to a flagon-shaped stomach. He adds a horizontal line at the junction of the two organs and identifies it by scrawling the word "diaphragm" alongside. Two further heavily drawn lines lead away upward from the diaphragm, and another two sideways. He continues, pointing:

"These pairs of lines represent two distinctly separate types of nerve, which stimulate movements of the diaphragm. The upper ones represent the pneumogastric nerves, arguably the most important nerves in the body. They allow the brain to communicate with the major organs of the chest and abdomen. These nerves also help to regulate muscular movements of the diaphragm which separates chest from abdomen – as during the quiet breathing that we do unconsciously. These other two lines represent the somatic nerves, which in contrast we can control ourselves quite consciously. Thus when we take a forceful deep breath, it is under influence of these somatic nerves that the rib muscles will expand the chest, and the diaphragm will descend. This increases the capacity of the chest cavity and allows more air to enter."

Claude had entered the packed amphitheatre only seconds before Magendie's arrival and had perched himself precariously the end of the front bench. His elderly neighbour was now taking a deep wheezing breath – as if to confirm the normality of his own somatic nerves.

"Now we will move to the subject of this lecture. You will be familiar with the traditional teaching that vomiting represents a contraction – even a spasm – of the muscular walls of the stomach, a process activated by the pneumogastric nerves. Now, is this explanation correct?"

Magendie's gaze again sweeps over the audience. At the same time Claude turns in his seat to survey the sea of eager faces behind him. Some of them appear to be students, like him. The majority are older men, probably practising physicians taking the opportunity of listening to the eminent lecturer. Even some women are present, wearing inconsiderately tall hats. Around half of the onlookers are nodding their heads in agreement with Magendie's challenging statement. The rest seem unmoved by the challenge. During this introduction, Magendie's assistant (identifiable from the notice board as his *préparateur*, Constantin James) had left the auditorium, and now returns propelling a long trolley with squeaking wheels. Two small dogs are strapped to it, their backs to the trolley, their bellies shaved of all hair.

"I will shortly inject this first dog with the drug emetine, which my esteemed colleague Pelletier has recently identified as the active ingredient of tartar emetic. Those of you who regularly consult my *Formulaire* will know how many people have died in France over from the use of tartar emetic. Accordingly, we are now keenly searching for safer substitutes with which to induce therapeutic vomiting".

As he speaks, he incises the upper abdomen. Some minor bleeding is controlled by the pressure of a moist cloth applied to the wound by his assistant.

"You there, I need your help for this."

Magendie points directly at Claude, who blushes to the roots of his hair and reluctantly approaches the front of the amphitheatre, where he is grasped none too kindly by the shoulders and manoeuvred to the left side of the dog.

"Now, place your index and middle finger through the incision. In a moment, I will ask you to describe to me what you feel."

After carefully filling a shiny metal cylinder from a glass vessel beside him, Magendie injects the contents into a vein in the hind leg of the dog. Within one minute Claude's fingers are bent forcibly, as what he assumes to be the animal's diaphragm descends abruptly against them. The dog meanwhile vomits the foulest material, some of which cascades onto his breeches and boots. Magendie asks Claude to describe to the audience what he had felt, and he is then permitted to return to his seat. His neighbours on the front bench obligingly bunch closer together; either to reward him for his recent ordeal by giving him more space to sit, or to distance themselves from the distasteful mess on his hands and clothes. Meanwhile, Magendie proceeds to address the audience:

"It is clear, is it not, that it must be the emetine-induced downward movement of the diaphragm, stimulated by the pneumogastric nerves, which plays the central role in vomiting. In doing so, it increases the pressure within the abdominal cavity. The stomach is compressed, and is thus obliged to eject its contents up through the gullet. But how might I now determine if the diaphragm is indeed the major organ involved in the process of vomiting?"

After a pause during which a murmur rustles through the audience, a resonant voice in the audience exclaimed:

"You could cut the pneumogastric nerves!"

Magendie identifies the owner of the voice, an elderly bearded man some three rows from the front, and nods towards him with appreciation. Continuously describing to his audience the exact steps in his procedure, Magendie locates and finally cuts the pneumogastric nerves through the existing incision in the abdominal wall. He now calls upon the man who offered his advice to join him at the front – and to place his own fingers within the incision. A second injection of emetine yields absolutely no response from the dog. There is no semblance of vomiting, and the 'volunteer' reports no impact on his fingers. Drawing himself up to his full height Magendie comments:

"We can now acknowledge the primacy of the diaphragm in the process of vomiting. Yet we cannot exclude that a contraction of the stomach itself might play at least some part in vomiting: after all, it too is supplied by the pneumogastric nerves. Another experiment is called for."

He moves to the other dog, which has a freshly sutured wound on its abdomen. He again addresses the audience:

"I operated on this dog before we came into the amphitheatre. I can assure you that I have left its pneumogastric nerves quite intact. However, I have completely removed its stomach and in its place, I have sewn a pig's urine bladder, an organ that you will know has less muscular tissue within its walls. Furthermore, whatever muscular tissue exists in the bladder is clearly not in connection with the dog's pneumogastric nerves. Mr James has just filled this false stomach with red liquid, using a rubber tube passed through the dog's mouth."

He indicates on his diagram on the board exactly how he and his *préparateur* had separated the stomach from the gullet above and from the small intestine below, replacing the original organ by the thin flaccid pig's bladder. With some ceremony, he now injects a vein in the dog's hind leg. In less than one minute, the dog begins to vomit forcefully: red fluid is everywhere. The audience gasps, followed by polite applause.

"It is therefore clear…" Magendie summarises, now back in his original position at the lectern, "…that whatever the role of the stomach might be in accommodating food and propelling it onwards into the intestine, it has certainly nothing but a passive part to play in the process of vomiting. The increased pressure within the abdominal cavity produced by sudden downward movement of the diaphragm is the event – the one and only action, I must emphasize – that brings about the process of vomiting."

There is a further brisk round of applause from the audience. With a bow of acknowledgement, Magendie dramatically leaves the auditorium. Behind him, Constantin James wheels out the trolley bearing the two animals, and within minutes the amphitheatre is empty. Claude remains in his seat, enveloped by silence. His eyes move from the drawing on the blackboard to the nauseating mess on the floor and once more back to the diagram.

CHAPTER 4

THE AWAKENING

It is raining miserably as Claude emerges on to the street outside the *Collège*. He hesitates, unsure whether he should return to his cold and dismal lodgings or to the warmth of the medical school library. At that moment, the massive oak door behind him opens abruptly and Constantin James appears, glances disapprovingly at the heavy sky and marches briskly down the *rue des Écoles* in the direction of the medical school. Claude follows, quickening his pace until he catches up with him.

"I must say, that was an impressive demonstration."

James stops; looks at him. "And to whom am I speaking?"

"Bernard, Claude Bernard"

"I would be happy to talk with you Bernard, but let's get out of this bloody rain?"

A few steps further a rather scruffy bar offers them protection against the elements.

"May I offer you coffee?"

They sit at a small marble-topped table, in silence until a surly waiter deposits two cups of steaming coffee in front of them. Claude again takes the initiative.

"Do you believe in scientific truth, Mr James?"

"What a strange question! Do I sense a passion for Cartesian philosophy?"

Claude ignores his comment. He does not want to impress James: only to discover the path that had led to his post as *préparateur* – which Claude has just decided will be his next goal.

"So much of what they teach us in medical school seems to be impression, guesswork – or at best somebody's observation. It's wonderful to be confident about the mechanism of at least one body process?"

James smiles condescendingly:

"Don't be so naive, Bernard. That experiment doesn't always work, much to Magendie's embarrassment. You should see the convoluted explanations he comes up with to explain his failures! Fortunately, today's demonstration was perfect; at least he has finally managed to convince most people about his theory of vomiting."

The rain is now falling even more heavily; the wheels of passing carriages dipping spectacularly into muddy depressions in the road. Content with the warmth of their refuge, James begins to reveal his own history at some length. Claude learns that he has a French mother and an American father: indeed he had received some of his education in Chicago, and being bilingual he had been helping Magendie with the French translation of some useful medical articles in the *London Medical Gazette*.

James continues:

"I've been his *préparateur* for the last three years and I also help with his clinical work at the *Hôtel-Dieu*. You know, he can be very direct – even rude; yet one has to acknowledge his deep wisdom. For a long time, he was almost alone in condemning the widespread use of leeches. He is also viciously critical of the way that his colleagues use drugs in so many diseases, without evidence that they work."

Claude is immediately alert:

"That's interesting! When I was training in pharmacy a few years ago, I tried to find out – usually without success – why certain medicaments were used. When I asked my *patron*, he was not too surprised at my questions: even once suggested that surgical operations often harmed more than they helped."

"Well then, you should know that Magendie originally trained as a surgeon? That bastard Dupuytren had just been made professor of surgery and saw Magendie's brilliance as a future threat; made life so difficult for him that he had to quit. He decided instead to work as a physician, and now uses his surgical skill only to solve the riddles of physiology."

The rain had at last settled to a mild drizzle, and James excuses himself abruptly:

"I must go, but I trust that we will meet again, Bernard."

Claude remains sitting in the *café* for some time, contemplating the discussion he has just had with James; more certain than ever of his new ambition of working with Magendie.

"It's remarkable, Casi! You must come next time. You know, I can see myself in Magendie's shoes – one day. There are so many theories about how the body works – and yet so few facts; it could keep me busy for a lifetime!"

"Aren't you rushing things a bit?"

"Not at all; I must have a goal. Can't you see how many people construct theories – and then follow them quite irrationally? They don't want to admit that they don't know or are uncertain? It is as if something is better than nothing, even though that something has no dimensions."

They are sitting on a bench in the central square of the medical school, as Claude drives home his ideas to his friend. Davaine is lost for words; trying to understand his friend's reasoning. He looks at Claude's serious expression:

"Alright; get the rest of it off your chest, Claude!"

"You know, I am only beginning to appreciate what I learned in Lyon; it's a fundamental scepticism about the treatment of illness. I left the pharmacy feeling that most drugs were used empirically – and sometimes dangerously, too. According to his *préparateur*, Magendie is of the same opinion – I am sure with good evidence behind him. I am also certain that surgeons are often just as irrational with what they do to people with scalpels! I simply can't commit myself to treating people until I really understand their illness; and I can't do that until I know how each organ works under normal conditions."

"How do you expect to do that?"

"Simple; it's just a matter of systematically examining each organ under different conditions – like Magendie demonstrated yesterday: I can't understand why it's not been done before. For example, do organs function together in some coordinated way or does each have a mind of its own? One surely has to answer those questions in healthy individuals before one can even begin to understand disease."

"You mean, experiment on people?"

"*Idiot!* On animals, of course! Vivisection is not such an evil thing if it helps us to treat humans better. Can you think of any another way of proving how organs act."

"You always speak of 'proving': can't you accept anything that anyone tells you?"

"Yes, of course; well provisionally anyhow. But I surely want proof before I can accept it as being true."

Davaine shakes his head; any further discussion is a waste of time. He takes Claude by the elbow and they retire to a bar for a well-earned drink.

The publication of his examination results in that cold November of 1836 is a big relief. Claude had passed – and for anatomy, he had won a special note of commendation for his expertise in dissection. After the short Christmas break, he would be an *externe*, attached to the services of physicians and surgeons in the Paris hospitals: some responsibility at last.

Davaine, who had also passed without difficulty is joyous:

"Let's go dancing somewhere! I think I'll invite that pretty girl who works with the *traiteur* in the next building. Go on Claude, you ask that librarian you keep telling me about - Yvette, isn't it?"

Claude was reticent about asking a girl with whom he had only had passing – and then only professional – contact. Davaine though is persistent; even teasing, and Claude feels obliged to approach her. The next day he takes his courage into his hands and visits the library on the pretext of re-reading one of Magendie's journal articles. She is wearing a very becoming red dress and greets him so warmly, that later in the morning Claude has no difficulty in issuing the invitation.

"I'm so sorry…" – but with the kindest of smiles – "…but I really can't accompany you. I think that my gentleman friend might take a rather poor view of it."

Claude, embarrassed, leaves the journal open on the table, mumbles thanks for her help and leaves the building on the pretext of an important engagement about which he had almost forgotten. Despite Davaine's suggestion that he should come alone, he decides that he will celebrate instead by going to the theatre. That year there had been a spate of productions featuring a young actress called Rachel – at seventeen already a star. At the *Théatre-Français,* Claude would see if she really lived up to the critics' enthusiasm.

The following day he visits his favourite bookshop to purchase Balzac's latest book, Père Goriot. He had been told that it dealt with life in a Paris boarding house, one of whose residents was Bianchon, a medical student. Balzac had apparently styled this character on his student friend Bouillaud, who had by now become an eminent physician at the *Charité*. Claude wants to compare the character in Balzac's book with Bouillaud himself, whom he had heard lecturing in an annoyingly didactic way.

In the hospital wards, his black apron clearly identifies him as an *externe*. It travels between his room, the medical school and the hospital, tightly bundled into his satchel with notebooks, pencils and often fruit. He is attached to the *Hôtel-Dieu* hospital and allocated to Dr Auguste Chomel, one of the hospital's finest physicians. The day begins with lectures; then a check on the progress of the half-dozen patients allocated to his care in St Agnes' ward. Had they eaten their diet, taken their prescribed medication; how do they feel? With the other *externes* Claude is directly responsible to the *interne*: a medical student some three years his senior. Rebot is a helpful young man, but expects that his *externes* should answer only to Chomel, an approach that makes his own life a little easier!

"This is Monsieur Vincent, whom you saw on your round last week".

Rebot reports to Chomel towards the end of the long morning round.

"The ulcer on his left foot has increased in size despite rest and the dressings that we are using. There is absolutely no pain in the foot, which is surprising when you note how deeply the ulcer involves the tissues."

Chomel looks pointedly one by one at his entourage as if expecting an immediate explanation for the paradox Rebot had voiced. More than a dozen people now crowd around the bed staring intently at the deeply discoloured foot, from which a large deep ulcer emits the foulest of odours. Monsieur Vincent himself looks hopefully from face to face.

Chomel addresses the group:

"This man has saccharine diabetes, in which one sometimes finds that arteries are obstructed. Hence, his foot is dark from impending gangrene. Putrefaction is now occurring. On top of this, saccharine diabetes appears to damage the nerves of the leg, something to which our attention was drawn almost forty years ago by a certain Doctor Rollo. Because of this, he fails to appreciate pain. In that sense, one can say that Monsieur Vincent is fortunate. Should he have surgery to the limb, he will of course suffer less, but that is small compensation.

"And his diet, Monsieur Bernard?"

"I can report that as from last week, Monsieur Vincent is being given a diet which limits both starch and his sugar intake."

Chomel nods approvingly:

"One of my colleagues, Dr Piorry believes that since sugar is lost in the urine in such large quantities, it must be replenished by feeding a diet which is *rich* in sugar and starch. I am not of that opinion, since I have observed lessening of the amount of sugar in the urine by the type of diet that Monsieur Bernard has just described to you. Perhaps more importantly, the patient feels better!"

Chomel looks meaningfully at his patient, as if he expects to be thanked for this part of his treatment, and asks the students to move away from the bed so that he can talk alone with him. Rejoining the group some minutes later, he continues:

"His outlook is bad, of course. As the putrefaction extends – as it must do – his body will become overwhelmed from the breakdown of his own tissues, and at that stage death will not be far distant."

One of the students asks whether an operation might save his life.

"I cannot feel the pulse behind the knee, so that we know that simple removal of the diseased tissue would not be followed by wound healing: there is simply not enough blood supply. Amputating his leg above the knee is a possibility, but his overall condition would probably not sustain it. I have told Monsieur Vincent of his predicament and he does not wish to have surgery. He has exercised his freedom of choice by allowing nature to take its course. The outcome is obvious."

They have come to the end of the ward round, and as is the normal routine the assembly of students accompany Chomel to the autopsy room on the lower floor, where he is to perform an autopsy on a patient from his ward. While they prepare their instruments, Chomel asks Claude to summarise the dead man's history:

"This fifty-year old man had a long-standing cough, er... apparently with copious blood in the sputum, a chronic fever, and ...actually, quite devastating weakness. Listening to his chest there is....or was...quite loud sounds, of a type er...."

Chomel looks up at Claude; impatient:
"Rebot, please…"
"Yes, sir. He had definite crepitations at both his lung bases: moist sounds indicative of infection, and probably consumption."
"Thank you, Rebot." Chomel again looks pointedly, but now disapprovingly at Claude, and opens the chest. He follows exactly the routine that Claude had observed during his very first dissecting experience at the *école pratique*. The man's heart is normal enough but when the lungs are removed their surface show myriads of solid white areas, typical (says Chomel) of extensive tuberculosis. Chomel points out similar white areas in the kidneys: clearly, the process is widespread.
"This man also may have had saccharine diabetes." adds Chomel. "People with that condition often seem to have concurrent tuberculosis. Did you by any chance arrange for his urine to be checked for sugar, Bernard?"
The answer is 'no'. Claude feels that he has made a devastating omission as the eyes of the other students swivel towards him.

Claude's two further years as an *externe* pass quickly enough: lecture followed by ward round; finally surgery or autopsy! He spends most afternoons in the dissection room at the *école Pratique*: fascinated now by the anatomy of the brain. He enjoys the technical challenge of dissecting the course of the cranial nerves as they pursue their tortuous paths through various apertures in the skull, heading towards their destinations in the nose, eyes, ears, face and neck. From the distribution of their many branches, he tries to deduce what their functions might be – before he looks them up in his anatomy atlas.

Claude's final attachment is at the *Charité*, to the service of Dr Pierre Rayer: a man who had written about many disorders – including diabetes. One of the patients for whom Claude is responsible is a young girl in her twenties. She had rapidly worsening eyesight due to cataract, an unusual complication of diabetes at such a young age. It had been diagnosed a few years earlier and was of a rare form which was not as progressive as usual. Rayer had found a diet which improved her condition to the point where she had been almost free of her thirst, a major symptom of the disorder. Yet, finding a solution to her impending blindness was not so easy: operations for cataract were notorious for the uncertainty of their outcome and many patients finished up losing their vision altogether. Claude is fascinated by her condition. When he learns that she has an interest in fine literature he offers to read to her – when he has the time. He finds himself becoming very attracted to her. One day, she sends him a way with a flea in his ear. Had he been a trifle clumsy in his attentions and offended her sensitivity with his rather personal comments? Was romance ever to come his way?

He takes every opportunity during his time as an *externe* to attend Magendie's lectures at the *Collège de France*, mostly meeting with Constantin James afterwards for refreshment at one of the nearby *cafés*. Today is no exception:

"I am glad that I saw you today. I've been invited back to America for a big family event. My grandfather has reached the remarkable age of ninety; he has invited all his family to Chicago to celebrate – at his expense, would you believe? Magendie told me yesterday that I can go, as long as I can find someone to replace me. I don't suppose you're interested?"

Claude does not hesitate:

"What a marvellous opportunity. I'd be a fool not to do it; but I am not so sure that he'll accept me."

"We'll see. I will arrange a time for you to meet him as soon as possible: I need to make my own arrangements quite promptly too."

James had arranged for the introduction to take place early the following week. Claude dresses up in his suit and highly polished boots; decides to take with him the record of his special commendation for dissection on the spine – fully aware that this was one of Magendie's major areas of interest.

"So, you are the young man James has told me about."

Magendie hardly glances at Claude; his attention fixed upon a rabbit the side of whose head he had been dissecting.

"Yes, I was hoping that you might allow me to take his place while he is abroad."

Magendie looks up at him, scrutinizing him carefully from top to toe, as if his appearance and dress were relevant to his appointment as a *préparateur*.

"Can you dissect, Bonnard?"

"It's *Bernard*, Monsieur; Claude Bernard. Yes, I enjoy dissection and I trust that this certificate will convince you of my ability."

Claude proffers the document that he had brought with him; Magendie leans over and looks at it intently.

"Signed by Cruveilhier I see. Did he actually examine you?"

"Yes; the preparation on which I was working at the time was a neurological dissection of the thoracic spine."

Magendie suddenly stops his own dissection, turns in his chair and looks Claude directly in the face.

"I suppose that I could do worse than take you on. Make sure that James takes you through the routine of the laboratory...." he hesitates. "...and you'd best come with him to my next lecture as well. Goodbye Bonnard!"

During the several week absence of James in the summer of '39, Claude commits himself to the hilt, foregoing some of his own dissecting sessions at the *école pratique* so that he can help Magendie prepare and present each lecture. What Claude appreciated was his mental flexibility. He did not accept the finality of a piece of information, as did most of his other teachers. He had a freshness of approach and a questioning nature that was immediately appealing. Sadly there was little warmth in their relationship and Magendie did not spare Claude from criticism if there was any slight lapse in his work, however understandable. However, during a presentation Magendie would never forget to publicly acknowledge Claude's part in the experiments. For the moment, that was enough.

Claude was sometimes disturbed by Magendie's approach. As he had experienced at the lecture on vomiting, Magendie often carried out an experiment in front of an audience to demonstrate a particular phenomenon; yet sometimes obtained a result that was different from what he had expected. Laughingly, he would dismiss the unexpected without apparently presenting or seeking an explanation. Furthermore, it was sometimes not clear with what purpose he had performed that particular experiment in the first place. Constantin James had once told Claude that Magendie believed that most men of science privately compared themselves to their personal hero: an Archimedes, a Newton, a Galileo or a Descartes. Magendie saw himself only as a humble rag-picker, a *chiffonier*. Just as the latter used his hooked stick to prod amongst the filth of the streets in the hope of finding an accidentally dropped gem or coin, so he would randomly explore a myriad of unknown scientific phenomena just to see what he might find.

1839 is a year that imprints on Claude the tougher side of research. Magendie defends his views on the origin of the heart sounds; the ones heard through the stethoscope that Laennec had invented just ten years earlier. Unfortunately, his theory – that all sounds are produced by the heart impacting on the inside of the chest wall – is shown to be incorrect by some other researchers. It appears that some sounds in fact resulted from the closure of the heart valves. There is now an even more unpleasant conflict. Achille Longet is only two years older than Claude; but is already a medical graduate with research experience on the brain and nerves – largely gained in Magendie' laboratory. He publicly challenges the credibility and originality of some of Magendie's most important work on the spinal cord and its nerves. It involves Claude as a witness and is never convincingly resolved: neither of the two contestants triumphs in the whole matter. For Claude, it is a harsh but realistic introduction to the politics and ruthlessly competitive element of research.

The year draws to an end, and with it Claude's status as *externe*. He begins to prepare for the important examinations that would decide his future – the transition from *externe* to *interne*. Keenly aware of the extreme importance of this assessment to his career, he is worried that he had committed too much time helping Magendie at the expense of his own studies. He knows only too well that only one out of seven *externes* was likely to pass: those who failed would have to gain their further experience by working long hours in hospitals outside Paris. On the other hand, if he succeeded, then as an *interne* in Paris he would not only have prestige, but also a lighter clinical workload and accordingly more time to commit to research. That experience would open wide the doors to his future career aspirations.

On a freezing day in mid-December he presents himself in his freshly washed black apron to an examination room adjoining the medical school library. He has with him two notebooks: one carries records of patients who had been under his care in the different clinics; the other holds details of the autopsies with which he had assisted. Outwardly he is calm and collected; inwardly he is trembling with fear.

"Your written papers were less than impressive, Monsieur Bernard..."

Such is the first comment as Claude takes his place on the uncomfortable wooden chair. On the other side of the table sit the seven examiners who will decide his future. Claude cannot identify two of them. But the man who has just condemned his papers is Jacques Lisfranc, head surgeon at the *Pitié* and obviously the chairman of the panel. Gabriel Andral is also from the *Pitié*, while Rayer and Fouquier (personal physician to Louis-Phillippe) are from the *Charité*, and Rostan from the smaller, recently constructed *hôpital de l'École*. Lisfranc continues:

"...but today, it is the purpose of this viva voce to assess the clinical competence which you have acquired as an *externe* – as far as we may in these surroundings (his arm describes a wide arc as if it might cause the austere surroundings to disappear). I see that you have had experience in a number of busy services, particularly at the *Hôtel-Dieu*, where of course we provide excellent instruction in acute medicine (the other examiners nod in agreement). If you will allow us to peruse your case book, we can perhaps discuss one of them in detail."

Lisfranc briefly leafs through the notebook and peers intently at Claude over heavy-rimmed spectacles:

"Let us discuss Albert Picard, Monsieur Bernard; your patient who died as a result of pneumonia."

Picard's case is also recorded in his second notebook: Claude had assisted at the autopsy performed by Chomel. As succinctly as he can he describes Picard's stormy ten-day hospital course: firstly the symptoms, and then what he heard when listening to his chest through a stethoscope. Finally, he describes the delirium that developed on the fifth day. By this stage, the patient had declined all food and fluids, and drifted into two days of restless coma from which he did not recover. Claude is aware that he is hesitating as he speaks; a sort of rambling uncertainty that always seemed to afflict him whenever he had to give an account of himself.

"Perhaps you can describe in more detail what you found when you examined the patient, and what you concluded from those findings?"

Claude begins tentatively; then more fluently as the examiners nod with what he hopes is approval:

"He was most distressed by chest pain... intensely breathless really, and coughing continuously with expectoration of blood-stained sputum. Speech was an effort....I actually had difficulty in obtaining a detailed history. His fever was 40 degrees Celsius and he had severe cyanosis, of the deepest blue I have seen....particularly of lips and face. He was generally unkempt....probably malnourished. With my stethoscope I heard loud moist sounds throughout his chest, and his abdomen was flaccid. Neither liver nor kidneys seemed to be enlarged."

"Thank you for your comments, Monsieur Bernard, but I would like you to tell me about the severe cyanosis you observed, and why you believe it was present."

Claude hesitates; swallows the saliva that had accumulated and continues:

"I believe his cyanosis to have been a result of the most extensive damage to both lungs from the pneumonia. Because of this, oxygen in the inhaled air could not diffuse into the blood that entered his lungs via the minor circulation. I reason that the arteries of the body, rather than being suffused with red oxygenated blood were instead full of darker unoxygenated blood. This gave his skin the blue colour of cyanosis which I observed."

"Thank you, Monsieur, and what type of pneumonia did you consider that he was suffering from?"

"I did consider the possibility of consumption – tuberculous pneumonia, but the short history suggested something more acute."

Following a signal from Lisfranc, Fouquier takes over the questioning, logically moving to the subject of Picard's treatment:

"Could you please tell us now what treatment he received?"

"Soon after his admission he was commenced on antimony....in the form of *kermès*. He developed the expected side effects of vomiting and diarrhoea, the latter of quite severe degree; and at the time of his death, his skin bore typical pustules. All these symptoms confirmed ....that the dose of *kermès* was at least sufficient. He was not treated by bleeding in any form, following the recent demonstration by Doctor Louis that the outcome of pneumonia is actually worsened by this procedure."

Fouquier continues, now leaning forward in his chair as if to show the extreme importance of his next demand:

"Please explain why you think that he died, rather than responding to such treatment."

Claude hesitates again; looks at his examiners one by one – guardians of the bridge towards his future career. He was uncertain whether he should say what was on his mind; conscious of the fact that it might jeopardise his chances if his remarks were to be misconstrued. After several seconds of silence he begins:

"Monsieur Picard had a most severe case of pneumonia; I suppose that he may have died simply because of this. However, I believe that his death was hastened...er....both by the antimony treatment he received as well as by a lack of oxygen."

Fouquier's face turns crimson with anger and he sits bolt upright on his impressive high-backed armchair:

"Are you implying that he was incorrectly treated by Dr Chomel? Explain yourself!"

Claude looks anxiously at the faces of the other examiners: expressions quizzical rather than disapproving. He feels the blood rising to his face as he takes a deep breath and continues:

"I am of course aware that antimony has been used for over one hundred years in the treatment of simple pneumonia. As I understand it, the principle is to bring inflammation to the surface – and also to purge the body. However, I am not aware of any proof that the medication works in this way….or indeed that it works at all."

He pauses; takes a deep breath and continues:

"Furthermore, Monsieur Picard was dehydrated, even at the time of his admission; he must have lost considerable fluid as a result of perspiring with his high fever. He was then obliged to suffer the expected severe diarrhoea resulting from antimony treatment. Throughout his illness, he was too ill to drink, which even further aggravated his dehydration: his lax skin and his fast pulse confirming this. I therefore believe that at least part of his delirium and coma was due to reduced blood volume from dehydration, which had deprived the brain of its circulation. It is fortunate that he was not subjected to bleeding as well: I believe he would then have died even sooner."

Since no-one seems inclined to interrupt Claude, he continues. Perspiration is accumulating on his forehead despite the bitterly cold room:

"On top of this, the presence of cyanosis indicated a degree of oxygen deprivation which would have interfered with the function of both his brain and his heart; tissues which we have been told in our lectures require oxygen for correct function."

One could hear a pin drop in the silence.

"I am aware that oxygen does not currently represent accepted treatment for pneumonia. However, I have read that already fifty years ago, Chaussier used oxygen treatment for newborn babies with respiratory problems. In cases of pneumonia, breathing one hundred percent oxygen might be preferable to the twenty percent found in natural air, particularly in severe cases such as that of Monsieur Picard. I also heard in a lecture at the *Collège* that tissue respiration – the combustion that creates carbonic acid from oxygen – is the process by which the body's temperature is maintained. Therefore with his high fever, I would reason that there might be an even greater requirement for oxygen – which was not satisfied in this particular patient."

There is no comment from the examiners, who simply look at one another, accompanied by the noise of restlessly shuffling shoes on the bare wooden floor. After a brief and hushed discussion between Lisfranc and the examiners sitting on either side of him, the former addresses Claude:

"We thank you for addressing us in this way, and would ask you to leave now. Your result will be posted, with all the others, at the end of the week. Good day to you, Monsieur Bernard!"

Claude leaves the room. Lisfranc lookes emphatically at his fellow examiners, one by one:

"I am inclined to agree with Fouquier's remark. I cannot tolerate arrogance from a student. What was good enough for thousands of physicians seems not to suit our Monsieur Bernard. Do you not agree, gentlemen?"

"I am not so sure, Jacques." Rayer, looking thoughtful. "I myself have often wondered whether antimony actually has all the benefits that our colleagues have claimed for it. I think that we would all agree that some mild cases of pneumonia would get better without any treatment. In the more severe cases, I find it hard to judge whether antimony has been truly beneficial. I would have to say that I hope that I will never need that awful treatment!"

Andral decides to add his comment:

"I must admit that I like his idea about oxygen. He seems to be quite an original thinker."

He swivels in his chair to the man sitting behind him:

"Monsieur Bouchardat, do you think that the pharmacy would find it possible to prepare a regular supply of oxygen. Our wards are full of cases of pneumonia at this time of the year, and we could look at oxygen treatment as an option for treatment. I could also talk to my colleague, Louis: he could now perhaps use his numerical method to assess the possible benefit of oxygen in that condition."

"I'll certainly look into it." comments Bouchardat; one of the observers unrecognised by Claude. Lisfranc's anger seems to be gradually subsiding:

"…and what do you think, Rostan?"

"I would have liked to seen Bernard emphasise treatment of the dehydration, which I think is just as important as the other factors he mentioned. Obviously, the patient was very ill, and perhaps nothing could have been done about this aspect. He may not know that ever since our cholera epidemic I have been experimenting with replacing fluids into the veins or under the skin. Yet I do agree that it was refreshing to hear some original and well-informed thought – after he managed to get over his attack of nerves! You know Jacques, I thought that he was totally honest and without any real disrespect. His arguments were also very well reasoned. Of course, we should have asked him about his autopsy findings, but I think we put him through quite an ordeal as it is. I doubt whether autopsy would have shed any further light on the cause of death."

Some two hundred students jostle each other in front of the main medical school notice board, trying to catch a glimpse of their names. Murmurs and exclamations emanate from the few happy and the many disappointed. Claude waits, in no hurry to read the truth of his performance in the examinations: obviously unsatisfactory in the written papers and a total disaster in the *viva voce*. Once the crowd has dwindled, he makes his way tentatively to the notice board. A mistake? Opposite his name is the number twenty-six. Of the two hundred or so students, only twenty-nine have satisfied the requirement to proceed to *internship*; and he, Claude Bernard is one. He looks further down the alphabetical list, first to Davaine – also successful, and then Lasègue – just there at twenty-ninth! He races back to his room, tears of relief and happiness coursing down his cheeks.

CHAPTER 5

IN NEW DIRECTIONS

The transition to the post of *interne* was a big one: more responsibility, more accountability. Claude's mounting self-confidence is very apparent in his first posting to the surgical service of Armand Velpeau. Sparks fly as he questions Velpeau's didactic approach, delaying ward rounds, but amusing the *externes*. Yet he is a valuable assistant during surgical operations. Velpeau never has to ask for the appropriate surgical instrument; Claude anticipates his every need. When permitted to make an incision, locate a specific blood vessel or tie off one that is bleeding, he also works with such speed and precision that Velpeau can only compliment him. Claude is nevertheless concerned about Velpeau's approach to pain. All his patients receive opium preparations prior to operation, but their groans and screams during surgery are still heart-rending. Sometimes Claude's main responsibility during surgery is to restrain the patient with straps, to prevent him from leaping off the table at the crucial moment.

Velpeau had written in one of his articles that *'...the idea that pain in surgery can be avoided is an illusion that should be abandoned'*. For Claude, such absolutism was unacceptable. One day, it prompts him to prescribe a larger than usual dose of opium for one particularly deserving woman. It almost kills her. Claude later comes across the work of Lafargue, and his new technique for introducing morphine directly under the skin via a specially designed lancet. Velpeau is unimpressed. He breathes a sigh of relief when Claude finally moves on to his next post with Pierre Rayer!

The *externes* had just been dismissed after a long and tiring ward round. Claude, now their immediate supervisor is also tired; he stands watching them disappear along the wide corridor, frowning. Rayer approaches him, places a hand on his shoulder and invites him into his office where they subside into two overstuffed leather covered armchairs. Through the window, Claude sees the *externes* sprawled on benches, exhausted from their long ordeal in the stuffy ward.

"You are doing well; yet you seem troubled and ill at ease. Is there something with which I might help you?"

Unaccustomed either to concern or praise, Claude is temporarily taken aback. That Rayer with his many commitments should take the time to be so personal is a surprise. At first tentatively and then with more confidence, he tries to put his worries into words:

"We have seen so many patients this morning in whom the diagnosis is not clear, and yet we offer them treatment with a certainty that hardly seems merited. Those treatments which we offer are themselves not without risk. Yet that man in the second bed, Rimbaud, the one who has all the typical features of pneumonia, is not being offered any treatment at all. I respect the point that you made, concerning your choice of '*traitement expectant*'. I also appreciated the comments that you made concerning the wisdom of the Hahnemann sect, and the fact that we may sometimes harm patients with our treatment – I was studying pharmacy in Lyon when my *patron* first made me aware of this principle."

Rayer nods but remains silent.

"I also understand that bleeding treatment for pneumonia is out of favour following the finding of Louis' numerical method. But this bothers me, too."

"Why, may I ask?"

"I have recently read Louis' article again. His conclusions are based on the fact that the group of patients in his analysis who were treated without bleeding survived as well as the group who were bled."

"Correct: do continue!"

"Amongst his sixteen patients whose normal treatment was supplemented by bleeding, eight appeared to recover from their illness rather quickly. However, there were an equal number of patients in whom there was rapid deterioration after bleeding, leading to their death. This means that there was fifty percent likelihood of recovery with bleeding treatment."

Rayer nods.

"In the group who were treated without bleeding, the survival rate was also fifty percent, so Louis' conclusions are understandable. But isn't it possible that those eight patients who died in the group treated by bleeding had some additional problem that we cannot yet define and which rendered bleeding particularly dangerous...."

"Yes, that's certainly possible."

"...and if such patients could have been identified and excluded in advance, then bleeding might after all have been shown to be useful treatment for pneumonia – in appropriate patients?"

Rayer looks at Claude thoughtfully:

"Good reasoning, young man! It is some time since I read Louis' report. Some of my colleagues still bleed such cases, but many more now say that it is to be avoided; Magendie, the next physician with whom you will be working is one of them; at least that's something about which he and I agree! I do believe that statistics can be misleading, and particularly if the numbers we are comparing are rather small."

Claude smiles with relief. He is pleased not to have made a fool of himself; also flattered that Rayer had considered him sufficient of a colleague to refer, albeit obliquely to a recent argument about contagious infection in which Rayer and Magendie had clashed.

"The philosophy to treatment is of course very complex. It raises many questions, for which we do not have the answers."

Rayer is is now peering out of his window into the courtyard. The students had by now dispersed:

"From time to time, I invite to my home people from various disciplines, both within and outside the field of medicine. We have interesting debates on various topics: so perhaps you might care to attend our next meeting. I believe..." he glances across at a diary sitting on his desk, "... ah yes, the next one is already on the Friday of next week. Can you join us?"

Claude is overwhelmed, immediately accepts the invitation and leaves Rayer's office, jubilant. As he leaves the hospital, he sees his friend Lasègue, and immediately tells him of the morning's happenings. Lasègue is amazed: Rayer's salons are highly regarded as intellectual events of note. For Claude, a humble *interne* to be invited is nothing short of remarkable. During the week Rayer makes no further reference to the invitation, although Claude receives an envelope in the *internes'* quarters specifying the address and the time at which he was expected to attend. He is uncertain about what he should wear. Of his friends, only Pelouze would have had experience of such a salon, and it is too late to contact him. From the formality of the written invitation, Claude judges that he should wear his finest outfit: the cutaway frock coat, his red waistcoat and high collared white shirt, topped by the new fashionably-small cravat that he would borrow from Lasègue.

The building in which Rayer lived was most unassuming from the outside: In answer to his knock, a maid in black dress and white lace apron opens the ornately-carved door. Rayer himself, wearing a black velvet coat and a beaming smile leads him by the arm to a room of generous proportions; tall windows completely hidden behind heavy blue velvet drapes matched by comfortable looking armchairs.

Some fifteen people are standing in small groups in different sections of the room, talking earnestly in hushed tones, as if their words were highly secret. Claude sees his friend Pelouze talking to a bearded man of about the same age: his stare is acknowledged by a smile and a nod. Rayer mingles with the other guests, leaving Claude to accept a glass of wine and tempting *petit four* from the rather attractive maid. He soon finds Pelouze by his side. He identifies for Claude some of the people present, in the same hushed tones that were apparently the order of the day. A tall man with a rather bulbous lower lip was Emile Littré, while the short man next to him with receding chin, red hair and bushy eyebrows was Charles Sainte-Beuve. Both had apparently started medicine but left medical school before graduating; both now in literary careers. Two of Rayer's physician colleagues from the *Charité*, Rullier and Maury were already familiar to Claude. Three men in dark business attire standing in one corner were identified as being from Paris' financial aristocracy, amongst whom Rayer had become the favoured physician. A man with rather noble features in clerical collar and black gown was sitting alone on one end of the room quietly watching the proceedings. Pelouze did not know who he was. The remaining men were apparently all physicians and surgeons from other Paris hospitals.

After a few minutes, Rayer claps his hands together for attention. There is a shuffle of feet as the guests subside obediently and almost in unison into sofas and armchairs.

Rayer's introduction is brief:

"For a few of you, Monsieur Littré is no stranger. He was, of course, my *interne* in '27, when sadly for all of us, personal events compelled him to give up his medical studies. He is now eminent in other fields; those of translation and journalism. As editor of our new medical journal, *l'Expérience,* he has even been kind enough to publish several papers that I have written."

A murmur of approval ripples through the room.

"His latest interest in philosophy may prove to be even more valuable to us in the field of medicine. He has recently become a strong advocate of *positivisme*, and this forms the subject of his talk to us this evening. As usual, we will have some time for questions at the end of his presentation."

Littré rises to his feet while Rayer retires to an armchair. With one arm extended against the mantlepiece – as if in need of some support for what he is about to say – he begins to speak: quietly and in rather halting phrases:

"We must admit to ourselves that we are often anxious to know both the fundamental and the final cause of any phenomenon; be it a disease, an element of human behaviour or some celestial event that might be observed through a telescope. Even some early philosophers believed that it was impossible ever to establish a 'final cause' – of any phenomenon. Accordingly, they did not believe that absolute knowledge would ever be within reach of anybody, and on any topic. There would always be more."

"Building on the beliefs of his predecessors, Auguste Comte was the originator of *positivisme*. All who like me follow his ideas embrace the idea that facts – and facts alone – should form the basis of our knowledge and awareness. Anything that we are rash enough to call 'truth' stems from facts and their relationships to each other. Progress depends on our observation, our experience of these observed facts and what we do with them. It is only experience that is the eventual source of whatever knowledge and awareness that we acquire. *Positivisme* also denies knowledge simply through belief and thus puts into question conventional religion."

He stops, mops his brow with a red cloth that he extracts from an inside pocket of his coat and sips water from a glass standing on the mantelpiece. Meanwhile he looks quizzically one-by-one at his listeners, who are whispering amongst themselves, evidently stimulated by what they are hearing.

"Of course when I talk about observed facts I am using the word as it applies to all our senses. I speak mainly of hearing and seeing; yet also our senses of touch and smell – elements that I clearly remember our host, Monsieur Rayer advocating to medical students as being fundamental to medical diagnosis. Since these senses are all employed in the course of scientific quest, it is through these that increments of knowledge will be achieved."

Littré looks meaningfully at Rayer, who acknowledges the reference to his teachings with a smile and a gentle nod.

"I am now sadly outside the field of medicine. Yet more than ten years later I retain an intense affinity for it. I am aware for example that speculation about disease and its management is still rife; speculation which is sometimes unsupported even by the most basic fact, and nevertheless uttered with total conviction. *Positivisme* absolutely insists that speculation is to be avoided at all costs. It is a barrier to our progress in whatever we are considering. That is not to say that hypothesis is inappropriate. On the contrary, hypothesis is the framework upon which we must build factual support – or acknowledge a lack of it."

Littré goes on to explain the views of some of Comte's philosophical forefathers; Kant, Saint-Simon and even Descartes. He finally concludes on a positive note:

"So we can summarize by saying that *positivisme* is a system of knowledge based entirely on facts – or discoveries – made through the physical or positive sciences. However it includes an assumption – in fact a conviction – that such knowledge is never absolute."

There is polite applause as Littré sits and Rayer takes the floor in order to initiate discussion:

"I would like to exercise host's privilege by asking Monsieur Littré the first question. I have a problem with the definition of 'fact', if that word is used as the simple result of input from one of our senses. Surely, our perception of a fact – or our observation – may be erroneous because we are human; and humans err. Moreover, a scientific experiment may also produce a false result for one or more reasons. As such, what is only an observation may all too readily be assumed to be a 'fact'. Have I missed something?"

"I think of *positivisme* as being based on certain important principles...."

Littré hesitates while gazing intently at an imaginary scene beyond the end of the room:

"...and one of these principles assumes that a 'fact' is exactly that, and not a spurious result caused by chance, careless procedure or poor scientific interpretation. Thus, one respects and indeed defines a 'fact' by showing that the relevant observation is repeatable, or at least statistically valid."

Rayer seems content with the firmness of Littré's reply. One of the 'financial' group is now on his feet, clearly wishing to speak. He is introduced by Rayer as a certain Monsieur Grell:

"Being a mathematician, I appreciate your mention of the importance of statistics and also that mysterious concept of truth. Of course the acquisition of knowledge has infinite dimensions. Expressed in geometrical terms, awareness of a subject can be likened to an asymptote, over time progressively approaching the horizontal plane of absolute knowledge – truth if you will – but in fact reaching it only at some point in infinity."

Littré smiles and acknowledges this comment with a smile, but before he can respond, everyone's attention is suddenly drawn to the tall figure of the cleric, who had leaped violently to his feet. Rayer barely has time to introduce him as the Abbé Dupanloup, from the nearby seminary of St Nicolas. Arms flung wide and in a deep, resonant voice he launches into a massive attack:

"You will understand that it is not possible for me to accept this. You are effectively proposing the removal of belief from the realm of religious trust. You are thus denouncing God, through the experience and wisdom of Christ as the source of divine knowledge. What concerns me almost as much – as an educator – is your lack of reference to intelligence, that ability to marshal facts and experiences into a usable framework. Surely, intelligence helps to define the dimensions of knowledge?"

There is silence, while Littré raised the glass of water to his lips, again gazing into the distance almost absentmindedly. Still holding the glass in his hand he responds with even more measured intervals than usual between his phrases:

"Father, you must first understand that I have only recently acquired the interest – albeit passionate – in *positivisme*. At this moment, I would wish for Auguste Comte – whom I have not yet had the pleasure of meeting – to be with us, so that he might answer you! While holding to the fundamental principles of *positivisme*, I am not convinced that we need to discard religion. Yet I still have some difficulty in accepting – what I could best refer to as – blind belief. As to the second part of your question, I have always perceived intelligence not so much in how we use facts – but rather the manner in which we interrogate the world in order to search for them."

Rayer had seen that Littré was beginning to fatigue. To protect his *protégé* from further attack, he calls the meeting to a close, amid excited murmurs from the assembled guests.

> *September 14th, 1840*
> *My dear Ronne*
>
> *I was devastated to hear from you about the floods in Vaise; and the turmoil of dealing with the consequences! How could Millet possibly find 15,000 francs to correct the damage and restock the pharmacy? As Mayor of Vaise, he must also have had plenty of other problems and challenges to deal with, although I am not surprised that he acquitted himself well in the crisis. What a fine man! But do you not wish to return to Villefranche and your family quite soon? You know, I can really imagine you in your own officine!*
>
> *Anyhow I just had to write to you! You cannot imagine the extraordinary evening that I have just had at Rayer's apartment: one of his 'salons'. For the privilege of just being there! The speaker was a man called Littré. Started medicine, but then gave it up to write – and to have time to think, I suppose. It was all about facts and the importance of truth. You know how I feel about Descartes. Have you heard of positivisme? Littré is so committed to this concept which a man called Auguste Compte has recently introduced into philosophical thought – all about the avoidance of speculation, and the principle of actually knowing rather than guessing. He so criticized blind belief that a cleric who was in the audience almost had a fit! It was music to my ears!*
>
> *Hearing all this has stimulated me and reinforced my own ideas – I probably won't sleep at all tonight! There were so many things that I*

would have liked to ask Littré myself, but I was by far the youngest there. I am sure that I will get another chance though, because like me, he was one of Rayer's internes and they have obviously stayed the best of friends.

I so enjoy being attached to Rayer's service. He has such a particular way of approaching a problem: not at all afraid to admit that he doesn't know something. When he discusses a condition, his thought processes are so clear that I can almost visualise what experiments would need to be done to understand the problem. Yet I find the practice of medicine irritating. How can one work with all those vague uncertainties – or with so many physicians who perpetuate them by confusing theory with fact?

You will remember what I wrote to you about Magendie. At the end of the year, I will be starting to work on his service. Of course I hope to make a good impression, since it is in his laboratory that I dearly wish to work. I am convinced that his type of experimental approach can yield answers that matter. Yet rumour has it that quite unlike Rayer he is not an easy man to work for. I must also tell you that when I thanked Rayer this evening for inviting me, he made a comment about me keeping in touch with him when I move to Magendie's service – perhaps by occasionally attending his ward rounds. Life has certainly become very interesting, not to say complicated!

Do write again soon about yourself and Marianne – and your plans!

Your ever friend, Claude

Claude is increasingly anxious about the prospect of leaving Rayer's service. Both he and his patients had provided Claude with much interest. Would Magendie be as helpful as Rayer? And would Claude be lucky enough also to work in his laboratory? If so, would he be obliged to follow Magendie's approach of random discovery rather than his own evolving principle of reasoned hypothesis? The latter was obviously an alien concept for Magendie who would consider that theorizing was a pointless contemplation.

Magendie's opinions and statements had been widely publicised throughout France. His views on cholera, his disapproval of bleeding as a form of therapy and even his scepticism about the efficacy of medical treatment had managed to find their way into the daily press. To his medical assistants he uttered such comments as: *'It is clear that you have never tried doing nothing'*. Or if a persuasive junior colleague wished to use this or that drug for one of his patients, he would say: *'Alright, if it amuses you, use it!'*

And so it is that early in 1841, Claude finally begins to work for him at the *Hôtel-Dieu*. From almost the very first day, he is afflicted by anxiety about his management of the patients. Magendie repeatedly disapproves of so many things not performed to his liking. If Claude prescribes a diet to reduce the weight of an obese patient, Magendie reverses the instruction on the basis that an ill patient needs more rather than less sustenance. If Claude confines a woman to bed because of severe shortness of breath, Magendie immediately and ostentatiously orders her to get out of bed and sit in a chair. In choosing the dosage of a drug, it is certain to be either too low – or more often too high – for Magendie's liking. The ward round finishes on a sour note, his lip curled in what appears to be universal disapproval of everything and everybody around him – and Claude in particular.

His demeanour only seems to soften in his direct dealings with patients. There he is tolerant and understanding. If a patient expresses concern, it is sure to be the nurse or doctor who is at fault. It is only after the ward round, when according to custom they move to the autopsy room that Claude seems to win some degree of approval. Magendie even sometimes takes a seat with the observing *externes*, while Claude proceeds with dissection and demonstrates the findings.

Claude has disturbed nights, worrying about his poor performance on the wards. A couple of his predecessors had assured him that they had been subjected to similar humiliation. Yet he begins to doubt whether he can continue to work with Magendie: he seriously considers requesting a transfer to another service. If indeed his judgement is as poor as it seems, perhaps he should even leave medicine altogether – like Littré, whose life had taken such a brilliantly successful literary turn. And so Claude's thoughts turn once more to his passion for the theatre; the possibility of performing *Rose du Rhône*, of rewriting *Arthur de Bretagne* – and of returning to his family who now seem more remote than ever from his new life. Burdened by such dark thoughts, he decides to share his concerns with Rayer. Leaving the *Hôtel-Dieu* on a bitterly cold afternoon, he walks briskly to the *Charité* and finds Rayer in his office, working through the proofs of his *magnum opus* on the kidney. Claude unburdens himself to a man whom he highly respects, and who is gradually assuming the role of his mentor. Slowly, and so kindly, Rayer persuades him to be more patient.

On the next day Claude decides to ask Magendie if he might again assist with some of the experiments at the *Collège*. Therefore, he watches Magendie as he divides this nerve or that in the spine, or pinches the third or fifth cranial nerve to see how a rabbit's eye reacts. He is allowed to apply electrical stimulation to the phrenic nerve of an old dog, just after it dies to see if the diaphragm still reacts – and it does. He watches Magendie divide the olfactory nerve of a rabbit, and together they record the effects that the resulting loss of smell has on the feeding habits of the animal. Every observation finds its way into one of his notebooks, either at the time or before he retires to bed. Claude decides to leave spaces – a few pages – into which he might later enter an afterthought or a sequel to earlier experiments. Leaving those few pages free will remind of unfinished work or an unanswered question that he needs to complete or resolve – at some time.

One afternoon, already fatigued after a long ward round at the *Hôtel-Dieu*, he finally completes an autopsy – on a young prostitute who had unusually died from the effects of gonorrhoea. The *externes* had dispersed, and Claude is now carefully washing the instruments that he had used. Magendie is sitting in the corner of the autopsy room completing the hospital records of the unfortunate woman. He sighs, gets up to leave, hesitates and turns towards Claude:

"See here Bernard, I want you to be my *préparateur*!"

Turning abruptly on his heel, he sweeps out of the room.

That unexpected offer – more correctly an order – is the turning point in Claude's career; a long bridge eventually traversed, and a gate opening into the arena of experimental medicine. It is to this rather self-righteous and idiosyncratic man, obsessed by his own correctness and so dismissive of the work of others that Claude would be delivering himself. How would he react to his new master's foibles? Claude certainly shares with him an extreme curiosity: that insatiable appetite for observation and the accumulation of facts. Yet he is determined to go beyond this. An observation would only justify being a 'fact' if it supported or dismissed a hypothesis, and could be almost infinitely reproduced – the first step towards what he would later call his experimental method.

"How blind my colleagues are!"

They are now sitting in the new laboratory of the *Collège de France* that had recently been allocated to Magendie; luxurious compared with the closet-sized space in which Claude had previously assisted him. Windows allow in light and air. There were two cupboards for instruments, marble topped tables for their experiments and a large reservoir of water suspended from the ceiling. From this, tubes lead to the tables and to an enamel basin from which effluent drains to the outside. The animal house adjoins the laboratory and accounts for the nauseating stench with which Claude would have to live.

"It is not simply a question of whether the drugs that we use benefit the patient. In most cases they actually worsen their condition. Drugs are basically poisons – just used in lower dosage! Do please keep this in mind, Bernard, when you care for my patients in Sainte Monique ward."

Claude nods agreement. His attachment to Magendie is in two realms; supervising his patients as *interne* at the Hôtel-Dieu, and acting as his *préparateur* at the *Collège*.

"By the way, I will leave it to you to decide how you divide your time between here and the hospital. I will only say that I have no-one else to assist me here at the *Collège*, whereas at the hospital I have Husson as well as that other interne – what's his name? – whom I am sharing with Doctor Piorry. The present lot of *externes* are quite capable, too. All I can say is that you will need to spend plenty of time in this laboratory if you wish to get ahead in your research career."

Claude is naturally aware of Magendie's arrangements at the hospital; pleased when he moves on to the subject of his laboratory responsibilities:

"I also expect you to manage the day to day running of my laboratory. That means purchasing the animals and their food. Lesage, our *garçon de laboratoire* has the responsibility of cleaning the cages and doing the feeds, but he needs help from time to time. By the way, we will be doing quite many nutritional experiments: you will need to find me some special nutrients from one of the suppliers. The most reliable is Lamereau, and you will find the list that I made over there."

He gestures towards an untidy pile of papers.

"Keep the books well: the authorities examine them quite often. I don't think that they trust me, even after all this time. I certainly don't know how they can expect me to come up with good research without money: we have barely four hundred francs to last us until the end of the year."

Claude nods; it has never occurred to him to enquire how research was funded.

"By the way, we need blood from time to time, so that it is convenient for me that you are also my *interne*. About three hundred millilitres is all we need at any one time. Use your judgement about which patients you approach, and ask one of the *externes* to do the bleeding. You know my attitude about bleeding patients as a form of treatment, but at least it will keep the *externes'* skills sharp, in case they move to the service of a physician who still believes all that rubbish! You will be here tomorrow morning by eight, won't you?"

With responsibilities in both hospital and at the *Collège*, Claude now had two modest incomes; enough to move into a proper apartment. He eventually finds two small rooms in the *cour du Commerce Saint-André des Arts* – a short passage-way just off the *rue de l'École de Médicine*. It had a small dark cellar where he hoped to keep a few animals and – time permitting – do some of his own experiments. The long but narrow living room was sparsely furnished: an old but comfortable armchair, a rough table and at one end of the room an obviously well-used fireplace which would hopefully warm the room during evenings spent writing.

On a rare, bright sunny day in December, he moves his belongings into his new home, close to the *Collège* and not that much further from the *Hôtel-Dieu*. Casimir Davaine, his first visitor points out that fifty years earlier Guillotin had lived just opposite:

"Did you know that it was here that he experimented on different animals to perfect his 'instrument'; it's really quite appropriate that you should be living here, don't you think?"

Public executions were in fact performed almost daily in the *place de la Revolution*, although Claude had so far not been able to bring himself to witness one.

Magendie had grudgingly agreed that Claude could still attend some of Rayer's rounds. On these occasions Claude would stand inconspicuously behind the group of *externes*, listening intently. He always had with him one of his small notebooks in which he made frequent entries, his tall forehead creased with concentration. On one particular day in the spring of '42, the round moves to the bedside of a middle-aged man who rapidly becomes the centre of intense discussion. The entire right side of his face, from the roots of his hair down to his chin droops miserably due to paralysis of his muscles, which also prevent him closing his right eye. His mouth is lopsided, his speech indistinct and saliva is dripping from its right corner.

"This man has a complete paralysis of the seventh cranial nerve on the right side." Rayer explains. "As we have seen, there is no evidence of other neurological loss, such as one might get from a brain apoplexy. I am almost certain that his problem lies within the facial nerve itself. Would anyone like to suggest what sort of process may be going on?"

One student suggests a cancer of the nerve.

That's very rare", says Rayer. "It is probably a form of inflammation. The sudden onset and the slow improvement conform to the pattern described by Charles Bell, an English physician; so we now call it Bell's palsy. It is interesting and quite puzzling that when he was admitted to hospital the patient complained that he couldn't taste properly. That combination of symptoms was first recorded by Montault, who used to work at the *Hôtel Dieu*."

Rayer's *interne* demonstrates the strange phenomenon: a drop of lemon juice applied to the left side of the tongue was recognized as bitter by the patient, yet not when it was placed on the right side. Other forms of sensation such as a pinprick or a heated spoon handle were quite equally perceived on the two sides of the tongue.

Claude remembers seeing a similar case at the *Salpetrière*. The mystery of taste loss lay in the fact that the seventh nerve was acknowledged as having only one action: the control of movement of the facial muscles. It had been universally agreed by anatomists that it did not possess any "sensing" function whatsoever: that was one of the roles of the fifth cranial nerve that in this patient seemed to be functioning quite normally. How then could a loss of taste arise as an apparent result of seventh nerve damage?

That evening Claude buries himself in his anatomy books and finds a description of a very small nerve called the *chorda tympani*, which for three centuries had been known to connect a branch of the seventh nerve with a branch of the fifth nerve. Anatomists had suggested that the *chorda tympani* stimulated the flow of saliva but apart from that, its function was unknown. Could it be that taste impulses passed backwards through the *chorda tympani*, into the facial nerve and thence to the brain? On the next day, Claude mentions Rayer's case to Magendie, who after some persuasion agrees that he can begin his own studies of this tiny nerve: his very first independent research project.

During the following year, he performs many experiments on the *chorda tympani* – in the cellar of his new dwelling, since Magendie did not approve of use of the college facilities for personal projects. Claude does however use his access to hospital autopsies to confirm for himself the nerve's most intimate anatomical details in the human.

It is on a day in early '43 that Magendie springs a surprise on him:

"I'm going to cancel all my lectures for the spring, Claude. That will give you some more time for your own studies on that little nerve. I've been asked by the government to look at the healing qualities of the health spas in southern Italy. Springing up all over the place, they are. There have been all sorts of claims of spectacular cures and miraculous recovery from even serious illness. I might even try a bath myself for my weary joints! Young James has not yet found a new post, so I have decided to take him with me. He has a good pair of eyes and much more energy than me. We should be able to complete our assessments and be there and back in a couple of months."

Claude is not certain how to react. On the one hand, he is apprehensive about carrying sole responsibility for the laboratory. On the other hand, Magendie's absence might allow him to perform more experiments under the better conditions at the *Collège*.

"Would you permit me to do my experiments here in your laboratory during your absence? The equipment here would make it so much easier."

"I cannot see why not." Magendie replies. "And if he has time you could even ask Lesage to help you. In return, I think you might help out on my service at the *Hôtel Dieu*. I cannot expect Piorry to do all the clinical work in my absence. It will do you good, too!"

Magendie duly departs in April. Claude wastes little time in settling down to his research. He performs studies on any available dogs, cats or rabbits discarded from other laboratories in the *Collège*. In his desire to fully understand the origin, derivation and purpose of the *chorda tympani* he performs dissections of the nerve in bats, hedgehogs, squirrels, moles, goats, reptiles and in a variety of birds including pigeons, turkeys, chickens and sparrows. In the large, and also some of the smaller animals he cuts the *chorda tympani,* comparing the animals' reactions to various chemicals (including citric acid) which he applies to their tongues before and after dividing the nerve. He closely observes both the animals' behaviour and the movements of their tongues in response to contact with the chemicals. In this way, Claude confirms that it is only in mammals that taste impulses pass through the little nerve – at least those impulses that arise from the front section of the tongue.

He fails to repeat the findings of previous researchers that electrical stimulation of the *chorda tympani* stimulates the flow of saliva from the lower salivary glands beneath the tongue and jaw. Claude records all his results and conclusions in a thirty-two page manuscript. When Magendie returns, Claude asks him to read it, and to his delight, only minor points of grammar require correction. It is promptly accepted for publication, the first article of many – just prior to his thirtieth birthday in May 1843. When he hears that it has been accepted, he has a vivid flashback to Girardin's comment all those years ago; when he suggested that he might have better aptitude for scientific writing!

Chapter 6

Painful Decisions

It is now nine years since he had commenced his medical studies, and Claude is obliged to submit a thesis for his *doctorat* – the official end of his medical studies. More important, within the next year he would need to undergo the more demanding assessment for the academic status of *agrégé* – a university lectureship: it would mean yet another thesis, yet another interview. He would be competing with other doctors for this prestigious appointment, and would need to demonstrate that he possessed not only the highest level of knowledge about anatomy and physiology as they related to illness, but also the qualities necessary to teach medical students. Success would also mean access to laboratory space, freedom to perform research on the faculty premises and some money for his research as well. It was the very substance of his ambition.

Claude hardly dared to dwell on the consequences of failure; it would mean an end to all his research. He would have to forsake academic life, move back to the Beaujolais and set himself up as a village doctor. There, he would derive his income from managing the minor illnesses of the local population: certainly not the life that he had envisaged! He had heard of a few researchers who had failed their *agrégation*; yet were able, by independent financial means to continue research in a corner of the *Collège*, the *Académie des Sciences* or some other institution interested in their ideas. Given his family circumstances, such an option for Claude was clearly out of the question; failure in the contest would place him into deep trouble.

The visit to Naples seemed to have given Magendie new energy for research: on his return, he embarks on even more studies on the spinal nerves, experiments on the circulatory system and much more work on nutrition. There is money to be gained from nutritional research, he says. The Gelatine Commission had been established to study whether gelatine could be used as a food supplement. It could be readily extracted from the enormous quantity of animal bones which would otherwise be discarded at the abattoir. Could gelatine fulfil an important function as a nutritional substitute or additive for the young, the ill and the poor? The newspapers had often dealt with this important subject. Magendie's research, his role on the Commission and his scepticism about the benefits of gelatine are regularly mentioned. Claude is interested in these studies too – stimulating his thoughts about the way that nutrients in general are absorbed and processed in the body.

It was inevitable that Magendie's work would become Claude's interest as well: so little was understood about the relationship of food to the chemistry of the human body! How could it handle such a variety of foods and extract from them the important nutrients that it needed? Claude is obliged to submit to the authorities in advance the subject of his doctoral thesis and soon decides that he will examine the part played by the stomach in the process of food digestion. He had never lost interest in the pneumogastric nerve; the one which Magendie had shown in his memorable demonstration to be important in the process of vomiting. Claude now shows convincingly that cutting this nerve causes acid production in the stomach to cease. More results follow: he finds that dietary sugar – sucrose – must be broken down by the gastric juice into the simpler molecule of glucose before it can be absorbed through the wall of the stomach or intestine. He also reasons from his results that it is not sucrose – but only its breakdown product glucose – that can be used by the body as an energy fuel.

In a wild moment, he even wonders whether the condition of diabetes might be caused by an excessive gastric conversion of starch and sucrose into glucose: an over activity of the stomach ferments. True to his principles, he does not put that vague theory into his thesis. However, he does rather harshly criticize certain French chemists whose opinions differ from his. Predictably, when it comes to his *viva voce*, the examiners disapprove of his attitude. He also has some difficulty in defending his conclusions. He knows exactly what he wants to say, yet his usual hesitant delivery spoils the flow of his argument. The well-established facts of his studies are nevertheless there to be seen: his thesis is accepted in its entirety and he is awarded his degree.

Claude Bernard, Doctor of Medicine in the University of Paris is a proud man; his parents even more so. Yet the far more challenging and critical examination is yet to come. With his appointment as *préparateur* concluding shortly, he will be obliged to sit his *agrégation* in less than one year – in October 1844. The busy period of preparation is not helped by the number of new projects that he had already begun. He has great difficulty in setting them aside.

In all corners of the medical school, in the *Académie*, in the *Collège* and in private laboratories like the one in Claude's cellar, research on animals is now being performed. The importance of vivisection in answering important biological questions is being rediscovered. As the public becomes aware of what is taking place, it reacts predictably, in horror at the experiments that are being carried out on such a scale. They find many ways of showing their concern. Paint is daubed on buildings where experiments are known to have been carried out: researchers identified as the perpetrators of vivisection are even physically assaulted in the streets. One morning, Magendie enters the room, a look of concern on his face. He sighs as he sits down at the table around which Claude, Pelouze and his assistant Charles Barreswill are awaiting him – as had become their weekly custom.

"I am sorry to have kept you all waiting, gentlemen, but I've just had a most unpleasant discussion. That man I was just showing to the door was a Quaker. In his quiet and gentle way, he was most upset about our work. He tried to talk me out of using animals for our experiments. We really must find a way of reassuring people that what we do is in the public interest."

Claude had before him a pile of papers and was pre-occupied with the outcome of some experiments. It is Pelouze who comments:

"I saw in *le National* that Grammont has become quite outspoken again about animal experiments. He wants to set up a society that opposes it absolutely. I think he will get a lot of support, too. I know that you Claude hold to Descartes' concept that animals have no feeling; and perhaps we have all been trying to convince ourselves of that. But Kant's 'escalation hypothesis' – that ruthlessness and heartlessness will increasingly permeate our society – is becoming widely accepted. Believe me, François...."

He turns to face Magendie squarely across the table:

"...no-one accepts that the experiments that you and Claude do on horses tied to a frame are without pain to the poor creatures."

Magendie had indeed also received another letter from a group of researchers in England who were extremely troubled by the animal experiments he had performed on his recent visit to that country. He is obviously concerned.

"You know gentlemen; I have some hopes for a chemical method of reducing pain. While preparing the next edition of my *formulaire*, I came across some interesting observations of an American physician by the name of Long. You all probably know about those absurd ether-sniffing parties that they have there – they were mentioned in our newspapers recently. Apparently Long noticed that when people fall about after sniffing ether they sustain quite severe bruising which hardly bothers them: they seem oblivious to the pain of their injuries."

"He has now reported giving ether to a young man from whom he cut away some cysts in the neck. The boy hardly noticed. If we could refine that approach for our animal experiments, it would surely reassure the public – not to speak of all the possible uses in human surgery. It would even make our friend Velpeau change his tune!"

Pelouze responds quickly.

"All very well, François, but how could we ever be sure that a drug like ether would not itself affect the results of an experiment?"

There is prolonged silence; no one knows the answer to that. Eventually Pelouze gets to his feet to conclude their meeting; turns to address Claude:

"I don't think that any of you were there, but last week Claude gave a paper to the *Académie* on the pneumogastric nerve experiments which he did with Charles. The results were very well received and he got a lot of applause."

Claude blushes at this acknowledgement, yet he knows that the fluency of his presentation was again not as it should have been. Pelouze continues:

"By the way Claude, I have received another batch of curare from my friend Goudet. He is just back from Peru with some curare-tipped arrows and some of the substance itself. I think that you were interested in trying to understand exactly how it kills. Would that be another interesting project?"

They all laugh; knowing that despite his many concurrent projects and the forthcoming examination for his *agrégation*, Claude would find it difficult to refuse.

"I would gladly get involved with curare if it wasn't for my work on the colouring matter in human tissues: the project for my thesis. That's enough to be getting on with! In fact, my experiments aren't going at all well, but it's far too late to change now."

Predictably, curare does occupy Claude's mind: his curiosity insatiable. During the following week, he asks Pelouze for some of his material, In his cellar laboratory injects a tiny portion into a frog. Half a minute later it collapses; apparently dead. He immediately performs an autopsy and is astounded to see that its heart is still beating: the frog is indeed not dead. Is it simply unconscious – or could it be totally paralysed? He quickly reaches for the equipment that he uses for electrically stimulating nerves and muscles. To his surprise, he finds that one of the frog's muscles totally fails to twitch when its nerve is stimulated – yet it twitches briskly enough if the current is applied directly to the muscle itself. After some minutes, its heart does finally stop beating: death has occurred.

He is surprised and confused by his findings, which suggest that the curare had somehow blocked the junction of the nerve with its corresponding muscle. He makes copious records in his notebook, determined that he would return to the study of curare as soon as time permitted. With the eventual happenings in his personal and professional life, that would not be for a further five years!

The important contest for his *agrégation* is every bit as challenging as Claude had feared. Doctors are not promoted lightly to the level of *professeur agrégé*, for which he discovers there are three other candidates on this occasion. From the very first moment he is made to feel uneasy. One examiner disagrees with his concept of digestion and challenges Claude to explain how his findings compare with those of the eminent research group in Heidelberg. The role of the pancreas gland was at that time clouded in mystery, and when Claude is asked about its function he says as much; for him, the existence of a duct which leads from that gland directly into the intestine simply supports the idea that it has a role in digestion. His examiners do not like this either: what about all the theories that had been proposed by other workers?

On the subject of spinal nerves, Claude finds himself caught between the conflicting findings and interpretations of Magendie and Longet – and as a result becomes completely tongue-tied. Knowing of his familiarity with research on gelatine as a food supplement, the examiners then turn to this subject. It soon becomes clear that they are biased in favour of gelatine being a useful nutrient: a view strongly promoted by a certain Dr d'Arcet – who unfortunately happens to be one of the present examiners. Claude cannot convince them that the carefully designed and detailed experiments which he had performed with Magendie provided no support whatsoever for the use of gelatine in nutrition.

When it comes to his thesis, they ask him why he had chosen to study the colouring matter in body tissues. Again he cannot express himself clearly, wondering – and not for the first time – why Magendie had insisted on this project for his thesis. There had been so many more exciting and relevant topics that had captured his imagination. Finally, one of his examiners, himself a chemist, decides to attack the analytical methods that Claude had used. While he had indeed performed all the chemical analyses himself, Claude is certainly not a chemist. The methods he had used were those developed by Pelouze and his colleague Barreswill. Accordingly, he finds it difficult to address the examiner's methodological questions.

He is asked to wait for what seems an endless time in a cold waiting room, while the examiners argue his merits or otherwise. It is no surprise when he is called back into the room and is told that he has not been successful. The vague and verbose explanations for their decision seem to rest mainly with his poor presentation; his inability to give a good account of himself. How could he expect to fulfil a serious teaching function with such a defect in his delivery? Most of their comments fall on deaf ears. He is holding back tears of anger and despair, his mind already reaching for a possible solution to a hopeless future.

Endlessly wandering the Paris streets does nothing to soothe Claude's disappointment and embarrassment at failing his *agrégation*. Can he face a future in the Beaujolais? He had talked with Magendie who understood Claude's predicament, but was already committed to his new *préparateur*: he reminds Claude to tie up some loose ends in his research before he finished at the end of the year.

However, Pelouze is helpful. Claude could certainly use an area in his laboratory on the *rue Dauphine*, even his animal house. But he would have to find the money for any animals, equipment and the chemical reagents he used. Claude was also welcome to continue collaborating with Charles Barreswill, with whom many new and interesting projects had already been discussed. The two men got on very well together and Pelouze knows that it is in his own, as much as Claude's interests to provide support for their ideas. He and Rayer had discussed at length what they might do to find support for Claude – perhaps an approach to a generous benefactor, such as had supported Michelangelo in his artistic pursuits!

His mentor Rayer is certainly upset by the situation but comes up with a suggestion which would grant Claude a temporary reprieve. A friend of his, a surgeon called Bougery was about to publish a new edition of his highly regarded anatomy atlas for surgeons. He needed someone to do a series of anatomical dissections that could in turn be drawn by Jacob, the eminent medical illustrator. Would Claude be interested? Claude accepts at once, and agrees to perform the necessary procedures in the first two months of '45. Rayer had also drawn his attention to a lectureship at the *Académie de Médecine*. There would be a strong field of applicants, but he had persuaded Claude to apply.

Just before Christmas, Claude receives a re-assuring letter from his mother. He should not feel that he was a failure; it was clearly God's way of deciding that he should devote himself to the lesser ills of man – even if that were to be in his own village. They were looking forward to welcoming him back as soon as he was able to leave Paris.

Pierre Rayer had always liked the annual January re-union with his fellow medical graduates of 1820. Henri Martin, placed next to him at the dinner is not a close friend, yet Rayer is enjoying being brought up to date with his successful life as physician to Paris society. Medical anecdotes – and even the details of his personal life – flow freely; tongue loosened by the excellent wine.

"Of course life treats me well, Pierre, and I cannot complain. I am busy enough dealing with the fashionable who have little wrong with them. The louder they complain, the less I seem to diagnose – I call it *'Martin's Law'*. Mind you, I don't know how you hospital doctors manage to fit it all in; your patients; your teaching… and then your research as well."

Rayer smiles. "I enjoy all those activities Henri, and more than anything else the contact with my colleagues and students. You know, the students are rather different from what they were in our time; they have so much more to remember. I'm sure they work harder than we did."

"I wish I could say that about my daughter." Henri replies. "I'll be glad to get her off my hands! I gave her a good education but she just sits at home like a little princess waiting for the impossible to happen."

Dinner, speeches and acknowledgements are over. Some fifty well-dressed and successful doctors with greying hair under silk hats make their way out of the hall and down the steps to the *rue du Colombier*.

"Henri, just a moment!" Rayer runs down the steps where Martin is about to step into his elegant carriage. "There's something on my mind that I would like to talk with you about."

"Why not come back to my apartment. It's not that late and I live just a few blocks away. We can have a cognac together in my new study: it would be a nice way to finish the evening. Ask your driver to follow me!" he adds, with an extravagant sweep of his arm.

They are now sitting in the deeply carpeted study; its walls entirely hidden by oak panelling and ceiling-high bookshelves. Rayer feels decidedly uneasy about what he is about to say.

"I was telling you about my students, Henri. One of them who recently qualified is a most unusual chap called Claude Bernard. I have been following his career with interest for some time. He also has his *doctorat* – but failed his *agrégation*."

"Can't be *that* bright then…."

"…if anything, quite the opposite. Claude has one of those analytical minds that never stops working; although that's also his worst enemy. He refuses to accept the unproven."

"There's plenty of that about, but we all have to work with it, don't we, Pierre?"

"Surely; but not *this* young man. I think that he will make a great contribution to scientific medicine, if given the chance. Now, hearing you mention your daughter…."

"…Marie-Françoise."

"Nice name. Yes. I just wonder if they might do each other a favour. Do you see what I mean?"

Martin nods slowly. There is silence for a minute or so while they sip cognac from large crystal goblets.

"What's he like then, Pierre?"

"Tall; quite a noble head, and carries himself well. He's not much for idle chatter, but he's probably more intelligent than you and I put together."

"Do I understand you correctly, Pierre? You would like to bring these two together – with a view to a mutual future?"

"I couldn't phrase it better myself, Henri. But tell me about Marie-Françoise?"

"Forget what I said before. Fanny – she prefers that name – is really a fine girl. She has unfortunately inherited my looks rather than that of her sadly-deceased mother, but she makes up for it by being shrewd." Martin adds as an afterthought: "She's probably shrewder than you and I put together!"

They both laugh heartily. Martin pours more cognac into Rayer's glass and they sit for a while without speaking; silence absolute but for the insistent ticking of the tall elegant clock set into a niche within the bookshelves.

"It is certainly something to think about, Pierre. I remarried last year, as you may know. I will try and separate Hélène from her busy social life tomorrow, and get her thoughts on the matter, too."

Every moment of Claude's day is haunted by the prospect of leaving an academic life that had started out so well. His very last hope had just been extinguished. He had indeed applied for the lectureship at the *Académie de Médecine*, but the successful candidate was Achille Longet, the man who had challenged Magendie about the originality of his findings on the spinal nerves. The final door had closed firmly behind him.

"I'm glad that you could both make it…." Rayer begins, apologetically. Magendie and Pelouze are sitting in the two comfortable chairs in his office at the *Charité*, uncertain of the reason for their invitation. "….. because it is about Claude."

They both nod, aware of the young man's predicament – and of Rayer's personal interest in his future.

"I want to discuss a proposition with you. It's a touchy situation, and I need your advice."

Rayer looks from one to the other.

"I think that I may have an opportunity to keep Claude here – by the rather devious means of an arranged marriage…" He hesitates briefly; allowing his idea to sink in. "….to the daughter of one of my more successful physician colleagues. Her dowry would of course enable him to properly establish his career in research."

"And what does Claude think about your idea, Pierre?" It is Magendie.

"He doesn't know yet: in fact I haven't even had the final word from Henri Martin…."

Pelouze interjects: "Isn't he the chap who looks after much of the Paris *élite*?

"Yes. That's him."

Rayer outlines the course of events that had led to his discussions with Martin, and explains that he simply wished to bounce the idea off his colleagues before he took any further steps. Pelouze is looking doubtful:

"Claude doesn't have much time for women, Pierre; he is so single minded about his work."

"I know, but don't you think it is worth a try?"

"I have to say that keeping Claude here in Paris would benefit the *Collège* – as well as the young man himself." Magendie, again. "Our council is getting rather concerned by our lack of productivity in the sciences. We actually need people like him. In fact *I* need him: he might be a good prospect for replacing me when my time comes."

The threat to the survival of the *Collège* as a direct competitor of the university was well known.

"Do I take it then, that you both support the idea?"

There is indeed universal agreement on the matter, and Rayer is pleased when he receives a response from Henri Martin a few days later:

Boulevard Saint-Denis, 34
February 19^h, 1845
My Dear Pierre

> *How nice it was to talk with you after the re-union. I have been able to make some independent enquiries about your young man from a friend who works in the medical school registry. What you said about him is amply confirmed from his record. He comes over as being a bit self-opinionated – but certainly not arrogant. Matched to his talents,*

that attitude is probably useful these days. I quite like the sound of him.

So let us move forward. Hélène and I would like to invite you to bring him over for supper on the 29th: that is if he agrees and it's convenient for you both. He is apparently a country boy at heart, albeit quite independent: so I am not sure how he will take to this approach. I have to say that Hélène is a little sceptical of whether it will work, but I'm prepared to give it a try.

We each need to undertake some sensitive and diplomatic discussions with our respective charges, but may I assume that if I don't hear from you we will see each other on the 29th? There are financial matters which we may discuss after that event.

With warmest good wishes,

Henri

The paths that wend their way through the Jardins des Tuileries had always been amongst Claude's favourites. He and Casimir Davaine had decided to meet by the noble statue of Julius Caesar near the *Grand Bassin*.

"It's been a long time since we did this, Casi."

Davaine smiles wrily.

"Only because of your obsession with working all hours that God gives you. It's sad that it takes a crisis in your life for us to meet in this civilized way. Tell me more?"

"It certainly is a crisis and I badly need someone to confide in. You know that I now have to give up my rooms on the *Commerce St André*. Charles Lasègue only has the one room and I really had hoped that you and Georgina might put me up for a short time: any corner will do?"

"Of course; but what about your cellar laboratory and the animals?"

"That's not a problem." Claude replies. "Magendie will accommodate my animals in his animal house: in fact he is allowing me to carry on with a few experiments at the *Collège*. I will just have to find the money for the animals and the necessary feeds and chemicals. I also have some bench space with Pelouze, so that I can work with Barreswill to finish off some of our earlier experiments."

They walk on in silence, past a pond where a few ducks are contemplating its partially frozen surface.

"But the real problem is me." Claude says quietly.

Davaine stops and turns to look directly at Claude's serious face; bloodshot eyes, deep furrows in his brow. Claude continues:

"Rayer has a friend from medical school days; a chap called Henri Martin who apparently treats half of Paris' society. He's really rather well-off."

"I can't say that I have heard of him."

"Well, neither had I, until I was invited to his home to meet his daughter."

"But why do you look so sad? It sounds interesting. What's she like?"

They resume their walking in silence until Claude bursts into an unstoppable torrent of words.

"Casi it's not like that! This has all been set up – like a performance at the *Ambigu;* like one of the crazy plays that *I* could have written! Rayer has decided that I must have a wife, and Théo Pelouze was the errand boy whom he sent to persuade me. This isn't about love or even affection. It's business! They want me to marry her!"

Claude's face is pale; his eyes awash with tears. Davaine puts his hands on his shoulders.

"Quiet now, Claude; take it one step at a time."

They sit down on a stone bench, remote from curious eyes. Claude draws a deep breath and mops his eyes.

"Casi, this is serious. I don't know what to do. The girl – Marie-Françoise is her name although she likes to be called Fanny – is not the Venus de Milo by any stretch of imagination…but then again I am no Adonis either! Of course I have only met her once, but she is so serious: not a hint of a smile the whole evening. The idea of this so repels me; as a romantic at heart I had hoped for something – well – more romantic. Pelouze knows the family too, and assures me that she has a strong character that would be wonderfully supportive, but her assertiveness has apparently frightened off all the previous men she has met. Can that be good?"

"But why are they doing this?"

"Come on! It's so obvious!"

Claude's voice had risen almost to a shout and a passing couple looks across at him quizzically.

"Rayer and Pelouze know that I'm at an impasse. I have no prospects at the medical school since I failed my *agregée*. I would have to wait another year until the next round of applications; and you well know how unlikely it is that I would even then be successful. They want to keep me here in Paris to continue research rather than returning to the Beaujolais as a country doctor. I should be flattered!"

There is silence for a few minutes while they mindlessly watch a bird on the other side of the path pecking through the leaves for an elusive worm.

"I still don't understand, Claude. How could you support this girl?"

Claude had been holding his head in both hands, and now turns to look at his friend with a mixture of alarm and anxiety on his face:

"Come on Casi, you must know how it works! The girl comes with money – and a lot of it, too – to be very exact a dowry of 60,000 francs and then another 5000 francs a year. That's the carrot that is supposed to attract me to the proposition! That this should happen to me!"

Davaine is looking down at his feet, thoughtfully.

"It could be worse Claude. If she is bright and intelligent, she may well support your academic dreams – personally, as well as the dowry. Moreover, you never know how you might grow towards each other. Marriage is after all only the start of a hopefully long relationship. Besides, what are your alternatives?"

It is a surprisingly warm and gentle affair. The formalities take place at the town hall – *le mairie*. Davaine is Claude's witness, attending with his girl friend Georgina. Charles Barreswill is present too, with Rayer, Pelouze and Magendie – together with their wives. There are also a few close friends and relatives of the Martins. Claude's parents could not come: his father had taken ill with pneumonia from which he was only just recovering, and his mother felt that her place was with him in St Julien. Afterwards there is a short service in a side chapel at St Sulpice, with a handful of other friends and colleagues. Martin had arranged a modest banquet for the thirty or so guests in a room of the *Café Cardinal* in the *boulevard des Italiens*. With the sun shining as they leave the restaurant, Claude is in buoyant mood. As was the custom of the day the whole dowry had been entrusted to him, to manage as he thought fit. Never in his wildest dreams had he considered that he would find himself in such a privileged position.

Before the wedding, he and Fanny had done a round of inspections of possible dwellings, and had finally decided on a pleasant apartment on the first floor of number five *rue de Pont-de-Lodi*. It had large windows that would catch the afternoon sun and apart from three bedrooms there was another small room, which he could use for a study.

At the start, it had needed a considerable effort on his part to raise a smile on Fanny's face. Nevertheless, when one evening he finally persuades her to attend a vaudeville performance at the *Ambigu*, their laughter continues into the cab, through the entrance to the apartment, into their bedroom and on to the bed. He later subsides into sexually satisfied sleep with a glowing contentment at the quite miraculous turn that life had taken.

Claude wastes no time in resuming his research. Magendie is happy to have him back as an associate (for whom he now did not need support from the *Collège*), and Pelouze is providing him with rather more bench space than before at his laboratories in the nearby *rue Dauphine*. There is enough money in Claude's new bank account to allow him to purchase pieces of equipment for his experiments: he even decides to commission some forged brass items from the instrument maker Breguet, which would be manufactured precisely to his own design.

Magendie's laboratory had by this time returned to the incompletely explored field of digestive secretions. Claude had no need to follow this line of work. Yet he had always been interested in the inconspicuous pancreas gland which lay behind the liver against the spine. Almost two hundred years earlier it had been observed to produce a liquid which entered the small intestine through a narrow duct. Logically therefore it had been assumed to have a digestive function. Yet it was only in 1844 while Claude was busy with spinal nerves and his work on colouring matter in the body that another Paris researcher by the name of Valentin showed that this pancreatic liquid could in fact digest starch into sugar; rather like the action of saliva or gastric secretions – but with greater intensity. Valentin even referred to the pancreas as 'the abdominal salivary gland'.

Everyone had now accepted that both saliva and pancreatic fluid were capable of breaking down complex carbohydrates like starch into absorbable glucose; but what of the other two main nutrients – proteins and fats? Nothing was known about how the body dealt with them; nor how they contributed to the nutrition of the body.

"Look at that." Claude comments to Barreswill one day after a consignment of rabbits had just arrived. "The urine in the bottom of the cage is completely clear."

"And why shouldn't it be?"

"Simply because rabbits are herbivores, and they always have cloudy urine which is alkaline. I have just analysed their urine and it is acidic; just like one sees in carnivores."

"Well, the poor things were probably not been fed while they were being delivered to us. Could they be breaking down the protein of their own muscles?"

"Very astute, Charles! I guess that's possible."

Claude is fascinated by his observation. He feeds a rabbit some meat instead of vegetable and confirms that the urine indeed changes colour and became alkaline – just as in a carnivore. He then kills it, opens its abdomen and carefully examines the abdominal contents. He is not too surprised to see white fluid in the so-called lacteal vessels leading away from the small intestinal wall; fluid which had been well shown by others to comprise products of digestion of fat. Yet there was no information on what actually emulsified the fat within the intestine so that it could be absorbed through the intestinal wall into the lacteals.

When he looks more closely, he sees to his surprise that not all the lacteals contain this white fluid – referred to as chyle. It was only in those vessels that drained the intestine below the point of entry of the pancreas duct.

Claude does an autopsy on another similarly fed rabbit, with identical results. He rushes into Barreswill just as he is closing up his laboratory for the night and almost drags him into the room where he has just performed his 'autopsy'.

"Look at those lacteals, Charles. It's only the ones below the point of entry of the pancreatic duct that contain white chyle. There can be only one explanation. Pancreatic secretions not only break down starch; they must also emulsify the fat in the diet."

Barreswill is astounded by the importance of Claude's demonstration – and its simplicity. They sit together throwing ideas at one another of how they might proceed further. Just how did pancreatic juice achieve its actions – and was it possible that the juice might also be responsible for the breakdown of the third nutrient – protein?

That night Claude returns to his apartment, anxious to share his discovery with his wife. On his arrival, Fanny is furious:

"They have left already. Do you know what time it is?"

Her face is flushed with anger as Claude checks the time on the magnificent grandfather clock that had been the Martin's wedding present. It has just passed eleven o'clock. Claude had both overlooked the time and completely forgotten the visit of Fanny's best friend and her husband. Claude tries to explain what he had discovered that day; Fanny is unreceptive.

"But it's every night, Claude; for one reason or another. Is this what our marriage is about?

"I'm tired, Fanny; please come to bed."

He takes his wife gently by the elbow and steers her towards their bedroom, hunger gnawing at his stomach. Fanny had indeed dressed nicely for their visitors. Claude observes that the dress had a tight-fitting bodice that suited her slim figure and her hair had been elegantly coiffured for the occasion. He feels very contrite about having neglected her. As they subside into their bed, Fanny turns to him, a faint smile lighting up her face: "I'm going to have a baby."

CHAPTER 7

MORE THAN ONE REVOLUTION

Claude's commitment to his research never interferes with his attendance at Rayer's ward rounds, which he considers an important stimulus to his own thought. He always stands behind the circle of *internes, externes* and visiting doctors; a notebook in one hand, a pencil in the other. On this occasion Rayer and his entourage stop at the bedside of a man; his cheeks hollow and his body so emaciated that he is hardly more than a skeleton. Rayer asks to be updated on his progress.

"Monsieur Lemoine is now without pain…." the *interne* reports. "… and he is eating quite well; yet no matter what type of food is offered, it is soon followed by severe diarrhoea."

Rayer addresses his students.

"As yet we do not have a diagnosis. There is a vague swelling in the upper part of his abdomen that I felt on my last ward round. Some of you may have confirmed this for yourselves: his thin abdominal wall makes examination of his organs rather easier. This finding is however insufficient to justify exploratory surgery. In any case, Monsieur Lemoine told me last week that he would refuse this option. I believe that his view of the situation is quite appropriate and we will just have to await developments. Any comments or questions?"

Claude coughs politely and indicates with a raised finger that he wishes to contribute to the discussion.

"May I ask if his faeces float on the surface of water?"

Rayer looks at Claude, and then at the *interne* who shrugs his shoulders: smiling, almost laughing at the seemingly pointless enquiry. Rayer looks back at Claude.

"A strange question, Doctor Bernard. Why would that be of interest to us?"

"He has lost a great deal of weight, despite apparently eating adequately. This suggests that food – and particularly fat – is not being absorbed from the intestine. Fat being of lower density than water one could reason that any fat-rich faeces would tend to float on the surface of water."

The nursing orderly who is accompanying the ward round comments that Monsieur Lemoine had passed a motion just prior to the round: it is still available in the sluice room for inspection, should Dr Rayer wish to see it. The entire group move to the sluice room where the orderly brings a pan containing a large quantity of yellow foul-smelling faeces. Claude uses a wooden spatula to transfer a portion of the faeces to the surface of a bowl of water where it remains, suspended. There is a murmur across the group as Rayer asks:

"Might it be a good idea if we examined a sample of normal faeces – for comparison?"

The orderly produces a bedpan containing faeces from another patient. Claude transfers a portion to the surface of another water-filled bowl, whereupon it immediately sinks slowly to the bottom.

"If I may, Dr Rayer," offers Claude, "our research studies have shown that both bile and pancreatic juice are capable of digesting fats from the diet, enabling them to be absorbed. Monsieur Lemoine does not have the yellow skin typical of jaundice: we can therefore assume that adequate amounts of bile must be entering the intestine. By exclusion, I would deduce that he must have severe pancreatic disease."

"Take note of that reasoning." says Rayer, turning towards his students, "And if Doctor Bernard is correct – and I have no reason to doubt it – we could move on and consider the diagnostic alternatives. The two most common diseases of the pancreas are cancer and chronic inflammation. In view of the swelling in the abdomen which some of us have felt, cancer is more likely. If this is the case then time will provide us with the proof, and quite soon at that! "

The round ends. Doctors and students disperse while Rayer and Claude stand together at the entrance to the ward.

"Thank you, Claude – as always. Once more you've helped with the diagnosis, taught the students and not least inspired me. Please never consider that you are anything but welcome on my rounds."

In May 1846, Louis-Henri is born, pathetically small and consistently refusing to take milk from his mother's breast. None of the doctors recommended by Fanny's father can find a reason. Claude discusses the problem with everyone he meets at the hospital but no help is forthcoming. Fanny is convinced that the Paris air is at fault; already in July so unbearably hot and humid. She decides to take the baby out of central Paris to Montreuil and stay with her aunt, even though it means being away on Claude's birthday. One morning she wakes up in her aunt's house to find Louis-Henri lifeless in the cot alongside her bed. Back in Paris she remains deeply depressed, irritable and subject to violent outbursts. Why – she says – can Claude not spend more time at home and provide her with emotional support? Are his dogs, rabbits and cats so much more important to him than his wife? Indeed, is he planning to spend the rest of his life this way, rather than being a proper doctor and attending to human suffering – as did her father? Why was that not good enough for him? Claude offers no answers.

Her moods gradually mellow and when she announces that she is again pregnant, happiness should have been everywhere. However, Claude now had other worries. His father had never properly recovered from the illness he had at the time of their wedding. His teaching had long since come to an end. Caroline was now seventeen and as with so many others, she could not find employment. Above all, it had been one of those bad years for wine. Claude discusses their predicament with Fanny, since he wishes to use some of their money – of her dowry – to at least repay his parents for their outlay towards his studies. She demands to see the figures. When the bank provides a list of their withdrawals she discovers that his research activities had already consumed more than one thousand francs of their capital.

"Must you insult me and our marriage by so obviously using my dowry for your selfish needs?"

Claude is uncertain how to deal with the confrontation that he well knows had to come eventually.

"Fanny, I don't think that we will suffer from the small amount of money that I have used. I wish you would see it as an investment in our future."

"What future? You don't love me; I don't feel that you are even interested in creating an amicable co-existence. Ours was most certainly an arranged marriage, but it seems that it was arranged only for *your* benefit!"

"I'm sorry, Fanny. I don't wish to neglect you and your needs. I promise that I will try to serve you better. As far as my family is concerned, I feel that I would like to repay the debt that I owe them. My income is necessarily modest at the moment; all I can promise you is to later restore what I have borrowed."

"Your income is only modest because you wish to pursue your own interests rather than the well-being of others. My father says that you are well endowed with intellect. Were you to use it for healing people, rather than your selfish pursuits, we would be far better off. It is all so one-sided!"

Claude feels unable to argue any further. He shrugs his shoulders and leaves the room, while Fanny bursts into tears and slams the door behind him with such ferocity that a crystal decanter on a sideboard crashes to the floor. For two days hardly a word passes between them. Claude's misery is complete when he receives news that his father had died. He considers returning to St Julien, if only to provide support for his mother. But in the letter which carries the bad news, his mother and Caroline insist that he should not make the trip. His mother adds that she is pleased to learn of his success and the expectation of a grandchild. She had finally accepted Claude's chosen path in medicine and made no further reference to the possibility of him practising in St Julien.

Jeanne Bernard is a pretty and contented baby. Her arrival almost erases the searing pain caused by her brother's tragic death. She blossoms on her mother's milk, and Fanny at last seems more content. They agree to employ a maid called Agnés who turns out to be a very willing helper. Claude finds it a pleasure to have the rather pert and decorative Agnés bustling around. Although he had been initially reluctant, he discovers that she can clean and tidy his study quite miraculously – without displacing any of his documents.

Beyond the Bernard household, France is in turmoil. Of all the revolutions in the Europe of 1848, the one in France is the most violent. The ineffectual Louis-Philippe is falling from grace, the corn harvest is spoiled by unremitting winter rain and potato crops are ruined by a blight that had spread from Ireland. With industrial output flagging and unemployment escalating, the country slides into recession. Louis-Philippe abdicates and sails for the refuge of England accompanied by Jean Vatout; adviser to the king – and of course Claude's first mentor. France is declared a republic. Workless starving Parisians take to the streets, storming the protective barricades in blind fury at the helpless government. In three 'red days of June' several thousand perish at the hands of soldiers under the command of Cavaignac, a man who has pretensions of winning the presidency of the republic by his decisive handling of the uprising. He was to be proved wrong. With the abdication of the king and the establishment of a republic, Napoleon Bonaparte's nephew, Louis Napoleon feels that his time has come. He makes a finely executed return to France from his exile in England to make a bid for the presidency. He brings with him the Napoleonic aura which still appeals, together with the promise of creating order and tranquillity. In four regions of France his charm and reason touch hearts and heads; by the end of the year his election machine has swamped that of Cavaignac. Louis Napoleon is elected prince-president, and by a handsome majority.

Claude's academic life flourishes in the early days of the republic. He is appointed to the *Collège de France* as deputy to Magendie, and will no longer need to use his 'personal' money to support his research. Magendie retires from clinical work at the *Hôtel Dieu* and continues only with a few lectures at the *Collège* during each winter session. Claude gives the summer series, and with his salary comes his rightful usage of Magendie's modest laboratory. There are whispers that he might assume the professorship of medicine at the *Collège* in due course. There is soon to be another bonus. Claude is awarded a prestigious prize in experimental physiology given by the *Académie des Sciences* for his work on the pancreas.

In the same year, together with some fellow scientists, Claude establishes the *Société de Biologie*, an association which provides a long-needed opportunity for aspiring researchers to meet those who had already made their mark in science. Pierre Rayer is elected its first president and Claude one of its two vice-presidents. Some cynics express the view that Claude had set up the society as a platform for presenting his own research. Indeed, a paper by him or one of his students is now read there almost every week; sugar in the vomit of a patient; experiments with atropine (a drug which acts as if the pneumogastric nerves have been cut); abnormal head movements in dogs after damage to a tiny area of the brain and even more work on the role of the pancreas in digestion. Through these various events, Claude's reputation in Paris rises rapidly. In parallel, his credibility in the eyes of the Martin family becomes at least partially restored.

There is one piece of research on which Claude cannot wait to report to his new Society. On that day in August 1848, Rayer, Davaine and Barreswill are present together with a dozen others, most of them now regular attendees of the new association:

"You will all know how Dumas insists that every chemical in the animal body comes from the food it eats."

Everyone present nods: it is not just the opinion of Jean-Baptiste Dumas, but a firmly imprinted notion that had never been challenged. Nutrients were the source of every chemical in the body.

"Well; it's just not true! Charles and I have taken blood samples from dogs that are fasting or have just been fed on meat; in other words just consuming protein. With his sensitive technique we can regularly detect glucose in their blood...."

A murmur runs through the audience.

"....and let me show you what happens when *I* don't eat!"

Claude produces a sheet of results from which it is clear that without food, his glucose level dropped a little in the first few hours, but then stayed absolutely level for the next two days of his fast.

"So glucose cannot just be coming from food! And the reason that Ambrosiani found that sugar was only in the blood when animals were fed is explained by the fact that his method back in '37 was just not sensitive enough. As you know he just depended on recognizing sugar crystals under his microscope!"

There is much more nodding and mumbling. Charles looks very pleased with himself while Claude continues, voice rising in pitch with excitement:

"I then took a dog that had been fed only on meat and opened its abdomen. Charles and I took blood samples from all sorts of blood vessels. Not only could we pick up traces of glucose in most of them, but in the hepatic vein that leaves the liver the levels were enormous, while in the portal vein that enters the liver there was none."

He shows them another sheet of paper with glucose results neatly entered opposite the names of various blood vessels.

"It seems that the liver is probably responsible for maintaining the glucose levels in the blood. Now Pierre, you always said on your ward rounds – as I seem to recall – that the liver has the single function of making bile. I have to report that you and everyone else have been wrong about this."

There is a buzz of excitement; Pierre Rayer is now sitting bolt upright on his chair, while Claude continues.

"I then killed a rabbit that had been fed only on meat. When Charles analyzed a sample of its liver, he found enormous amounts of glucose in it. We have now looked at livers of rats, mice, cats and dogs; and from our local butcher we obtained the livers of cows, pigs and sheep. In every single liver, Charles has been able to identify that sugar; and masses of it!"

Pierre Rayer cannot restrain himself.

"That's extraordinary Claude. The great Lavoisier was obviously wrong. He claimed that the synthesis of nutrients occurred only in plants. Animals are supposed only to use what plants have produced for us. You have turned whole concepts of biology upside down. The great Xavier Bichat was wrong, too about his claims of 'one organ, one function'. My goodness, how many students have I wrongly instructed!"

Two months later, on his return from St Julien Claude presents his results formally to the *Académie des Sciences*. The audience is amazed – and skeptical. His findings will surely be contested; yet Claude is convinced that he is right!

It is Magendie who ensures that awareness of Claude's research achievements reaches the highest circles of the new government. He notifies the Minister of Education, the Comte de Falloux about Claude's groundbreaking discoveries with a recommendation that he should receive appropriate recognition. One day Constantin James visits Claude in his laboratory smiling broadly, a copy of *le Moniteur* tucked under his arm.

"It seems that they have at last accepted your contribution to the musical world, Claude."

"What nonsense are you talking about?"

James shows him the announcement in *le Moniteur*.

'*Claude Bernard (of Villefranche) is named Chevalier of the Legion of Honour for his excellent work on the musical properties of the pancreas.*'

Claude does not know whether to laugh or scream. Was that a joke at his expense? James is able to calm him down with his assurance that it is Magendie who had indeed nominated him for the award. It is only unfortunate that the newspaper had made a misprint. Nevertheless, Claude does not rest until it publishes a formal correction and retraction later in the year; with 'medical' in place of 'musical'! All is forgiven when he is presented with the appropriate medal suspended from its little red ribbon.

Not long after this event Claude is at a family dinner in the Martin's home. They are sitting at the large mahogany dining table superbly laid with Meissen china, tall elegant glasses and highly ornamental silver cutlery. Claude had made a special effort on arrive on time. Fanny was in good spirits, having been collected from their apartment by her father's carriage; quite confident that Jeanne (whom they had decided to nickname Tony) was being well cared for by Agnès. Dr Martin was in a genial mood.

"So what do you think of our new Prince-President, Claude? Is he going to make your life easier?"

"Probably no more than yours, Henri."

Claude is certain that his father-in-law's highly independent and successful professional life is unlikely to be affected one way or the other by political machinations at the Elysée. Claude continues:

"The medical school, the *Collège* and all the academies try to keep away from that type of politics, and Louis hasn't yet announced any change to education policy. There's quite enough mischief in medical politics to keep me on my toes. There are some people who think they should have won that physiology prize rather than me – and they are letting me feel it!"

"You are right to keep looking over your shoulder Claude. Rayer has given me quite an insight in what happens in his various committees. It's quite easy to get trampled on if you are not careful. I am lucky to be outside those matters. By the way, I am almost certainly going to have to take on an associate soon: some energetic young man who can take over the practice from me in a few years time. I don't suppose that you would re-consider my proposal of joining the practice? It would be an honour – and an easy escape from the medical politics you refer to."

Claude shakes his head and smiles wryly at yet another attempt by his father-in-law to lure him away from his experiments into the lucrative life of private medical practice.

"I wish you wouldn't press me so, Henri. You must know that I am committed to my branch of medicine – and it's beginning to show results."

"What branch of medicine?" Fanny interrupts. "What does your torture of those poor animals have to do with medicine, Claude?"

Claude is exasperated. The evening had started out so well. When Fanny smiled it was wonderful; but now her mouth was set in a tight line and her features had hardened. Her wrath was clearly set to continue:

"According to an article yesterday in *le National*, half of Paris thinks that your sort of work is unnecessary and brutal. I'm also ashamed to tell my friends about what you do. Why can't you help people like my father does?"

Claude is silent. He looks from one to the other. Both Fanny and her parents are wondering how he will respond.

"I have had some time to think about all your concerns since we last discussed this – on your birthday Madame – if I remember correctly."

Claude looks at Madame Martin – then back at Fanny.

"Let me try to explain. I have often told you about my commitment to scientific truth, Fanny. It's what drove me to do research in the first place; so much medical treatment remains a matter of guesswork and false concepts. Tell me Henri, which medicines are you truly confident will result in cure of a patient?"

Martin is not fazed by the challenge.

"Well, all those we use for coughs and diarrhoea; and of course the ones we use for pain relief too. There are so many that I wouldn't really know where to start."

Claude's response is rapid and assertive.

"No Henri. The types of medicine you mention only relieve symptoms; the common conditions that cause those symptoms mostly get better by themselves – yet doctors get the credit for it! Of course, there are serious disorders like cancer, apoplexy, consumption and pneumonia that threaten life. I doubt whether you have evidence that any drug which you use alters what eventually happens to *those* patients."

"You may well be right about all that Claude...." Martin responds, looking somewhat ill at ease, "...but you must also admit that there is an art to caring for the ill, even if it is just the symptoms which we are treating. Reassurance and explanation are surely worthwhile in our profession!"

Fanny interjects; her face crimson with anger.

"...and caring is something you could occasionally show towards people and not just towards your animals!"

"Fanny, if I didn't care for people I wouldn't be working so hard. I have tried to explain why I do what I do but still you don't understand. Yet my medical colleagues – and I think I can include your father in this – appreciate its relevance. I wish you could trust me."

Claude turns towards his father-in-law.

"Henri, you mentioned *art*: but art cannot take the place of scientific medicine? Art is about creation; a writer for his stories, a painter for his pictures; a composer for his music. So, what do doctors create then? Only the side effects of the ill-chosen medicines they prescribe. I suppose that there may be an art to the process of reassurance. But is it really honest reassurance, or a platitude based on doctors' ignorance of what is actually happening to their patient – or even just deceiving the patient about their real predicament?"

Claude is exhausted. Doctor Martin's face is thoughtful; while his wife's is blank as though she had not understood a word of what had been said. Fanny is crying; her face buried in a lace handkerchief. Claude stands, distressed too.

"I think we had better go Fanny. Henri, I am so sorry that I allowed myself to be provoked just when you were trying to be kind and helpful. *Madame*, please forgive me for spoiling a wonderful meal. May I just say that I am giving my first lecture at the *Collège* on my birthday, July 12th? I think I am going to explain a little of my philosophy towards medicine and science; it will be a good introduction to what follows in my later lectures. As you know these lectures are open to the public. I would be really honoured if you would come; I'd really like to hear your reaction and thoughts afterwards."

There is silence in the carriage during their return to their apartment. Claude tries to take Fanny's hand, but is rudely rejected. This was not at all what he had hoped for.

Claude's gives his inaugural lecture at the *Collège* to a full amphitheatre, in which Dr Martin and his wife are indeed present. Fanny had made her excuses on grounds that she and Agnès were preparing his birthday dinner to which the extended family had been invited afterwards. On their return, Fanny's parents report to her that Claude had received much applause: they were proud to have been there.

The next day, Charles Barreswill comments to Pelouze that the content of Claude's talk had been interesting although he thought that his delivery had been marred – as always – by his rather hesitant manner. He recalls that it had been this very aspect of Claude's presentation, which had snuffed his chances of success at the contest for his *agrégation* five years earlier.

Claude makes his annual trip St Julien in September, only this time by train. Already in July, bookings had been accepted for travel on the inaugural passenger train service to Lyon; the first section of a railway line which would eventually reach as far south as Marseilles. He had looked forward to introducing Fanny to his family and giving his mother the pleasure of seeing Tony. However, at the last moment Fanny had announced that she was pregnant again; they had agreed that it might be wiser for her to stay in Paris.

His mother is overjoyed to see him and Claude is pleased that the cottage is in good repair, thanks to the money that he had sent her. Caroline now carried the surname Cantin and looked well and happy. She and her husband Jean lived in Pouilly-le-Monial – only some ten kilometres to the south and were therefore still able to keep a watchful eye on their mother. Tired from his labours at the *Collège*, Claude was only a bystander at the harvest this year. The vines were providing a rich harvest and with the hot summer that had passed, everyone was optimistic about the quality of the vintage. The only concern was the Oïdium – powdery mildew – which some of the *vignerons* in other wine-growing regions of France had reported. It was now spreading east and south and a few vines in neighbouring Macon had already been affected.

Claude visits his father's grave and spends many hours wandering through the vineyards and around the familiar haunts of the village. He wonders if it would prove possible to bring his family back to the Beaujolais each year: escaping from Paris each summer would be bliss; he might even be able to write reports, lectures and articles on his research. On a bright Sunday, Ronne and Marianne visit him with their two young children in a carriage drawn by the most handsome white horse. They look so prosperous and happy; both the pharmacy and their relationship were obviously in good shape. Ronne plies him with questions about Fanny, but Claude decides that he will not spoil the occasion of their visit by sharing his concerns about his marriage. He is really sorry when the time comes to leave St Julien for Paris after his ten day stay.

Claude eventually manages to persuade Barreswill and Pelouze to regularly set aside some time at the end of the week. In this way they could jointly discuss research; ideas and reflections on what they had discovered and where it was all leading. Rayer and Magendie had agreed to come if possible. On this occasion, Claude wished to discuss his last few months' observations concerning sugar levels in the blood for which Charles had recently perfected a more sensitive and rapid measurement. He knows that Rayer's considerable experience in diabetes will be an asset to their discussions. Davaine is also present; now working closely with Rayer on infections, and particularly with the mysterious lung disease Charbon – also called anthrax – which had affected so many workers in the abattoirs. Claude wastes no time in reporting his latest research findings.

"A couple of months ago Pierre, you had an unfortunate young man on your ward who had diabetes and drifted into coma. When you performed his post mortem, we were all surprised that he had a brain tumour. You may remember that we had a big debate about whether it was the tumour or the diabetes which actually caused his death."

"Of course! You even wondered if the brain tumour might somehow have caused the diabetes." Rayer smiles kindly. "You quite delayed the ward round that day with all your different theories!"

"I'm sorry about that Pierre. But that case did prompt me to do a few experiments on the subject. I used a fine needle to produce small areas of damage in different parts of the brain of rabbits and dogs. I then looked for any changes in their blood sugar levels. You will remember that one edge of your patient's tumour involved the fourth ventricle. I have discovered that if I stimulate the floor of the fourth ventricle with such a needle – a *piqûre* – blood sugar levels invariably rise. I was not able to show this reaction in any other part of the brain. Charles did the actual measurements of course."

"The levels were really quite high." Charles adds. "They went from about one gram to almost three and a half grams per litre after Claude's little manoeuvres."

Rayer sits forward on his chair, clearly excited by the findings.

"That's truly remarkable. Those are just the sort of blood sugar levels you have measured in my patients with diabetes. You're not suggesting that you have identified the cause of diabetes, Claude?"

"Not *the* cause, but perhaps *a* cause. The control of blood sugar levels seems to be a very complicated business. There must be a very good reason why levels of sugar in the blood are normally kept so very constant and there could be quite a few ways by which the body achieves this. Perhaps even the brain has a part to play in the matter!"

"How did you manage to get so deep into the brain?" Asks Pelouze.

"I've started putting my animals to sleep with ether using Long's method – do you remember François mentioned it some time ago? I just add small amounts at a time to a cloth placed over the rabbit's nose. I no longer need that complicated frame that Magendie developed to immobilise rabbits. Ether works well on dogs too by the way. Immobile animals allow me to place the lesions with so much greater accuracy."

"And it seems much kinder to the poor little beasts as well," comments Barreswill. "By the way, Claude, are you quite sure that the ether isn't itself raising the sugar levels?"

"Yes, I checked that possibility."

Rayer joins in the discussion:

"Didn't you also suggest on my ward round that the pneumogastric nerve might somehow influence the sugar level?"

"That's right. That was only because its nerve fibres start near the fourth ventricle of the brain. I did look at the effect of cutting the pneumogastric on two animals in which I had induced diabetes; but that didn't alter the sugar levels at all."

Davaine feels that he ought to add to the discussion.

"What about the interesting experiments on the liver which you reported last year, Claude? It may not be via the pneumogastric nerve, but could the brain nevertheless have an effect on the liver?"

"We actually have had some remarkable results on that, Casi. It started when we injected plain water into the blood vessels that enter the liver. When Charles analyzed the fluid from the blood vessels leaving the liver, he found sugar in the fluid; and lots of it too. When I did my *piqure* of the fourth ventricle, even more sugar appeared in those vessels. However, it is clear the 'message' to the liver is not carried by the pneumogastric nerves. There are of course other nerves which I have not yet examined."

After the meeting, Rayer offers Claude a ride home in his carriage. Claude does not hesitate: he is exceptionally tired and the idea of walking does not appeal. During the last month he had even sometimes stayed overnight in the tiny, damp laboratory; either because he needed to take blood samples from his animals during an extended experiment, or simply because he was too tired – perhaps even too afraid – to return home.

"Aren't you pushing yourself too hard, Claude?" Rayer offers. "You're making wonderful progress with your research; so many important findings which are beyond everyone's expectations. I also hear that your lectures are well attended. You must be putting an enormous amount of work into them. How about Fanny, though? She can't be seeing very much of you these days. And Tony…?"

"Yes. Fanny complains bitterly; her objection to my work with animals has become a matter of principle. It comes up in conversation almost every day. I cannot decide whether it is out of sympathy for the animals or just disappointment that I am not a successful practicing physician like her father. Perhaps it's both!" Claude adds. "I have to face the fact that our marriage is not succeeding Pierre."

Rayer feels sweat breaking out on his forehead; the arranged marriage had made it possible for Claude to contribute uniquely to medical science, as well as giving him both satisfaction and recognition. Now Rayer can clearly see that a heavy price is being paid for that success – and by everyone. They travel on in silence until they reached the *rue de Pont-de-Lodi* and the carriage comes to a halt.

"This is all very upsetting Claude. Is it worth risking your marriage and your health just to make yourself successful in research? Isn't there more to life than that?"

"It's probably too late Pierre. I enjoy what I do and I am getting results. I cannot turn back; in fact I am not sure that I wish to!"

With that, Claude steps down from the carriage, turns towards Rayer and puts a hand on his knee.

"…and Pierre, please do not suffer anguish over this. I am sure that you and Théo acted out of your best motives. It is up to me to find a *modus vivendi.*"

Claude despondently climbs the stairs to his apartment. Research indeed represented his whole existence now. He had no confidence in any other ability within medicine; and certainly nothing would persuade him to become a practicing physician. It was an excellent discipline to join Rayer's ward rounds, and he could often contribute to a diagnosis by using his detailed knowledge of physiology. Nevertheless, for him the clinical problems on the wards were there for one main purpose: to act as stimuli for his research ideas.

Apart from a lamp burning in the salon, the apartment was in darkness: Fanny had evidently retired for the night, presumably again disappointed by his absence. Claude removes his coat and boots, slumps into his comfortable armchair and within a minute he is asleep.

Several evenings later, Fanny and Agnès are trying to pacify Tony who is listless, crying and feverish. She had been completely well in the morning and her symptoms had developed only during the afternoon. Claude had not yet arrived home and time was moving on – soon too late for Fanny to attend the meeting which she had earmarked for this evening. Illness was unusual for Tony who was now a robust two year old and normally full of joy and good spirits. Fanny is haunted by visions of their first child's illness and death for which no explanations had been forthcoming.

"Do go Madame." Agnès pleads. "You can do no more than me at the moment. I will give her some cold compresses and make sure that she drinks. And anyway I am sure that Monsieur will be home shortly."

"I am not so sure he will, Agnès – if the last few weeks are anything to go by. My meeting is in the hall next to St Sulpice. However, if he does arrive and Tony gets any worse than this, please come and fetch me immediately."

Fanny makes her way to the hall, taking a short route, which takes her through the dismal unlit side streets where she is at risk of assault. She breathes a sigh of relief when she arrives. The hall is only half-full, mainly with women. On an elevated platform, the speaker had already commenced his talk. His delivery is forceful; accompanied by emphatic gestures.

"...and we cannot afford to be complacent. The torture and unshackled demolition of animals whose voices cannot be heard must not be allowed to continue. It is for this and this alone that I have this week submitted for consideration the text of a law which will be debated early next year by the *Assemblée Nationale*."

The Comte de Grammont's face is flushed with the intensity of his delivery. His enthusiasm is rewarded by modest applause as he continues:

"Fines of between five and fifteen francs will be imposed as a first deterrent; my committee's restraint has made these lower than I would have liked. Yet we have agreed to recommend a jail sentence as a consequence of non-payment of fines. I will be happy to keep you all informed of our progress with the bill using the kind offices of the SPA. Until then, I must remind you that we need your financial support. The costs of printing leaflets and organising personal appeals to those who are abusing God's creatures are high. I would ask you all to dig deeply into your pockets to help the cause that I know you all support."

Some of the women in the audience begin to ask questions, but Fanny's mind is now only on her child. She leaves the hall after depositing several coins in the box beside the entrance. When she arrives home, Claude is sitting next to Tony's bed, a frown of concern on his face.

"She is sleeping peacefully enough, Fanny. I think it would be best if we get some sleep now. We can see how she is in the morning. I don't think that her fever is so very high anymore."

Reluctantly Fanny agrees. For the first time in weeks they retire to bed together; and for once with minds and souls focussed on a matter of mutual concern.

The following morning finds Tony without fever. She had perspired freely during the night, her eyes had regained their sparkle and she had just devoured her breakfast with almost normal vigour, all much to her parents' delight. Claude doesn't think to enquire about Fanny's absence the previous evening and leaves for the *Collège* with his usual sense of urgency.

Claude spends many hours with colleagues discussing his results on *piqûre* diabetes. Although he was wedded to the principle that nerve activity also controlled organ function – and might therefore also be responsible for organ dysfunction – there was in fact no real proof that a lesion in the brain was the cause of most cases of diabetes.

On the other hand, he is fascinated by his remarkable discovery of production of sugar by the liver. Could it be that an over-activity of the liver was responsible for the elevated glucose levels of diabetes; and how might he pursue this idea further? With little existing knowledge of how the liver functioned, he could not see a way forward. His observation was not enough to construct a hypothesis; and without a hypothesis, he could not design the relevant experiment. Accordingly, he makes sure that he has fully recorded all his latest results on 'glucose' in his notebook. He then leaves the following five pages blank as a reminder that he needed to return to the subject at a later date; hopefully when he had inspiration about how to proceed.

CHAPTER 8

Arrows Find Their Mark

Fanny announces in the New Year that she was again pregnant. As with her previous pregnancies, her temperament had become so much milder. She found it easier to smile; less likely to react badly to his late arrivals in the evening. Surprisingly, she was now taking some interest in the results of his work. That was indeed fortunate since he was busier than ever with his research. His innovative probing and the resulting important discoveries were becoming widely known; students of the highest calibre were writing to ask for the privilege of assisting with his research. Lurking in the back of his mind is the puzzle of curare that he had begun to unravel five years earlier. Why not take the opportunity of having the help of students to advance his understanding of that fascinating poison which caused paralysis and certain death? Ever since he had made his original observation on curare, he had wondered if studying poisons might provide insight into the way the body worked. He suddenly comes upon the term 'physiological dissection' to describe this concept.

A further stimulus for this move is a patient whom he had seen on one of Rayer's ward rounds at the *Charité*; a young woman with rheumatic heart failure. She had died as a result of an overdose of medicine containing digitalis leaf. The case reminded Claude of both Millet's and Magendie's conviction that every medicine was potentially a poison – if one gave it in large enough doses. But what about the converse situation; could a known poison conceivably work as a useful medicine – if one gave it in *small* enough doses? It really was high time that he worked on those curare-tipped darts and the pure curare that Goudot had brought back from Peru. Claude looks back in his notebooks of five years earlier; at his first experiments on frogs. There had been a puzzling fact about curare which had been bothering him for some time. To help him solve the riddle he decides to share his thoughts with one of his students.

"Don't you think it strange, Jean", Claude comments to him one day, "That the natives in Peru can safely eat the meat of animals that they have just killed using curare-tipped darts? Wouldn't you think that such a powerful poison would also harm – even kill – someone eating the meat?"

The student's reply is rapid.

"Unless any poison within the meat is destroyed by the acidic contents of the stomach."

"A good thought Jean; and one which I would like you to test as soon as possible. I suggest you start by giving rabbits increasing doses of curare through a gastric tube – and see what happens."

It does not take long for Jean Bardet to report that even if he gives a dose of curare into the stomach much higher than that needed to kill a rabbit by injection, there is no discernible effect on the rabbits. He is triumphant about the confirmation of his theory.

"Before you get too excited, there is of course another possibility." Claude observes. "After you administer the curare, try leaving the tube in place for about half an hour; then withdraw the contents of the stomach back through the tube? I want you to then inject a small part of that fluid back under the skin of the rabbit."

Bardet returns later that day, a baffled expression on his face.

"I tried it three times. The same result each time," he adds. "Even the tiniest amount of stomach contents injected into the rabbit was fatal within a few minutes. The stomach acid is obviously not destroying the curare!"

Together with Bardet, Claude performs some further experiments of this type; different doses of curare and different timing of withdrawal of the stomach contents. Yet every time a sample of the fluid is injected either into the same or another animal death follows.

"So what can you deduce from those experiments, Jean?"

There is silence for a couple of minutes.

"I can see only one explanation. If it is not the stomach acid which destroys the curare, then it must be that curare cannot be absorbed through the lining of the stomach or bowel. Perhaps the molecule is just too big..."

"...and the proof of that?"

His student smiles broadly.

"I'll report back to you tomorrow, Monsieur."

When Claude arrives the next morning, Bardet is already waiting in front of the laboratory for him, and judging by his bleary eyes he has been up all night. Yet he is looking most pleased with himself; a grin stretching from ear to ear.

"Case proved! I gave the same dose of curare to two rabbits by gastric tube. However, I operated on one of them a couple of hours before giving the dose; I opened its stomach and made several shallow incisions in the lining of its stomach before closing it again. After giving the doses by tube the animal with the damaged stomach died in a manner typical of curare poisoning; the other one is still alive and well!"

"Well done Jean. I think I would like to repeat that last series of experiments with you. Assuming the results are the same, you might then record them in the style of one of my earlier articles – perhaps the one I wrote on pancreatic juice in '47. We'll have a fine paper for you to present at the next meeting of the *Societé de Biologie*!"

And that was Claude's approach. A project had to begin with an observation. This was considered carefully, and was then discussed with a student or colleague. From this, a hypothesis would emerge. The experiment that followed was constructed and performed with a purpose (not on a whim as Magendie might have done). Whether the outcome was positive or negative it would need confirmation, further experiments and finally a firm conclusion. Claude trusted his assistants to work carefully, but he would always verify an important result personally.

"I had some excellent results today Fanny." he announces as soon as he enters the apartment that evening; mood buoyant. "Let's celebrate by going to the theatre. Hugo's *Notre Dame de Paris* is at the *Théatre-Français* tomorrow: I've never seen it on stage."

"Look at me, Claude! Women who are expecting a child in three months are not to be seen in public! Go without me: I doubt that I would enjoy it anyhow. By the way I see in *le National* that Hugo, whom you so admire is most outspoken against vivisection – he utterly condemns those who commit such a crime against nature: he is even planning to set up his own anti-vivisection foundation in due course."

Claude does not know how to respond to the challenge. He hangs up his cloak, walks into his study and closes the door behind him with far more than necessary force.

Marie-Louise's birth is uneventful; she is a healthy robust child and Fanny is now quite happy to busy herself with the needs of her two daughters. Claude feels little need to be involved in that aspect of his domestic life; he decides to dedicate himself fully to understanding exactly how curare kills its victims. He begins by re-reading all the explorers' stories about the poison, beginning with the sixteenth century descriptions of Sir Walter Raleigh and ending with the vivid documentation in the early 1800's by Waterton and von Humboldt about how people died after accidental poisoning. He reads about the fate of a Peruvian hunter who had been scratched by one of his own darts. The man had recognised the inevitability of what would happen and took time to carefully set down his load, lie down by its side and peacefully await the arrival of death. There appeared to be no more gentle way of parting with life.

Claude decides to try using smaller and smaller amounts of curare. He eventually finds a dose, which paralyses the muscles of the legs without affecting the muscles which control breathing. The animals are only temporarily paralysed and recover within a couple of hours with no apparent after effects. He also finds that if he provides artificial respiration until the effect of curare has worn off, he can give even larger doses – with complete recovery. Claude is pleased with his work that attracts much interest from his visitors. The picture is clear. Death from curare had but one simple cause; the temporary but reversible paralysis of chest muscles and the diaphragm – which led to death by asphyxiation. His conclusions are momentous and form the basis of a number of lectures.

"...and I must emphasize that neither the natives of Peru who accidentally injure themselves with the poisoned darts – nor the beasts whom they pursue for food – die as peacefully as Brodie and von Humboldt have led us to believe."

There is utter silence in the packed amphitheatre in the *Collège de France*. "Instead, theirs must be the most agonizing death of all. Whether man or beast, may I ask you to imagine the torment of suddenly losing the ability to breathe; choking on one's own breath as it were and being able neither to move nor to utter a cry for help. Yes, consciousness is in no way affected by curare. The intellect in curare poisoning remains totally clear; the mind is terrified until the moment of death."

With this dramatic statement, he concludes his lecture and offers to respond to questions from the audience. The first of these comes promptly from a man sitting in the centre of the amphitheatre.

"Monsieur, you have made clear to us the way in which curare poisons the body. If there are indeed no adverse consequences, could not curare in the lesser doses you described have certain benefits in relaxing the muscles? Suspending movement may be an advantage in certain medical conditions."

The comment fascinates Claude; totally in line with his philosophy toward poisons and their future for medical treatment.

"We all accept that effective medicines given in excess are poisons. Conversely, poisons given in much smaller quantities may indeed prove to be useful as medicines – like the poisonous digitalis leaf, which in small doses helps the heart to beat more strongly. Curare may certainly be useful in some disorders, but I have no personal experience of using it in this way."

Another man in the same row of benches springs to his feet.

"May I comment on that point, Monsieur Bernard? My name is Doctor Vella from Torino. Since I visited your laboratory earlier this year, I have managed to procure some curare. I have now examined its value in treating the devastating muscular contractions of tetanus that occur as a result of war wounds. I believe that my treatment with curare has saved some lives. Of course, one is aware that breathing must be supported during its use, and we use bellows and a tube connected to the mouth for that purpose. One of my colleagues in Torino is trying this treatment also in severe cases of epileptic convulsions."

A murmur of interest rustles through the auditorium during which another hand is raised, in the front row. It is the surgeon Armand Velpeau, with whom Claude had worked as an *interne* some fifteen years earlier. He rises slowly to his feet and turns to address the audience.

"Monsieur Bernard will remember that when he worked with me, I said that I doubted that painless surgery would ever be possible. Yet a few years ago chloroform and ether became available for anaesthesia and obliged me to change my views."

He turns again towards Claude and continues:

"Listening to you now, I foresee the prospect of a further advance in surgery. If curare can be given safely, combined with artificial respiration to the lungs – as Doctor Vella has just described – then operations within both the chest and abdominal cavities might be made much easier – and safer. Since I am to retire shortly, any such progress will be for the benefit of my successors – and of course their patients. I congratulate you, Monsieur Bernard."

Just as Claude is nodding and smiling with appreciation, a woman in the back row leaps to her feet; shouting, almost screaming:

"Shame on you Monsieur, and on the rest of you who experiment on animals. May you rot in hell for the undeserved punishment you cause to God's innocent creatures with your experiments! How can you continue with your daily murder?"

There is a hush in the audience, the members of which look first at the woman and then at Claude, no doubt wondering how he will react to this challenge.

"Madame, I mentioned how the native populations of South America are nourished mainly by food obtained from their use of curare. Not only can we not prohibit them from using it in this way, but also we must try to understand, for the ultimate benefit of mankind, just how curare acts. The sacrifice and suffering that I have necessarily imposed on so few animals is paltry when compared with the deaths that have been caused over centuries by the widespread use of curare. I understand your concern, but may I ask if you can suggest any other way in which we might proceed to answer important questions which I am sure will benefit our patients?"

There is no response from the woman, and her outburst seems to stifle any further questions from the rest of the audience. Claude notices that the hour allocated to his talk has already passed. He bows briefly and leaves the amphitheatre accompanied by a murmur of voices. As he leaves he wonders – and not for the first time – whether the attendance of the public at his lectures was always such a good thing.

September of 1850 finds Claude, Fanny, Tony and Marie on their very first visit to the Beaujolais *en famille*. They had previously travelled by railway to Versailles, but there was now the added excitement of a lengthier travel to a part of France into which Fanny had never ventured. Claude is interested to see the new five-kilometre tunnel through the *Mont de Blaisy* between Tonnerre and Dijon, which shortened the trip by almost one hour. Unfortunately, Fanny becomes anxious when the train inexplicably comes to a grinding halt inside the tunnel; she remains flustered and irritable for the rest of the trip.

The atmosphere in St Julien is initially awkward. While the grandchildren find an immediate affinity with Claude's mother, Fanny remains aloof and detached. When Claude enthusiastically carries Tony on his shoulders into the vineyards Fanny stays behind, claiming that the chill of the countryside had to be treated with respect. An invitation from Lombard is rejected by Fanny despite Madame Bernard's offer to care for the children for a couple of hours. Fanny mostly stays in Claude's old room with its window looking on to the front garden – or at best joins Madame Bernard by the fire where she seems to prefer reading to talking. In the course of the next week, there is a slight thaw in her attitude; she agrees to join Claude at a second invitation from Lombard; perhaps more at ease in the elegance of his manor house than in the family cottage.

Their stay is cut short by one week: the chill of an early autumn prompts Fanny to declare that travel in the rather draughty railway carriage might prove dangerous for the children as well as uncomfortable for her – should they delay their return to Paris any longer. Once on the train, Claude attempts to engage her in conversation, but she wishes to sleep at the same time as the children. She later finds little positive to say about his beloved Beaujolais – or its inhabitants. Yet again, she reproaches Claude on the matter of her dowry – and its use for his mother's benefit.

Both Magendie and Rayer had earlier put forward Claude for membership of the *Académie des Sciences*. When he arrives back in Paris, he learns that he had not been awarded a seat in that prestigious institution even though for two successive years it had awarded him the prize in experimental physiology. Unfazed, he returns with full vigour to his research and particularly his lectures. The latter require much work and every spare moment as he tries to eliminate the hesitant way of speaking. He had been prepared to spend some of his time in St Julien composing his talks for the coming semester, but Fanny had informed him quite forcefully that she would find this most antisocial. She had presented her disapproval to Madame Bernard as being only in Claude's interests – to ensure that he relaxed as much as possible after the difficult year that had passed, and in preparation for the year ahead.

One morning Claude is at his usual place at the back of the group of students and doctors on one of Rayer's ward rounds at the *Charité*. They are standing around the bed of a middle-aged man who had an obvious swelling in the left side of his neck.

"It has apparently been enlarging for several months," reports the *interne*, "but one of the interesting things we noticed was his small left pupil and drooping left eyelid."

In turn with the others, Claude leans over the patient to peer at the left eye in which indeed the left pupil is so much smaller than the right.

"Has he any other evidence of nerve damage?" asks Rayer.

"He does seem to have some weakness of the left arm as well, especially affecting movements of the shoulder girdle."

Rayer sits on the bed to examine the lump in the man's neck. In traditional fashion he also tests the corresponding muscle groups of the man's left and right shoulder. He nods in agreement with his *interne's* findings and addresses the round:

"Most interesting! This combination of signs was described by an Englishman named Selleck Hare – about ten years ago, as I recall. The swelling is probably compressing the nerves supplying the upper arm as they leave the spine – and in addition the sympathetic nerve. These nerves all run very close to each other exactly where this man has his swelling."

"Is my anatomy correct, Monsieur Bernard?" He adds, smiling.

"Quite correct Monsieur Rayer. I don't think that there is any area of the body which has so many nerves concentrated in such a small area! The students here may be interested to learn that almost a century and a half ago there was a French army surgeon with the picturesque name of Pourfour du Petit who used the injuries of war to help him discover how the body worked – you could almost call it 'accidental vivisection'. He was particularly interested in the injuries to that part of the neck. With the support of some animal experiments, it was he who discovered that some fibres of the sympathetic go to the eye; and that is why we see those particular ocular signs."

Claude is not to be stopped:

"Monsieur Rayer, I have been interested of late in understanding why damage to nerves sometimes cause temperature disturbance in the areas of the body which they supply. I have a broader theory that nerves might even play a part in controlling body temperature. From that point of view, would you mind if I examine him?"

"Of course not; please go ahead." Replies Rayer.

Claude takes Rayer's place sitting on the edge of the bed. Using the back of his hand – traditionally considered its most temperature-sensitive part – he compares the temperature on corresponding areas of the left and right sides of the man's upper chest, neck, cheeks and forehead. He frowns and turns to Rayer.

"Monsieur Rayer, would you care to compare the temperature of the skin on the two sides of his face?"

Rayer copies Claude's technique carefully and then stands; to deliver his verdict, and with a puzzled expression on his face:

"The left side of his face seems warmer than the right. Is that what you found – and what your theory leads you to expect, Monsieur Bernard?"

"It is exactly what I felt. I have been working on the theory that since nerves, and particularly the branches of the sympathetic seem to so closely follow the course of arteries, one might expect that any interference with their function should cause the tissues beyond to be cooler rather than warmer. It will be interesting to set up some experiments to answer the question."

Various other students and doctors on the round carefully feel the man's face and nod in agreement with what Claude had found; the difference in temperature was indeed quite striking.

Claude wastes no time in acting on his idea. That very afternoon he returns to his basement laboratory at the *Collège* where it is even more humid than usual after two days of heavy rain. He decides to use a rabbit for his experiment, since he knows that in the cat and dog the sympathetic nerves run most inseparably from the pneumogastric nerve, damage to which would only confuse his results.

He insists that Lesage immediately stops what he is doing so that he can assist Claude. The operation is performed quickly under ether anaesthetic. Skin temperature is continuously read and recorded by Lesage from thermometers taped to each ear of the rabbit. The findings are clear. Soon after Claude cuts the main sympathetic nerve on the left side of the neck, the temperature of the ear on that side rises by some four degrees centigrade and remains elevated. Claude also confirms that the pupil on that side had become smaller, as Pourfour du Petit had shown one hundred and thirty years previously – and as Claude had so often demonstrated in his lecture-demonstrations at the *Collège*. Yet why had neither he nor anyone else previously observed the temperature change?

Claude is excited by the findings and the next day he repeats the experiments several times with identical findings. To confirm the significance of what he had found, he stimulates the sympathetic nerve with a modest electric current: the pupil on that side becomes larger – and the ear temperature falls. To his onlookers in the laboratory he explains that this test represents a counterproof to his theory; an important element of his research philosophy.

Two days later, he visits Rayer in his office at the *Charité*.

"It's remarkable, Pierre. The temperature change in the skin is absolutely reproducible. The extraordinary thing is that no one has noticed it before. That experiment must have been done thousands of times in the one hundred and fifty years since du Petit first described it."

"It's quite important that you document it as soon as possible, Claude: it's possibly one of the most important things that you have discovered."

Claude is excited: "You know, sympathetic nerve activity could explain all sorts of phenomena, like the facial flushing of excitement or the opposite: the pale face of shock. I have also been wondering if a restriction of the circulation to the skin may be the way the body conserves its heat in cold weather; that could be due to the sympathetic nerves, too. If you take it one step further, if the flow of blood to organs and muscles is controlled by the sympathetic, it could be the way in which activity of the organs is altered."

"What are you going to do with all those notebooks?" Pelouze asks Claude one day as the group finish their meeting somewhat earlier than usual.

Claude had indeed acquired yet another notebook to add to the existing twenty, which he has almost filled – except for the numerous blank pages awaiting completion of earlier projects. Unlike the others, his new one had a red cover. It did not contain results of experiments, but instead random ideas and thoughts resulting from his work and that of others. Here he had also briefly noted the experiments that he might perform in the future; also philosophical ideas about the principles of experimentation and about the body and the way it related to its surroundings. Some of the entries consisted only of a few words: other ideas extended into one or more pages. This *cahier rouge* always travelled with him. If he attended a meeting that had finished its business before its allocated time, he would sometimes refer to his notebook and introduce a new idea into discussion with his colleagues.

"Théo, I need to write down my thoughts to help me understand for myself – and later explain to others what I do, and why I do it. I am convinced that it is this approach to research that is getting me results."

Charles Barreswill decides to tease Claude.

"Why not tell us a bit more about your approach, Claude?"

Claude smiles and blushes.

"Many of my experiments start either with some intuitive idea or with an observation, thanks to Pierre and his ward rounds."

He looks directly at Rayer with a smile that reflects the depths of gratitude to his mentor and friend.

"Where I don't have the benefit of an observation I need to generate one; or at least generate a fact on which I can base a hypothesis. That isn't easy, but there must be a starting point somewhere. Like my work on curare. We could have sat down and dreamed up all sorts of ideas and theories about how it works. But I felt that the only way forward was to give it to an animal and see what would happen. It is my main justification to God and anyone else for performing experiments on animals."

The little group smiles and nods almost in unison.

"I believe that a hypothesis is fundamental to planning an experiment, but it must not be too rigid – and one must not be too disappointed if experimental facts do not support it. Don't we often hear from our colleagues about a 'failed experiment'? I would *never* say that! Surely, it is better to regard it as an 'unexpected result'. One must accept the facts, and look again carefully at the original hypothesis; if the facts don't fit, the hypothesis must be modified."

Claude stops, gulps down a glass of water and resumes.

"Let us say that I have had a result which confirms my hypothesis; yet when I try to confirm that result by repeating the experiment the result is different. Should I keep on repeating the experiment until I get the same result as the first time and then breathe a sigh of relief? No! I hold to the view that such an approach can lead us astray…"

Magendie looks rather ill at ease, recognizing full well that this is exactly his approach. Claude continues:

"...and if that happens, it means simply that the conditions of the second experiment were not the same as the first time. I must use those differing results and try to identify – by restructuring the experiment – those different underlying conditions. In a nutshell, if one has identical conditions in two experiments then the outcome – the results of those two experiments – must also be identical."

Claude looks from one to the other of the group.

"Are you sure you want me to continue?"

His audience nods almost in unison: now that he has begun, they want to hear the rest.

"There is another important principle, related to statistics. We all agree that it is important to repeat experiments a number of times, and then take the average of the results from which to derive a single numerical conclusion...."

He looks directly at Magendie.

"...but have you noticed that there are no limits to the broad range of results from which some of our colleagues calculate that average? Ever since I read Louis' results on the use of bleeding, I have been convinced that statistics blur – even destroy – the significance of a study. The use of statistics hides those very important conditions that explain the variability of results. We also cannot naïvely continue to attribute variability to that crazy notion of *vitalisme*. There will not be progress until that concept is finally put to rest."

"I surely agree with that." Comments Rayer. "I don't know how we have accepted the idea of such a vague ethereal force for so long: just as a way of hiding our ignorance!"

There is silence as Claude takes another sip from his glass. His colleagues look at him with interest. He could continue, but decides that he has imposed enough on their time and patience.

"I'll bore you another day with more of my silly notions!"

Rayer's response was brisk and positive.

"We would all be happy to hear from you at any time Claude; and there is no question of boring us. However, there was something that crossed my mind as I heard you speak now about different results and their underlying conditions. I was reading again recently about one of Laplace's concepts: the predictability of events based on knowledge of contributory elements – or conditions as you refer to them. I think that your notions about research correspond to his concept of scientific determinism. Gentlemen, I do believe that we have a new philosopher in our midst!"

The laughter that follows is kind and totally free of ridicule, and they agree to meet again the following week.

February 29ᵗʰ 1851

Cher Ami

> You have probably almost forgotten your old friend Laurent – it must be at least three years since we last saw each other. Not that much has changed. Despite this ever busier, noisier and dirtier city, Juliette and our two sons manage to stay healthy – which cannot be said for me. A year ago I was in the Hôtel Dieu with a bout of pneumonia which almost carried me off to meet 'Dieu' himself! When we meet I must tell you what it is like to be a patient in that so-called hospital where you once worked! On a happier note, Lambert and I decided last year to open a law practice together: after a slow start we are now most busy and having to turn clients away!
>
> This letter to you was prompted by something which took Juliette's attention in last week's issue of l'Illustration. I enclose the two relevant pages for you: perhaps you even saw them yourself if you are regular reader of this wonderful journal. Of course we were proud to see your name with a description of the important research on the pancreas gland that you presented to the Académie des Sciences. There are not many people who are honoured by being mentioned in such a way in that prestigious journal.
>
> But the supreme co-incidence was an article about Girardin on the very next page! It so vividly reminded me of our supper at Bobino's – I think it must have been almost twenty years ago – when you were depressed by his harsh criticism of your dramatic masterpiece. It seems from the article that you have certainly not been alone in your misery; that leopard doesn't change his spots!
>
> Please write if you have time between your important discoveries. We would much like to see you and Fanny – perhaps at Bobino's for old times' sake.
>
> With warmest wishes, from your friend.... Laurent

Claude re-reads the letter carefully. How had he managed to lose contact with his old friends? He had also not heard from Ronne for at least one year: but then again, he probably had forgotten to reply to his last letter. And when had he last written to his mother and Caroline? He had arranged for them to receive regular amounts from his bank account to make good his late father's longstanding debt. However, that was the bank's responsibility, and Claude was quite unaware of how much was still owed. Fanny's repeated complaints about that financial commitment also echo uncomfortably through his consciousness...

...and of course, he had not read the articles in *l'Illustration*. His only reading for years had been the scientific articles and books relevant to his research. He realises that even if Fanny would have bought copies, it was unlikely that he would have been aware of it. Pierre Rayer's comments on his over-commitment to his work re-surface. Had he detached himself too far from everyday life? He had certainly mastered the art of separating himself from his domestic difficulty by immersing himself in experiments and lectures. Yet he now begins to wonder if his single-minded commitment to work might indeed be contributing to his marital disharmony?

Now he carefully unfolds the two pages torn from *l'Illustration* and spreads them out side by side on his desk noting that the date – February 22nd – was all of four months following his presentation to the *Académie des Sciences*. He reads with interest and admiration the detailed and interesting way that the journalist had summarised, in lay language, Claude's findings on the digestive actions of pancreatic juice. He wonders if he could possibly have described his own work quite as succinctly.

The other page contains the article about St Marc Girardin; its author had examined the continued success and high esteem in which that critic was still held. However, he quite harshly expressed disapproval of the way in which the noted professor in the faculty of arts targeted young aspiring minds: their progressiveness squashed by his conservatism – their romanticism trivialized in favour of his obsession with classicism.

Nothing had changed in almost twenty years! Had *Arthur de Bretagne* after all been cruelly misjudged? Moving to the bookcase that filled one entire wall of the study, he rummages behind the books on its uppermost shelf and locates his now-dusty manuscript. Casually he leafs through the pages, the heat rising in his cheeks as he re-reads Girardin's terse comments in the margins. Might there still be a chance of having it published or produced?

CHAPTER 9

SWEET SUCCESS, SOUR DISCORD

Louis Napoleon fills the vacuum left by the abdication of his one-time jailer, Louis-Philippe; first as Prince-president and now – three years later and with the help of a bloody *coup d'état* – as Emperor of the Second Empire. The violence that Louis employs to ensure ultimate authority compels Victor Hugo, once his staunch supporter, to take voluntary exile in Belgium and then in the Channel Islands. From there he rounds on his *Napoleon le Petit* with his famous literary skill. Needing a better social image, the self-styled Napoleon III decides to relinquish his embarrassing mistress, Elizabeth Howard and marries the beautiful Spanish-Scottish aristocrat Eugénie de Montijo.

Claude typically gives only passing attention to this picturesque catalogue of events; unaware of their future relevance to his search for scientific truth. For him, the year 1852 is the one that ushers in a flow of admiring scientists from abroad. A surgeon from America helps him to re-examine the control of the salivary glands; not by the tiny *chorda tympani* nerve that had established Claude's early research career, but the sympathetic nerves that he increasingly regards as central to the control of many body functions. Then there are the physicians from America and England wanting to acquire Claude and Charles more precise method of measuring glucose in the blood; a fundamental necessity both for the researcher and any physician with responsibility for people with diabetes; for how else could they accurately assess the impact of treatment?

Later, physiologists from Germany and the most eminent of French doctors and scientists begin to flock to the *Collège* so that they can watch, and then emulate Claude's animal experiments. Some come just to hear about his discoveries or his ideas; all of which he is prepared to share. For their research, most of Claude's visitors together with his bright student volunteers are obliged to squeeze into his airless, cold, moist and confined laboratory in the basement of the *Collège*. Those who are more interested in the chemical aspects overflow into the more spacious laboratories of Pelouze or Barreswill.

The ageing Magendie had by now decided to retire completely from his teaching duties; even his research activities were minimal, thus creating welcome extra space. Acknowledging Claude's exceptional research productivity, Magendie makes a successful plea to the *Collège* – that they provide Claude with an extra one thousand francs to help upgrade his dank workplace.

Much of Claude's work in those two years is spent consolidating his earlier experiments; inspirations about how he might address old questions; answers which will fill the blank pages of his numerous notebooks. He has a number of research assistants to help him satisfy his thirst for this knowledge:

"Jacques," he would say, "let us try stimulating the pneumogastric nerve electrically, and compare the different effects on the heartbeat if you either cut the nerve or leave it intact."

To another he would say:

"William, you have now mastered the method of measuring sugar in the blood; but we now need to try to do the measurements on smaller quantities. Try and find out by how much you can reduce the sample size without losing accuracy."

And then: "Sylvain, use Blondlot's silver cannula to make a stomach fistula in a dog and see what galvanic stimulation of the sympathetic does to the amount of acid which is produced.

With one student, he sets up experiments to compare the effects of strychnine and curare on body temperature. With yet another he compares the effect of bile and pancreatic juice both separately and together on the digestion of fat. There seems no end to the variety of projects and experiments he needs to perform – and there is no lack of enthusiastic and capable assistants to carry them out. He enters the profusion of results into his notebooks and finally assembles them into a form suitable for presentation; to the *Societé de Biologie*, to the *Académie des Sciences* and the countless other conferences and symposia which are blossoming in this era of Parisian-led medical research.

Claude's mind often dwells on the generation of glucose by the liver. What is the substance – and the process – that gives birth to what he now considers to be the most important nutrient of the body? One day at the *Collège*, he meets a young chemist by the name of Marcellin Berthelot. At the ridiculously young age of twenty-four, he had been appointed assistant to the professor of chemistry. Claude explains his discovery, and his pressing need to know the nature of this mysterious substance:

"If you have some spare time, you might like to find out for me from what substance – or substances – glucose is created in the liver!"

Berthelot laughs at Claude's rather vague challenge:

"You will have to give me some idea of what you are looking for, Monsieur. By the way did you see the paper by Mialhe in the proceedings of the *Société de Hydrologie?*"

"No. It's not a journal that I often get to read."

"Well, in the most recent issue he says that your claim that the liver makes glucose is nonsense – or words to that effect. He claims that rather than manufacturing it, the liver simply accumulates glucose from ingested food – and then releases it at the appropriate time."

"Does he provide any proof of his claim?"

"No. It's just his opinion; but he is highly thought of – as you are aware."

"He may be the great professor, but unless he provides proof, it is all a lot of hot air!"

Nevertheless, Mialhe's criticism disturbs Claude, for he will have to find a way of providing further proof for his own theory. From time to time he leaves another piece of fresh liver in Berthelot's laboratory for him to work on. When their paths cross at the *Collège*, Berthelot mentions this or that idea – but no results. Without more of an idea of what he is searching for – he repeats - analysis is a tall order.

St Julien, 12th May, 1853
Dearest Claude

I was so pleased to get your last letter. I am not surprised to hear that so many important people are visiting you; I know that your father would have been as proud of you and your achievements as I am. Do you remember sending me those two articles from l'Illustration a year or two ago: about your research and the one about that man Girardin. I suppose he probably did you quite a favour by putting you off the idea of writing! Well, I have these articles pinned up on the wall near where your father used to sit. I show it to all our friends when they pay a visit! Moreover, talking about your work on diabetes, Madame Valdet in the village has just contracted diabetes and is quite ill. I told her that you were doing research in that area: obviously, she hopes that you might come up with a cure for it soon!

I am writing this letter to say that I have had some advice from Lombard: he is actually quite a nice man and it is such a pity that your father did not get on well with him. He has suggested that I donate part of our property to you now rather than waiting until I am no longer here. Who knows how much longer I have in this world; goodness knows, I am almost sixty-five! Anyhow, it seems that I can save you and Caroline quite a lot in the way of inheritance tax if I transfer some of my possessions to you now.

I have decided to leave the cottage to Caroline and her family when I die. It would not be much use to you with all your commitments in Paris and she does not need it right now: they all seem very happy in Pouilly. However, I would like you to have, already now, the five hectares of vines and of course the pressing and bottling rooms. Also the 'vignerons' cottage - where Morel and his family now live (mind you, he is getting on a bit, too). I hope you will not mind getting more involved with the winery: it is doing very well now. By the way, we hope to eliminate the Oïdium from the vines this year; we have just given the first treatment with sulphur and we will give another two treatments during June and July.

As you can see, I am still able to keep an eye on things, but I know how you adore that side of our life. The railway now makes it quite easy for you to get back and forth. In addition, I hope that you will not always be so busy! Under the agreement, you will benefit directly from all the profits and in turn, I would be happy if you paid me a pension; we can work out the details of this when you come here in August.

Well, I am sure that you will agree that I have done the right thing by everybody. Moreover, I am sure that your father would have approved.

With much love from... your Maman

Claude is amazed, both at his mother and at Lombard. What excitement he feels about his future ownership of the vines. He had maintained his interest in their productivity, always hoping that one day he might be able to involve himself personally with the business of wine. He is now confident that he can carry the necessary responsibility. Later that year he would spend rather longer in St Julien in order to discuss some of the implications of her decision. He would then return to Paris in October; the proud owner of a Beaujolais vineyard and a winery of his very own.

The year of 1854 is an important one for France. It is not immediately clear why Louis-Napoleon decides to join Great Britain and enter the Russian-Turkish battle over the Crimea. Some say it is to support Catholic interests (the custody of Holy Places was one of the issues of the war). Others remark cynically that a triumph over injustice would remind the world that France was once more a world power.

Claude achieves his own small victory in that year. His mentors had made previous attempts to have him elected to the *Académie des Sciences* – to which he had presented so much in the way of important research results. With the support of Magendie and Rayer he is at last successful. Welcome prestige of course, although Fanny does not hesitate to remind Claude that prestige did not pay the bills!

Rather more dismal is another epidemic of cholera that sweeps through Europe claiming the lives of almost ten thousand in Paris alone. London too is affected, but a certain John Snow changes the future of millions of people by a brilliant piece of detective work. He discovers that cholera hardly affected anyone who had consumed water provided by the pumping plant upstream from where sewage was ejected into the

River Thames. Those people most affected lived in houses whose water was taken from another pumping plant downstream from that point.

Baron Haussman, the Prefect of the Seine appointed by Louis Napoleon in '53 to replace Rambuteau immediately recognizes the importance of Snow's findings. He acts as swiftly as bureaucracy allows. If Vatout had the benefit of 'bottomless purse' during the reign of Louis-Phillippe, then Haussmann had even more at his disposal now for the benefit of Parisians: the equivalent of a whole year's national expenditure. Even so, not until '59 would he gain Senate approval to create the one hundred and thirty kilometer aqueduct needed to convey the safer uncontaminated drinking water from the rivers Dhuys and Vanne.

One afternoon in the early spring, Claude suddenly realizes that he is ill; during the whole of the previous week his head had ached and his chest had felt heavy. Now a pain in his left loin and lower abdomen made it difficult even to stand at his laboratory benches. He had no idea what was wrong with him, but staying in the laboratory was not an option; there were some reports that he could complete more comfortably in his apartment. He leaves the *Collège* and slowly makes his way home. He makes a small detour to Pelouze's laboratory on *rue Dauphine* to deposit the draft of an article on curare upon which he wants his friend's comments and turns into the *rue du Pont-de-Lodi*. An ambulance carriage is drawing away from number five, while outside the building a small group of women is standing, talking animatedly.

"What's happened?" Claude asks a bystander.

"It was the woman on the third floor, Madame Bliet. Someone smelt smoke – burst into her apartment – must have fallen asleep in her chair – didn't notice her chimney was not drawing properly. She was stone-cold dead when they found her."

Relieved only that the problem had not involved his own family, Claude climbs the stairs to his apartment and finds Fanny by the window from which she has been watching the dramatic events below.

"And what brings you home so early?" She asks roughly.

"I'm not feeling very well. I'm probably better off here; it's so cold and cramped in the laboratory now. Even my own table is occupied by a student on one of my projects!"

"I can't remember ever having seen you home this early. Agnès is not well either, so there are quite a lot of things for me to do in the apartment. If you are not feeling too badly you might help with the children's supper. You could even tell them a story – you told me once that your imagination was quite fertile!"

What and how much did the children normally eat? Painfully he climbs the stairs to their room from where laughter is spilling into the narrow corridor. When he opens the door, they fall suddenly silent and look at him in amazement.

"It's Papa's turn to give you supper tonight. Let's go down to the kitchen."

"Where's Maman? Tony asked.

"She's busy with some other things; come on then!"

Reluctantly the children follow him down the stairs. On the kitchen stove is an earthenware crock from which emanates a pleasant and rich aroma of stewing meat and vegetables. Claude judges an appropriate portion each for Tony and Marie who are already sitting and waiting; watching him wordlessly. Claude begins to leave the room.

"Maman sits with us while we eat."

Claude hesitates. "You will have to eat alone tonight: Papa's not feeling well."

He leaves the room and at the other end of the corridor enters his study, closing the door after him. He sits at his desk, head pillowed on folded arms. He must have fallen asleep because he is suddenly aware of a gentle hand resting on his shoulder. He looks up to see the concerned face of Casimir Davaine – Fanny meanwhile is standing in the open doorway, looking puzzled.

"Sorry to wake you up, my friend, but I called in to Théo's laboratory just after you saw him. He told me that you looked ill so I came to see what was wrong."

"It's kind of you Casi. I think I need some new lungs! My abdomen does not like me either. No diarrhea, thank goodness!"

"Let me examine you Claude? I must say that you don't look at all well."

"I'm not sure I deserve your concern, but thank you."

Davaine draws Claude out on his symptoms, carefully examines him and finally sits down opposite him in the seldom-used wicker chair. Fanny had meanwhile left.

"Not much to find, Claude. I think it most likely that you have a bronchial inflammation; perhaps also an infected urinary system, perhaps mild enteritis. I think you should give me a urine sample and I will see if it contains any albumin or inflammatory cells. May I suggest that you stay indoors for a week or so?"

"I think I'll be alright to…"

"Claude, I'm not going to treat this lightly. For once, your crowd of admiring followers can manage by themselves. I am meeting Théo again on Friday so I will call here on my way. I'm not going to suggest any medication for you…" He smiles knowingly, "…I expect that you wouldn't take it anyhow. But I hope that you don't object to drinking three litres of fluids each day?"

"Of course I'll do that Casi – and thank you for caring."

The two friends sit and chat for some time. Davaine is tempted to ask about more personal matters but judges that it is neither the time nor the place for such confidences. He takes with him the sample and leaves.

Later that evening, Fanny summons Claude to the kitchen where the table is laid for the two of them; he supposes that the children are already in bed. Claude eats slowly, without appetite and in complete silence. Eventually Fanny breaks the silence.

"Our fireplace is not as it should be either, Claude. The chimneysweep came last month but it still does not draw properly. If you ask me, there is a fault in the flue system of the whole building: in fact I'd rather not spend another winter here. We also need more space for the children now."

Claude remains silent. Fanny had indicated her displeasure with the apartment on more than one occasion. It was either the noise from the apartment above, or steepness of the stairs. At other times, she had complained about the coldness of the children's bedroom, or the fact that the windows rattled when it was windy.

"We can't afford to move at the moment Fanny." Claude finally responds. "I think that Magendie is going to formally retire quite soon. I suppose that there is a chance that I might get his chair at the *Collège*; then we could certainly move to a nicer place."

"What about the money that you are getting from the winery now?"

"I've told you before that it is not very much. There were quite lot of expenses to settle this year in St Julien, and we are not at the point where we can use that income to better our life in Paris. Please try to be patient. I don't think that the children are suffering too much…."

"…and how would you know that since you're hardly ever here – and what about *my* suffering?"

Claude does not finish his meal, and quietly leaves the kitchen for the peace and seclusion of his study.

The next days of enforced rest seem endless. Claude finishes his reports but cannot summon the energy or interest to read or write – his eyes ache terribly although his earlier symptoms seem to be easing. He spends most of the day on his bed, deep in thought. To be sure he had neglected his family, but Fanny's harshness towards him was becoming unbearable. He could not find a way of pleasing her; neither was family life providing him even with the warmth that he received from colleagues and students. He realizes that his laboratory had virtually become his home. Of course, he had been far too engrossed in his work: satisfying as it was, he knows that he had been neglecting other interests. He had not been to the theatre for almost two years, nor had he visited the *salons*: the annual presentations of painting and sculpture. He had recently read about the construction of buildings for the great *Exposition Universelle*, which would be opening later that year; might that provide him with an opportunity to re-acquaint himself with a world beyond physiology? Their social life was also non-existent. They seldom ate in restaurants, and since his colleagues were well aware of his discord with Fanny, they were rarely invited out. For her part Fanny openly disapproved of his work now – and accordingly of his colleagues as well – all tarred by her with the same brush. She had made it quite clear that neither they nor their wives were welcome in her home.

When Davaine returns to see him at about noon on the Friday, Claude answers the door. Fanny is still away at the children's school where it is her turn to assist with preparation of the midday meal.

"You're looking much better, Claude."

"I do feel better. I followed your advice and I have to admit that the rest may have helped too. Tell me Casi, by what mechanism do you suppose that rest confers benefit – assuming of course that it does?"

"I have no idea. Does it matter?"

"I've been thinking about it. The problem is that I cannot even conceive of an experiment that would help in understanding such a complicated phenomenon as rest. Anyhow what did the analyses tell you about me?"

"I found albumin as well as cells in the urine sample. It suggests some degree of inflammation. I really think that alkalinizing the urine would help you."

Davaine examines Claude, nodding with seeming approval, and then sits on the edge of his bed.

"I think I've told you about my theory of infection; that a predisposing weakness of the body is probably more important in creating the infection than the germs themselves. You know, I visited your laboratory at the *Collège* yesterday: the conditions under which you work are absolutely disgraceful. The humidity and cold there are without doubt weakening your resistance. I could not believe how all your people there are rugged up with scarves and hats while they work – and its not even winter yet! I am surprised that your animals are not all dead by now! You must do something about it. The wardens of the *Collège* can surely find you somewhere better."

"Casi, you should have seen where I was working when I first joined Magendie as his *préparateur*. It was not much bigger than a large cupboard. I'm actually quite well off now."

Davaine shakes his head: "How can you be so wise when it comes to your science – and then so foolish when it comes to your own body?"

Claude looks suitably contrite about his naïveté, and they both burst into hilarious laughter. Davaine's face becomes serious again.

"So tell me about you and Fanny. What is happening?"

"I really don't know which way to turn. I probably should never have married – and certainly not Fanny! I can't please her, and she certainly doesn't please me. We argue about everything – and at the same time nothing! Of course, I am quite prepared to admit that I am working too hard – and according to you, now under the wrong conditions."

"You know Claude, I have often thought about the way your marriage was arranged."

"Rayer and Pelouze meant well, Casi."

"Of course; but has it occurred to you that there may have been a selfish motive?"

"I'm not sure I understand you."

"Surely you remember! At that time Théo had precious few projects in hand and Magendie was fed up with a succession of less-than-enthusiastic *préparateurs* – apart from you of course! You were the potential feather in their cap. They needed you and your ideas; they *had* to keep you in Paris for their own sake as much as yours – for the glory that would reflect on the medical school and the *Collège*."

Claude shakes his head in disbelief.

"If you are trying to make me feel better, you've failed, Casi; you're even more cynical than I am!"

They continue talking for a few minutes until Fanny's arrival home acts as a mutually understood signal that it was time for the friends to part. Davaine places a bottle of bicarbonate that he had brought with him on the corner of Claude's desk and leaves the apartment.

Davaine and Pelouze are sitting together in the latter's laboratory some minutes later.

"His body is certainly better, Théo. Now his soul is the problem. I don't wish to criticize you and Pierre for arranging his marriage to Fanny, but it really is a catastrophe. Was it really the only option?"

"I cannot tell you how much time I spend reflecting on those weeks – what would it be – almost ten years ago. I know that Pierre feels badly about the marriage failing: it is probably one of the reasons that he – and Magendie as well – are helping Claude to climb the ladder of fame. Not to say of course that he doesn't deserve it... "He smiles "...or indeed might actually manage it himself! However, guilt does motivate us all. I sometimes wonder how Henri feels about it. He must be aware of the situation."

"Claude hardly sees Fanny's parents these days. Of course they know that Fanny is not what you would call an easy person otherwise they would not have been so keen to get her off their hands in the first place. They must often ask themselves what *they* have done!"

Their discussion is not yielding any answers and Davaine leaves for his own laboratory at the *Charité*. He had his own problems, though only about his research on anthrax. It had claimed millions of lives – of both sheep and men – since biblical times. He had been studying that fatal disease of the lungs for some time, and a couple of years earlier he had identified under the microscope some rod-shaped structures in the blood. They were quite unlike anything that had been previously seen in man – or in sheep. What did their presence in the blood mean? Were they actually a product of the disease? How could he clarify this enigma? Unfortunately, it represented only one of the heavy commitments to his new laboratory where the still-narrow science of bacteriology was being slowly expanded; routine hospital duties and his patients always prioritized over his research.

During his days of enforced rest, Claude's mind drifts to the poisoning of his neighbour by her blocked chimney. It was not the first time that he had applied his mind to the problem. Ten years previously, a

French chemist called LeBlanc had identified carbon monoxide as the culprit gas of coal fumes, but no-one actually knew how it affected the body. Claude had also seen some patients with less severe poisoning in Rayer's ward back in '46; most whom had recovered after a week or two.

Prompted by this, Claude had taken his first experimental step: deliberately poisoning a dog with carbon monoxide. At its autopsy, he was astounded to see bright red blood not only in arteries (where he would expect it) but also in veins (whose blood being without oxygen would normally be much darker). Not knowing how to proceed, he made his usual notes and left the following pages blank in the hope that he would meanwhile get some inspiration. That was all of eight years ago.

His illness had now given him a God-given opportunity to redirect his mind to the problem; to at least establish a hypothesis. From the work of the great chemist Lavoisier at the end of the last century he knew that oxygen absorbed from the lungs was distributed to the body by arterial blood, the redness of which was said to be due to its oxygen content. Was carbon monoxide preventing oxygen from being released in the tissues so that it remained in the blood, imparting the bright red colour also to venous blood? In other words, were people simply dying from a lack of oxygen? Taking note of Davaine and Rayer's earlier warnings, Claude wisely decides not to proceed immediately with the necessary experiments. He adds his ideas to the next blank page of one of his notebooks; he would test that hypothesis when the time was right.

A few days later his colleagues, visitors and students welcome him back to the *Collége* with an almost ceremonial atmosphere. With the help of a local *traiteur*, they had arranged a small buffet with wine in the anteroom of the laboratory. Pelouze and Magendie were there; and Rayer arrived somewhat later. Once they had all dispersed Rayer takes him by the arm and steers him into the area of the laboratory that Claude uses as his 'office' – when not occupied by a student or visitor.

"I have some excellent news for you."

Claude looks at him quizzically and waits.

"I don't suppose that you knew that one of the chairs of botany at the Sorbonne fell vacant earlier this year?"

Claude shakes his head, wondering at the relevance of his comment.

"Last week there was much discussion on the Council – on which I sit, as you know – about whether it is really necessary to have two chairs of botany. A couple of members said that they felt that physiology was of increasing importance – I should say, thanks partly to your contributions.

In fact, your name came up in the discussions from several members of council. To cut a long story short, it has been agreed that a chair in general physiology is to be created in place of the vacant one in botany – and you're going to be invited to apply for it."

"That's wonderful Pierre; and I'm flattered. But what does it involve."

"It's a busy program of straight lectures that Council has in mind. There may be a problem for you in that there is no provision for demonstrating – or for a *préparateur.*"

"To whom would I be lecturing?"

"Principally medical and veterinary students. Because there is a defined curriculum, the Sorbonne wants quite a didactic course which you might also find a little tiresome; you won't be able to chatter on about all your theories – or your research." Rayer smiles. "But I think you will be interested in the salary."

Claude remains silent.

"It's seven thousand francs a year. Even that's to be increased next year I'm told."

"Pierre, I don't know what to say. It would obviously be foolish not to apply. I suppose I could keep pressure on the council to give me an assistant; it is hard to imagine teaching physiology without practical demonstrations. You know that up to now I have closely followed François' model – it works so well at the *Collège!*"

Rayer's face darkens a little.

"By the way, I meant to tell you that François hasn't been well. Did you notice that he hasn't been his usual boisterous self?"

"Yes, now that you mention it. He is also coughing quite a lot. Has he asked your opinion?"

"He has; and I have suggested that Casimir could do some analyses in our new laboratory at the *Charité.* François simply refuses. He could well have tuberculosis; or perhaps it's just the heart trouble that he has had now for some years. It will not surprise you to know that he has also rejected the idea of any additional treatment, so it is probably reasonable not to chase the diagnosis too vigorously. He isn't giving lectures at the moment, so I suggested that he should go to his house in Sannois; the air is certainly better there."

"I hope it is not as serious as you think, Pierre. But you have brought me some marvellous news today: you can let the Council know that I would consider it an honour to be invited to apply – and would certainly accept."

Despite the sobering effect of the news about Magendie, Claude feels that he is walking on air as he takes his usual route home that evening. The honour bestowed on him by a post at the Sorbonne – the University of Paris – was substantial, although there would be much preparation involved for a new series of lectures. Fanny would be pleased about the additional salary; hopefully accepting his need for additional commitment to his work and perhaps even proud of him.

As he is telling her the good news Claude sees the frown that perpetually creased her forehead gradually dissolving. Her dark eyes light up and even her voice acquires a timbre of such intimacy that Claude can only wonder about the flexibility of human nature. Dark thoughts of his marriage melt away and in a flood of affection, he promises her that as soon as he receives his additional salary he will make enquiries about a more spacious apartment, with larger rooms and better facilities.

William Pavy is not a newcomer to the laboratory. Soon after qualifying as a doctor in London, he had become fascinated by the subject of diabetes, and had visited Paris to learn how Claude and Charles Barreswill measured blood sugar. On his return to London, he had established the technique in his own laboratory for use with his patients, and finally reported his results to the journal Lancet. Here he had made a *faux-pas* by failing to acknowledge the source of his method; something which is not appreciated in scientific circles. Recently, he had again written to Claude to see if he could assist with his studies on sugar and the liver. Claude had almost refused; yet overall he felt there was more to be gained than to be lost from having young Pavy work with him; Claude would be able to take that part of his research a step further. Pavy certainly seemed to have a good mind – and a good pair of hands.

They are now standing facing each other across a dissection table. Claude is repeating the experiment of six years earlier in which he had originally found sugar in the liver. This time they are carefully taking samples from different parts of a fresh calf's liver, which he had brought from the butcher that morning: Claude wanted to know if sugar was evenly distributed within that organ.

"What do you really think is the cause of diabetes, Monsieur Bernard?"

Claude does not speak for a time; his mind occupied both with the job in hand – and with formulating a reply.

"That's such a big question. Some years ago, probably while you were still in medical school I showed that at least some of the sugar in the blood – which we now know to be glucose – comes from breakdown of cane sugar and starch in the stomach and intestines. I did wonder at the time if high blood glucose levels in people with diabetes were due to a more rapid breakdown of carbohydrates in the intestine."

"And you tested your theory?"

"At the time I didn't see how. Now that we can measure glucose in the blood on smaller samples it might be easier, but of course it would need to be done on patients suffering from that condition. On the other hand, since I have now found sugar in the liver, diabetes could also be due to excessive production of glucose by the liver."

Claude thoughtfully places a further piece of liver tissue in a bottle while Pavy presses him further on the subject:

"It occurred to me recently that in people with diabetes, their body cells and tissues might not be able to absorb glucose – or perhaps they can't burn it once it gets there, for some reason. Might that be yet another cause of the raised glucose levels?"

Claude looks thoughtfully at his youthful colleague.

"An interesting idea William, but probably even more difficult to prove! Some years ago, I tried to understand how tissues of the body dealt with glucose. I decided to take blood samples from the arteries and the veins in various animals, and measure the temperature of the blood in these vessels. I found that the blood leaving the lungs was no warmer than that which arrived there; Lavoisier's idea – that the body's heat comes from combustion of oxygen in lung tissue – was clearly quite incorrect. When I compared the levels of sugar in the arteries arriving in the lungs with that in the veins leaving the lungs I found that they too were quite similar; sugar was not undergoing combustion there to any significant degree."

Pavy's comment is immediate:

"…but what about the levels in other arteries and veins?"

"Ah! That was quite a different story. In the legs, glucose levels in the veins were always lower than in the corresponding arteries. My current belief is that this is due to glucose being used – burned as you say – in the muscles. Now if your theory was correct, you might expect to find that in people with diabetes glucose levels in arteries and veins were more alike."

Pavy smiles. "I don't think that my patients would be very happy to have those sorts of experiments performed on them!"

"Of course not. That is why I always pursue my research in animals. Anyhow, to get back to your question: in order to confirm the meaning of those differences of blood glucose in the legs, I measured the temperature in those same arteries and veins. I found that blood leaving the legs in veins was anything up to two degrees warmer than blood arriving in the arteries! Therefore, I am convinced that muscles are a major source of animal heat. The liver is too, by the way; when blood from the liver joins the vena cava on its way back to the heart, its temperature rises by almost two degrees. Now wouldn't the control of temperature in people with diabetes be a fascinating study?"

Pavy's face shows great interest.

"Are you going to do that?"

"We don't know if diabetes exists in animals, and as you know I don't feel that any experimentation on humans is justified. I even feel that medical treatment of a patient is often nothing more than an experiment. Look how often people prescribe drugs without real proof that they are effective; that was one reason why I decided not to practice medicine!"

Claude realizes that he is spending far too much time talking.

"I know that I haven't fully answered your question. I can't tell you from my studies whether muscles and other tissues of a diabetic are defective in the way they absorb and burn glucose. You are right of course. In theory it may be a reason why blood glucose is elevated in people with diabetes, but we certainly can't pursue that theory in animals."

Chapter 10

A Mounting Controversy

June always creates a special type of sunshine that melts away people's worries and brings smiles to their faces. Henri Martin had retired – unable to find a successor. That morning he and his wife had collected Fanny in their carriage so that they might spend the day together; a sort of celebration, since Fanny had revealed that she was again pregnant. Claude returns home to find his jubilant wife waiting excitedly for his arrival. Her parents had taken her to an apartment that was for rent within the *Hôtel Rigaud*; a building designed ten years earlier by Louis Visconti. He had been Louis Napoleon's Imperial architect, but had died soon after accepting the appointment. Situated in a lively commercial centre of the city, Fanny had been immediately won over by the building's impressive frontage to *rue de Mogador*.

"The rooms are quite a bit larger than these ones, Claude. It will be wonderful when the baby arrives. Big windows too, facing west, so that it all seems wonderfully bright; and there is gas lighting in all the rooms."

"What about water?" Claude asks. It had often been his task to bring up additional pails from the basement of their building.

"Well, it is piped to a fountain on the ground floor, so there is only one flight of stairs to negotiate; there is even talk of extending the water supply pipe direct to the apartment itself. By the way, they told us that Mademoiselle Mars and your favourite artist, Eugene Delacroix live quite close by. It's really quite a smart area."

When Claude sees the apartment two days later he can understand Fanny's enthusiasm. He also acknowledges how easy it would be for her to maintain close touch with her parents, whose home lay almost exactly to the east along a new omnibus route. She had also anticipated his concerns about ease of access to the *Collège* and the Sorbonne:

"There's an omnibus quite close by which takes you directly to the left bank and failing that there are so many cabs in the area that I am sure you won't have any difficulties. Who knows, we may even have our own carriage one day!"

By September, they are well settled in their new home. The children are pleased with their new rooms, and Claude with his new study. Agnès too finds the apartment much easier to keep clean and tidy. She looked even more attractive in a new blouse with a deep cut *decolleté*. When she brings Claude some tea one day while he is working at his desk, he feels an unfamiliar stirring in his loins. Was there some deeper significance to her cheeky half smile, he wonders?

Fanny is content and some good-natured banter begins to make life at home pleasurable again. Indeed all France is joyful in that month of '55. In the Crimea, Sebastopol had fallen to the allied forces of the British and the French. Both at home and abroad, the victory nicely polishes Louis-Napoleon's image; already so bright from the success of the recent *Exposition Universelle*.

A letter from Magendie, sent from his country house, arrives at the laboratory the very next day. It is brief:

Dear Claude

I do not think that I have much longer: indeed, such is my discomfort that I truly wish for the end. Claude. I do admire you – and your methods, and if I had been younger and less stubborn, I would have learned from them and adapted myself to them. How sorry I am not to be given the chance to see what you still have in store for the world of science.

Last month I wrote to the Collège. I made my feelings quite plain; that I want you to have my chair. There is clearly no one else who could do the job as well as you. *The reply that I received only yesterday leads me to believe that they will honour my request, and I hope that you will accept. Then I can then leave this earth knowing that it won't go to some spineless young fool bereft of original ideas.*

Yours ever, François

"Pardon me, but I'm looking for Professor Magendie."

Claude turns in his chair to see a rather smartly dressed young man standing at the doorway of his room.

"I'm sorry; he's not here at present. May I help you?"

"I'm his new *préparateur*."

The previous occupant of the post, whom he and Magendie had shared ever since Claude had taken over the responsibility of the summer lectures, had left some weeks earlier for some personal reason that Claude no longer remembered. The vacancy that this generated was one reason why Claude had been content to have Pavy come from London to join him in his laboratory for a second period. He vaguely remembered a discussion about another *préparateur* who might later be available. Presumably, communication from the office had broken down because of Magendie's illness.

"Please sit down, Monsieur...?"

"Tripier; Auguste Tripier."

"Unfortunately the professor is very ill. Frankly I don't expect him to return to his work here..."

Tripier looks crestfallen.

"...but our work continues, and I would be most happy to have you join our little family here. I am certain that the *Collège* will honour the offer that it made to you."

"That is most kind. I have been looking forward to being here ever since I heard the Professor's lectures..." then adding a diplomatic afterthought "...and of course yours, too."

Claude smiles as he recalls his own early days, and the remarkable change of heart that he had experienced after hearing Magendie's impressive lecture on the mechanism of vomiting.

"You may not believe this, but you have arrived at a particularly opportune moment. My work load is likely to increase, and I would quite like to discuss with you a rather different approach to your responsibilities which you might enjoy – although perhaps at the expense of a rather heavier commitment!"

Tripier sits forward on his chair, eager to hear what Claude has in store for him.

"We are fortunate in producing prolific and – dare I say – quite valuable results from our research. However, they have to be accurately recorded and combined with a commentary into articles that are either published, or pushed under the noses of the *Académie des Sciences* or the *Collège*. We survive on what you might call publicity; one way or the other it determines the money which we are given to continue our further research."

Tripier says nothing.

"Our reputation is also based on lectures – which must also be published. It is the management or – if you like – the secretarial responsibility for handling these texts which I would like to offer you as a means of increasing our efficiency and becoming more productive."

Tripier responds very quickly:

"That sounds most interesting. In fact, I learned shorthand before I started medical school: it was useful for recording the lectures in medical school. I could easily record your lectures too – as you give them."

Claude is delighted. Up until now, he had been writing his lectures word for word beforehand. It had certainly helped his fluency, but if Tripier was indeed able, the new approach would allow him to be much more spontaneous in his delivery. They talk further. Tripier was already a fully-qualified doctor, but admitted that he was uncertain about which line he should follow within the profession. He wanted to explore the option of research; and how better than at the *Collège*, he adds?

Magendie dies, his towering reputation justifying a burial of privilege and honour at the cemetery of Père Lachaise, almost alongside the tomb of the famous Bichat. Extensive obituaries appear in all the newspapers. The *Académie des Sciences* sends its recommendation to the Minister of Education that Claude should succeed him at the *Collège*. At the age of forty-three, Claude Bernard, professor of medicine at the *Collège de France* and professor of physiology, University of Paris is at the peak of his career. He had become widely recognized for his inspired discoveries, and the conclusions that flowed from them had been largely unchallenged.

He is soon back at work on the liver. While he had the help of his English guest, William Pavy, he wanted to repeat and enlarge on what he referred to as sugar-washout experiments; those which he had first performed some six years earlier. They are now at the dissecting table, and

Claude is flushing water into the artery leading into a fresh pig's liver; he had bought it that morning from the local butcher. He takes repeated samples from the vein leaving the liver, while Pavy analyzes their glucose content. Eventually Pavy reports that no further glucose is detectable in the samples: the washout is complete. They record their results, and tired from their labours, leave the liver and their instruments on the table for Lesage to clear away.

The next morning they arrive in the laboratory to find the pig's liver still lying on the table: Claude had forgotten that he had allowed Lesage to leave early the previous afternoon! On a whim, Claude suggests that they repeat a 'washout' on that same liver immediately. To his surprise, even more glucose is washed out through the veins than on the previous day. There could be only one conclusion: glucose had been freshly generated in that liver – overnight.

Now he had absolutely no doubt that the liver manufactured – and not just stored – glucose. Of course, there had to be a precursor – a parent compound in the liver that was making the glucose. He decides to give it the provisional name *glycogène* and is even more determined to press the young chemist Berthelot – whom he had originally approached almost two years previously – to identify it chemically. Meanwhile, he prepares his results for presentation at a meeting of the *Académie des Sciences*. He knows that Louis Mialhe, the physician who had previously challenged his liver theory will be at the meeting. Claude is looking forward to providing the proof that the liver did indeed make glucose – and not just store it, as that clever Mialhe had claimed.

The auditorium of the *Académie* is full, as usual. The chairman is Jean-Baptiste Bouillaud, who rather blandly announces Claude's recent appointment to the chair of medicine at the *Collège* and invites him to present his paper. Claude outlines the background to his work on glucose: the absence of glucose in blood vessels reaching the liver, the profusion of glucose leaving it, and the vast amount which is present in the liver itself. He then reports his latest findings on his washout experiments:

"....and to conclude, *mesdames et messieurs*, this compound which I have called *glycogène* appears to generate the glucose in the liver. In turn the glucose is released into the blood circulation to provide nutrition for the body tissues. I would also like to propose that an excessive breakdown of this *glycogène* causes the condition of diabetes.

Unfortunately we do not yet have the means to confirm this hypothesis. Thank you."

There is brisk applause; but even before it subsides, a bearded man in the middle of the auditorium springs to his feet:

"My name is Figuier – from the faculty of pharmacy. I must report that unlike Monsieur – I mean Professor Bernard, I have shown conclusively that in dogs fed only meat there is indeed glucose present in the blood arriving in the liver in the portal vein. I have used a new and more sensitive method for measuring glucose, to which perhaps the professor does not have access. Not only this, but I can rarely detect glucose blood leaving the liver. Therefore, far from the liver being an organ which makes glucose as he claims, my research confirms that the liver actually consumes it."

There is an understandable disturbance in the amphitheatre of the *Académie*. Such was the acrimonious way in which Figuier had presented his challenge, that Claude is almost lost for words. However, the eyes of many in the audience turn towards him, anxious to hear how the new professor will respond to this attack. He climbs gingerly to his feet:

"As researchers, we can only submit our findings. Mine have meanwhile been supported by the work of the eminent German physiologist von Liebig, and I can only suggest that others might determine if Monsieur Figuier's claims can be substantiated."

Another man springs to his feet; rather better known to the audience. It is Achille Longet, who doesn't even bother to introduce himself:

"I am not surprised by what I have just heard from my colleague, Monsieur Figuier. In fact, I have recently discovered a compound in the blood reaching the liver – an *albuminose* – which interferes with the ability to measure glucose. Almost certainly, this is the reason that Professor Bernard has not been able to detect glucose in the portal vessels. I must agree: we are a long way from being able to support Professor Bernard's idea – which is nothing more than a vague theory! The long-held principle that the body's glucose comes only from our nutrition – indeed from plants – still remains true."

Claude is almost speechless. This was not what he had wanted for his first presentation after being promoted to the chair of medicine. Now there is another hand raised; another question from the audience and a familiar face, too:

"My name is Pavy, William Pavy. I have the honour of working with the professor at the *Collège*, and I can certainly vouch for the care and precision with which he is working. However, I must emphasize that all our experiments are performed on what I would call dead or dying tissue: that which has been removed from the animal. Most certainly I can agree that glucose is being manufactured in the liver by a parent substance – which he chooses to call *glycogène*. However, I most humbly believe that this reaction is simply a post-mortem phenomenon, and has nothing whatsoever to do with what happens during life – let alone being the cause of diabetes."

Pavy sits down again. Claude is livid with embarrassment and anger: a painful knot has developed in the pit of his stomach. After a few seconds, he stands up slowly and moves to the lectern:

"*Mesdames et messieurs,* I think that the last word on my theories and discoveries has yet to be spoken. I will be pleased if perhaps this academy is prepared to exercise an independent examination of this problem – and report back to this assembly in due course."

The meeting having been officially closed by Bouillaud, the audience disperses. Claude remains seated; face pale and sweating and is joined by a concerned Rayer. Claude looks up at him:

"What did I do to deserve all that, Pierre? Who was that Figuier chap; I've never seen him before?"

Rayer shakes his head. "He's a bit of a publicist: also writes for *la Presse*, I believe. I didn't know that he had an interest in glucose, although I suppose he is allowed to dabble – like our friend Bouchardat!"

"Of course, it is possible that he has developed a more sensitive glucose analysis, although again Charles has been trying to do it for years now. But I cannot understand that he gets completely opposite results to me."

"What do you think of Longet's outburst, Claude?"

"His hot air worries me less than Figuier's: he's just repeating other peoples' concepts, and that story about *albuminose* is old hat, too. He knows what he is talking about: after all, he has just been made the professor of physiology at the Sorbonne! Yet he must also know that by heating the samples, as I surely do, *albuminose* is destroyed. It's a complete red-herring – and at least the twentieth time that he has challenged me about something or other at a meeting like this...."

"...but as you know, Claude, it's not just you whom he attacks."

"No, but it still irks me: he has had it in for me ever since that debacle about the spinal nerve roots. It's Pavy who really saddens me. He has talked to me about his reservations about experiments on isolated organs; but to air them like that in public is a real slap in the face: I feel like sending him back to London where he belongs! You remember that after his last visit he published *my* methodology for blood glucose analysis in *The Lancet* – as if it was his own work!"

Claude suddenly grimaces and bends forward, gagging as if to vomit. He shakes his head helplessly as Rayer puts his arm around his shoulders:

"You know, you are too kind and generous to all your visitors, Claude."

Claude straightens himself slowly.

"It's part of our job, isn't it – like others have helped me." He attempts a smile at Rayer. "We build bridges for others to cross – to go further than we have been able; but sometimes I wonder...."

Rayer remains silent; takes Claude by the elbow and they move out into the fresh air.

Despite Tripier's help, it is not all success with his lectures. Certainly, Claude enjoys those that he gives at the *Collège*. There he is relaxed: sometimes even humorous. Supported by his demonstrations his words flow naturally. The mature and often-informed audience acknowledges and visibly shares his enjoyment – both of his novel presentations and his discoveries – else they would not come from so far afield to fill the amphitheatre. By contrast, he almost dreads his sessions at the Sorbonne. He knows that his lectures there are lack-lustre. Since he has no laboratory there, he cannot support his talks with practical demonstrations. As if this is were not enough, the restriction placed upon him to present material within a curriculum of so-called facts cramps his style – which becomes more and more hesitant. Students vote with their feet; the auditorium is at best half full, and the sight of sleeping students fills him with dismay. Longet is sometimes a shadowy witness – in the very back row, unsettling as ever. Another regular *auditeur* is Louis Pasteur whose presence Claude welcomes, whether at the Sorbonne or the *Collège*: he often sends an appreciative note afterwards.

Claude's personal life also continues to burden him. He is initially elated beyond words when Fanny gives birth to a boy in January. His daughters had that special affinity with their mother, and the notion of a son-and-heir gives an enormous boost to his morale. However, Claude-Henri is not a healthy child; his weaknesses seem to mirror those of his departed younger brother and his lack of appetite and slow development trouble both Fanny and Claude.

On one Sunday morning, he takes Marie-Louise and Tony to the end of *rue de Mogador*. There, in a small park where the new Church of *la Trinité* was to be built, people often met and chatted on rather uncomfortable benches. Claude-Henri was again unwell, and Fanny had decided that she would keep him indoors: the girls would be a sufficient handful for Claude: the walk providing an opportunity for them to dissipate their seemingly endless energy.

The park seemed to attract people with dogs that also wished to socialize! While Claude is sitting on a bench enjoying the sight of his children at play around the fountain, a small spaniel nuzzles up to him. No sooner had Claude bent forward to stroke it than Tony descends upon him, screaming:

"Leave him Papa; don't touch him!"

Frightened, the little dog runs to his mistress who looks at Claude with distaste and suspicion. Tony sobs while Marie-Louise stands at a distance uncertainly nibbling the forefinger of her right hand.

"Whatever's wrong, Tony?"

Silence. Claude tries to take her on his knee to calm her tears but she brushes him aside and runs to her sister. Meanwhile the people who had been enjoying the autumn sunshine stare at them curiously. Only reluctantly, the girls allow themselves to be taken by the hand, and they silently return home. Claude assumes that Fanny must have told the girls that he experimented on dogs. Later that day he asks her to come into his study and closes the door:

"I know," says Fanny, "the girls told me – and they are still upset."

"But you must have said something to them for Tony to have had such a reaction?"

"How can you expect them not to know that you experiment on dogs? Children are inquisitive, and since you are not here most of the time, it is left to me to answer their questions. Do you expect me to lie to them about what you do?"

"Perhaps yes! I do many things besides my research on animals. You could speak about my teaching at the University; that I work on committees; that I write books and simply that I do experiments in order to discover how the body works and why it goes wrong. There is no need to frighten them at their age about some unpleasant necessities of my work – and most particularly about me."

"Is the butchering of animals what you call a 'necessity'?"

"We have had this discussion before Fanny, and I am not going to justify my research yet again. For the sake of the children though, it would be surely better if you didn't alarm them." He hesitated. "I recently came upon a comparison that I might actually mention to the girls – that research is like having to walk through a hot, smelly kitchen to reach the final satisfying meal at the dining table."

"*Bah!* What an absurd comparison!"

She turns on her heel and leaves the study, slamming the door behind her. Claude sits for a while staring out of the window. If he had a problem at work, he could mostly devise a solution or at least a way forward. Why does he feel so impotent to resolve the present situation at home – and why again does he have this cramping pain in his belly?

Tripier had just arrived back in Claude's new office – Magendie's until earlier in the year. Claude had re-arranged the simple furnishings. The large bookshelves remained where they were, but he had moved the desk close to the window from where he could more easily gaze beyond his four walls, as if to summon an inspiration or a new idea from outside.

"Monsieur, I've brought you the results of the oxygen analyses from Monsieur Pelouze."

On the previous day, they had killed a dog with carbon monoxide using a piece of equipment that Pelouze had helped to design. The unfortunate animal was one that Claude had obtained from the local veterinarian; it would anyhow need to be 'put down' after suffering an irrecoverable back injury from the hoofs of a bolting horse. Claude preferred the use of such animals if possible.

There had been nothing notable about the animal's death, which certainly appeared peaceful enough. However, he would not be misled; prior to Claude's research, people had also mistakenly assumed that death from curare was peaceful! The colour of the dog's arterial blood had been a normal bright red. Yet, as Claude had noted so many years before, rather than being dark, the venous blood was just as red as the arterial blood.

Tripier now holds a single sheet of paper in his left hand, held aloft as if to tease his master:

"You had expected the venous blood to have the same high oxygen content as the arterial blood. Is that not so?"

Claude nods: "Well, that is certainly what I would expect if carbon monoxide is indeed stopping the oxygen from being released into body tissues."

"Then you will be disappointed. Monsieur Pelouze could find only a trace of oxygen in both the arterial and the venous blood."

"There must be some mistake; that the crimson colour of venous blood must be due to oxygen. We need to repeat that experiment as soon as possible."

Later that week, they are able to repeat the experiment on another dog whose head had been injured by the wheels of a carriage. When Tripier brings the results from Pelouze, the findings are identical. Claude sits for a while, alternately staring through the window and doodling on a piece of paper in front of him.

"My friend, I think we need to discuss this with Barreswill and Pelouze; I have another idea!"

The four men are now sitting around a table, and Claude cannot wait to present his idea. Before they begin, Barreswill congratulates Claude:

"I have just seen Dumas' report – on his committee's evaluation of Figuier's claims." He says. "You have been put in the clear: they support *your* findings."

"Yes, I've heard: but I would have liked them to have used Figuier's new glucose method as well as mine. I am going to have to repeat all those studies some time soon."

"Well Claude, you may not have heard that Figuier has just resigned his post. He's in disgrace in his faculty."

Claude shakes his head slowly.

"That is the side of research that I loathe: all these attacks. Everybody just wants to attract attention to themselves, and diminish the credibility of their colleagues. It's a nasty game, and we all suffer!"

There is silence, eventually broken by a deep sigh from Claude:

"Well, let's get back to carbon monoxide! My first theory was obviously wrong, and the only explanation for your findings, Théo, is that carbon monoxide is mingling with the blood, and somehow stopping oxygen from doing the same. I have reasoned that carbon monoxide – rather than oxygen – is responsible for the red colour of the poisoned animal's blood. After all, why should oxygen be unique in that sense?"

Barreswill nods. "I follow your reasoning Claude. Have you thought of an experiment which we could do to test your new hypothesis?"

Claude looks out of the window – and then back at his colleagues.

"Let's just see what happens to the oxygen content of blood if we mix carbon monoxide with blood in a flask. We don't need an animal experiment for that!"

They spend the afternoon setting up the necessary stands, rubber tubes and glassware. Late into the evening, they repeat one experiment after another. The results are consistent and conclusive. As they shake up larger and larger amounts of carbon monoxide with the blood in the flask, so the blood sample releases more and more oxygen into a side-tube. There was presumably a substance within blood that trapped all the gases to which it was exposed – yet somehow preferring carbon monoxide to oxygen! They try adding more oxygen to the blood sample, but it is consistently rejected.

The interpretation is clear: carbon monoxide was rendering blood useless as a vehicle for transporting oxygen to the tissues. The poisonous gas had coloured the blood red, displaced any oxygen that was already present, and stopped all further oxygen from attaching itself to the blood. People dying from carbon monoxide were simply asphyxiating.

Claude looks at his colleagues, one by one:

"You know, gentlemen, I doubt whether death from carbon monoxide is any kinder to its victims than is curare!"

The results of the research do not immediately cast any light on possible treatment but they do provide a powerful insight into the way that gases behave in the body. Claude had always maintained that the main value of his research with poisons was the way it would help him to understand the normal functioning – the physiology – of the human body. There was no better example of that than the work they had just done.

He arrives in St Julien for his usual autumn visit; immediately struck by the suddenness with which age had become woven into the fabric of his mother's body and mind. Like his late father, her hands had become deformed by arthritis and she had become quite stooped; her lined face less inclined to be moulded by smiles. The family cottage was clearly too large, cold and moist for her health – and now rather neglected too. Claude wonders about other more comfortable options for her to spend the twilight years of her life. He was glad that he had taken on the lion's share of the management of the winery. It was doing well.

His sister Caroline and her family arrive for a visit. Jeanne is now nine years old; just a few months older than Tony. Their life in Pouilly-le-Monial seems pleasant enough, but the distance from St Julien makes it difficult for them to be fully attentive to Madame Bernard's needs.

Claude observes how relaxed and healthy Jeanne seems in comparison to his own children; always so pathetically pale and thin, and he wonders how Fanny would feel if he at least brought the children into the healthier countryside for part of the summer. Of course, his mother was certainly now too old to take a hand in their supervision, and he had also developed his own routine which he was reluctant to forego. His writing in the earlier part of the day was entirely devoid of interruption and therefore highly productive, while in the afternoons he would involve himself with the business of the winery, or spend it with his mother.

One afternoon he meets Lombard outside the manor house; he sees that the shutters have recently been repainted a deep green.

"Do you like the way we've done it?" Lombard asks.

"I have always liked your house – with or without the new paint!" Claude replies. "To live here would be as close to paradise as I could imagine."

"That's not impossible, you know. The house is far too big for us. We now only use the downstairs bedroom; no one ventures upstairs any more and we are too old now to have house guests."

"Are you suggesting that I might rent the upper floor then?"

"I'm thinking more radically. My family in Chuzelles wants us there, so they can better keep an eye on us! I am considering putting it up for sale."

Claude is silent for a few moments. Hands deep in his pockets he looks first at Lombard, then at the house, then across the vineyards to the long valley beyond which he is sure that he can today make out the silhouette of Mt Blanc. Finally he looks at Lombard again, his head cocked sideways.

"If only I could. My mother needs a healthier place; having her bedroom downstairs would be much kinder to her poor bones and joints; and I would have more space to work and relax too. I don't need to tell you how I would feel about having the additional vines; I suppose you'd sell those with the house?"

"Probably, but don't get too carried away Claude. We have not yet made up our minds; yet for many reasons it would give me much pleasure to think of you living here. May I write to you in Paris when our plans are a little firmer?"

Lombard invites Claude into the cellar to taste the earliest pressing of his grapes. As always, it causes that special tingling on the back of Claude's tongue and brings a smile to his face.

"I don't think that you have my new address in Paris; we are now in the *rue de Mogador*, number ten. May I ask you to be so kind as to let me know what you decide to do with the house – and when? Please do stay with us too if you visit Paris. Haussmann is playing havoc with the old streets and buildings but the result should be wonderful. You will be amazed at how much has changed since you were last there. When was it actually?"

"More than ten years ago I'm ashamed to say. Don't you remember; you were about to be married?"

No more is said. Claude is due to return to Paris later that week, and busies himself with minor chores. Each time he passes Lombard's house, he looks at it with affection and longing. Only one thought plays on his mind, immovable even during the ten-hour train trip back to Paris.

His mind cannot resist pursuing the theoretical possibilities. How much would Lombard's property be worth: surely no less than fifty; perhaps as much as one hundred thousand francs? That was rather more than he had any prospect committing in the next year or two. Yet he wanted that house; and not the least attractive element was the chance of expanding his holding of vines. And how would Fanny react to the idea? With her patent dislike of the countryside, there was no way in which she would benefit from the purchase.

He reflects on the failed venture of his father almost thirty years earlier. Could such an enterprise after all be financially successful? Within a day, barrels of wine could now be transported easily and rapidly by rail from Villefranche to the great Paris warehouses at Bercy; the wine would not have to suffer the long journey northwards on the rivers and canals. He had heard that the cooperative was also discussing a railway line extending from the commercial wine center at Beaujeu via St Julien to Villefranche; that would make for even greater efficiency.

Now back in Paris, reality dictated that he must put aside his dreams and concentrate on the immediate needs of his lectures. Having Tripier to help him was an enormous bonus. As Magendie had deputed Claude to help demonstrate at his lectures, so he in turn involves Tripier with numerous presentations. The young man always rose to the occasion with impressive technical skills. His recording of results and documentation was also almost flawless and together they publish articles and reports in a steady stream, still with time to plan and pursue the numerous projects which Claude dreamed up with startling ease.

The nature of *glycogène* had now become the principal subject both of Claude's thoughts as well as his discussions with Tripier, Pelouze and Barreswill. Claude knows only one thing for certain; it was not water-soluble; otherwise it would have been completely flushed out with the first washout; and no further glucose would have been obtained by further 'wash-outs'.

He is sitting at the table in his room, gazing out of the window in deep thought. On the other side of the table Tripier sits slumped, chin on chest, utterly tired from endless hours of fulfilling his commitments to Claude.

"Mother nature is wonderful Auguste: we should spend more time studying it!"

"I'm not sure that I understand."

"Let me give you some facts. We know from our own work that the starch that we get from eating vegetable matter is broken down by intestinal ferments into glucose?"

Tripier nods.

"Now, in plants the starch is also broken down into glucose, which of course sweetens the leaves and the fruit – and contributes to growth."

Tripier nods politely. He has no knowledge of plant biology and is confused by the direction of Claude's thinking.

"We have shown that glucose is actually created in the liver – which of course destroys the concept of the great Lavoisier – that it is only plants which can create nutrients."

Tripier indeed knows that other researchers in France and in Germany have now fully confirmed his *patron's* remarkable findings. Like Claude, they are also actively pursuing the chemical source of the glucose in the liver. Claude takes a deep breath and continues.

"If chemical processes in plants and animals are indeed so similar, then perhaps we should look towards plant biology for telling us how to proceed."

"I follow your arguments, but what is your hypothesis?"

Claude smiles; pauses only for a moment:

"Simply this: *glycogène* may itself be starch – or something very like it? As I said, plants and animals may not be as different as we think!"

Tripier's response is typically enthusiastic:

"That would mean that the liver has the same ferments for breaking down *glycogène* that you identified in the intestine for breaking down dietary starch?"

"Well, they wouldn't need to be *exactly* the same."

They sit in silence, digesting the ideas that Claude had expressed. Tripier speaks first:

"How can we test your hypothesis?"

"To start with, we simply need to know if there is starch-like material in the liver. Now that we know what we might be looking for, perhaps Berthelot can actually help us."

At the *Collège*, the laboratory is soon set up for the experiment, the first part of which is the responsibility of Claude and his assistant. After grinding up pieces of liver, and a few steps of separation, filtration and drying, they are left with a white powder. Berthelot arrives, wearing a big smile on his face.

"We're in luck. I have managed to get a particularly pure form of Payen's *diastase végétale*. This ferment is so powerful that it can break down two thousand times its own weight of starch into glucose! If there's starch in your extract, we'll find it!"

Rolling up the sleeves of his coat, he arranges the necessary glassware and tubes with remarkable adroitness and begins the experiment. The powder that Claude has extracted from the liver is dissolved, the 'ferment' is added and the resulting product filtered.

"Now be kind enough to pass me some of our friend Barreswill's reducing agent, Claude. We will soon see if there is anything in your extract that Payen's diastase has been able to convert into glucose."

They all hold their breath. No sooner had the reducing agent been added than the filtrate turned a characteristic blue-green: glucose was present – and in vast quantities! Their shouts of joy would have been audible throughout the *Collège*: *glycogène* was none other than 'animal starch'.

Over the next few weeks, Claude examines the liver of every animal on which he can lay his hands. In every species it is the same: the starch-like material is universally present in liver. The only livers in which he is unable to find it are from patients who were emaciated at the time of their death. Perhaps, he reasons, *glycogène* had not been replaced because the patients had not been eating.

It had been a particularly harsh winter for Claude-Henri. At the age of almost eighteen months, his lungs could not deal with the winter infections. Each attack seemed to drag his frail little body into greater depths of misery; and one day he simply does not respond, despite all the loving care and expertise bestowed upon him. His death fills Claude with a sense of depression and hopelessness; a son-and-heir was clearly not to be. Fanny is less scathed by the disaster, her mind and soul apparently responding to the practical necessities of her daily existence, and that of their daughters now age ten and seven respectively.

"It's all well and good that we now have a more satisfactory apartment Claude, but I can't stay within its four walls all day."

Fanny clearly had something in mind.

"Must I always depend on my father's help or wait endlessly on cold pavements for a cab to pass by? Even then, they are so poorly maintained and draughty; it is no wonder that the children fall ill. I think it is time that we afforded ourselves our own carriage."

On the ground floor of their building was a broad entrance giving access to a cobbled courtyard, three well-appointed stables and cover for an equal number of carriages. There was also simple accommodation for coachmen. Claude is himself tiring of the difficulty in reaching the left bank where the *Collège*, the Sorbonne and all his colleagues' activities are concentrated: cabs were not always available and transport by omnibus was both slow and uncomfortable.

Henri Martin, knowing well about such matters, is able to help Claude with the practical details of purchasing a horse and carriage. For his part, Claude recalls the bell system that Millet had used in his pharmacy for summoning help from his apprentices. He improvises a rope that extends from a cupboard in their pantry down to a bell attached to the wall of the driver's quarters. If they needed his services, Claude or Fanny simply tugged on the rope. To acknowledge the call Jean-Paul, their newly appointed coachman responded by tugging on his end of the rope, whereupon a second bell in the pantry sounded his affirmative response. The freshly harnessed horse and carriage would be duly waiting below a few minutes later. The arrangement worked well and their quality of life had improved dramatically.

Claude was always flattered to be invited to comment at scientific meetings, and to sit on many influential committees. He had even received an invitation from the Ministry of Agriculture to help investigate pneumonia in cattle: another to examine applications received by the *Académie des Sciences* for a lucrative prize for cholera research. However, no invitation gives him as much of a thrill as the one that arrives towards the end of '59:

From the Maison de l'Empereur, Palais des Tuileries, 20 October 1859.

Monsieur Claude Bernard,

By the order of the Emperor I wish to inform you that you have the honour of being invited to spend seven days at the palace at Compiègne, from November 22nd to November 28th.

Court vehicles will be waiting to transport you to the Palace on the 22nd, on arrival of the special train which will depart from the Gare du Nord at two o'clock in the afternoon.

Please accept, Monsieur, the assurance of my distinguished sentiments,

Signed: The First Chamberlain Vicomte de Laferriere.

Pierre Rayer smiles knowingly when Claude shows him the invitation.

"Interesting, my friend. Their majesties started these *salons* a couple of years ago; they refer to their prestigious events as *Les Séries de Compiègne*; I went last year after Louis appointed me as his court physician. It was certainly an experience!"

"It sounds rather special."

"It certainly is – although it is a bit of a military operation! You visit their wonderful gardens at such and such a time; at another, you have to talk wisely to people who feel obliged to listen politely. Later you join in a hunt of which you disapprove. You finish the evening dancing with someone whose chatter doesn't at all interest you and upon whose sensitive feet and finely crafted shoes you cannot avoid stepping."

Claude laughs. Rayer's description only serves to heighten his interest.

"And what sort of man is our Emperor – or are you forbidden to speak about him"

"Why not? I would certainly not divulge matters of health. I think you would like him – that is, if you get the opportunity to speak with him; there will be at least fifty others there for that week, all wanting that privilege! His interest seems genuine enough, but meeting the Empress will alone be worth your visit; she is exceptionally beautiful. She may have aristocratic origins, but her manner is commonplace enough to make you feel quite at ease."

When Claude tells Fanny, she is initially disapproving and cynical. Was the royal couple not aware of Claude's sinister activities; and why had she not been invited – as she had read was usually the protocol? Claude accepts the invitation and a week or so later, he receives detailed instructions for the event. Amongst other details, he notes that servants were expected to accompany their masters to assist with dress and necessary errands within the chateau. It was worth a try.

"Might you part with Agnès for a week, Fanny?"

"And who do you expect to care for the children, Claude – and do the cleaning and cooking, while you are away enjoying yourself?"

"Perhaps your mother could stay here with you."

"What, and look after the apartment as well! How absurd! No, I have thought for some time that we need an extra pair of hands. Agnès has too much on her hands; this apartment is so much bigger than the one we had in the *rue du Pont-de-Lodi*."

"No Fanny, we have just taken on Jean-Paul to look after our horse and carriage; we certainly don't have the money for yet another servant."

"Well I'm sure that all your colleagues have at least one or two more servants than we have."

Claude chooses to ignore this observation, although it is possibly correct: it is something that had never occupied his mind. He is obliged to think rapidly:

"I suppose that I could always ask my laboratory assistant Lesage to accompany me. He's not the youngest any more but he comes from a good family in Chartres and knows his manners well."

Indeed, such was the experience of a visit to Compiègne that many a friend was known to volunteer their services as valet or maid; just to be present at such an occasion. His loyal assistant deserved a little shine in his life; his work could be readily performed by Tripier during his one-week absence.

Chapter 11

Event Extraordinary

The *Gare du Nord* was alive with excited travellers, their shouts and laughter almost obliterating the hiss of locomotive steam. Pungent coal fumes trapped beneath the glass gables irritate Claude's nose, prompting him to wonder what the concentration of carbon monoxide might be in the air he is breathing. Jean-Paul is puffing and red-faced with the effort of unloading the baggage as Claude realizes that he has spent far too much money on new clothes for the event; items which he was most unlikely to use again. Jean-Paul transfers care of the numerous cases and boxes to a very disgruntled porter. Claude extends his theory by considering that the man's grumpy mood was caused by a shortage of oxygen resulting from carbon monoxide fumes.

At the quieter end of the station, platform number one carried a large sign *Reservé – Impérial*. People were already filing through the gates assisted by the porters with their awkward trolleys. It was all orderly enough. The guests were shepherded into the front three carriages bearing the Imperial blue livery and gold eagle emblems. The servants were in the next three carriages, the baggage of their masters and mistresses carefully stowed with the help of porters in the last two. Lesage had been delighted with the invitation to assist Claude, and was looking forward to his own unique experience at the chateau. Meeting the other valets and attendants – he had told Claude – would give him a marvellous insight into how the other 'half' lived.

The richly carpeted interior into which Claude now steps is certainly unlike anything he had previously experienced. Instead of the hard benches of the Lyon trains, there are brocade-upholstered armchairs separated by low tables on which magazines sit in orderly piles. There appear to be many couples, causing Claude to wonder why indeed the invitation had not been extended to Fanny.

Almost imperceptibly, the train moves off. Grey buildings gradually give way to even darker autumn landscapes as the train gathers speed for its ninety-minute trip north. Claude diverts his attention from the dismal countryside to the colourful dress and lively conversation of the other occupants of their carriage. He overhears a heated and largely disapproving discussion about Louis Napoleon's military support for Victor-Emmanuel, King of Lombardy in his campaign to re-unite that province with the rest of Italy. Behind him, two men are criticizing Haussman's architectural revolution and debating Garnier's plan for the new opera house that will be built quite close to Claude's apartment.

"Is this your first visit to Compiègne?"

He had not taken particular notice of the somewhat older man who had taken the seat next to him.

"Yes, it is actually – and already quite an experience!"

"I know what you mean: not exactly one's everyday activity! Have we met before? My name's Hector Berlioz."

"Mine's Claude Bernard. We've not met – but your name must surely be known to every Parisian – if not every Frenchman!"

Berlioz smiles, modestly. An article in *l'Illustration* about his Imperial Cantata had caught Claude's attention some years earlier. It had been given its *première* at the great *Exposition Universelle* of '55; more than one thousand artists – musicians and choristers – had taken part. Claude had been impressed by the necessary invention of a couple of mechanical 'conductors' that copied Berlioz' movements; thus enabling all the participants to keep time accurately.

"Tell me," Claude asks, looking around him, "do these people actually have anything in common with one another?"

"Of course not; and that's the point. Their majesties thrive on hearing what they must consider intelligent talk. I think they imagine that if eminent people from different backgrounds are obliged to sit and speak with one another, then some marvellous ideas will eventuate. Actually I shouldn't be so cynical about it all; you'll find that it's worth the effort, if only for the privilege of meeting the wonderful Eugénie!"

It was Claude's turn to smile; it must have been the third time that he had heard the beauty of the Empress mentioned. He was becoming quite keen to draw his own conclusions.

"Is the lady so very special?"

"You will have to judge for yourself; beauty is so subjective. She is certainly charming. However, it is such a strange game that they play, those two. Let us face it, they are not particularly popular in our country – or even abroad when it comes to that. He speaks French with a German accent that he acquired during all those years in Switzerland – and English with the American accent that he captured during his exile. Eugénie is Spanish with a touch of the Scottish. With all his affairs before and since his marriage, he is also hardly a model for our young men. She is apparently quite flirtatious – but next to him, she is a saint! I think that these events at Compiègne are a way of capturing the necessary goodwill amongst people who matter!"

Claude is fascinated by the gossip and smiles at Berlioz' description of their forthcoming hosts.

"Well, I'm not sure that I matter so very much. In fact, I cannot see what I will be able to contribute to the gathering. I just do research into how the body works."

"Don't be so sure about that. They had that young fellow Pasteur here a couple of years ago; the last time I came. He was quite entertaining with his microscope and his frogs. After he left the castle though, I gather that the maids were upset; they found a bag of slimy frogs pushed under his bed! By the way, I too dabbled in medicine for a couple of years – just to please my father; until he gave up the fight and let me study music!"

Berlioz also tells Claude about *The Trojans*, his recently completed five-act opera for which he could not find a theatre willing enough to present it.

"I am hoping to get the ear of the Emperor while I am here to see if he can intercede on my behalf." He hesitates, glances left and right and then winks at Claude: "To be honest, I think that most of these people dream of leaving with a small bonus!"

Berlioz' mention of Pasteur reminds Claude that he had to complete a report as soon as he returned to Paris. He had for some time sat on the *Académie des Sciences'* awards committee. Now as its Chairman, Claude was obliged to provide a detailed report supporting the committee's decision to award a prize to Pasteur for his elegant work on fermentation. That announcement would be made in the New Year. Noting Claude's immersion in his own thoughts, Berlioz excuses himself.

Seemingly the whole population of Compiègne was at the station to meet them; inquisitive eyes trying to identify visiting celebrities. A long string of carriages drawn by fine white horses was waiting; impatient to take the passengers and their baggage to the chateau: a military operation indeed, as Rayer had forewarned. Claude is allocated an apparently mute, uniformed and wigged orderly who guides him ceremoniously to his three-roomed suite; 'quarters' perhaps a better term for the austerity, bare boards and lack of heating.

Lesage's room was on the floor above Claude's, and apparently almost as well appointed. He had now laid out on the bed for Claude the prescribed evening dress of white silk stockings, black velvet breeches and the cutaway high-necked green jacket bearing his Silver Star and red ribbon. Lesage gives him his 'stamp of approval' and at seven o'clock in the evening – by the clock – Claude joins the guests in their descent towards the impressive *salon des Aides de Camp*.

The women are splendid in their crinolines, deeply revealing *decolletés* emblazoned with jewels; and now ushered into a single row. They face the array of ogling uniformed men wearing medals that wink in the shimmering light of the ornate chandeliers. The Emperor and Empress arrive in the hall, walk slowly past their guests, smiling. The Emperor stops occasionally to greet people he presumably recognizes; his wife likewise, the women so addressed responding with particularly low curtsies. The Empress is wearing a flowing white tulle dress in a simple design. Her narrow sparkling tiara encircles a bouffant hairstyle that sets off her fine facial features. Claude wonders if her personality could possibly live up to her appearance.

The two rows then merge and follow their Majesties, now arm-in-arm into the splendid *galerie de bal*. Here they will be served dinner at an infinitely long table glimmering with polished silver and crystal. The brightly uniformed *Cent Gardes,* standing at attention on the periphery of the immense room would see to it that the guests consumed their splendid five-course meal within the hour allocated by the Emperor!

Claude's placement at his table had been clearly defined by a seating plan that would be in effect for the entire week. He finds himself flanked on the left by a woman who introduces herself briefly as Madame Simonet, and is thereafter dominated by the man to her left. On his right is a place – still unoccupied – identified by its ornately inscribed place card as being for the Princess Mathilde; Claude knows that as the Emperor's cousin, she had an apartment in the chateau; presumably she alone was permitted the privilege of arriving in her own time. Escorted by one of the *Cent Gardes* the Princess eventually arrives, and quite soon the conversation flows easily enough:

"You are here alone, Monsieur?"

"Yes; we still have quite young children; it's probably better that way."

The princess takes a sip of the excellent wine and is silent for a minute. If Claude's wife had indeed been invited, she would have come; they all managed it somehow!

"Strange, is it not? Their majesties have been welcoming guests to their salons now for several years, but I have yet to understand why they invite some people to come alone; yet others with their spouses. I must say that I do enjoy meeting the wives of important people; it gives one quite a different insight into their lives...."

She turns to look him straight in the eyes.

"...and what might your wife say about your life?"

Claude is puzzled, yet unfazed by her frankness.

"I suppose she might say that – like most scientists – I spend too much time in my laboratory: it's quite easy for one's passion for work to take precedence."

"Yes, it is either work or other women that create unhappy marriages. In my case it was the latter: but enough of that! Will you be telling us about your work during this week; I'm sure you do not wish to spoil this nice dinner by any serious talk now."

"Unlike Monsieur Pasteur, I did not come equipped with my microscope, but if the opportunity presents itself, I would be happy to speak about my research; I often find that in return I get quite some ideas from my audiences, however remote from the world of science they may be."

"That's done then: I will be sure to tell my cousin that he should not forget you."

On that first evening, no program had been arranged. After dinner, the guests were wandering aimlessly through the ornate rooms, familiarizing themselves with their surroundings for the forthcoming days. Claude discovers Berlioz in the *salon des Cartes* examining a map on the wall. He smiles:

"I wish I had your luck; believe me, it's neither mistake nor a coincidence that you have been placed beside the *Princesse*."

"I was rather wondering why I had been given that privilege."

"Yes; puzzling. She sees herself as the *Notre Dame des Arts*. Perhaps she wishes to graduate to a similar position in the sciences! Have you by any chance seen her magnificent collection of paintings at the *rue de Courcelles?*"

"No, I've not had that pleasure."

"Mind you, they say that it was her friend Nieuwerkerke who decided what she should hang on her walls! I haven't been to her chateau at St Gratien, but what she hangs there is her taste – and that's pretty awful! What she sees in that horrible painter Giraud I do not know. Perhaps it is because his portraits flatter her!"

"I thought Nieuwerkeke would be here by her side; aren't they married now?"

"Never! She'd lose the immense settlement that she got when she and Demidoff divorced all those years ago. Weren't you dazzled by the Demidoff diamonds that she was wearing tonight?"

"I am ashamed to say that I didn't notice them. Who was Demidoff?"

Berlioz tosses his head back and laughs.

"Let me enlighten you about our hostess. When she was only fifteen, Princess Mathilde was briefly engaged to our esteemed Emperor. It didn't last long, because she decided to marry Count Demidoff; by the way, he got his title from Czar Nicholas I, who just happened to be Mathilde's uncle! It's *who* you know that matters in life, don't you think? Anyhow, Demidoff was a horror: unfaithful and brutal to her. She appealed to the Czar and he dissolved the marriage six years later. He decided that Demidoff should pay Mathilde two hundred thousand francs each year for the remainder of her life – as long as she didn't remarry."

"How extraordinary; I had no idea!"

"Well, I'm off to bed; we have quite a week before us."

Feeling very tired himself, Claude soon follows. He had again been suffering from almost daily abdominal spasms over the previous week. He decides that he will ask Casimir Davaine to examine him as soon as he is back in Paris.

Claude had not slept well. Throughout the night he had been pursued by a wild black horse around the grounds of the chateau. He had woken up in a lather of sweat just as he tripped on a tree root and the horse was about to trample on him. It was still quite early, and he draws open the curtains to a grey, unwelcoming dawn. Although Lesage would be disappointed, Claude chooses his own wardrobe for the morning. He dresses; descends the dimly lit stairs to the *salle des Jeux* where an obliging attendant in wig and livery provides him with a herbal infusion which gradually coaxes away his anxiety.

Outside, the air is moist, and the chill finds its way easily through the thick cloak that the attendant had produced from a cupboard in the lobby. As he skirts the chateau, he has the absurd sensation of a hundred pairs of eyes staring at him from still-shuttered windows. His thoughts pursue wild and apparently disconnected paths. What is he doing in this unreal world? Why indeed had they not invited Fanny? Then, would he have wanted her there: to embarrass him in public as she had done elsewhere on so many occasions over the years? And what is he to do with his domestic life? The more he tries to warm to his wife and children, the more distant they make him feel. On more than one occasion, he had asked Fanny why she was so opposed to him and his life. She had invoked God and religion, and quoted passages from the bible to support her distaste for his work and his way of life. She had certainly become more devout, and was often at St Sulpice or its nearby hall. The children would accompany her with boisterous enthusiasm, while any activity that he suggested was rewarded by sullenness and monosyllabic rejection.

Moreover, when had their bodies last enjoyed each other? She seemed to shrink from any little tenderness that he offered her, as when one of the children was ill recently. Tentatively he had offered legal separation as a solution for their meaningless, even painful co-existence. His proposal had only inflamed Fanny the more: the disgrace and shame (she said) would kill her and maim the children for life. His mind drifts to St Julien and the tranquility that enveloped him whenever he was there. The grim reality of his life in Paris – outside his laboratory – was now so clear to him that he had to fight back tears of dismay – and again he was aware of the gnawing ache in his belly.

He re-enters the chateau; hardly warmer there than in the chill of the still-frosty terraces. At one end of the *Salon des Cartes* a group of men is sitting, one of them holding forth exuberantly. Berlioz is there too, and seeing Claude, beckons furiously:

"I say Bernard, come and join us: I'm sure a clear-thinking scientist can help us out of our dilemma!"

Claude is introduced to the others. There was Gustave LeGray – the eminent photographer and Sainte-Beuve the literary critic whom he now remembers having seen at Rayer's salon almost twenty years earlier. Sainte-Beuve had been sitting at Princess Mathilda's right arm at the previous night's dinner. Viollet-le-Duc was an architect, the Emperor's personal adviser, and is introduced as masterminding the rebuilding of the nearby *Chateau de Pierrefonds*. Finally Claude shakes hands with the artist Theodore Rousseau. Claude wonders how these people could remotely benefit from his participation, but he obligingly takes his place in the one remaining unoccupied armchair.

"We were just observing," says Berlioz, "that art benefits considerably from science, while science is free to progress – and does so without reference to, or support from art. What is your experience as an eminent medical scientist?"

Claude rapidly understands the nature of the conversation that must have led to this question. He knows that Le Gray has pioneered – with the help of chemists – his collodion-on-glass method of fixing negative images. Viollet-le-Duc's advanced use of iron in his designs is also well known as are the advanced engineering methods he had demonstrated in so many of his adventurous projects. Claude wonders in a fleeting second about Rousseau. All he knows is that he had taken refuge in Barbizon at the edge of the forest of Fontainebleau – shunning studios in favour of painting subjects outdoors in their natural light.

All eyes are now on him.

"I think that the division between art and science has been rather exaggerated. One need not look beyond Leonardo da Vinci to appreciate the support which visual art has given to the medical and other sciences. As scientists, we cannot expect to convey our ideas to others without expressing our findings and conclusions by the written or the spoken word – and what is that if not an art? I believe that we seriously lack training in that art of expression."

While stating this Claude looks intently at Sainte-Beuve who now leans forward urgently to respond:

"I can certainly see how the best scientists might be those who can communicate their findings in the most convincing manner. Perhaps it is also that such an art cannot easily be taught – perhaps it is a gift, as is the art of painting."

Claude smiles:

"Then I can understand why I have such difficulty in convincing both my students and my critics about the importance of what I have discovered!"

There is a ripple of kind laughter at this show of modesty.

"Monsieur Bernard, do you consider imagination to be a tool for the scientist, as it is for the artist?"

The question comes from the Princess Mathilde, who had obviously decided to join their group. There is a brief lull in the discussion as Sainte-Beuve pulls up a chair for her, providing Claude with a welcome opportunity to gather his thoughts:

"I am sure that I am not alone in believing that imagination is the phenomenon which most closely binds arts to the sciences. I doubt Madame, whether the advance of science is aware of its debt to imagination: the real origin of an idea or a theory is so rarely stated."

The princess nods slowly as she absorbs his words. Le Gray adds his thoughts:

"I would have thought that it is more the gradual accumulation of organized knowledge which creates scientific advance – rather than imagination."

Claude's reply is prompt.

"Well, that is classical Kantian view to which I cannot subscribe. To me it is intuition, surely an element of imagination, which is the real origin of – and sets the scene for – a scientific theory. Then it is the hypothesis – the organized excursion into imagination – which we must construct to examine and subsequently prove or disprove our theory. I think that imagination is a more valuable tool with which to advance science than is knowledge. In fact, I believe that it was Goethe who said that a truly great experimenter in the natural sciences cannot exist without imagination."

There is silence in the group as they digest these ideas. Presumably finding it too difficult to reason, even more so to contest this view, Rousseau abruptly changes the direction of the discussion:

"Surely the great distinction between arts and sciences is the creative element. Does science ever truly create?"

It is not the first time that people had confronted Claude with this question, although he still found it difficult to provide a coherent reply. Yet having just attempted to unify arts and sciences he was bound to respond with something better than ignorance.

"In its simplest sense we scientists do create. From the galvanic cell, the physicist creates electricity. In the test tube the chemist creates a molecule. One still hears discussion about so-called spontaneous generation; the spontaneous development of new life forms which might explain the origin of disease. I have seen little evidence to support that concept, but in my view the advance of science should in due course make it possible to create completely independent life forms. After all, whether in a plant or an animal, the biological cell is composed of definable substances. In turn, these possess a chemical composition that is open to analysis. Logically then, such substances should, in due course all be amenable to synthesis. To answer your question, science is not yet truly creative. Yet I am convinced that it has the capacity to be so."

Claude suddenly looks thoughtful.

"Your question has just reminded me of an argument that I had with my father-in-law; a well-known physician…." He pauses. "….it must have been almost fifteen years ago. He claimed that there was an art to practicing medicine. I strongly disagreed with him, because I insisted that any form of art must be creative. I maintained then that there was little that was created by doctors, except the evil consequences – the disasters of ill-performed surgery and the side effects of medicaments carelessly and unjustifiably prescribed!"

There are smiles and nods from his listeners as he continues:

"I don't believe that anything has happened in the intervening years that would prompt me to change my view. Quite simply, the word 'art' is used far too readily!"

There is a ripple of laughter and Berlioz gets to his feet.

"I think we have challenged our friend enough. Monsieur Bernard's logical thought might actually be of great value to those of us whose day-to-day existence depends on being creative. I rather wish that some of my music could be 'spontaneously generated' through some technical advance, and thus save me considerable trouble!"

There are more smiles and generous applause as the group breaks up and its contributors disperse. Claude finds Sainte-Beuve by his side, gently holding him by the elbow:

"I know that you must be a busy fellow, Bernard, but I arrange a sort of dining club with a few people of various interests; no doctors, I hasten to add. If you can find the time I am sure that we would all like you to join us."

"Most kind of you. At the moment life seems to be particularly busy…"

"No, no! I well understand. However, keep it mind. If the opportunity arises, please drop me a note; you'll always be welcome."

Claude feels flattered by the open invitation, which he might be inclined to take up later.

The afternoon would provide several options for the guests. The *chasse à courre* – the hunt for stags on horseback in the forest of Compiégne – was an activity led by both the Emperor and the Empress. However, it would certainly not prove attractive to all the visitors. One alternative was a visit to the town of Pierrefonds some ten kilometers away at the southern end of the forest. On the orders of Louis Napoleon, the imaginative even bizarre fairy-tale reconstruction of the ruins of its castle had been entrusted to Viollet-le-Duc who had recently taken up residence in a nearby house for the duration of the immense project. His drawings of the projected development had been placed for all to see on an easel at one end of the *Salle des Jeux*.

With three others, Claude is now sitting in the plush seats of a comfortable black carriage drawn by two white horses. It is being whisked through the forest on broad tracks tunnelling through towering beeches and oaks. A dozen similar carriages follow hard on their heels. His immediate travelling companions introduce themselves. Next to him is the ageing engineer Séguin, whose reputation is based on his innovations to the steam traction engine. Prosper Merimée is an author, a committed archeologist and the Inspector of Historic Monuments. He had been a friend of the Montijo family in Spain and had known Eugénie since she was a child. Accordingly, he was there every week during *les Séries*. The final passenger is the artist Corot, clutching a sizeable sketchbook that he explains will be used to chronicle the development of Pierrefonds. This will be the third time that he would paint the ruins, hoping that the

Emperor might purchase at least one canvas from him and so set him on the route to real fame.

The day is magnificent and Claude easily puts behind him the languor and negative thoughts of the previous day as the carriage comes to a halt at the *Vieux Moulin*, in a clearing at the halfway point, so that the visitors can take refreshments. He and Merimée are the last to alight from the carriage:

"So Monsieur Bernard, and what do you hope to get from your week with the master and mistress of the House?"

Claude is temporarily taken aback by Merimée's question.

"Don't look so shocked, my man. They are a generous couple. They only invited you because of your worthy contributions to society, and would therefore consider it reasonable to give you a reward or support of some type. Give it some thought, I beg you; you may only get one chance!"

With that, Merimée turns away and strides off in the direction of a long table; wine and Scotch shortbreads are appetizingly displayed, and other guests are now gravitating towards it. Less than an hour later, they arrive at the village of Pierrefonds, attractively situated around a large pond in which water lilies were thriving, despite the chill of autumn. Clouds now cover the sky and the ruins of the fourteenth century castle on the hill opposite seem so dismal: hardly worth the undoubtedly enormous investment. Claude wanders off towards the building that houses the thermal baths at the edge of the pond. A trickle of people issue to and from its uninviting doors as Claude wonders whether his old friend Constantin James is still Inspector of Thermal Baths and Spas. He would almost certainly have visited this installation at some time in the past. Not for the first time he wonders about the mechanism by which the waters conveyed their healing powers – if indeed they did. Some years ago, Pelouze had been involved with analyzing spa waters for their chemical content, and Claude makes a mental note to have a look at his results in a spare moment.

On the return journey, his mind drifts back to Merimée's frank question, and he wonders whether he will indeed be made some sort of offer. Moreover, how should he react? There was never enough money for research, so how did one really define one's needs? He had always performed his work on such a modest budget.

A mist is slowly closing in as Claude looks out towards the park, stretching beyond the terrace in front of the chateau. On its lawns, the townspeople of Compiégne were gathering around flares set into the ground, having cleared away the debris of the afternoon fair, which was always such an important part of the *Fête de l'Impératrice*. All was in readiness for the fireworks display, which would also be viewed by the guests who had assembled in groups behind Claude. At the far end of the terrace, Claude sees Lesage in animated discussion with a small group of men and women. While Claude was being assisted with his dressing earlier that evening, Lesage had regaled him with anecdotes gleaned from his fellow valets and maids. Claude imagines that they were now exchanging more of the same. Guests had dressed extravagantly for the occasion, billowing crinolines occasionally swept into unusual shapes by the gusting wind despite the restraining effect of heavy cloaks. The Empress herself, supremely elegant, was standing in the midst of a group of laughing women at the head of the stairs that led down to the park.

"And what, may I ask was your reaction to the Pierrefonds folly in which my dear cousin has so indulged himself?"

Claude turns to look at Princess Mathilde who had appeared out of the shadows to stand beside him, her slender Bonaparte hands applied lightly to the top of the balustrade as if she was about to play the piano.

"Impressive I suppose, Madame. It is hard to put into perspective the reconstruction of a historic site when measured against all the other demands which are made on the state coffers."

"Ah, but that's the point, Monsieur. He is paying for it himself – for himself and his lady. And thus a 'folly' it indeed must be."

Claude nods slowly, not at all certain where the conversation was taking him.

"I have hardly seen the Empress since I arrived: has she been unwell?"

"Not at all! However, the women's program is rather different to yours; it is after all her main responsibility during these weeks. The only activity which she insists on following is the hunt; and she is indeed an excellent equestrian. She and I are agreed however, that we prefer to associate with the men; they do have more to say for themselves, you know."

Claude is silent for a while as a series of rockets trailing white sparks sweep in a massive arc into the sky above them, finally descending earthwards in the form of glowing red balls.

"I was speaking to the Emperor earlier today about our conversation and the ideas which you expressed yesterday about the interplay of art and science…"

Claude looks at her, a half-smile enhancing her regular facial features in the glow of the spent rockets.

"...and he was most impressed. The advancement of science is much on his mind. He said that he would like to meet you in his study one evening before dinner, in order to talk further. Would tomorrow be convenient?"

"I am honoured that he wishes to talk with me, but I would have thought that there were others here who would be in a better position to provide him with information."

"I can assure you that it is to you that he wishes to speak. It seems that he is already somewhat familiar with your activities through one of his private physicians; Doctor Rayon, I believe?"

"*Rayer* actually. Pierre is rather prone to praise his colleagues, which is no bad thing. But some of us have a hard time living up to it!"

The Princess smiles, and Claude realizes that it was surely Pierre Rayer who had recommended that he be invited to Compiègne.

"I would of course be delighted to meet him."

"That's done then. I shall arrange for one of his guards to collect you from your apartment at five tomorrow. By the way, I hope that you have found everything to your satisfaction, Monsieur Bernard. Do reassure the Emperor if you feel you can; he and his Lady do like to know that their little program is successful."

The princess smiles generously, holds a delicately perfumed hand aloft to be kissed and then melts away into the ghostly shadows.

There is genuine warmth in the handshake with which the Emperor greets Claude, his eyes scanning Claude's face as if searching for some lack of symmetry. In return, Claude observes that his host is indeed quite short, an impression heightened by his large head and beard and the quite high desk behind which he now subsides with a deep sigh.

"Do excuse me for a moment Bernard, but I really must sign these documents; otherwise my army will be in revolt!"

Claude takes the opportunity of glancing around the study. Massive bookcases occupy two walls, while a third is shared between a large map of Europe and a tall, uncurtained window giving on to the terrace and a magnificent view of the park beyond. Two rather inviting ornate armchairs upholstered in green, red and gold brocade are to his left separated by a low marble-topped table. The desk is bare except for a neat pile of papers and a small bronze of a horse carrying a rider who might have been the host himself. He eventually hands the sheaf of papers to the guard who has been standing by his side, and who now leaves the room, soundlessly closing the enormous door behind him. The Emperor looks up at Claude with a benevolent smile, pushes back the massive high-backed chair, and gestures invitingly towards the armchairs into one of which he now transfers himself.

"Well, I trust you are content with all our arrangements so far?"

"A wonderful experience, Your Majesty: I have all but forgotten my commitments at the *Collège*."

"You will rediscover them soon enough. I understand from my cousin that you know Pasteur, who has also entertained us here in the past."

"Certainly; a fine scientist. Since I sit on the awards council of the *Académie des Sciences*, I can tell you that he has recently been well rewarded for his work. I was told about the demonstrations which he gave while he was your guest. I regret that I will not be able to perform as he did with his frogs!"

The Emperor smiles:

"Never mind – yet you do much research with animals, I believe?"

Claude hesitates briefly, uncertain as to which line he should adopt.

"Indeed I do. I believe that there is no substitute for the living animal when we still understand so little of normal physiology – let alone pathology. There are those of my colleagues who prefer to practice medicine as if the human being was the experimental model, and I must say that I strongly disapprove of that."

"But is it certain that a rabbit or a dog is an appropriate experimental model for man?"

Claude can only admire the sharpness of the question,

"Within limits, yes. I have spent much time discovering the similarity of chemical processes and reactions between different species. Of course, there is a quantitative difference in their chemistry, even beyond such matters as variation in the size of the animal. But then again, I expect that we will also discover large differences in the way that different humans respond to medicaments – or indeed to the toxic substances and poisons which so interest me."

The Emperor is silent for a short time, staring out of the window while he digests Claude's comments.

"Disapproval of animal research is actually quite rife, is it not?"

"It is indeed! I must often justify the nature of my work to others."

"I would guess that such attitudes might also exist within those chambers that decide on whether and how to support your work?"

"That may be true, but in any event support for research is always difficult to come by. My late mentor Doctor Magendie, such a fine and productive scientist, worked for many decades in the most absurdly cramped and unhealthy conditions. Many have felt that this led to his final demise."

The Emperor's face clouds over momentarily. He seems irritated, even pained by Claude's comment.

"I understand Bernard; I already accept that we must look after our scientists rather better. How are your own working conditions?"

"I should not complain; my laboratory is undoubtedly better provided for than that of my late master. There is however vast complexity in a scientist's responsibility. I and many others sit on government committees reporting on such matters as public hygiene, cholera, glanders and the like. Then we have our substantial teaching commitments, above all to medical students. Then there is the administration: endless reports and interviews. In between all this our research must be pursued."

There is a further pause in their discussion.

"Tell me, does the general public have access to your lectures?"

"Certainly, all our lectures at the *Collège* are all open to the public. In fact, I enjoy those the most and receive some interesting comments – even suggestions – following them. It is quite a challenge to present my material such that the lay public may appreciate it."

"I am so pleased. It has long appeared to me utterly useless to educate our young without ensuring that their parents – the older generation – shares in the progress of knowledge. I have often tried to persuade Rouland that he should initiate a national program of adult education along these lines. I am quite distressed that he is so unenthusiastic."

Louis is looking grim. His mouth is set in a firm line and Claude decides that he would not wish to oppose this man: he is enjoying the discussion more than he would have ever thought possible.

"I wish I could fully understand the scientific mind Bernard. Tell me, with all the ignorance and uncertainty which you imply exists in the field of medicine, how do you first approach a problem."

It is Claude's turn to gaze out of the window. The Emperor's eyes follow, as if he wished to share any inspiration that his guest might derive from the glorious view of the park. "Intuition mainly. It really does begin with intuition, you know – and I wish I could explain that, even to myself!"

The Emperor's eyes light up and he suddenly sits forward on his chair, enthusiastically.

"Wonderful, Bernard. I must tell you that I share that concept – almost a dependence – on intuition and instinct. But how can I convince my generals and my ministers that these are important sentiments?"

He shakes his head from side to side while Claude recalls the interesting discussions which he had two evenings previously with Berlioz and the others about intuition and imagination as starting points for both art and science.

"There we share a problem too, Your Majesty; convincing others of the correctness of our theories and actions. In science I believe that we must always provide proof to support our ideas and theories. Yet even with proof, it is often difficult for others to accept. Jealousy and envy are rife in our profession – as I expect it must be in yours."

Louis-Napoleon smiles, nods and now gazes intently at Claude as if to penetrate his innermost thoughts.

"May I ask how you spend your leisure time, Bernard?

"I have little of that, so that I am lucky that work gives me much joy. My family seat is in the Beaujolais, and when I return there, as I do almost every autumn for the several weeks of the harvest I feel the greatest peace and tranquility. There too, I can extend my understanding of biology. I have recently begun to compare the chemical reactions that are common to plants and animals: they are not as different as you may think. Apart from this I love the theatre and the art which Paris offers in such abundance." He hesitates: "Sadly, my wife does not share those interests."

"And do you share her interests, Bernard?"

Claude immediately regrets his mention of Fanny, and seeks further inspiration from the view of the park. He then responds slowly to the question:

"Your Majesty, there are those in the world whose sole pleasures derive from their family and their household activities. It is not for me to criticize those values, yet I find it difficult to participate as fully as I might in domestic matters."

He is not going to say more. From both Princess Mathilde's comments on the first evening and now the Emperor's question, Claude is certain that his hosts must have had foreknowledge of his problems. It is logical that Pierre Rayer – if he had indeed been behind Claude's invitation – might also have been obliged to provide some personal background. Suddenly he wishes to be away; back in his laboratory with Lesage and Tripier – even at home with his family. Does he really have to endure three further days of this gilded, unnatural existence?

The Emperor's eyes had switched to the ornate clock on the mantle shelf. It seems that he had to attend to other important matters. He raises his body briskly from the comfortable chair, at the same time extending his arm for an even warmer handshake than the one with which he had welcomed Claude:

"I have enjoyed our discussion more than I can say, Bernard. I trust that we may have many further opportunities."

Within seconds, he had escorted Claude to the massive door, which the guard outside now closes silently behind him.

"What do you think of all this Maurice?"

Claude had returned to his room to find Lesage standing by the bed on which he had neatly arranged every item of his outfit for the evening: shirt pressed, shoes polished, medals shiny. Claude had come to appreciate this aspect of his stay. In his own home, he had always chosen apparel that came most easily to hand. From Fanny's comments as well as the glances of his colleagues, he was aware that while not exactly shabbily dressed, his appearance was not always as it should have been. He makes a mental note that he will put more attention towards this aspect of his life.

"Quite remarkable, Monsieur. I appreciate that you invited me along in this capacity, but I would in no way wish to exchange this life for my one in Paris."

Claude had not visited Lesage in his home, but from his conversations with him, it was apparent that it was very modest. His wife had died many years ago, and when not occupied in the laboratory, he was forever helping others with their problems; a widow's paper work, her son's arithmetic, a sick man's meals and so on. It was out of respect for his benevolence that the prefix '*père*' graced the name of Claude's now-ageing laboratory assistant.

"I share your sentiments completely, my friend. They may be fine people, but their concerns are on such a different plane."

"May I say that those concerns are well beneath you? The scandals and gossip which I was obliged to listen to from the valets and maids do not bear repeating; even about the Emperor himself. Was your meeting with him useful?"

"It is so difficult to say. What is said to one's face is always open to interpretation; yet our Emperor appears sympathetic enough to science. I also know what you mean about the wagging tongues. I would be happy to do without the gossip, yet it is quite useful to know something of these people's lives, so that one does not put one's foot in the wrong place."

They both laugh at the imagery, and Claude realizes that he feels so much greater affinity with Lesage than with anyone that he had met since his arrival in Compiégne. He faces his assistant squarely, placing his hands on his broad shoulders:

"I may not have told you often enough how much I value you as a person, Maurice. I fear that you may think that I take your commitment and good nature for granted; and that is certainly not the case."

There are tears in Lesage's eyes as he turns away from Claude:

"Come Monsieur, you will be late for dinner."

The last three days were by no means tedious, yet he was now looking forward to leaving. Certainly, he had enjoyed freedom from commitment. The abdominal pains that had so troubled him on arrival in Compiégne had totally disappeared, and his appetite had never been better. Was it his imagination, or were his trousers a little tighter around the waist? Claude had discovered one of Descartes' minor works in the library, and had spent several hours the previous night reading it, rather than sleeping. He did not avoid the company of others, but kept such a low profile that the question of giving a talk or lecture never arose. He took a back seat in any discussion groups, and demurred from making anything but the most superficial comment – even when challenged. He thoroughly enjoyed a performance of a comedy by Scribe, which was given by a group from the *Théatre Français* in the intimacy of the chateau's theatre, constructed during the era of Louis-Philippe. The appreciative audience was accommodated on well-tiered benches loosely covered with regal-red linen. The excellent acoustics allowed him to appreciate every syllable of the actors' fine diction – yet the performance tweaked uncomfortable memories of his own failed aspirations.

On the last evening, he could not avoid one dance with Princess Mathilde to the accompaniment of an incompetently handled barrel organ. Aware of his clumsiness he is most apologetic.

"Do not be distressed, Monsieur Bernard," she says later. "Perhaps you will join me at the *rue de Courcelles* or at St Gratien where one might practice a little. I also have my ladies to tea sometimes; it would give me great pleasure to welcome your wife on one of those occasions."

Claude hardly knows how to respond to either of these proposals. He has no wish to complicate his life any more than it already is. The charm of Princess Mathilde is undoubted. Yet somebody – was it Merimée or Sainte-Beuve – had told him that when asked whether she missed having a child of her own, the princess had responded that she would rather start one hundred pregnancies, than carry one through to its natural conclusion!

Of course, he was grateful to her for introducing him to the Emperor – although no offer of support had yet been forthcoming. Berlioz on the other hand was wearing a sickening smile; he had received a solid agreement from the Emperor that he would intervene on his behalf: a venue for *The Trojans* was now assured, granted in return for the memorable performance of his Imperial Cantata in the *Exposition Universelle* four years earlier. Corot too had been promised that his latest painting of Pierrefonds castle would be purchased – for permanent display, and at a fine price.

CHAPTER 12

NO PLEASURE WITHOUT PAIN

Davaine is standing beside Claude's bed; his facial expression a mixture of confusion and concern.

"I should be able to tell you what is wrong Claude, but I can't. Your lower abdomen tenderness and the diarrhea can only lead me to assume that it is some form of enteritis or colitis – certainly not cholera though."

"...and not tuberculous consumption I hope, Casi?"

"I doubt it: you haven't lost weight and there's no fever."

The abdominal symptoms had returned with considerable force a few days after his return from Compiégne. With enormous effort, he had prepared and given two lectures at the *Collège* – unhappy with both. He had also spent short periods in his laboratory to check progress on his projects.

"And how are things with Fanny – and the children?" Davaine asks, tentatively.

"No better than you would expect. She was suspicious of my activities at Compiégne; of course. I had to admit that it was essentially a social event, but she brightened up a little this week when she received an invitation from Princess Mathilde to one of her salons at the *rue de Courcelles*."

"And no 'offers' yet from His Majesty, I suppose?"

Claude smiles; shakes his head. Soon after his return to Paris, he had told Davaine about his interview with the Emperor – and the good fortune of some of his fellow guests at the chateau. His reward was obviously not to be.

"Claude, I am going to ask Pierre to see you."

"Do you think that it is that serious?"

"Well I might give you some bismuth and magnesium which would help your symptoms, but we need to have a diagnosis. It's so strange that you had so few symptoms when you were away; while now they are occurring daily. There must be something in your surroundings: yet I cannot imagine that it is the water, or the food you eat."

There is silence between them for a few moments and Claude decides to change the subject:

"And your research Casi; anything new?"

"Not really. I have put aside my studies on anthrax for the time being: Pierre and I are still not sure what causes those strange rods to appear in the blood of patients and animals with that condition. Pollender in Germany has also seen them in the blood of animals suffering from anthrax; it is useful to have that confirmation. Anyhow I must go. I expect that Fanny will be back at any moment."

After he leaves, Claude reflects on his comment about the absence of his symptoms while he was in Compiégne. He tries to recall whether he had been free of pain during last autumn's visit to St Julien?

A few days later Rayer appears, and Fanny conducts him to Claude's bedroom where he is still in bed at eleven in the morning.

"I should have invited myself along to see you before now." He begins. "I rather wondered why you had been avoiding my ward rounds!"

"I am sorry Pierre. I would have been there if I possibly could."

They talk at length: about Claude's family, his research, his writing, and his lectures – and again about his family. Rayer examines him, a frown creasing his broad forehead. His fleshy jowls shake as he sits down wearily at Claude's bedside again.

"Casimir is right, of course. It's something about here and you!"

As he says this, he throws his arms expansively about him while looking thoughtfully at Claude, and then to the mountain of books and papers which totally obscures the top of a large table at his bedside.

"I am not sure that I understand, Pierre."

"I see quite a number of patients Claude, whose intestinal system seems to – how shall I say – over-react to their hidden emotions with painful spasms. It is like the heart palpitations that some people have when they are upset.

"Do you mean…?"

"Yes, I do. Your laboratory conditions are a disgrace and your domestic situation is a mess. All that controversy about your research – those challenges – they don't help either. In addition…," he adds, "…you are pushing yourself to achieve even more than is reasonable – and quite why, I am not sure."

Claude is silent, digesting Rayer's comments.

"Assuming you are right Pierre, what can you possibly do about it?"

"Not *me* Claude, *you*! You have the problems; you have to decide what you want to do about them, although I am desperately sorry about your personal life, particularly since I had a hand in moulding it."

Claude is looking steadfastly at his knees which are creating two symmetrical mounds through the counterpane.

"I would like to think that you are right Pierre – and that it's nothing more serious."

"*Bon dieu*, Claude, this is serious! In its own way, just as serious as an infection. Look what it's doing to you!"

Rayer puts his hand on Claude's arm and looks at him intently.

"Give some thought to a longer stay in St Julien. You are obviously not much good to anyone here now; being away will do you good. If nothing else, just take time to consider your options. I do not know about your relationship with your mother, but it might even be helpful to talk to her frankly about your marriage. Knowing you, I suppose that you will also want to do some writing while you are there, so you can still be productive. Our mail service seems to have improved recently, so I expect that you can also keep in touch with your laboratory people. And if it takes rather longer, Casimir or I will visit you: actually I rather fancy a spell in the country!"

Rayer looks at the heavy watch gracing his paunch and leaps to his feet.

"…but I must leave you now: please tell me what you decide to do?"

Fanny is furious.

"You've just got back from a holiday, Claude; and now you are to be away again?"

"I got back three months ago, actually; and this is different Fanny. You know that I am not well, and both Pierre and Casimir think that I need a complete break. I must follow their recommendation."

"Can't you take some medicine like everyone else?"

"You also know that I have tried that; both Casimir and Pierre have prescribed mixtures for me but they don't seem to help."

"Then, why don't you ask my father? He seems to get people better again very quickly. Anyhow, why can't we go away together – as a family? Other equally busy and successful people seem to manage it."

Claude was silent and thoughtful, uncertain whether he should confront the situation now – as it would have to be confronted at some time. He takes a deep breath:

"You and I have a problem Fanny. No doubt you consider that it is all my fault, but I believe – and we have discussed this before – that we are simply unsuited to live with one another. You cannot seem to accept those aspects of my life and work which others appreciate, and I am simply not prepared to change them by...."

"....but you expect me to change my attitudes!"

"That is what I am trying to say; I do not expect you to. We discussed a possible separation before; I still believe that is what we should do."

"And you want me, as a good Catholic to sustain the wrath of God – having supported you and your children over all these years? Just as you are at last allowing me to mix in socially acceptable circles, you wish to embarrass me by throwing me out. And then, what about the children?"

"Firstly, I am sure that you will find other women at Princess Mathilde's salons who have been separated from their husbands – if those are the 'socially acceptable circles' to which you are referring. Fanny, you must also know that the likelihood of failure is greater in an arranged marriage such as ours. As far as the children are concerned, our incompatibility has not been helped by the fact that you have turned them against me. I find that so painful. My relationship with them might actually improve if we live apart."

Fanny strikes the table at which they were sitting with both clenched fists.

"You are not going to break up a family for which I have suffered so much and worked so hard! Have you conveniently forgotten that it was my father's money, my dowry that originally supported your grisly research – as well as sustaining your tiresome family in the wilds of France?

Suddenly she stands up, knocking her chair to the floor. "You may go to hell as far as I am concerned!"

Fleeing the room, Fanny slams the door behind her. A tidal wave of emotion rises within Claude. He feels his eyes bulging with tears that cannot escape. He wants to yell with anger and despair but his tongue refuses to move. His abdomen feels as though a horse has kicked him, and he vomits uncontrollably over the white tablecloth.

Claude spends an exhausting day in the laboratory in preparation for his anticipated absence. With considerable effort, he had reviewed the two recent manuscripts written by Tripier, and they are now discussing the minor modifications that will be necessary before publication. He also discusses with two of his students a project on the functioning of the parotid salivary gland that sits within the cheek, and which he wants them to carry out under Tripier's supervision.

Just as Claude is leaving his room, Lesage announces that a certain Monsieur Rouland wishes to see him – if he was not too busy. He shows a well-dressed man into Claude's room where he takes the seat on the opposite side of the desk, disapprovingly glancing around the austere room.

"I trust that I am not inconveniencing you." He begins. "I quite often visit the *Collège* in my role as the Emperor's Minister of Education. I have just had a meeting with the Dean here in connection with some plans for next year. I was hoping that you might be free for a moment, and thus save me a separate visit."

He smiles disarmingly as Claude recalls how Louis-Napoleon had mentioned Rouland's lack of enthusiasm about more widespread introduction of adult education. The reason for his visit soon becomes apparent.

"The Emperor has sent me here with an offer to support your work: he was most impressed with what you had to say to him last November. Of course I should have come sooner, but as you may be aware, His Majesty has very many ideas. They keep us all much occupied."

Claude can feel his heart accelerate with excitement. Rouland fumbles in a case that he had perched on his lap and extracts a sheet of paper from which he proceeds to read to himself, mumbling incoherently as he scans the extensive text. Eventually he looks up at Claude:

"It is a little unusual actually. Put simply, the Emperor says that I am to offer you a sum of money to enable your 'personal goals' to be achieved: I quote his words quite precisely."

Claude is not sure how to respond to such a generous, yet vague offer.

"That is unbelievably kind, and I would be most happy to prepare a document – even perhaps with your assistance – in which I could outline our exact needs here in the laboratory. We do have quite ambitious plans for the next few years."

"That is quite unnecessary." Rouland replies, clearly irritated. "I have just spoken with your Dean about expanding and improving your facilities so that you may become even more productive. You certainly won't have cause for complaint once you see the extent of that support."

Rouland shakes his head slowly from side to side, as if he disapproves of what he is about to say to Claude.

"No, it is about your *personal* goals that he has asked me to see you. What the Emperor has in mind is a direct bequest to enable you to pursue your ideas – outside your laboratory. Exactly how you use this bequest is for us to neither suggest nor approve. He has therefore instructed me to pay to your bank the sum of ten thousand francs."

Rouland finally looks up from his paper to study Claude's reaction to the news. As expected, he looks quite stunned. Rouland is already on his feet:

"You must excuse me, Monsieur Bernard but I have another meeting at the Elysée – and quite soon. Please do me the kindness of letting me have your banker's details so that we may transfer the money soonest: I do so dislike unfinished business. My compliments, Monsieur"

With that, he quietly leaves the room. Claude subsides into his chair and as is his way, he gazes for almost one hour out of the window. His mind is buzzing with excitement; one thought uppermost in his mind.

Each time he takes the train to Villefranche, it seems quicker; the journey shorter. He pushes from his mind Fanny's vitriolic parting comments and mesmerized by the contrapuntal rhythm of steel upon steel, he allows his mind to drift. He would find the period of rest that his friends had prescribed difficult to follow. Indeed, he had taken with him a microscope and equipment for dissecting and for mounting slides. He also had with him his *cahier rouge* that was now almost full of tightly packed handwriting embracing his ideas, theories and reflections on life, health and disease. Little had changed in Chatenay since his autumn visit the previous year, but he delights in seeing the swelling buds on the vines, some already in leaf. His mother had become even more stooped in that short period, and she had a large bruise on her forearm from a fall on the stairs two weeks previously. She was lucky that her arm had not fractured.

"In your last letter you told me of your maladies Claude, but there was no mention of the children. Are they well? I do so miss them."

"They are very well, and so active, Maman; they almost make up for our other two tragedies from which Fanny has still not recovered. She and I have had……"

"Yes, well go on upstairs and tidy up so we can sit down and have supper."

Madame Bernard clearly did not wish to know about anything involving Fanny: their dislike for one another could never be undone, and certainly not by Claude. However, he cannot wait to tell his mother of the good news; over supper, it comes tumbling out; like a child recounting a windfall of Christmas presents:

"You did receive the letter that I sent you immediately after my week in Compiègne?"

"Of course; didn't I reply?"

"I don't believe so, but it doesn't matter. It just so happens that my long talk with the Emperor has borne fruit. Apart from a major donation to the *Collège* – which I hope will provide me with more space – he has given me ten thousand francs for my personal use."

"My goodness Claude, I am so proud of you! But what will you do with all that?"

"I must really use it in the spirit with which it was given to me; to further my personal goals – the Emperor used exactly those words. I don't suppose that you have been speaking with Lombard recently?"

"He has not been well, you know. I think it is more than just his arthritis. He and his wife left for Chuzelles after Christmas to stay with his family and he has only been back here once since then. He told me that he will be coming back some time this month to check the property. Did you notice how wonderful the vines are looking at the moment?"

Claude smiles.

"You know Maman, he mentioned to me last year that he was thinking of selling his house – with his vineyards of course. He thought it would fetch around sixty thousand francs, so all I could do was to dream. Together with my savings and a modest mortgage, the Emperor's bequest now makes it possible for me to buy it. I could alter the rooms so that you could live on the ground floor level and never need to use the stairs again; and I would have somewhere to come – to experiment as well as write. I think that I could easily convert one room into a laboratory. And the vines....."

"But such a large house! How could we look after it?"

"It certainly has more rooms, but above all they are larger and more airy, which would suit us both better. As for help, with the proceeds of the harvest we should be able to afford someone to live in the house and care for it permanently: when I am in Paris it would give me a marvellous feeling to know that there is someone to keep an eye on you."

"Well, talk to Lombard if you must but I won't leave this cottage. You know that it was my parents' gift to me and your father; it wouldn't be right to have someone else living in it."

Claude looks crestfallen: not for a moment had he considered that his mother would take that view. They finish the meal in near silence.

Barely one week later, Claude sees that the shutters of Lombard's house are wide open: he cannot resist knocking at the door. Lombard answers it himself, and leads Claude into the salon, hobbling with the aid of a gold-headed cane.

"I'm glad that you're here Claude – in more ways than one."

Lombard's face is grey and drawn:

"It's time for us to leave; my family insists that we join them in Chuzelles as soon as possible. If you can see your way clear to buying it for the sixty thousand francs for which it was recently valued, it's yours!"

Claude cannot believe his ears. Lombard takes him for a tour of the house. Paint is peeling from many of the walls but the structure seems without any fissures or other major defect. In the cellar below, the presses are in working order, the wine vats without leakage. At the back, a large covered shed houses Lombard's carriage, his horse well stabled in an adjoining barn.

For two full days, his mind is only on the purchase of the manor house. What a wonderful dimension it would add to his life! The space and light alone would boost his morale. He would also have a wider access to nature. He could do without the stray cats and dogs of Paris; there would be frogs from the creeks and rabbits from the fields, and he could study the teeming life of the ponds. His revelations about the similarities between the starch of plants and the *glycogène* of animals had made him aware that he had to study the complete spectrum of nature. Even the vines might furnish him with material for his ideas on comparative biology. In the back of his mind, the publication of a major treatise on the subject was already taking shape. The Emperor would definitely approve of that 'personal goal'!

Claude's mother was pleased. If this meant that she would see more of her son then it was well and good, just as long as he did not place any pressure upon her to move from the cottage that held the fond memories of her earlier life. Claude suddenly realizes how well he feels; mind and body both liberated. Although there were still occasions when his abdomen felt a little distended, he is entirely free of pain. He returns to Paris three weeks later, having barely glanced at his notebooks.

Louis Pasteur had arrived in Paris in 1858 from Lille to work at the prestigious *École Normale Supérieure* as its administrator and director of scientific studies. No doubt, it was his important scientific contribution to the wine and beer industry that had paved his way to this appointment. It was a growth of yeasts on grapes, he had firstly discovered, which allowed fermentation of sugar to alcohol – and not those so-called unstabilizing vibrations, which had been the dominant theory until then. Later, he had been retained by a brewing company in Lille owned by a Monsieur Bigot, father of one of his students. Pasteur had found that bacteria were infecting those yeast cells, thereby causing the unpredictable yield of alcohol that was threatening not just Monsieur Bigot, but the whole French beer industry.

Claude had been most impressed by the report that Pasteur had recently submitted to the *Académie* on his fermentation experiments. He also knew with what primitive laboratory facilities the *École* has provided him: so much so, that he had persuaded his friend Berthelot to offer Pasteur some space in his laboratory. Claude is now delighted to see Pasteur who has called in: *"….on the off chance that you would find time to speak with me."*

They had now been talking for some time about his discoveries, during which he is again struck by Pasteur's quiet confidence. No wonder he had been so well received in Compiègne!

"I really wanted to pay my respects. I well know that as chairman of the committee, you guided the decision of the *Académie* in awarding me that prize."

"Well, your research was quite beyond reproach, Louis…." Claude hesitates, smiles. "…although I have to say that I still believe that it is the chemicals made by the yeast rather than the living yeasts themselves that provide the stimulus to fermentation."

Pasteur leans forward in his chair: "I had quite a disagreement with Berthelot about that recently: I must tell you that all my work indicates that yeast cells *must* be alive for fermentation to take place." Pasteur's face becomes quite solemn. "But there is something else I wanted to talk with you about; even perhaps enlist your help. Felix Pouchet has again claimed that his experiments on putrefaction support that ridiculous concept of 'spontaneous generation'.

"Yes. I know. His new book *Heterogenesis* is sitting on my desk at home. I am afraid I cannot bring myself to read it!"

"Exactly! Well, I think that it is about time that we finally put that idea to rest: I even wonder if the *Collège* might have a part to play in it: his claims confuse the whole theory of contagion by organisms; they will surely hamper any research on prevention of infection. How can anyone in their right mind still believe that the maggots in decaying meat are somehow generated by the meat itself: I imagine that he will soon propose that crocodiles develop from the mud in which they live! Are we still living in the age of Aristotle?"

Claude is amused at the vehemence of his colleague, especially since he knows that before moving to Paris, Pasteur himself had been quite a staunch supporter of 'spontaneous generation'.

"I know what you mean, Louis. But surely Pouchet doesn't support Aristotle's claim that living beings can arise from earth, air, fire and water?"

"Not quite that – but almost as bad! In his book, he claims that literally any type of organic matter can give rise to entirely new forms of life – certainly germs and yeasts – providing there is oxygen present! He believes that his latest experiments are conclusive."

Pasteur again leans forward eagerly in his chair, his eyes staring intently at Claude. "What he did was to heat animal tissue in a series of glass flasks. On half of them, he then sealed off the neck so that air could no longer enter the flasks. After a few days, he observed that putrefaction occurred only in those flasks that were not sealed. He now claims – with such erroneous logic in my opinion – that it is only the entry of oxygen that permits putrefaction to occur, by allowing 'spontaneous generation' of microbes within the tissue. What's more, I hear from my colleagues that he is submitting that work to the Academy for next year's Alhumbert prize."

Claude knows that Pasteur too is submitting his work for that coveted prize; important both to pocket and prestige in the competitive world of French science. They sit for a while in a silence finally broken by Claude:

"It seems to me that you will need to exactly repeat his procedure – yet at the same time find a way of showing that it is the entry of germs rather than oxygen which allows putrefaction to occur. But how to do that best, I...?"

Claude's voice trails away as he suddenly remembers some of his own early research. His eyes light up.

"Do you remember a few years ago, Louis, there was a lot of discussion about microbes circulating in the air. I was interested at the time in the properties of sugar solutions, and in particular, in the mould that often develops when a mixture of gelatin and sugar was left in the open. I found then that heating up the air that entered a flask containing that mixture prevented the mould from forming. Perhaps one could look at the putrefaction process the same way – heating the air presumably damages any microbes that are present; but it shouldn't affect the oxygen, should it?"

Pasteur looks thoughtful.

"That might work. I actually thought of narrowing and bending the glass tube that conducts air into the flask. We now know that many microbes are carried on dust particles: I would expect any dust to be deposited on the deformed walls of the tubing as the air enters. So the microbes would be held back with the dust – but not the oxygen."

Claude looks at his watch.

"That's ingenious. May I make a suggestion? Would you allow me to make a few experiments myself using my heating method? We could compare our two methods."

They shake hands on their decision and Pasteur leaves. Claude decides to perform his part of the deal in St Julien when he returns in June to sign the documents for the purchase of Lombard's house. He rather liked Pasteur: a trifle serious and intense perhaps, but clearly a fine scientist who deserved as much help as he could give him. Their mutual interest in wine might even become a bond to be nurtured in Claude's new life which lay ahead.

Claude is tired; yet it had hardly passed four o'clock. Tripier, Lesage and Sechenov, his recently arrived Russian visitor had already left for the afternoon and Claude decides to return home early himself: he could spend some time playing with the children, whom he had hardly seen since his return from St Julien. Earlier that morning he had asked Jean-Paul to collect him from the *Collège* – but only at seven o'clock. If he took a cab now, he would be home in plenty of time to cancel the arrangement. The combined effect of warm afternoon sunshine and a cool breeze lifts his spirits. The cab crosses the Seine by the recently constructed *Pont de Solferino* and in less than half an hour deposits him in the *rue de Mogador*. As he enters the apartment, he hears voices coming from the salon and is about to enter the room when a certain caution prompts him to halt in his stride, and listen at the door:

"...not really getting anywhere. The Society seems to be involved with too many other animal issues."

The voice is deep and resonant, unrecognizable to Claude.

"That's exactly why we need an association which deals directly with anti-vivisection issues: people who are willing to take action themselves. Grammont's law will never be fully ratified for anything other than domestic animals. Even then, the fines are ridiculously small!"

That emphatic voice was Fanny's – and she had more to say:

"Grammont tells me that he has estimated that last year alone almost twenty thousand animals were killed or maimed in the name of science – and that's just in Paris. It must stop!"

"Have you talked to your husband then – the famous professor? He seems to be one of the main culprits; it's not surprising that others follow his example?"

The new female voice had an icy edge to it, but now it is Fanny's voice again:

"Not all of his research involves animals, you know, and I do continue to remind him of his religious and moral duty. In time, I think he will relent. When he does so, he will of course be the perfect example to hold up for the world to see."

Another male voice springs into life:

"I read in *l'Illustration* last month about Pasteur's marvellous work. Apparently he uses very few animals for his research: perhaps we should persuade him to join our association as its figurehead or patron?"

"It's a fine thought and indeed he might accept..." Fanny's voice again! "...but I am also in continuous touch with Victor Hugo by letter. He has promised that when he eventually returns from his exile in the Channel Islands, he will be the patron of our new association."

Claude turns on his heel and leaves the apartment, quietly closing the door behind him. His head is bursting, his chest thumping. Bile rises in his throat as he wills himself to suppress the urge to vomit and defecate. He has no notion of the direction that his legs take him, or of his destination. Some hours later night has fallen, and his body feels frozen as he stares into the waters of the Seine swirling beneath him. Rain begins to fall and he realizes that he is not far from Davaine's house. The door is finally opened in response to his insistent banging a few minutes later. Once he is settled in front of their fire, he recounts the events of the evening. Davaine and his wife listen patiently; relieved when he agrees to spend the night there. They make him comfortable in the attic room.

Claude is gazing out of its high window when Davaine knocks on his door the next morning.

"Casi, I cannot take any more of this. It is destroying me. While I was in St Julien I took your and Pierre's advice and considered what I should do – but I still imagined that by some miracle the situation would improve."

"Georgina and I were discussing it all last night after we settled you down. Would you consider staying with us until you have a firmer view of what you might do? You are welcome to use this room. As you see, it even has a table at which you can work – if you wish! Young Jules shouldn't disturb you too much."

"My good, kind and wonderful friend, I would like nothing more."

They agree how they would approach Fanny. Davaine would call and see her, explaining that during a meeting with his colleagues, Claude had become very ill with severe abdominal pains. Davaine had of course wanted to care for his good friend, and since it had been so late, he had taken him home in his own carriage. Might Fanny kindly allow him now to take with him some clothes and books to keep Claude occupied during his recovery? Fanny was unlikely to be wholly convinced by the story but it would have to do for the moment. Davaine returns from his visit later that day with the necessary items. Fanny had not queried his explanation of Claude's absence: after all, he had increasingly spent nights away from home – in his laboratory, she had assumed. Without emotion or real sincerity, she simply said that she hoped that he would soon be better.

After his sound sleep, Claude has little difficulty in planning a way forward. He would spend a week in the laboratory with his assistants and students during which he would allot the necessary projects for them to complete in his absence. He would use the evenings to prepare his lecture scheduled for Friday afternoon, the last lecture of the academic year. It was an important one: more general than most and essentially an introduction to the winter program on experimental pathology. He would then set off for St Julien, in the hope that he could move into the new house somewhat earlier.

If the authorities at the *Collège* and Sorbonne were agreeable, he would then spend most of his time in St Julien, returning only when necessary for his lecture courses and to supervise his staff. He certainly did not wish to return to *rue de Mogador:* Davaine's attic room would be a convenient and welcome *pied-à-terre* until he could establish something more permanent for himself. The onus of day-to-day supervision at the *Collège* would rest on Tripier's shoulders, but they were broad enough: the challenge would help mould his character. He could always be in touch by mail; after all, it now took only three days for a letter to pass between St Julien and Paris. All that remained was for him was to frankly discuss a way forward with Fanny. A letter, a visit? He would attend to that in a day or so.

Claude had just finished eating supper with Davaine and his wife, and had shared his decisions with them: "May I also tell you how I hope to deal with my marital problem?"

"Of course, Claude!"

"You see, I believe that Fanny knows full well that our marriage has no future. I cannot see that she holds any affection for me: and after what has happened, I cannot say that I have affection for her either. For my own well-being, I have decided that I must now live apart from her. A legal separation would be logical, but she refuses on religious grounds and ..."

"I didn't know that she was so religious."

"She wasn't. Even her father is surprised just how devout she has become. She seems to have acquired a deep belief in order to support her attitude towards my animal work. I have to acknowledge and respect that attitude in a way, since I am not blind to the fact that the wider public is so very uneasy about animal experimentation."

Davaine's wife decides to interject:

"Have you considered stopping or at least reducing your animal work in order to please her – and perhaps others?"

"Quite simply Georgina, it wouldn't work. I don't believe in human experimentation as Casi well knows, and I can assure you that there are questions that only experimentation on living animals can answer – contrary to the views of my critics."

"You must understand that I am not taking Fanny's side Claude, otherwise I could not support Casimir in the research he is doing; but could you not satisfy your academic thirst by working on projects that do not require the use of living animals – or at least do so less often. There must be so many areas of ignorance?"

They are silent for a while, the insistent ticking of a large grandfather clock so intruding on Claude's thoughts that he has difficulty in forming an answer to this most obvious of questions. His answer is accordingly oblique:

"You have to understand that I do have sympathy for animals – I am not callous in my approach. I now use anaesthesia during my procedures and if possible, I sacrifice the animal later in order to save it from suffering. I can only say that I believe that what I do is important for future researchers and to advance human welfare in general."

Georgina feels that she is not going to get very far on that topic.

"And what about the children?"

"You know that Fanny is turning them slowly but surely against me, and I cannot stop that. I would need to speak with Fanny about seeing them separately – if they wished it. Alternatively, perhaps she will have the kindness to occasionally have me visit their home for a meal."

Davaine and his wife look at one another trying to hide disbelief at his naively optimistic view of his future personal life. Claude breaks the silence with a typically abrupt change of subject.

"You know Casi, I had Pasteur with me for a long time earlier this week; in fact just before my recent crisis. He has been doing some fine research, some of which rang a familiar bell in regard to your work on anthrax."

"I have put all that aside for the time being, Claude?"

"Yes, but you might still find this of interest. In his research on wine fermentation, he has seen under the microscope some small rods that sound rather like the ones you identified in animals dying from anthrax. However, he has demonstrated quite clearly that it is actually these rods that damage the yeast cells and stop the wine from fermenting. You always thought that the microscopic rods that you saw were the *result* of the disease, didn't you? Well, isn't it possible that they are actually the cause? Couldn't your little rods be damaging the cells of the lung and skin just as Pasteur's rods damage yeast cells?"

"It's certainly possible. In fact, that was also suggested by Pollender about five years ago but I don't think he has done anything more about his idea."

"Well, I think you should look at that problem again."

"That's easy for you to say Claude, but we haven't had any cases recently and with my recent clinical work, the laboratory isn't really set up to do those type of studies. However, it's nice of you to think of my problems when you have so many of your own. I will of course discuss it with Pierre."

He takes a deep breath as he enters a packed auditorium of the *Collège*. Explaining his ideas on the organization of the human body would be rather different to his usual lectures. Claude would explain how he built on solid facts to create theories capable of being tested: specific experiments which led to generalizations, and ultimately to better understanding of health and disease.

It had all begun, he explains to the hushed audience, with his work on *glycogène*. He had shown that this substance was present in the liver, to be broken down – on demand as it were – into glucose. The liver then delivered that glucose directly into the bloodstream where it was distributed as a fuel to nourish other body tissues. It was the first time that an organ of the body had been shown to manufacture a substance and then deliver it into the blood for an effect elsewhere. He then proposes that the thyroid and the suprarenal glands, as well as the spleen – whose functions were still unknown – might also release chemicals into the blood stream at appropriate times. What could these chemicals be, and what effects might they have? What function did these organs – of what he called 'internal secretion' – actually serve?

This leads him to outline his concept of regulation within the body. Again, he bases his comments on the glucose model. He had measured it in the blood of animals and humans under so many different circumstances and conditions. Was the audience not puzzled how day after day, the level of glucose in the blood stayed within such a narrow range: so that only in the condition of diabetes was the level invariably high? So just how did the liver know when to stop its breakdown of *glycogène*. Indeed, was it the liver that was at fault in people with diabetes?

So little was still known, he says, about blood constituents other than glucose, yet blood undoubtedly had functions that went far beyond simply conveying oxygen and nutrients like glucose to the body tissues. One could presume that elements like sodium and potassium, and substances like urea were not just to be found in the urine, but were present also in the blood. These too were probably kept within quite a narrow range of values. Why did he say this? Because one had to reason – using the example of glucose – that the body probably worked best if levels of chemicals bathing the tissues were kept within a certain range.

If one considered what a hostile and fluctuating environment animals often lived in, one would argue that blood and other body fluids were like insulators or buffers: supplying the cells of the body with what they needed, taking away what they had jettisoned – and fundamentally ensuring that they would always be bathed by a fluid that was friendly to them. Much work still needed to be done, probably by others in the near and distant future. However, he had decided that henceforth he would refer to these important body fluids collectively as the *milieu intérieur*.

The applause is initially only modest, as if the audience is still digesting the meaning of his proposals. With the usual time to spare, Claude invites questions from the audience. They immediately fasten on to his concept of the 'hostile environment', and a young woman in the front row immediately attracts his attention:

"The challenge of environmental heat and cold is always with us, and more so in lower animals. Would you say, Monsieur Bernard that constancy of blood temperature is part of your *milieu intérieur*?"

"Probably yes. However, in that instance the constancy is achieved both by physical and chemical means."

Claude pauses, wondering how he might improve on his answer without taking up too much time.

"I have confirmed by the insertion of thermometers that the temperature measured in the mouth or rectum is almost independent of the environment; as you know its level is indeed held within very narrow limits: in man, between 35 and 37 degrees Celsius. Much of this constancy is achieved through activity of the nervous system. Some of you will have heard me lecture about sympathetic nerve activity. By constricting blood vessels, such activity directs blood away from the skin, reducing the loss of heat – and so raising body temperature. There is undoubtedly also a chemical element which influences body temperature, but of that our knowledge is more rudimentary."

"Yes, but how does the sympathetic nerve know whether to exert its effect?"

The woman is greedy for information, and Claude is happy to satisfy her:

"There are heat-sensitive nerves which conduct impulses back to nerve centres in the spinal cord and brain, which then correspondingly vary the sympathetic nerve activity. It is in fact just another type of reflex."

The rest of the audience has now had time to digest Claude's thoughts and there is a veritable sea of hands waving in the air. A male voice to his left asks:

"What about the water content of the blood – indeed of the whole body? One assumes that this too must be kept constant."

Claude smiles. That was the sort of question that gave him so much pleasure.

"A totally valid assumption. The concentration of any chemical within the bloodstream logically depends on two things: firstly the actual quantity of that chemical that is present; and secondly the volume of water within which it is dissolved. If there is indeed an ideal concentration for each substance in the blood, then there should also be a mechanism within the body that dictates to our brain when we must drink and when we must stop drinking. I reason that without such a mechanism the concentration of those constituents would be much too unstable for the good of the body. Presumably a parallel mechanism ensures that a relevant message is sent to the kidneys instructing them whether they should retain water or allow it to pass out in the form of urine."

Claude hesitates briefly. "You might well ask if that message is conveyed by a chemical agent or a nerve impulse? I don't know: it could even be a combination of the two. If I were called upon to design a system capable of withstanding the 'hostile environment' within which the animal kingdom lives, I would definitely consider that something as fundamental as the body's fluid control should not be entrusted to a single mechanism!"

A buzz of whispers is rippling through the audience; a sign, now so familiar to Claude that his ideas had reached their target. It was now time to bring the discussion to an end:

"I trust that you have found my observations and theories of interest." He says. "Much still needs to be done to explore and confirm these ideas. This work is important, because you will now appreciate just how difficult it is for doctors to understand illness; to conceive treatments for disease until they know how the normal body functions – its physiology."

He looks at his watch.

"I regret that we must terminate our discussion there, *Mesdames et Messieurs*. I do thank you all for your attention – and for your interesting comments and questions."

As a single body the audience, nodding and smiling with obvious approval, rises to its feet and applauds loudly. Claude blushes, bows and leaves the lecture theatre with that acknowledgement ringing in his ears. Somewhat later, he is on the point of leaving his laboratory with bulging satchels under each arm, when Tripier asks:

"I hope you won't mind, Professor if I comment that this afternoon's lecture was the best I have ever heard – anywhere and by anybody."

"I am flattered but a little surprised to hear you say that Auguste. On what do you base such a generous compliment?"

Tripier is silent for a few moments, looking above Claude's head as if the ceiling would tell him how to reply to his master:

"Normally you use facts and figures in your lectures to very precisely support your conclusions and hypotheses. It's always very convincing, too. That wasn't apparent today, and might have been a negative point. Yet you showed how logic and intuition lead to hypotheses. If I had the resources, I would this very evening start researching the areas upon which you touched. Indeed, I am sure that there were some present who will do exactly that!"

"Sadly, not all subjects lend themselves to that sort of analysis and presentation, Auguste. Many people also prefer to hear facts and firm recommendations. I find that getting the balance right is quite difficult, but I truly appreciate what you are saying."

Claude smiles, shakes Tripier's hand warmly and leaves the *Collège*, his head held high.

The children had not yet returned from their school, and Fanny and Claude are facing each other across a bare kitchen table.

"Fanny, I will come straight to the point. I have decided that it would be best for my work, my health and my peace of mind if I spend some time away from you. I am not going to justify what I am doing – we have amply discussed our difficulties. Perhaps that way you too will feel less threatened by my activities."

"So you are leaving me to fend for myself."

"Not permanently, I would hope."

"Where will you live?"

"For the moment – and now that it is summer – I will use the peace and quiet of St Julien both to write and to do my experiments. I will spend little time in Paris and when I need to be here Casimir will accommodate me. Beyond that I have no plans at the moment."

"And our children?"

"You may wish them to have a summer holiday with me in the Beaujolais which of course would …"

"…in your grand new mansion of course!"

"Well, it would certainly give me and my family much pleasure: it must be all of three years since my mother has seen them. I also trust that I may come and see them here from time to time?"

As he is speaking, Fanny's face becomes deeply etched and furrowed. She does not reply to his last question. After some minutes of uneasy silence, he leaves the table: perhaps there is indeed nothing more to be said. Back in his study, he throws some books and papers into a satchel and in his bedroom he fills a small case with clothes. Quietly, he leaves the apartment, head and heart overflowing with countless mixed emotions.

CHAPTER 13

A NEW WAY OF LIFE

Wine had blessed France both with prosperity and a certain romance; but like humans, vines become ill. Frosts may ravage them if they are grown too close to the ground, while winds batter those which are too tall. Yet illness is not just climatic. Again as in man, infection creates the biggest threat to the life of the vine – and then the livelihood of the winemaker. In the early 1850's, the *oïdium* fungus had spread through vineyards the length and breadth of the country. Sulphur was found to be both curative and preventive – but another disease, phylloxera had yet to rear its ugly head! Louis Pasteur's contribution to winemaking had begun with his discovery that fermentation was triggered by yeasts, and not by the *vitalisme* that so conveniently explained the un-explainable. It was also Pasteur who had found that bacterial growth interfered with the action of these yeasts and so accounted for the disastrous variability in taste and alcoholic content of both wine and beer. It was that discovery which had now earned him his award from the *Académie des Sciences*.

In the Beaujolais meanwhile, Claude has no cause for complaint. Shortly after his arrival, the formalities of buying the manor house are completed and he moves into it from the adjoining cottage of his birth. He again tries to convince his mother that it would be sensible for her to join him – but fails. He also needs a maid and housekeeper, and a certain Madame Josephine who lives nearby with her husband Jean-Pierre and their son seem ideal for the job. She is happy to stay in a room just off the upper corridor whenever Claude is in residence. Claude also makes sure that she devotes some time to helping his mother.

As with his family's vineyards, Claude ensures that his new acquisition of vines have been treated with sulphur. He feels able to leave the further welfare of the vines to Morel and his family: the nine hectares would enable him to generate a good additional income. His almost daily meanderings through the vines have now diminished to a weekly walk at random between well-tended plants now heavy with fruit, allowing his mind to turn to more immediate and pressing matters.

He has gradually developed a rhythm to his life to suit his head – and his abdomen; his pains have gradually subsided after only two weeks in the Beaujolais. He spends the mornings diligently applying himself to experiments and a little writing. For the latter he uses one ground-floor room as his study; bare except for a set of bookshelves, a table and a chair. From here, he can cast sidelong glances at a lawn – which he has decided to cultivate as a bowling green – and beyond this to some magnificent yew trees which are in full leaf.

An upstairs room next to that of the maid Josephine is ideal for his experiments; easily accessed from the main house. It already houses a dissecting table that he had constructed himself: facing it, a bench where he would in due course set up his microscope with its supporting paraphernalia. Downstairs there is a shed in which he can house animals; initially field mice that he will catch with a series of ingenious traps. In Villefranche, he now purchases a range of chemicals and equipment for the laboratory, using the horse and trap that Lombard had thrown in with the sale of the house. He also visits his friend Ronne. He duly admires the recent modifications to his pharmacy on the *rue Nationale* and invites him to St Julien for the following weekend.

Claude's first task is to solve Pasteur's dilemma: is it germs or oxygen that creates putrefaction of animal tissue? He brought with him the special glass tubes that he had made and used several years earlier in Paris for his sugar-and-gelatin experiments. Each tube has a short section surrounded by a ceramic cylinder which could be heated to a very high temperature by a small oil-fired furnace through which the tube passed.

He sets up six flasks containing pieces of this muscle tissue taken from a readily-available field mouse. To the mouth of each flask, he attaches one of his specially modified tubes that conduct air to and from the exterior. In the three flasks whose inflowing air has been conducted through heated tubes the tissue is little changed after two days. In the three whose air had been conducted through unheated tubes the tissue has undergone marked putrefaction. The nauseating smell is ample proof, but Claude also studies the deranged muscle cells under his microscope.

The results are clear: he wastes no time in writing to Pasteur. It is not oxygen that allows putrefaction to occur, but – he presumes – germs derived from the air. Claude mentions in his letter that he will not be in Paris before October, but will be delighted to hear in return from his colleague about what had transpired with his "bent-tube" experiments.

He now finds himself dreaming, unaware of time and place; only an empty feeling in his stomach reminding him how much time had elapsed. The words of Tripier resound in his ears, and he realizes that it is time for him to commit to paper the principles of his research that have provided him with so many useful answers. He would like to begin immediately, yet he would need all his notebooks and for that he would have to wait until he returned to Paris.

The next day the sun is shining out of a deep blue sky more appropriate to the Mediterranean coast. Ronne arrives in the morning in a smart trap drawn by a handsome horse with a long mane. After a long walk, and an excellent lunch prepared by Josephine for which they had been joined by Claude's mother, the two old friends are now alone in the garden in front of the house enjoying the late summer warmth. Ronne's face is unusually serious.

"It can't be easy, Claude."

"I'm not sure what you are referring to."

"Your family matters, of course. You are married – but it would appear only in name. The fact that Fanny is manipulating your daughters against you must make you feel awful. What are you going to do?"

"I wish I knew. In Paris the sadness of it plagues me constantly. But here…" He gestures nonchalantly towards the house and vineyards, "…I somehow find it easier to distance myself from my difficulties. I am amongst my vines, the fresh air and with my country folk – people with whom I still have much affinity. I can simply please myself. Perhaps I should have become a village doctor after all – and made my parents happy in the process!"

Claude pauses for breath.

"You know Ronne, much of what I do in Paris is obligation towards completing what I have already begun; a sort of a treadmill really. Dealing with the administration of the *Collège* and the Sorbonne is also not easy. A year ago I was promised money to enlarge my laboratory – a so-called direct grant from the Emperor. First, the money did not come because the treasury claimed they needed it for the new *Opéra*. Then it got as far as the *Collège*, who delayed, on the basis that they needed the money urgently for essential repairs to the roof. So what can I do? Write to the Emperor?"

"That's sad. I don't see how you can give of your best."

"Exactly! I just bury myself even more in my work in my little dungeon that they call a laboratory. I hardly go to the theatre now, and visiting the *salons* to see the latest paintings is a thing of the past. My social life in Paris – such as it is – consists of attending formal dinners that give me indigestion, while I sit next to people who either bore or irritate me. I feel closer to my *garçon de laboratoire*, Lesage than almost anybody else."

They both sit in silence for some minutes.

"To answer your question though; I guess that I will continue to press Fanny into having a legal separation, but I think I wrote to you that she consistently rejects the idea. By the way, do you remember what I said to you all those years ago about women and me?"

Ronne nods slowly. "Only too well, Claude, and it doesn't make me any happier to hear you remind me of it now. Most of us need a woman to balance and give meaning to our life."

The early evening chill dictates that they return to the house. Claude proudly shows his friend his newly equipped laboratory and his study. Ronne's attention is drawn to a book on the table with the title *Handbuch der Chirurgischen Operationslehre mit Einschluss der Chirurgischen Anatomie und Instrumentlehre*. The authors' names, *C. Bernard* and *Ch. Huette* are engraved on the cover.

"That title is quite a mouthful, isn't it? I didn't even know that you could speak German."

"I can't write, speak or read German – at the moment, at least. That's a recent translation from the book that Charles Huette and I published years ago when I was unemployable! I am now using it to try and teach myself German…"

He points to an open notebook lying next to the thick volume. Ronne sees various German phrases with their French counterparts neatly entered side by side.

"...but unfortunately I don't seem to have a good sense for languages. I'm not finding it at all easy. By the way, I was only reponsible for the dissections used for its illustrations. The publishers only added my name to the authorship in later editions, when they realised that my name might help them to sell more copies!"

"What are you writing at the moment then?"

"I am planning something that blends the principles of research with my scientific philosophy. I'm sure you know that saying – that a pygmy sitting on the shoulders of a giant can see further than the giant himself."

Ronne nods, smiling.

"Well, I have this notion; that my role in research is to create bridges that other researchers can cross – and which enable them to explore further and deeper into unknown territory. To be durable and reliable, those bridges have to have strong foundations; in other words, one has to perform research according to indestructible principles. I have in mind a title something like *Principles of Experimental Medicine*. I'm going to describe my successes in solving scientific problems – and all my errors, too, which are probably even more instructive!"

"Interesting, Claude; I look forward to seeing it in print!"

Later that day the two friends part company, and Claude promises to visit Ronne and his family in Villefranche on his way back to Paris if time permits.

Claude's lecture series on experimental pathology at the *Collège* had gone well. He had expanded his ideas on the importance of the *milieu intérieur*, and was pleased about the audiences' reception of his ideas. He had made careful distinction between what was known and what still remained to be proven and could sense the excitement that he had thereby managed to create. There had been a good response in the form of questions from the audience, which he always found re-assuring. Between lectures, he had been able to perform some long overdue experiments with Tripier on artificially altering blood temperature to see how it affected nerve function: he would soon be able to present that work to the *Académie*. Many of his colleagues had heard of his indisposition and had shown concern for his welfare, especially since he appeared to have lost weight in the six months since his last attendance. He had received many invitations to dine with them, from most of which he excused himself. However, he does not wish to miss the weekly dining club arranged by an ex-colleague, Dr Jean Bouley; like Claude, he had wide-ranging interests that extended to literature and art.

At one such dinner, he finds himself sitting next to Edward About, author, playwright and journalist. He had achieved some notoriety because of his irreverent attitudes to the establishment and his whimsical *reportage*. They are discussing the exciting evolution of art and science that they were all witnessing.

"Wouldn't it be wonderful," About announces to the gathering, "if every now and then one could hibernate like a squirrel – but for as long as a decade – and so extend one's life! Imagine the wonders of seeing how our artistic and scientific world was evolving over a couple of centuries."

"Not so impossible, really." offers Claude. "If you believe Darwin, we have primitive ancestors that can do just that!"

Ten pairs of eyes swivel towards Claude.

"Go to any pond and you can find amongst the weeds little creatures no more than one millimeter in size, complete with digestive system, a primitive brain and even fins. Some are called rotifers, some tardigrades. One can dehydrate these little fellows quite easily and thereby suspend their life. Months or years later one can simply bring them back to life by rehydrating them."

"But for how long can you continue doing that?"

The question comes from the artist Paul Chenavard.

"I don't know; possibly for hundreds of years. One can also freeze them and restore their life thereafter by thawing. Actually rotifers were one of the first living things that van Leewenhoek saw through his microscope one hundred and fifty years ago."

There is complete silence around the table for a few moments as the group digests Claude's revelation.

"What a wonderful theme for my next book!" exclaims About. "I can't wait to get started."

He leaps from his chair as if to leave, amid much laughter from the other guests.

Claude's personal life is not proceeding along such humorous lines. He feels very restricted living with the Davaine family, despite their warmth and generosity. At Georgina's pleading, he visits *rue de Mogador* to see Fanny soon after he returns to Paris. The children are at school, and the severe expression on Fanny's face promises to make any discussion difficult.

"Of course I see the difficulty which you have in accepting my research. Georgina partly shares your views and has helped me understand why you so object to my work with animals."

"But it is not just that. I feel used, as if I am just a housekeeper. I carry all the decisions and responsibilities in this house. You don't even seem to hear if I mention one of the children's difficulties or my annoyance with the stove that refuses to work. Your head is always somewhere else. And how do you think Tony and Marie feel if you never volunteer to walk or play with them – or show any interest in their activities?"

There is silence as Claude absorbs these recriminations, which he has to admit are completely valid. He cannot think of a suitable reply and chooses to sidestep the issue.

"There is something which you need to know, Fanny. The animal experiments that I now need to do personally are few in number. I have reached the stage in my career, where I can better serve science by describing the principles by which I do research and reach conclusions."

The stern lines around Fanny's mouth soften somewhat while he is speaking, encouraging him to continue:

"I have actually started on this writing project and it is going to be my main objective while I spend time in St Julien…"

"And that's another thing. Why do you have to spend so much time there rather than here in Paris – with us? What sort of a message do you think that sends to your children – or what's left of our friends?"

"With respect Fanny, the anti-vivisection meetings which you hold in our home also send a unfortunate message to our friends; nor do they improve my relationship with the children. I cannot forbid you to pursue your beliefs, particularly since you appear to base them on your religious principles. However, I would hope that you would honour my self-respect by not having any further meetings here. As far as St Julien is concerned, you have to understand that I am not well. Perhaps it is just the absence of responsibility that helps me – or the air of the Beaujolais, but I do feel well there. I have to tell you that my abdominal pains have returned in the last week or so, and both Pierre and Casi have insisted that I leave for St Julien again as soon as possible."

Fanny raises her arms and lets them fall despondently on her lap. She shakes her head and gazes out of the kitchen window towards the building that faced theirs across *rue Mogador*. Claude continues:

"You know, it is really very lovely now in St Julien with our larger house. I would really like you to join me there during the summer; it would do you and the children so much good. I know that you do not get along with my mother, but we are now quite separate from her; not cramped like we were last time. It would give her such pleasure to see her grandchildren, too. Perhaps I can move back with you after the summer and we can give our marriage a further chance."

They look at each other across the kitchen table with bland expressions on their faces; neither of them convinced by his optimism.

"I'll think about it. In the meantime, please do try and find time to spend with the children."

Claude had little confidence that a return of their relationship would be anything other than superficial and temporary. As he walks down the stairs from their apartment, he can only regret the fact of his marriage – for himself, for Fanny and not least for his children. Yet, what would have been his alternatives?

Pasteur had earlier sent Claude the detailed results of his experiments. He had found that he could prevent putrefaction in the flasks both with his 'bent-tube' studies and his version of Claude's heating technique. He is now sitting opposite Claude, as he had done six months earlier; this time a smile was creasing his usually serious face.

"I do so appreciate how you have helped me to examine the nature of putrefaction, Claude. And may I congratulate you; I heard last week of your recent election to the *Académie de Médecine*?"

"Thank you Louis. Strange it may be, but I feel very little elation at joining that elitist society. Why are physicians often so smug – so full of themselves – as if they have yet again achieved some magnificent cure in one of their patients? Don't they know that their patients are probably recovering despite, rather than because of their treatment?"

Pasteur laughs at Claude's cynicism: being a laboratory chemist, he had little insight into the limitations of medical treatment. Now that his research was becoming more medically orientated, he wonders if he should be spending some of his time doing rounds with a physician on the hospital wards – as he knew to be Claude's custom.

"Forgive my ignorance, but is treatment still so rudimentary, then?"

"Certainly! As I say to my students, until we have full knowledge of physiology we will probably not make much headway. On the matter of our results, Louis, the fact that both sets of experiments implied an airborne agent in the causation of putrefaction certainly seems to put yet another nail in the coffin of 'spontaneous generation'. A communication to the *Académie* is surely your next step. Yet I suspect that we are still quite far from the end of the story."

"I agree; Pouchet does not give up easily. He is now planning a trip to the top of a volcano – Etna I believe – where he presumes there are no germs; he will repeat his experiments there, hoping of course that putrefaction still occurs! I actually thought of doing the same thing – perhaps on a glacier just to show that he is wrong!"

Claude shakes his head disbelievingly, convinced that challenge and counter-challenge will continue for some time. Important as it is to demolish the two-thousand year concept of spontaneous generation he is disinclined to participate further in either tedious debate or experiment.

"You know Louis, ever since I got those first results which confirmed germs in the air, I've been thinking about other implications of our heating experiments. I am sure that the effect of heat on germs needs to be investigated further. I have been attending Trousseau's rounds at the *Hôtel Dieu* since Pierre Rayer has been ill. There are so many cases of severe and dehydrating diarrhea that come into the wards. And not just the occasional case of cholera either."

"I'm surprised that you still get the time to go to the wards."

"It is not always easy; but so important. It stimulates my ideas. I even sometimes have a suggestion to offer; physiology and pathology are not so far apart, you know! When I see all those cases of diarrhoea in the wards I find it hard to escape my suspicion that food might be a major carrier of germs. So, if heat can kill germs in the air, then why not use heat also to improve the safety of food?"

"Using heat to protect food isn't new, Claude. Joblot and Spallanzani showed more than one hundred years ago that boiling could preserve food longer, and Appert got his twelve thousand franc prize in 1810 for showing just how long his heating-and-bottling procedure could preserve food for Napoleon's army!"

"Yet fifty years have gone by since then, and what has been achieved? You have already shown that it is germs that damage the all-important yeast that ferments wine and beer. So perhaps heating wine and beer at some stage of the process might solve that problem; that is, if it does not affect the taste! You might become France's big hero!"

"Yes: we could even test that idea in our vineyards."

Claude smiles knowingly.

"As far as I know, we haven't had too much of a problem with that in the Beaujolais – at least for the moment; but you could perhaps look at milk. From the health point of view it's possibly more important than wine."

Pasteur looks at him quizzically, but remains silent, allowing his friend to develop his idea:

"Just think of the conditions under which cows are kept – and the way that milk is handled. We already know that illnesses can pass between animals and from animals to man. I am convinced that milk is a major carrier of disease – and yet it is potentially such a valuable food. Perhaps a heat process applied to milk may render a great service to nutrition."

"If only we knew a little more about the relationship of germs to disease processes we could have more to go on."

Claude has a reply for that, too.

"I think we have quite a lot. You showed a couple of years ago that germs in milk generate lactic acid, which in turn sours its taste. Your 'friend' Pouchet recently identified the *vibrio* that causes cholera. It's certainly to be found in water contaminated with sewage, but it might also be present in milk. I would guess that we will also discover one day that the typhoid germ is carried in milk; and perhaps even the tuberculosis germ. Personally, I never touch milk, and there must be many like me who are deprived of its valuable nutrition for fear of contracting illness."

"But if milk carries harmful germs, the relationship between milk and disease would surely be more obvious."

"Not necessarily, Louis. I remember my *patron* in Lyon telling me, even thirty years ago, that cholera was much more common in the badly nourished. I also wonder if a tendency to certain infections may be hereditary. Those factors might well explain why people have such difficulty in connecting the cause of a disease with its development."

Pasteur is now sitting bolt upright.

"You have given me a great deal to think about. I know you are very busy with your research and lectures, but would it be presumptuous to suggest that you might work with me if I experimented in that area – perhaps first with wine?"

"I am leaving for the Beaujolais shortly but if you would like to do some initial experiments and keep me in touch with your findings, I would be delighted."

The two men part with a firm handshake. Pasteur is beaming at Claude with a mixture of admiration, gratitude and deep affection.

"I have to tell you that I have some concerns about Louis."

Claude had spent the latter part of the afternoon at Berthelot's laboratory where they had just finished discussing an idea about how they might synthesize glycogen. Claude hopes that his friend might pursue the project while he is in St Julien.

"In what way, Marcel?"

"I suppose he is sound enough in his techniques here in the laboratory, but he seems to get an idea, and then desperately needs to support it even if the facts tell him otherwise."

"You are not suggesting dishonesty?"

"Not quite, but take this matter of fermentation. We know and accept that living yeasts ferment sugar – and so on. Of course we must give Louis credit for that important finding. Yet based on our own, dare I say solid experiments, we suggested that soluble extracts of these yeasts also ferment under certain conditions – and that living yeasts are not necessary for fermentation. Yet without reason or experimental proof to the contrary, he simply opposes this – and so loudly. I heard him at the *Académie* recently. He projects his ideas so well that he can readily convince the audience that his ideas are correct – even without factual support!"

"I know what you mean. In the early 1850's he actually supported the concept of spontaneous generation – until something clearly swung his opinion. He is now almost obsessed with the need to denounce the concept! I often wish that I had his powers of rhetoric: he is a fine speaker – and a good publicist – which certainly helps in this day and age!"

Berthelot's brow is deeply furrowed:

"What also irks me is that he knowingly accepted a prestigious appointment at the *École* – knowing full well that there were little or no laboratory facilities there. He then accepted what I thought was my quite generous offer of space for his research. Now, he is challenging my work and my conclusions on fermentation under my very nose – and publicly as well! Am I just being too sensitive?"

"So understandable Marcel, but he did tell me recently that he hopes to soon have some unused attic space at the *École* converted to a small laboratory. He has also written personally to the Emperor asking for financial support for his research – which he well deserves. It will be interesting to see what response he gets!"

Claude suddenly looks disturbed; his face flushed with suppressed anger:

"Speaking of laboratory space, Marcel, you may remember that after I was in Compiègne, the Emperor granted the *Collège* money to improve *my* laboratory. That money is still being used by the *Collège* for other purposes. When I challenge them, all they can say is that they will 'look into it'."

Berthelot takes Claude gently by the elbow:

"Of course: there may be a reason. Had you considered that some of our colleagues may be very envious of your success. To your face they are kind, but behind your back, they may be up to all sorts of mischief. But, let me tell you something good for a change. Do you remember that earlier this year we were at one of Jean Bouley's dinners, and you told us all about your little rotifers?"

"Certainly. Edmond About got quite excited about them."

"Well, I happened to see him yesterday at the *Café Boroni*. His new book called *The Man with the Broken Ear* has just been accepted for publication by Hachette. If I understood him correctly, the story concerns a French colonel who falls into a frozen ditch during Napoleon's Russian campaign. A mad scientist who has worked with rotifers and tardigrades decides to dessicate the officer to one-third of his usual weight, and keeps him in this semi-frozen, dehydrated state for fifty years. He then reverses the process, whereupon the soldier promptly sits up and declares: *Vive l'Empéreur!*"

Claude bursts into laughter:

"There you are Marcel, next time I see the Princesse Mathilde, I will be able to give her another example of how generously science supports the arts!"

Berthelot looks at him, puzzled.

Tripier had left a number of newly arrived letters on his master's desk at the *Collège*. One was from Claude's old student Willi Kühne, inviting him to Heidelberg to give a lecture, another from Constantin James. The final letter was on fine yellow paper and in an envelope sealed with red wax.

rue de Courcelles, Paris, July 14, 1861

Dear Monsieur Bernard (or do you prefer Professor?)

I feel remiss in not having written to you before this. I so enjoyed meeting you at Compiègne – was it really eighteen months ago? Of course I had the pleasure of meeting your wife shortly afterwards, but it was Hector Berlioz who graced my salon last month and reminded me that I have neglected you – and my promise to invite you. Hector tells me that you are doing wonderful things for science: I do believe that he sometimes regrets his own dismissal of his father's wish that he should complete his medical studies! And so it would indeed give me pleasure to welcome you here for tea on August 8th at 4.00 p.m.

I do so hope you can join us, and with sincere good wishes

Mathilde

Claude smiles to himself. He would have liked to accept, were it not for the fact that he would be in St Julien at the time; a return trip to Paris just for that event would be just too extravagant. He immediately pens a letter to Princess Mathilde emphasizing how keen he would be to come on another occasion, perhaps in late autumn. He could not resist adding the anecdote concerning About's new book.

On a particularly hot day towards the end of July, he visits *rue de Mogador*. He had asked Fanny for a date on which the children were likely to be at home. Claude decides to walk from the Davaine's house and as he crosses Paris his route is deviated by road closures and vast *chantiers* operated by hundreds of workers; ever-present evidence of Haussman's vigorous restructuring of the city. Accordingly he arrives late, and as he approaches the apartment he feels the familiar knot tightening in his stomach. He need not have worried. Perhaps Tony and Marie had been charged with the need to be gracious to their father; certainly, Fanny is politeness personified. Claude is struck by how the girls have grown. Tony, at age fourteen is quite the young woman in a swirling skirt and tight bodice, while an immaculately-coiffured Marie-Louise sits obediently by her side, hands folded neatly in her lap. After initial pleasantries, the conversation becomes rather stilted and Claude feels perspiration breaking out on his forehead as he carefully chooses his words:

"As I said in my letter, I can't say how much pleasure it would give me if you would all join me in St Julien at the end of August. Indeed if the girls wished, they might like to stay and help with the harvest: they could enjoy meeting others of their generation from nearby families."

Tony and Marie look at each other with obvious displeasure at this last suggestion. Fanny's response is both prompt and surprising:

"We have discussed it Claude, and would like to come, on condition that you do not expect us to follow you in your daily pursuits. You have a carriage, I presume?"

"Indeed; and a fine mare to draw it, too. Josephine's husband sometimes helps me with errands and I am sure would be only too pleased to take you about the area; even down to Villefranche where there is a quite wonderful patisserie – still owned by the same family that I knew when I was the girls' age."

The most difficult step was yet to come, and Claude hesitates:

"As you know, I found it necessary to distance myself from you for a period. Perhaps it was as important for you as it was to me that we were apart for these months. There were parts of our lives that did not then fit together. I would like to think that time has helped to soften our differences. I would very much like to return here afterwards."

There is no reaction – no response whatever to his proposal. After a few moments during which Fanny and the children avoid his eyes he adds:

"Well, I don't expect that any of us can make a decision about that right now, but I am delighted that you will come to St Julien. We can discuss it all again there."

Claude takes Fanny aside to discuss some financial matters and then leaves with the feeling that at least he had achieved something. How pleased his mother would be to see her grandchildren! He is actually relieved that Fanny and the children would follow their own program while in St Julien: he had some ideas that he wanted to pursue on the parallels between animal and vegetable life. He also wanted to begin work on his book; the first publication that would examine the principles, the methodology and the philosophy of the science to which he had dedicated his life.

There was only one thing that he had to do before leaving.

Pierre Rayer was looking better than he had expected. On his last visit, his fleshy jowls were drooping badly, his appearance that of a sad bulldog. Neither Davaine nor Andral could identify a cause for the loss of appetite, weight loss and fatigue.

"I expect to be back at work next month Claude, but I trust that you will be away by then."

"Certainly. I still get my abdominal symptoms, but I hope that the summer break will do the usual for me. I have to say that I would welcome a longer absence, but I am afraid that neither the *Collège* nor the Sorbonne would be happy about it. You cannot imagine how much better I feel away from Paris."

There is silence for a while. Rayer scrutinizes Claude's face as if he is looking for something that he had previously overlooked. His heavy lids are blinking slowly.

"I will speak with Casimir, Claude – and then perhaps have a word to the council of both institutions, now that I am back on my feet. I have to say that your young man, Tripier seems to get on with things even in your absence...", and as an afterthought, "...and you too are most productive when you are in the Beaujolais. Perhaps it is the wine which inspires you!"

"You're most kind, Pierre"

Claude is delighted that Rayer is regaining his positive spirit and good humour. Tripier had indeed been an enormous help to Claude. The *Collège* had already agreed to him providing lecture-demonstrations in Claude's absence; in return, Claude is now permitting him to undertake some of his own experiments on electrical stimulation of different tissues; an idea which Tripier had adopted from their studies on nerve function.

"By the way, I thought you would be pleased to hear that Fanny and the children are joining me for a couple of weeks during the summer; we're going to try to make amends. I may even move back to *rue de Mogador.*"

"You've really made my day now." Rayer replies. "Be off with you, and let this old man have his afternoon rest!"

The seeds for his truce with Fanny had been sown during the two weeks during which she and the two children were with him in St Julien. As Fanny had requested, he had initially left his family to find their own way around the area. Yet lacking local knowledge, they finally accept his offer to show them the surroundings. They also visit Villefranche where Ronne and Marianne received them very warmly. Their children had established a rapport of sorts with Tony and Marie, and together they indulged in much unhealthy eating at the wonderful patisserie of Monsieur Malonet in the *rue Nationale*.

Claude is not able to persuade his daughters to help with the harvest. However, Fanny declares herself interested in the winemaking process and Morel enthusiastically explains to her the use of the many tools and devices – aided by some tasting of the previous year's product. Of course, Claude's writing lapses for the three weeks of their eventual stay, but he feels that his participation in the family activities is the better option. Fanny avoids visiting her mother-in-law at the cottage, but is courteous enough when Madame Bernard, milder and more good-natured than ever, joins them for the occasional meal in the new house. In September, when Fanny and the girls leave St Julien again for Paris, their parting from Madame Bernard is remarkably warm.

Mostly alone during the winter, Claude had the joy of a one-week visit from Davaine who could only marvel at how well and relaxed Claude seemed to be. Pierre Rayer also visits him, to Claude's delight confirming that both the *Collège* and the Sorbonne had agreed to his extended absence. Josephine cooks some fine meals for them; in return, Pierre invites him for an exquisite meal in a neighbouring village from which they return in the highest of spirits. Claude's sister Caroline, her husband Jean and their daughter Jeanne visit from Pouilly-le-Monial on two occasions. In that relaxed atmosphere, Claude establishes a particularly close relationship with his niece Jeanne: highly spirited, intelligent and with a curiosity that really appeals to him. Claude concludes his stay by compiling detailed accounts relating to the expenses of his buildings and vineyards; pleased that the receipts from the sale of his excellent wine comfortably exceed all his costs.

CHAPTER 14

MOST COMPLEX EMOTIONS

How Paris had changed during his six month absence! Construction of Haussman's new *grands boulevards* was well underway, with a new complex of drains beneath. Above ground, there were more of the new shiny omnibuses, attracting visitors and an expanding population to the smart shops, *cafés* and restaurants that flanked the broad avenues. Prompted by the Emperor's insistence on adopting the 'London model', Claude finds two new squares in the process of construction. Even more were to come. The *orangerie* had sprung up in the Tuileries and the *Parc Monceau* had been completely replanted. Three new theatres had been completed and work had begun in earnest on Garnier's opera house, the structure of which was now well above ground level.

Claude is again living with his family in *rue de Mogador*. Despite some initial awkwardness, modest harmony had been re-established. Claude had read an enthusiastic review of one of Molière's plays in which the new star Sarah Bernhardt was playing the leading role. Fanny had somewhat hesitatingly agreed to see it with Claude, but seemed to derive little pleasure from the experience.

"I'm truly proud of the way that you carried on in my absence."
"Thank you, but I do have some problems to tell you about; and some questions."

On the first day of his return to the *Collège*, Tripier had joined Claude in his room, and for the whole afternoon they discuss the happenings at the *Collège* during his absence.

"You will not be very pleased to hear that having received the approval to enlarge the laboratory, about which I believe I wrote to you...."

Claude nods.

"...the *Collège* has at the last minute again decided to withhold your money because, they say, your health problems may yet prevent you from being able to use it."

Claude's face becomes white with fury. Tripier had never seen him like this before:

"That's madness. Rayer and Davaine both consider the terrible conditions in our laboratory to be a *cause* of my illness; as indeed I am sure it was for Magendie."

"I am sorry: I know how much this means to you."

There is silence for a minute or so during which Claude gradually regains his composure, so that Tripier feels safe to continue:

"But I did manage to complete a whole series of electrical stimulation experiments; both on the spinal nerves as well as on the salivary glands. But perhaps it is best if we deal with those results later this week?"

"There's certainly no hurry Auguste, and I do look forward to hearing about them. Tell me about the lectures you gave. Were they well-received?"

"I tried to emulate your style of course, and perhaps the most successful presentation was one on spinal nerve reflexes. Following that talk, a man – whose name I do not recall – asked me a very interesting question about electrical stimulation of whole organs. I had no answer, but over the last few weeks I have researched the literature in this area and I indeed found rather little on the subject."

"You are quite right; there's much to be discovered."

"I was thinking that when I finish my attachment with you in a year's time, I might pursue that idea – even in the human clinical situation."

After all, if I use low voltage stimulation there is not likely to be much hazard involved..." He hesitates briefly. "...because of course I do know how you feel about human experimentation."

Claude nods and wonders – and not for the first time – whether he had deprived himself of useful results by his tight adherence to this principle? Of course it was too late to change his tune; he could hardly retreat from the powerful arguments that he had voiced in countless lectures. Yet...

"What organs had you considered looking at?"

"It seems as if it would be best to choose those which are reasonably accessible; perhaps approaching the prostate via the rectum and the female pelvic organs through the vagina. Complaints in those organs seem to be common enough and most of them are at present not very amenable to treatment."

Claude is shaking his head, troubled by Tripier's rather impulsive approach to human research.

"It sounds rather vague and empirical, if I may say so? Have you a theory; a hypothesis?"

"I have put together a few ideas which I would like to show you – when you have a moment, of course."

"Had you perhaps considered doing some formal training in that area of practice, at the same time; I should be able to introduce you to one of the relevant surgeons."

"That's most kind."

"Now that I think about it, Auguste I wonder if there is an electrophysiological aspect to childbirth; it could be a fertile area of research – if you forgive my pun."

They both laugh.

Claude's next appointment is with one of his 'pupils'; a young man called Paul Bert whom he had first met when examining him for his degree in Natural Sciences in '60. He had then so impressively presented his comparisons of the anatomy of monkey and man that Claude had offered him a place in his laboratory during the last three years of his medical studies – which he had just completed. They are now discussing his doctoral thesis – about vital properties of tissues and the possibility of transplanting them. Claude is pleased by just how well Bert had drawn together the conclusions of his different experiments. He feels sure that unless he had an unexpected problem with his *viva voce* the Sorbonne would approve his thesis. Claude also knows that Bert is hoping to become his *préparateur* when Tripier finishes his 'tour of duty'.

He had done quite enough for his first day back at the *collège* – and was still smarting from the news of his laboratory finance. While in St Julien, he had decided that he would leave the *collège* early each evening whenever possible: getting home earlier would give him a chance to develop a warmer relationship with his daughters. On his arrival home however, he discovers that they are embroiled in preparation for some examinations and do not at all welcome his intrusion. He enquires after Fanny's activities of the day; an abrupt reply prevents any further dialogue. He wonders whether she might have attended yet another meeting of her anti-vivisection society.

The following afternoon he is sitting in his room carefully setting out the year's laboratory accounts for the *Collège* treasurer when there is a knock at his door:

"May I introduce myself – Ernest Renan? I hope that I am not disturbing you?"

Claude knew of Renan's recent appointment to the *Collège* as its Professor of Hebrew. At age eighteen, Berthelot had been one of his students at a private college. He had so impressed Renan with his precociously sharp concepts of scientific philosophy that teacher and pupil had become bosom friends. Marcel had mentioned Renan's arrival in a letter to Claude while he was in St Julien.

"Not at all. By all means come in and sit down."

Renan eases himself into a chair and approvingly scans the walls of books which surround them.

"I am doing as Marcel instructed." He begins. "No doubt you have heard that I disgraced myself in my first lecture; the waves of disapproval are beginning to hit the shore and may just swamp me! I am in dire need of a friend!"

Claude smiles at Renan's frankness. He had indeed heard that during the lecture in question, Renan had referred to Jesus as an "incomparable man". Seen as sacrilege by the college elders, his course had been immediately suspended; even dismissal was now a distinct possibility. Two years earlier, when the post had originally become vacant, no lesser person than the Empress Eugénie had blocked Renan's appointment because of his lack of religious education and academic achievement.

It was said that the Emperor himself had more recently interceded in order to make Renan's appointment possible!

"Fear not. What support I can ever give you will be generously offered. But what will you do in the absence of your course?"

"My passion for writing knows no bounds. If the *Collège* decides in its wisdom to strip me of my noble post, I suppose I could survive on my adoring public readership: they seem to thrive on my taste for disrespect and search for truth."

"Truth is hard enough for me to find in science; how you do it in religion and history is beyond my imagination. What are you writing currently?"

"I've given my new book the title of *A Life of Jesus*. Its virtually finished, but in view of the *Collège's* reaction to my lecture I have to say that I am rather apprehensive about ever delivering it to my publisher."

"Would you allow me to read the text? I am ashamed to say that religion occupies precious little of my daily thought. Science challenges belief in so many ways that I am almost scared to introduce religion into an already confusing bag of worms. But perhaps it is time for me to become enlightened."

A big grin spreads over Renan's plump face.

"It would be a pleasure to give you the first section of my book."

He suddenly looks down at his fob watch and springs to his feet:

"For now though you will have to excuse me; the Berthelots are expecting my wife and I for supper. Please let us speak again at some length; one of the main reasons I joined this venerable institution was to rub shoulders with other thinkers; and Marcel has been so full of praise of your work – and your ideas."

He gets up to leave:

"Speaking of ideas, Sainte-Beuve tells me that some years ago – I gather at that horrible place, Compiègne – he gave you an open invitation to join us at one of our dinners. Do come if you can: they are always on the last Friday of the month. I would be most happy to escort you!"

He clasps Claude's right hand warmly between both of his and disappears, the door closing soundlessly behind him. Claude also has an appointment and hurries off in the direction of the *Académie* where Pasteur will be presenting his material for the coveted Alhumbert Prize for '...*work shedding light on the nature of spontaneous generation*'. Claude had been invited to join the judging committee, as its secretary.

Pasteur performs with characteristic fluency and conviction, and no one in the large audience is left in any doubt about the consistency of his findings in relation to putrefaction. He produces sealed containers of blood and urine for the judges to examine. Seeing his detailed results they cannot fail to be convinced that it has to be 'corpuscules' in the atmosphere which provide the source of microbial growth in organic matter. In their absence, no growth is to be seen. Pasteur concludes that there is never a need to invoke spontaneous generation as the cause of putrefaction; his work (he says) provides the 'final blow' to the concept of spontaneous generation. To Claude's embarrassment, he mentions to the judging committee that they can accept the integrity of the experiments since... '...*the eminent physiologist Monsieur Claude Bernard was so obliging as to preside himself over the experiments*'.

At this disclosure, the judges look at Claude quizzically while all that he can do in acknowledgement is to nod. They award the prize to Pasteur. Yet it is sadly no 'final blow': his presentation is only the prelude to many years of ongoing argument and dispute; challenges from his longstanding rival Pouchet, as well as another highly respected chemist by the name of Béchamp.

Far beyond this privileged world of research and academic politics, sinister events are taking place that would determine the fall of Louis Napoleon; the collapse of the Second Empire. The first step is Otto von Bismarck's appointment to Paris as French ambassador. After only a few months in office, he writes to King Wilhelm that: "*...viewed from a distance, it (France) seems very impressive. Close at hand, you realize that it is nothing.*" French art and science may have been at their peak, wooing the rest of Europe, if not the world, but it was clear to Bismarck that the joyous and somewhat dissolute French would be no match for serious Prussian power. Wilhelm promptly recalls Bismarck to be Prussia's Minister-President. Together they quietly plan for a greater German Empire which would take into its bosom the southern German states, Austria to the east – and of course, France to the west.

Claude's autumn visit to St Julien in '62 is briefer than usual. By day, he walks amongst the vines watching the enthusiastic harvesting activity. He attempts to comfort his mother whose advancing age is now creating uncertainty and anxiety in them both. He uses the soft evenings to prepare his winter lectures. In October, he says farewell to his mother with definite misgivings.

Once back in Paris, it is not long before his abdominal symptoms return, sometimes keeping him from attending the *Collège*. Their pattern is becoming crystal clear to Rayer, Davaine – even to Claude himself when he takes the time to think about it! If demands on him are high, or when he is frustrated by events that do not move in the direction that he wishes, his symptoms re-emerge. If he does not immediately distance himself from problematic issues, a second more intensive symptom complex sets in – with vomiting, diarrhoea and extreme lethargy. No medications seem to help. When he is confined to his bed, Fanny helps him with reasonable grace but little heart. The smile with which Agnès brings him his meals and her gentle and almost intimate touch on his shoulder do infinitely more for his well-being. As for Tony and Marie-Louise, they are not to be seen unless he ventures out of his bedroom. Claude tries again to bridge the gap in his relationship with them. Providing he is well enough, he will take them to the *Cirque d'Hiver* later in the month to see an equestrian display that Fanny had seen favourably reviewed in *Le Temps*.

Claude is dreading the departure of Tripier: in his wonderfully methodical way, he had completed the documentation of Claude's lectures. He had also put together their many studies on the great sympathetic nerve so that they were ready for imminent publication. Claude is pleased that he has finally managed to secure for Tripier a training attachment to an eminent surgeon in the new field of gynaecology. Now it is up to him to create his own path into future science. With a great deal of urging, the *Collège* had duly approved his replacement by Paul Bert as *préparateur*, and by April he would be 'in office'.

For two centuries, the *salon* of paintings had been artistic event of the year until Nieuwerkerke, superintendent of *Beaux Arts* at the Louvre and intimate friend of Princess Mathilde had reduced it to a biennial event. This year the jury had rejected no less than fifteen hundred works of art, resulting in a major uproar from the disappointed artists. Their strident appeal against 'injustice' finally reaches the ears of the Emperor – who comes to see for himself. He may have been less dedicated to these matters than his cousin Mathilde, yet he also considered himself to be a true patron of the arts. He now insists on seeing all the rejected works. To make his point he purchases two of them and then instructs

Nieuwerkerke to offer the unsuccessful artists the opportunity of exhibiting in a neighbouring hall of the *Palais de l'Industrie*. Whether through pride or pique, only about half of the rejected artists accept, and the newspapers had recently given varying assessments of the works to be seen in this new *Salon des Refusés*. Late one afternoon Claude decides to see them for himself and sets off to the *Palais*.

For many of the works on show, he can but agree with most of the critics; just more of the same. However his eye is taken by a particular style of painting in the last room he visits; simple representations of everyday rural scenes, people and places. No deep significance, no religious connotations; just simple appeal to the eyes, heart and soul using colour and form. Some had been painted by a man called Millet; others by some artists by the name of Cézanne, Pissarro, Degas and Manet. Camille Corot whom he had met at Compiègne also had two canvases on display. He wonders about Gustave Courbet, whose tent outside the *Exposition Universelle* he had visited in '55. Sure enough, there are several examples; his *realisme* had obviously become a separate entity; now adopted by other artists.

On his way home, he passes his two favourite antiquarian booksellers and enquires – unsuccessfully – for a copy of William Harvey's *De Motu Cordis* for which he had been searching for some time. He finally arrives at the apartment to be met by flaming hostility from Fanny.

"Is it really asking so much for you to remember your responsibilities? Cannot you put some priority towards your family? Today was the last performance at the circus – and just look how nicely the girls dressed for the occasion, too."

"I'm sorry, Fanny; it must have slipped my mind. I was…."

"Don't tell me. A very important meeting with your very important colleagues, was it? Or do your rabbits still need more attention than your daughters?"

Fanny gestures towards Tony and Marie-Louise who indeed are very smartly dressed. The tirade to which he is being exposed seems neverending, and the bitter tears of the girls are now as much due to Fanny's screaming as to their disappointment at being let down by his forgetfulness. He escapes to his study and buries his head in his hands. He feels the familiar tightening in his belly and seconds later vomits into a bowl that stands in the corner of the room.

Never before had he been this ill. Severe abdominal cramps return every hour or so. They were becoming worse too and barely eased by passing thin watery bowel motions. His repeated vomiting had resulted in a painful inflammation in his mouth from regurgitation of little more than acid; he had hardly consumed any food for three days. Each night murderous meaningless nightmares woke him repeatedly. Davaine is again with him.

"You should really be in hospital."

"No offence intended, Casi, but I'd prefer to stay here and fill myself up with opium!"

There is silence while each digests their own thoughts about the situation. Since there was little likelihood that he could change his friend's mind, Davaine decides to change the subject.

"By the way, I want to thank you for giving me your thoughts on those little anthrax rods a few months ago."

"Have you started research in that area again then?"

"Not yet, but you may have heard that there has been an outbreak of anthrax in sheep near Dourdan. The local doctor there, Diard was one of my students a few years ago. He sent me a blood sample from one of the affected animals earlier this week. Sure enough, I again saw those tiny little rods in the blood."

"Fascinating; and what now?"

"Dourdan is less than an hour from here on that new railway line. I thought that I might fetch some more samples from him and try injecting material into other animals – perhaps rats or rabbits. It's one way of finding out if the rods are the cause or the result of anthrax infection."

Davaine duly departs, but returns at dusk with Pierre Rayer. Claude is feeling a little better, and had just managed to consume a bowl of chicken soup prepared with great care by Agnès. After carefully examining Claude's rather distended abdomen it is Rayer who speaks first:

"My best guess is that you have chronic enteritis – even perhaps an aftermath of a mild cholera attack; all of this of course aggravated by your circumstances; your work and your relationship to Fanny. There is only one thing that seems to benefit you; being away from Paris."

"I know; but I can't spend my life in St Julien."

"Certainly not; but we have to take one step at a time. I have this afternoon spoken with the *Collège* and they are prepared to release you from your courses for a whole year. Likewise, Jacquemin at the Sorbonne is in agreement with this approach, providing Paul Bert can give a physiology lecture there from time to time."

"But what about my research then – my pupils?"

"You will have to arrange that with Bert; but it might be a good opportunity for the *Collège* to actually get on with improving the state of your laboratory. There are just too many people squeezed into that unhygienic hole-in-the-ground. I doubt whether there are many prison cells as unhealthy as that!"

"Paul certainly seems competent enough to manage by himself; perhaps it will give him a chance to get on with his own research, and also let the university see what a fine lecturer he is."

Rayer and Davaine looked at each other with smiles of relief.

"That's done then Claude. Let's get you better from this acute episode and then away with you."

Over the next few days, his condition slowly improves. Paul Bert visits him at home, where they map out a plan for the following year; including yet another appeal to the *Collège* to release money for the renovations; and this time supported by an insistent letter from the influential Rayer. It is in mid-August that he finally journeys to St Julien, leaving it open for Fanny and the children to visit him – if they wished to.

The sun is streaming on to his desk; in wonderful silence broken only by the chatter of birds outside his study. Claude's first task is to construct an introduction to what will be his treatise on experimental medicine. It dawns on him that this vast project is the closest he has come to creative writing since the ill-fated *Arthur de Bretagne*. Thirty years of his life and more than one hundred articles, reports and comments had been devoted to discovery. Those were exercises in the annotation of facts; placing them into context with the expanding knowledge of animal biology. Now the time had come to explain to others how his mind worked; exactly how and why he did the experiments that had led him towards his many discoveries; his 'truths' of medical science. Once the introduction is out of the way, he could deal in more detail with the principles and techniques involved – a substantially larger task that would have to wait until he could set aside more time.

Even for the introduction, there is much ground to cover. He would need to explain an important progression: physiology toward pathology, health toward disease. Each was a natural extension of the other. Much of the scientific community was still under the spell of the highly regarded Cuvier, who had claimed (with so many others) that *vitalisme* was a major factor explaining health and disease – life and death; and that it had no physical or chemical explanation. He would therefore need to tackle that vague and totally invalid entity. He decides that his introduction would have three sections: the first would deal with an approach – his approach – to experimental reasoning.

He would begin by emphasizing the importance of the initial observation. What (he will ask the reader) was the difference between an observation and an experiment? When Pascal did his measurement of barometric pressure: first at the foot of the *Tour St Jacques* and then again at the top of the tower, one might say that he had simply made two observations. Nevertheless, the thought behind it, the hypothesis, the comparative nature of the study and the logical conclusion made it a proper 'experiment'. By contrast, Jenner had painstakingly observed a cuckoo through a spyglass – so as not to frighten it. That was a mere observation (Claude would insist) because he had not compared his sighting either with the same cuckoo on another tree – or with another cuckoo on the same tree! Medical research should therefore not continue simply as a science of observation; at the very least each experiment should consist of one or more *induced* or comparative observations.

Claude decides that he will further explore the concept of the initial 'idea'; the importance of intuition as a starting point for any research (he smiles to himself as he recalls Louis Napoleon's reaction at Compiègne). Of course, an observation, an idea or simple intuition was well and good; but one then needed to construct a hypothesis. Based on such a hypothesis one could then design a properly-structured experiment, exactly as an architect might design a building. That was the way forward in science. That was his experimental method.

Each day he writes until his wrist pains him, and then before dark takes a long walk through the vines, into the village or up into the hills. The harvest had again been a rich one and on his return he meets with the *vignerons* to check progress with the wine processing. In the evenings, he either invites his mother to dine, or if she is too tired, he calls in to the cottage to be sure that all is well before she retires for the night. He is as happy as he has ever been. Above all, his illness had diminished to a daily grumbling abdominal discomfort with occasional diarrhea. No longer was he tired. How wonderful too it was to be remote from Paris – from the anxieties of home and laboratory.

"You are looking so much better, Claude."

He looks across the stained and etched kitchen table towards his mother who is sitting in her favourite posture: elbows on the table and chin cupped in hands gnarled by arthritis. How little this room had changed since he was a boy. Even his father's wicker chair stands in the same spot, now covered by a colourful woven wool blanket, as if to keep his memory warm. Had he ever seen his mother sitting there?

"I cannot pretend that I am anything other than content, Maman. The relief at being so free of pain is wonderful – and after all, I am home again!"

"But your family: however often we may have spoken about it, I still can't understand what has gone wrong – that you can't find a way of creating harmony with Fanny."

"Ah! How I would wish for that harmony, Maman. When she was here, you saw a person with manners and some grace who has given you two wonderful grandchildren. But I have told you of our difficulties and you must believe me that I have tried over the years to be the husband and father she is looking for."

"And what sort of person is that?"

Claude thinks for a while: a question that had often passed through his mind.

"I would think someone like her father, whom of course you have not met. Henri is certainly a very civilized man. He was highly respected in his profession until he recently retired with his health problems; and quite knowledgeable in a superficial way too. He's a good family man, full of kind gestures and above all very sociable."

"And you then, Claude?"

"I would like to think that you are proud of me – as a scientist and hopefully as a son. However, there is not much else. As far as my family is concerned…" Claude hesitates, contemplating first his hands and then his mother's, as if to wonder whether he would be similarly deformed in later life. "… I suppose that under other circumstances I would feel different, but the effort required of getting closer to Tony and Marie is almost more than I can muster – but I will continue to try."

"I am worried about you Claude; it doesn't seem to be a normal, natural life that you lead; so isolated."

"Maman, you mustn't worry so. I am sociable, but only towards people whom I respect. You must know me well enough to understand that

I cannot pretend – about anything. Much of Paris life, even in science and medicine is about pretence, and I find this difficult to tolerate. So I withdraw from it, get on with my research and restrict my contacts to those with whom I work. It's that simple."

"Is it really your work with animals that so offends her."

"I still don't know the answer to that, Maman. Many people must wonder about my commitment to animal experiments. It is probably not what a wife would be proud of in a husband."

"And for the sake of your family, could there not be another away of satisfying your curiosity – because that is what drives you Claude; and all the time, too! I so clearly remember that when you left Thoissey, your college report was full of it – your curiosity, your skepticism...."

That was a word that Claude found disagreeable:

"No Maman, not skepticism but doubt. There is such a difference, and just what I am writing about at present: one is negative, the other positive. My search for truth is almost like a religion to me. Fanny has her religion and I have mine. Sadly, I doubt that they can ever come to terms with one another."

There seems little more to say. Madame Bernard knows better than to question the longer-term impact on Tony and Marie-Louise's lives. She had thought that she understood her son; had struggled so hard to accept the idea of his arranged marriage. Once the marital knot had been tied, she had expected more flexibility from him. Now she sees the futility of the situation – and so embarrassing to explain to her family and to her friends.

By the time the grey, cold New Year of '64 arrived, Claude had settled into a routine in which he felt that he could continue indefinitely. He was receiving many letters, and enjoyed the leisure to reflect and compose a response. Indeed, in mid-winter there was little in the Beaujolais to distract him from pen and paper! He had no difficulty in keeping in touch with the happenings at the *Collège,* and was even able to provide advice as and when necessary. Paul Bert was providing a steady flow of reports, and Claude could not comprehend that he was actually enjoying lecturing to the medical students at the Sorbonne. He also seemed to be doing a fine job of maintaining the various experiments which were in motion at the time of Claude's departure, and had even managed to pursue one of his own ideas; trying to achieve successful skin grafts between different animal species.

Fanny had written to say that her father's health had suddenly deteriorated; he had been losing weight for some time without obvious explanation and the doctors had just found him to have a large abdominal growth. Glands around his neck were also enlarged from presumed deposit of the tumour, and his attending doctor thought that he was unlikely to live much more than three months. She also mentioned that Tony and Marie-Louise were both well, but of course upset. No other details were forthcoming.

Claude also receives an enthusiastic letter from Renan. Before leaving Paris, he and Claude had become quite close; Claude had indeed joined him, together with a bevy of other so-called intellectuals at one of Sainte-Beuve's dinners. Renan turned out to have an encyclopedic knowledge of both the sciences and the arts and could converse intelligently about many topics; like Claude, his curiosity knew no limit. Claude had read Renan's *Life of Jesus* during his recovery and is pleased when Renan now mentions the remarkable sales of his book; some sixty thousand in the first three months since publication. As anticipated however, it had sent shockwaves both through the *Collège* and through the religious world: even the Pope had declared it the height of blasphemy.

Pasteur had just written to say that he had given an evening lecture to the Faculty at the Sorbonne; he wrote modestly that he had now '... demolished the concept of spontaneous generation'! His talk had been well publicized so that the Emperor's new Minister of Education, Victor Duruy had been present; also the writers Alexandre Dumas and George Sand – and not least Princess Mathilde who was now very obviously extending her patronage to the sciences. Louis felt that his demonstration had gone particularly well. He had also done a few more experiments on heating wine. Indeed, the growth of germs had been inhibited, and fermentation by the yeasts seemed to proceed more reproducibly. Of course, one still had to do much work to be sure that the heating process would not impair its taste. He went on to say "......*and you will be pleased to hear that the Emperor responded to my letter and has encouraged me (with both words and money) to pursue the diseases of wine. After this last harvest, I took some of my students from the École with me back to Arbois where my vignerons have had such trouble with their wine. Through my trusty microscope, I have seen different germs according to each aberration of taste. Would you believe, it has even got to the point where I can identify each little villain and predict to the vignerons how it will affect the taste of the wine? Our idea of heating might indeed be the answer. I shall keep you in touch.*"

Claude smiles to himself as he reads the last sentences. In the same post, Casimir Davaine had written ecstatically about his results with the new samples that he had brought from Dourdan. He had injected the blood from the anthrax-ill sheep into a rat and two rabbits. The rat was unaffected but both rabbits had died! Then wonder of wonders, he had examined the blood of the rabbits and had found it teeming with those little rods (which he had decided to call *bactéridies*). It was an extraordinary finding, because for the first time his experiment showed that they were the cause; not the result of the disease.

Somehow, the letters from Pasteur and Davaine spur him on to accelerate his writing of his 'Introduction'. He decides that its second section should deal with his approach to experimentation on living animals. What was actually the role of the physiologist, he would ask the reader? Surely to take apart the living machine using tools and processes borrowed from physics and chemistry and to measure phenomena that would enable laws to be formulated.

This brought him face to face with attacking *vitalisme*: such a ridiculous concept. Claude would argue that it was nothing but a mythical cloak for scientists' ignorance. It was up to physiologists to reduce it to its fundamental physical and chemical components using proper processes of analysis. Yet analysis was only a step; not a proof in itself. Analysis of a phenomenon into its constituents had to be followed by the converse – synthesis. One had to examine whether the original phenomenon could be re-created: counterproof, as it were. Yes, he liked that term; after all, it represented what he had always tried to do in his research. When he cut a nerve and showed that it caused paralysis in a muscle it was one thing – but not everything! He then was obliged to stimulate that nerve electrically, to see if the corresponding muscle contracted. That then was the counterproof!

In addition, how could he deal with the element of curiosity; like little children, scientists always want to know 'why'. Claude himself was more inquisitive than most, so how could he explain that the search for 'why' was unrealistic – even greedy? Scientists had to understand that they must first use experiments to discover 'how'; the immediate cause of a phenomenon.

Then, what would he say about that commonly used phrase 'the unsuccessful experiment'. Claude was committed to the idea that an experiment only failed if it was ill-conceived or poorly performed;

otherwise, there was no such thing. If one experiment succeeded and an apparently identical one performed the next day failed, there had to be a reason. The conditions of the second experiment must have been different. Then one had to urgently identify the previously unrecognized condition or factor that was responsible for the difference. Of course, that way of thinking represented the scientific or experimental determinism that had become sacred to him; so very dear to his heart and mind. He would have to ensure that its importance was not lost sight of throughout the book.

He would also have to question why scientists felt the need to reduce experimental facts into mathematical equations. Why succumb to that almost universal temptation of applying statistics? How science suffered when statistics hid from view the very individual variations and differences that could be so useful when investigating phenomena and their causes.

Finally, back to experiments on animals – vivisection? Did scientists have a right to use this approach? Yes – absolutely! Did not society already use animals in so many harsh ways: for their labour, for their furs and pelts and for their meat. Therefore, why not use them for purposes that could ultimately benefit understanding of the human body? Experiments were needed; either on man or on animals. Physicians certainly experimented on their patients often enough by using unproven remedies and surgical operations. Surely then, it was preferable to first do such experimentation in animals.

Throughout history, man had often experimented on man. Had not experiments been performed on willing tuberculous patients, doomed because of their illness? Morals did not forbid this. Claude smiles to himself as he realizes that in every day life, people did nothing but experiment on one another – psychologically and physically – even though morals forbade doing ill to one's neighbour. He would conclude that experiments that could harm should be forbidden; those that were innocent should be permitted and those that might do good were obligatory!

Most patiently, and one by one, Claude commits his ideas to paper; his neat writing contributing rapidly to the tall but orderly stack of loose-leaf sheets that he hoped his publishers would accept. He still needed to write the third and last section of his introduction. He would base this on his individual research projects and discoveries, so that the reader might understand how the principles enumerated in the first two sections had actually influenced what he had so methodically done in practice

Two new letters arrive simultaneously from Paris. The first is a brief note from Fanny to say that her father had died, and without too much discomfort. She appreciates that Claude would have been unable to come to the funeral, from which she had just returned with the children.

The other letter is from Casimir Davaine:

> "...and I am so glad to hear from you that your symptoms have (again) resolved. I suppose that you will be coming back to Paris later in the spring. You mention nothing about Fanny and thus I assume that all is well there – or at least satisfactory. Should this not be the case you must know that you can always stay with us – as you did before.
>
> I must now tell you about my further studies with the Anthrax bactéridies. I collected even more blood samples from Dourdan (the train trip there and back has become almost comfortable!). I injected some blood that had been standing overnight into the rabbits and nothing happened; I then discovered that blood must be injected into the animals within ten hours in order to get a reliable occurrence of the disease in the recipient. I also took blood samples from the recipient rabbits at hourly intervals following the injection. Claude, those bactéridies actually increase in number by the hour. They seem to reach a critical number at which the rabbit perishes so quickly that it is positively frightening. There can surely be no doubt that I have identified the causative agent of anthrax.
>
> It seems as if the process is then a sort of putrefaction, yet occurring in living tissue. The germ theory of disease is three centuries old, but I do believe that I have discovered the first example that provides its proof. Is it possible that what I have found might be not be unique to anthrax; Bactéridies of one type or another could explain contagion and epidemics as well. Please let me have your thoughts on all this.
>
> Your very good friend,   Casi

Spring had arrived, and Claude makes the painful decision to return to Paris. He had not quite finished recording his ideas for the last section of his book, having been diverted from his writing by a wish to reread Comte's philosophical writings on *positivisme*. He had spent much of this time in his garden planting flowers, including his favourite violets and periwinkles that he could watch from his study. He had also created a plantation of medicinal herbs, but without any intention of using them! The parallels between plant and animal life had again surfaced in his mind; an interesting project for him to follow in his Beaujolais laboratory at the next opportunity. He decides that when he has the chance he will analyze every similarity and difference between these two biological systems, and write a book on the subject.

Morel had been very helpful in both Claude' as well as his mother's cottage garden, where he now finds her as he visits to say goodbye. She is sitting in a comfortable garden chair that Claude had found in Villefranche; it had a clever mechanism that allowed the back section to recline. Her face was rosy red in the warm sun; the deep lines of ageing had somehow been smoothed out. He was pleased that he had instructed Josephine to spend rather more time seeing to her everyday needs during his absence.

CHAPTER 15

ANOTHER VISIT, ANOTHER CHALLENGE

Claude is looking approvingly at the minor changes that had taken place in the *Collège* laboratory during his absence. The larger windows were a step forward; the extra light would reduce the eyestrain that he always felt at the end of the day. There were now partitions, which rather cramped each working area, although the resulting privacy would make it easier to concentrate. Paul Bert had just shown him how the improved ventilation in the animal house worked; a benefit both for the animals and the researchers! It was of course not the enlargement the *Collège* has promised him, but with the needs of the other professors, perhaps his expectations had been too high.

Bert takes the opportunity of showing Claude one of the rats in which he had grafted skin from one thigh to the corresponding position on its opposite thigh three weeks previously; the graft had obviously 'taken'. They now retire to Claude's room to discuss Bert's ideas.

"I really feel a bit despondent about those grafts, *Monsieur*. As I just showed you, I can transplant skin successfully from one to another part of the same rat, guinea pig or a rabbit; but Baronio did that already fifty years ago. When I tried to graft from one animal to another of the same species, it was rejected after only a few days; in fact almost as quickly as if I transferred skin from a rat, say to a guinea pig."

"Well, I presume that even within a species each animal has its own identity; which is why the graft does not survive."

"Yes, but I asked myself whether that 'identity' – as you call it – was something in the blood circulation or in the tissues. Therefore, I tried some parabiotic experiments. I joined the main *vena cava* of one rabbit to that of another before doing the skin graft, so that the blood circulation of the two animals mixed completely. I also gave belladonna each day to the recipient animal; I based that on your work showing that it increases blood circulation through body tissues. I thought that together these techniques might help the graft to survive. But it didn't seem to make any difference."

"A *système Siamoise* such as you describe would only have a chance of working if the differences between individuals resided within the blood stream. Those results tell you that the rejection of the graft is due to something in the tissues themselves. What about trying to increase the oxygen level in your animals?"

"I'm not sure that I understand."

"When I was a medical student, I was interested in the idea of using oxygen treatment for a patient with very bad pneumonia. I found some work on compressed air that had been described two hundred years ago by an Englishman – I think his name was Henshaw – or perhaps Henman. He claimed that it helped recovery of people with pneumonia. In fact you must have read that this type of treatment is coming back into fashion; there are clinics springing up all over France claiming that high pressure chambers can cure all sorts of vague conditions."

"Yes; there was actually an article about it in *le Moniteur* last week, but I don't quite see its relevance to skin grafting."

"My hypothesis is simply that having more oxygen in tissues may improve blood circulation to the graft and so increase the likelihood of its acceptance. I'm not an empiricist as you know, but since you are

ANOTHER VISIT, ANOTHER CHALLENGE

using small animals, it wouldn't be too difficult to construct the necessary chamber and do a comparative study to see if your grafts survive longer."

"Well, I don't have any other ideas, so I will certainly try out your idea."

"And how did your lecturing go?"

"I had no difficulties, but you might find it better to ask people who attended! Like you though, I prefer the audiences here at the *Collège:* the students at the Sorbonne seem to want to be entertained rather than educated. By the way, I heard that they are at last trying to find the money to give you a laboratory and a *préparateur* at the Sorbonne: that would be a great help, because you could perform experiments in your lectures rather than being restricted to just speaking."

Claude nods tolerantly. He would only believe that when it actually happened.

Later that week he receives – for the second time – an invitation to *Les Séries*. Recalling his negative sentiments on leaving Compiègne five years earlier, his immediate reaction was to decline. Nevertheless, he had little to lose; some of the people he had met there had been quite stimulating. He decides to accept and is even able to persuade Lesage to accompany him again as his valet. As the date of his visit approaches, he has some doubts about whether he would indeed be able to go, since his abdominal pain had returned with considerable severity. However, he had found that staying at home when he was ill was actually more distressing than if he continued to work, since his family seemed to avoid him at all costs. It might just be his imagination, but even Agnès seemed less attentive than before.

Claude also had more confrontations with Fanny. She now insisted that their apartment was too small for them. Furthermore, she had to take the carriage for shopping of any quality; *rue de Mogador* was no longer a fitting address for someone of Claude's status. She also resented his recent invitation to Compiègne: she had not been welcomed to any more of Princess Mathilde's salons and was clearly jealous of his social *milieu* and the frequent invitations he alone received to attend this or that function.

The repeat visit to Compiègne turns out to be more enjoyable than he had anticipated. As Berlioz had befriended him in '59, so the author Gustave Flaubert and Claude now find themselves enjoying the same activities. The courts had just excused Flaubert for the social and sexual frivolity of *Madame Bovary*, and he was enjoying the success of his recent work, *Salammbo*. Merimée is there as usual, and Nieuwerkerke is present this time, so that Claude does not have Princess Mathilde as a dining partner; she is flanked by Nieuwerkerke and Sainte-Beuve. Nevertheless, she greets him warmly enough when they come across each other after the splendid banquet that distinguishes the first night of his stay:

"Monsieur Bernard! It is good to see you again, my scientific friend?"

"Thank you, Madame. It was an honour to be invited again."

"And have you made any important discoveries since we last met?"

Claude had difficulties in answering that type of question, laced as it was this time with a little sarcasm. Is it his sensitivity, or is the Princess challenging him to compete with his friend Pasteur whom she had heard lecturing again earlier in the year? He looks to left and right, rather hoping that they might be joined by someone who would release him from the need to respond. He is unsuccessful; now obliged to reply:

"I believe that you would need to ask others about that. Because of my last visit here and the Emperor's subsequent generosity (for which I did thank him most warmly) it was possible for me to extend my work to the Beaujolais. I have a small laboratory there now and above all the opportunity to write and so share my ideas with others."

"I believe my cousin would like to hear that directly from you. May I take the liberty of arranging it?"

"With pleasure, Madame."

"May I comment however, that you are not looking quite so well as on the last occasion that we met?"

"That is possible, Madame. My health has not been as good and I am afraid that my physicians are typically finding it difficult to make a diagnosis in one of their colleagues. However my sojourns in the Beaujolais work wonders."

They exchange modest bows and the Princess circulates towards some other guests.

Claude enjoys his day trip to Pierrefonds. Since his last visit, there had been obvious progress in the construction of the last two massive towers. Workers are scurrying about on ladders between platforms precariously attached to the now towering walls and turrets. In the setting autumn sun, the warm colour of the stone creates a wonderful atmosphere. He makes a mental note to enquire whether Corot had made any further paintings of the remarkable edifice. Back at Compiègne, Lesage was apparently enjoying himself more than on the last occasion; he had encountered an old friend who was now a maid to one of the Rothschild family of bankers – also a guest for the week.

Claude felt much more relaxed on this visit; able to participate in and simultaneously enjoy the company of the other guests. Of course, he was now somewhat of a celebrity: many people to whom he is introduced readily identify his name with one of his discoveries that they had read about in the newspapers, or from a lecture that one of their friends had heard him give. Claude knows that sensation-hungry journalists sometimes attended his lectures at the *Collège*.

Louis Napoleon is clearly not in good health. His cheeks are somewhat sunken, his step is less lively and the handshake with which he greets Claude does not have its previous firmness.

"It is kind of you to accept our invitation again, Monsieur. I hope that you are enjoying meeting your fellow guests."

"Indeed, your Majesty. It is every bit as enjoyable as my last visit. And I must not let a moment pass without thanking you again for your generosity following that visit."

The Emperor pauses to look down at the single sheet of paper before him, apparently refreshing his memory:

"May I be so bold as to ask how you were able to use my modest donation to your well-being?"

"Quite simply it enabled me to complete the purchase of a house in the Beaujolais within which I have equipped a small laboratory and a fine study. For my chronic illness, Dr Rayer recommended extended periods away from Paris. With what you granted me I have therefore managed to remain productive, at the same time as regaining my health. By the way, I gather that you know Dr Rayer quite well."

The Emperor nods."Yes indeed. He is my physician too, although I am not happy about the incomplete resolution of my health problem. Perhaps a stay in the Beaujolais would do me some good, too. Do you suppose that it was the local wine that helped your recovery?"

They both laugh, but the Emperor's face suddenly becomes serious:

"Speaking of wine, that excellent scientist Pasteur was our guest here again last year. He obliged us to open some of our wines from the cellar. Of course, there were a few bad ones amongst them, and in each of those he showed us germs through his wonderful microscope. The 'good' wines were quite free of them. A wonderful demonstration! We have decided to give him a special laboratory in the Arbois so that he can find a solution to the problem. An expensive problem too; millions of francs are at stake. I have actually had a report from him recently to say that heating the wine before bottling may be the answer. Would you believe it?"

All Claude can do is to nod wisely while the Emperor looks again at the paper before him.

"What about your laboratories then?"

"That seems to be less successful, your Majesty. I suppose that I should not complain about my territory since our work continues quite well. However the *Collège* has certainly not yet apportioned the money for all the alterations that I had planned."

Louis Napoleon draws himself up to his modest height in the chair behind his desk. His face is flushed.

"It was Rouland's duty to follow that up: I cannot expect you to do battle with your own administration. Rouland has gone now and thankfully his replacement, Victor Duruy is quite a different matter; he and I see eye to eye. I will ask him to call in and see you."

"That is kind of you, but there is a larger problem which I should mention. I do not have to tell you that France currently leads the rest of Europe – perhaps the world – in scientific research, especially in the biological sciences. However, those of us who keep in touch with matters outside France see Germany and Russia forging ahead of us. It is not their scientists that are better; it's their facilities. The most wonderfully equipped laboratories have now been constructed in all their major universities. It is these which also attract our very best minds away from France."

The Emperor suddenly seems restless; obviously keen to end the discussion:

"I think we must stop there, Bernard. I will not forget your last comments. In fact, I will ask Duruy to speak to you about a report on French science, which we need to compile quite soon. Perhaps you will be so kind as to accept this as a commission."

"I would be most happy to see your Minister and help provide such a report."

Louis eases himself very slowly out of his chair. His parting handshake is warm enough but there is no trace of a smile. He looks tired and worried as he ushers Claude to the door.

By the end of his week in Compiègne, Claude finds himself looking forward to his return to the laboratory. He had used some free time to complete the third section of his *Introduction*. It would contain many examples of his scientific thought and his unswerving commitment to scientific determinism and counterproof. He would use as models the specific projects and research challenges from the preceding fifteen years. He had also decided that his three hundred and fifty pages of *Introduction* justified publication in their own right. He would write another volume on his *Principles* later.

The Emperor had reason to look worried. After a period of blissful progress in his domestic affairs, things are not going well for him. Haussman is doing wonders for Paris, but at what expense! The provinces are complaining about being neglected. Claude's mention of German scientific supremacy had reminded Louis yet again that there were issues with Germany that he had to resolve. His war ministry was now even murmuring about taking Germany to war. However, the Mexican affair was an embarrassing fiasco; he was uneasy that his best troops were still on the other side of the Atlantic. He had achieved absolutely nothing from that expensive exercise; Diaz and his guerrillas would always be able to out-manoeuvre them. It was not helped by the fact that led by his penis, the commander Bazaine had become so infatuated with a Mexican girl, that he had completely lost his judgment. If only he felt better, the Emperor might be able to deal with all of this: the doctors all seemed to agree that he had gonorrhoea – the price paid for one of his few pleasures – but that crippling pain over his bladder....!

The Emperor sends Victor Duruy to see Claude, and quite soon after his return from Compiègne. His manner is indeed quite different from that of his predecessor:
"I have come to apologize for the problems you have experienced with your laboratories, Monsieur. The Emperor values your work and that of Pasteur as those which deserve most support in the medical sciences."
"I am delighted to hear it."
"...but as someone who has devoted his life to education, I would like to add my own compliments towards your highly respected public lectures at the *Collège*. I understand that you are even gaining international repute for these."

Claude acknowledges this by a small bow and a smile, while Duruy continues.

"You may know that I place the education of the public high on my agenda: how can we expect the nations' children to excel if their parents are not educated and informed? I would like to see much more of that and I am hoping that I might persuade the newspapers to devote more space to matters of literature, art and the sciences. Tell me, have you also written for the public, so that they may better understand what you have achieved?"

"Very little. One article on curare and another on the heart were published in the *revue des Deux Mondes,* and my book shortly to be published on my studies of experimental medicine may be considered to fall into that category. I will be interested to have your views on it in due course."

"Who is publishing it for you?"

"Baillière."

"We deal mostly with Hachette, but Baillière is a fine publishing house and I certainly look forward to reading it. On the matter of writing, as the Emperor no doubt mentioned, we would like to invite you to contribute to a review of our Nation's progress in physiology; he wishes to publish these to coincide with our next *Exposition Universelle* in '67, so you have plenty of time. Indeed we will shortly be establishing an advisory committee to guide us in our choice of material for that exhibition; perhaps you would also care to join us in that project?"

"You're very kind; I would be happy to help where necessary."

"I also understand that you have needs for laboratory and appropriate personal assistance for your lectures at the Sorbonne. I consider these of no less importance that those at the *Collège* and I shall do my best to provide you with the necessary support."

Duruy's visit comes to an abrupt end with the usual glance at his watch and a shake of the head. Claude is left with an impression of goodwill, but remains cynical of his prospects for better facilities; how easily words fell from the tongues of the well-educated who were in positions of power.

The new apartment at number 24, *rue de Luxembourg* was indeed larger; and with better access to the Sorbonne and the *Collège.* Fanny is glowing with happiness at being close to the shops of *rue St Honoré,* and only a stone's throw from the gardens of *les Tuileries.* In his large and airy study, Claude enjoys planning the definitive lectures in experimental medicine that he would also use for his new book. He spends little time in his laboratory: Bert had furnished it with new equipment and with the assistance of Bouchardat is immersed in studies of high-pressure oxygen and its effects. Is it his imagination, or had his health significantly improved since he had distanced himself from that damp cold area. On one of the rare days in his laboratory, he has a surprise visit from Pasteur – in buoyant mood:

"I'm delighted to see you looking rather better, Claude."

"Thank you Louis – probably because I am now spending so much less time in this little dungeon."

"Mine at the *Ècole* is hardly better: I'm becoming so weary of complaining, although thanks to the Emperor they have invested heavily in my facilities at Arbois; our wine industry now seems to be his main priority. Actually, that is why I am here. Later this month I am addressing the *Académie* with my latest results."

"I'm certainly looking forward to hearing about them."

"I was hoping that you would be at the *Académie* when I present them, since I have you to thank for setting me in that direction. If wine is heated to fifty-five degrees for several minutes one gets no germ growth. That's it! More important, the wine experts in Arbois have carefully studied the taste; they can't tell the difference between the treated and untreated wine. One of the experts is coming to my talk, by the way."

"It's a shame that we don't have an instrument to measure taste yet; I always hope for something better than the human palate for testing the sweetness of the grapes before we harvest them. How useful it would be for your research too! Anyhow, it's marvellous news and of course I will be at the *Académie* to listen to you."

"I must also tell you that I have been asked to undertake some studies on a disease called *Pébrine*."

Claude's blank face expresses his total ignorance of the disorder.

"Aha! I thought that would be your reaction! Silkworms are apparently dying in massive numbers because of the condition. The problem with wine was enough; now this disease is threatening to ruin the silk industry. The Ministry of Agriculture is convinced that it's an infestation of some sort – hence their request to me."

"Now that you mention it, there was something about it in *le Moniteur* recently, but I didn't give it much attention."

Pasteur outlines for Claude how the silkworms are dying and some of their abnormalities that scientists had already recorded. He would soon be on his way to the town of Alès near Nimes where the problem was rampant, in order to make some initial assessments. He admits to Claude with a smile that until recently he had not even realized that silkworms hatched into moths! Claude's memories of Lyon, its silk workers and the devastating cholera epidemic of '32 flash through his mind as Pasteur is speaking; he wonders how the silk-weavers on the hill at Croix-Rousse would deal with the impending silk crisis.

"Talking of infections Louis, Pierre Rayer mentioned to me recently that there are lots of cases of cholera in our hospital wards again; they are even talking of another epidemic spreading up from Marseilles. It occurs to me that we might try to sample the air from one of the wards to see if we can identify the *vibrio*. There is still little knowledge of how it is transmitted other than contaminated water. What do you think?"

"I would be happy to talk about it at another time, but I must go now. I have arranged to meet my wife at the *École* to go through the results of all my wine studies: I am shortly to give a more general lecture on the subject to a society of *vignerons*. Marie is such a help to me these days; it's quite wonderful how she catalogues all my research work."

With that parting comment, Pasteur leaves. Claude had his own appointment to keep; the senior editor at Baillière had asked him to call in and pick up the proofs of his *Introduction to the Study of Experimental Medicine*.

As one of his responsibilities, the *Académie des Sciences* had also asked Claude to visit a village near Perpignan in the south-west of the country. The purpose of the trip was to dedicate a statue to the memory of an eminent astronomer. François Arago had died in '53 and during his latter years had devoted himself to popularizing science and later still to politics. In his earlier years he had worked with Fresnel doing important studies on the polarization of light; a subject which had particularly fascinated Claude at college in Thoissey.

On his way south to Perpignan – more correctly Estagel, which was Arago's birthplace and the location of the statue – Claude had interrupted his journey in Villefranche, lunched with his friend Ronne and spent two days in St Julien signing some important documents in connection with the property. He had enjoyed the prospect of returning only a few weeks later for his usual autumn visit.

Claude is happy during the long return journey despite the heat, wondering why he had not spent more time exploring the wider countryside using the ever-expanding railway network. Sitting with him in the same compartment are a father and son who had also been at the ceremony in Estagel. The rather frail Monsieur Barral senior had recently completed a thirteen-volume review of Arago's works; together with his son Georges he also owned a bookshop in *rue Jacob*. The young Georges makes an instant impression on Claude. He had recently graduated from the Sorbonne and had only one ambition – to write. A shiver runs down his spine as he recalls his own passionate wish to commit himself to paper all those years ago; rarely had Claude come across such a lively, inquisitive and probing mind. He finds himself laying bare his own beliefs and achievements to the young man, in a way that he would never have thought possible. Time simply flies by until they reach Paris.

During the following night, Claude is awoken by excruciating abdominal pain; almost worse is the watery diarrhea. By morning, his mouth is parched and he can hardly raise himself from his bed. He immediately sends Jean-Paul and Agnès to fetch Davaine, who is soon at Claude's bedside.

"Your circulation is poor Claude, and really just from dehydration. I will take a sample of your stools with me to see what I can discover: but my suspicion is that you have mild cholera. Yet…" he hesitates, "…with your previous problems, I can't be sure. You certainly need fluid urgently – and put directly into a vein."

"I'm not going into hospital, Casi, if that's what you mean!"

They look at each other for a moment without speaking.

"Please be reasonable Claude. Bouchardat's formulae for these solutions are now very good. And you need treatment for your pain."

Claude hustles his friend out of the room while he urgently discharges foul bowel motions into a chamber pot. Some moments later Davaine returns to a resolute Claude, breathing heavily from his recent effort.

"I'll take my chances at home Casi. Without being able to measure what is happening in my blood, no one can possibly know how much of a given chemical to pour into my veins. I will drink water with some sugar and salt added and let my stomach and bowel decide what they want to absorb. If my body's own judgment on the matter fails, then…… Oh! I'm really too weary to discuss it further!"

Claude is tiring quickly, and Davaine realizes that no amount of persuasion is likely to convince his friend.

"Alright Claude. I will arrange to get you some morphine for your pain, and I only hope that vomiting does not set in. May I have you agreement that if it does, you will come into my ward at the *Charité?*"

"If I must...."

Claude remains desperately ill for over a week. He instructs Agnès on the exact amounts of sugar and salt that he wishes her to add to the reservoir of water which sits on his side table. From this he drinks hourly by the clock, in amounts dictated only by his own feelings. Rayer and Davaine visit him once or more each day pleading that he might nevertheless agree to hospitalization; but to no avail.

A week later, his stomach is tolerating very thin soup; anything more substantial is promptly vomited. Gradually his diarrhea eases; his pain subsides and sleep is again possible. It is only at the end of the third week of his illness that he is able to spend any time out of his bed; twice he had fallen over in his attempts to care for himself, and a large bruise now extends over his right flank. Neither Fanny nor the children are to be seen.

His instinct is to return to St Julien as soon as he is strong enough to make the journey: that haven of peace had so rapidly resolved his health problems in the past. However, at their visits both Davaine and Rayer are insistent that proximity to a hospital remained essential, in case of relapse. Despite regular examination of his blood and stools they find nothing that suggests a diagnosis. He is visited by his recent acquaintance, Georges Barral, who tells him that the elder Barral had become similarly ill following his return to Paris; because of his age and the insistence of his doctors, he had been hospitalized and treated with intravenous fluid. After a worrying first week, he was now showing some signs of recovery.

That winter proves to be one of the harshest on record. Claude's weakness remains profound and his appetite returns only slowly. He hardly leaves the shelter of the apartment, and he knows that it will be impossible for him to give even a part of his winter course at the *Collège*. However, he does receive a steady stream of colleagues, allowing him to keep up to date with proceedings of scientific meetings as well as the activities at the *Collège* – Bert's research results in particular. Fanny always stays in the background during these visits; Agnès supplies any refreshments that he wished for his visitors.

The endless hours of forced inactivity means that there is little that he can do except read. He tries to explore areas that would not normally interest him; the latest novel by Baudelaire or a new historical review. Nevertheless, reading for recreation is not for Claude.

The young Georges Barral is only too keen to supply him with this and that from the library, so that he can continue to satisfy his unbridled curiosity for science. He had always wished to learn other languages – particularly German and English – so that he could read articles in foreign journals. And so Barral brings him books on foreign language learning. Yet it seemed that he had a singular inability to acquire language skills; it simply added to his already immense frustration.

"I can't go on like this, Casi. I could tear my hair out – what is left of it – with the boredom of it all."

Davaine smiles understandingly as he concludes his examination of Claude's emaciated abdomen. He is sitting at the side of Claude's bed, his hand resting affectionately on Claude's shoulder where he can feel the contours of each bone. Below, the deltoid and biceps muscles are so wasted that the upper arm is totally shapeless; its skin hanging in folds. His cheeks are hollow, pale and almost transparent as he now looks up at Davaine with bloodshot eyes. There seems so little remaining of the elegance, pride and distinction of stature that had always impressed everyone who met him.

"I want to go to St Julien." He pleads, like a little child.

"I understand Claude, and I'm not going to oppose you. I now believe it to be a safe move. In fact, Pierre has had the agreement from the *Collège* that you should be awarded an unlimited sabbatical to enable you to recover completely. They are of course under no illusion but that you will continue to put pen to paper! But your lectures at the *Collège* and the Sorbonne will have to be set aside yet again."

"I should be grateful I suppose. However, there is so much that needs to be done – I cannot delegate to others *ad infinitum.*"

"One step at a time Claude! You may indeed make a more rapid recovery in the better air of the Beaujolais; until then everyone will just have to manage. So please would you allow me to accompany you there – perhaps next week?"

Claude attempts a smile. "I can think of nothing nicer."

Claude had much to arrange before he could leave. He had intended to discuss with Paul Bert some ideas for experiments that could be set up in his absence. However, when he arrives at the apartment the next day, Bert informs Claude excitedly that he had been invited to fill the chair of physiology in Bordeaux. In offering him the post, the university council was hoping that he might take up the position quite soon. Claude of course had known that Bert's promotion was possible – had even provided a glowing reference for his *préparateur* some weeks previously. He would have little choice but to close down the laboratories until he felt well enough to take up his proper function again. Lesage could keep the remaining animals under supervision, while helping Berthelot in his laboratory. Claude suddenly feels terribly empty, as if one chapter of his life had come to an end – and without any thought as to how the next chapter might begin.

His mood is not helped by Fanny's attitude. It is as if she again resented the fact that he was going to St Julien. Yet he had received precious little attention from her – or his daughters – during his illness. He would have to make some difficult decisions about his marriage and home life over the next months.

It is on a wonderful spring day in '66 that Claude and his good friend arrive in St Julien. For the first time he had been able to forewarn his mother exactly when they would be arriving, using the telegraph system that now had a reception point in St Julien. Accordingly the 'red carpet' had been laid out for them in the form of an enormous dish of Claude's favourite *bugnes*, which he reluctantly had to leave for his friend – concerned that they might upset his own still-fragile digestive tract. Claude is shocked at how his mother's health had deteriorated; her spine bent even further, her gait unstable and her vision clearly poor when the light was bad. He tries – again unsuccessfully – to persuade her to move permanently to his house. Davaine's two week stay was a blessing and a joy for Claude. His face had also acquired some colour and Josephine's cooking had somehow captured his interest in food again. Yet his spirits remained very low.

Davaine takes the train back to Paris; still seriously concerned. Time is so much better at healing bodies than souls, he decides. The illness had provided his friend with too much opportunity for reflection and self-examination. He distracts himself by dwelling on the conversation that he had with Claude just before he left:

"I wonder," Claude had said, "if your little anthrax rods might behave like rotifers."

"Do you mean they might survive drying?"

"Exactly," Claude had answered, "and like we did with our studies on putrefaction it would be interesting to see if heat kills them so that they no longer cause disease. After all, that's how Louis Pasteur has decided to save the French wine industry!"

Ronne appears un-announced one afternoon in mid-summer on his way back from visiting a distant relative in Blacé, a small village just beyond St Julien. Claude's spirits are temporarily lifted by the surprise visit, and the two of them are sitting on the terrace in deep discussion about their respective lives, two glasses and a bottle of Claude's vintage wine separating them across a rough-hewn table.

"You are still not your normal self, Claude."

They look at each other without speaking for a full minute. Never had there been anything but full confidence and openness between them.

"Perhaps I'm just tired of battling against the world."

"I had always thought of you as standing astride the world, like a colossus!"

"Simply an illusion, Ronne. I have had successes but it is my failures which burden me."

"With your marriage? Yes. I can see that. But professionally you have surely had nothing but triumphs."

"Well even that is not so, although I would have to admit that failure of my family life does hang most heavily on my conscience. Strangely it is my scientific writing that now comes back to haunt me...." Ronne looks at him quizzically: this is not the Claude that he is used to. "....like my work on the *chorda tympani* nerves which others have now shown not to be entirely correct; or my argument with Figuier about glucose levels in the portal vein. Not to speak of my so-called original discovery that artificial respiration will keep alive people with curare poisoning..."

"....and doesn't it?"

"Of course it does; but since I have had more time to read, I have just discovered that Brodie made that observation thirty years before me!"

"Surely those are such minor matters."

"Nothing is minor when you preach truth, and a structured methodology that you hope the scientific world will adopt. It is all of one year since I wrote my *Introduction*. Even that has not had the success I had hoped for – well at least not in the scientific circles towards which I had directed it."

"I thought that it had been well received."

"Ah yes, by the philosophers and perhaps even the literary fraternity; they quite liked it. I care little for those reviews. What bothers me is that it has hardly received a mention from the scientists and the journals; after all, it was for scientists that I wrote the book. There have been disparaging – and even worse, condescending – remarks made in the medical press about it."

"What about the sales of the book, Claude; that should tell you something."

"They have only been modest; I mean, nothing like Renan's *Life of Jesus*. Of course, it has provocative elements: not least my views on vivisection. I also went out of my way to destroy the mysticism of *vitalisme* that the church has so revelled in; and they have had their say about the book too! Perhaps I cannot expect popularity if I go out on a limb in that way."

Ronne nods. It is clear that his friend's mood is at an all time low.

"I understand Claude, but you must surely have provided the scientific world with so much that is good, that these minor matters – and I insist on calling them that – fade into insignificance. Even your marriage problem is not only of your doing. Blame your friends, Rayer and Pelouze if you wish – or Fanny's intransigence, but I am convinced that your role in the affair is again minor and subsidiary."

Claude smiles.

"Your visit today has done me so much good Ronne. Let's wander through the vineyards together – like we did forty years ago!"

By harvest time, Claude is beginning to feel a little of his former self. He decides that he will try to solve an issue which had troubled him for many years; the measurement of the sweetness of the grapes. Before he left, Davaine had helped him set up his laboratory; Claude's aim is to measure the sugar content of grapes using the same technique that he had developed with Barreswill at the *Collège*. However, he realizes that he needs to measure not just glucose but also fruit sugar – fructose. He eventually receives from Barreswill his suggestions about how he might adapt the method.

His first experiments are almost farcical. He runs between vineyard and laboratory with his samples that have to be macerated and weighed before measurements can be done. He cannot decide whether to include the seeds in this maceration: their fibrous content is playing havoc with his test tubes and seemingly distorting the results. The *vignerons* are amused by his antics, and assure him that they will not be taking the slightest notice of his results in their final decision for the timing of harvest!

He soon establishes a routine for each day. As it had been during his previous stay, he uses the mornings for writing. His first priority is the report on progress of general physiology in France, which the Emperor had commissioned for the *Exposition Universelle*. Claude had brought with him a folder full of references for the purpose; yet he hardly had to use this material. What he needed was there, in the front of his head. Over the next few weeks, he puts pen to paper: the groundwork laid by Laplace and Lavoisier, the writings of Bichat and the monumental contributions of Magendie; even his controversy with Longet. He finds a place for Milne-Edwards' and Brown-Séquard's contributions as well as Pasteur and Béchamp's work. However, it is his own twenty-five years of research that occupies a significant part of the document; the contribution that he believes he can truly vouch for.

The report takes less time to compile than he thought it would. When he re-reads it a few days later he finds little to alter. He decides to add a final note: France's achievements were all well and good (he writes), but how much better they would be with laboratory facilities specifically geared to the needs of the physiologist.

Midday usually signalled a meal with his mother, if she felt well enough to join him. Before her afternoon rest, they would sit and talk; about the vineyards, his health, Paris and above all his professional life. Madame Bernard had noticed that whenever the discussion drifted towards Fanny or the children, he deftly changed the direction of the conversation. One day Claude seems particularly morose and pre-occupied, and she decides to grasp the nettle.

"You are avoiding any discussion about Fanny and I must know why. Please tell me what is happening between you both."

Claude looks at his mother who suddenly seems so very old and frail. Her pleading demands an honest response.

"Things have not changed Maman. In fact, you will be disappointed with what I have to say. I have given the matter much thought since I arrived here. I have decided that after twenty years I can no longer maintain a relationship with her. I am afraid that our marriage is doomed."

There is silence as the reality of the situation embeds itself in her mind. Her shoulders slump and Claude puts his arms around her shrinking body, feeling the sobs emanating from deep within it. She looks up at her son's impassive face through tearful eyes.

"Is there really nothing you can do? Do you try and speak with her about how you might find some common ground?"

"We can never have common ground, Maman. Indeed, there is probably no-one with whom I could find that. It would surely have been better for me never to have married."

He hesitates:

"There is little point in going over the past though. I have already suggested to her that she might be happier living without me and I must tell you frankly that I would be more content without her. I face the fact that my place as a father probably has little future either, although I pray that when I no longer live with Fanny, my relationships with the children might improve."

"You are really going to leave them all?"

"Yes. I made the decision earlier this week. I suppose that I will write to Fanny in the next few days, and at least get that unpleasant step off my mind."

His mother looks at him steadily. How calm and detached he seemed about such an important decision. Was it really about his animal research after all? Had Fanny really tried to be a good wife to him? Moreover, what sort of a husband – and father – had he been towards *them*? Despite all their talking, she realizes just how little she knows of her son's life compared to that of her daughter. Perhaps she should ask Caroline to persuade Claude to defer his decision; he seemed so resolute. Her afternoon rest that day is anything but peaceful, and she is cursed with such pain in her spine and legs that she has a completely sleepless night.

"Monsieur!"

Josephine is outside his study door upon which she had just knocked. He opens it to find her holding an envelope bearing the charactcristic insignia of the telegraph office.

"It's special, Monsieur!"

Claude opens it eagerly:

Dear Bernard,

News of your indisposition has reached me. I wish you rapid recovery and prompt return to Paris to continue illuminating your colleagues and the world with your scientific wisdom.

With warmest good wishes,

Louis Napoleon

Claude smiles at Josephine's excitement; the telegraph system might well be useful, even efficient; but for confidentiality it left much to be desired. He is sitting at his table and for what seems an age looks across the lush grass towards the distant horizon. With the telegram, Josephine also brings him the day's mail, amongst which a rather thick envelope eventually attracts his attention. It contains a short note from Ronne inviting him to spend a night in Villefranche on his birthday. Enclosed with the letter is a substantial article from *le Moniteur* dated November 7th. His note concludes *"...and I hope that this cheers you up when you read it, as indeed it should. It makes me proud to be your old and good friend, Ronne.*

He spreads the sheets across his table. The article is entitled *Claude Bernard: idée de l'importance de ses travaux, de son enseignement et de la méthode.* The author is none other than his friend Louis Pasteur. He blushes as he reads it. Pasteur compares him to the great scientists of the past and summarizes some of his better-documented research findings in relation to diabetes. It refers to his quality as a teacher and an original researcher, drawing attention to his scientific 'eminence' and the wisdom of his *'Introduction à l'Étude de Médecine Expérimentale"* – even to his physical attributes! It quotes a recent article by Duruy and the eminent chemist Dumas that described Claude as *"...not just a great physiologist; he is physiology itself."* Finally, it draws attention to his recent illness with the hope that he might soon be welcomed back by his friends and colleagues.

Claude is greatly touched by the initiative of his friend and colleague, and immediately writes to say how delighted and flattered he feels. At the same time, he offers his condolences on the recent death of Pasteur's daughter from typhoid fever, which Berthelot had mentioned in a recent letter. Pasteur had already lost two daughters in the preceding seven years from infections. What hazards was he inflicting on his family by his research on infective agents?

During the following weeks – and clearly because of the article – Claude receives many goodwill wishes from colleagues; with these his self-esteem and generally positive mood returns. However, just as he is regaining his self-confidence in the early summer of '67, he is dealt another blow. He notices that the shutters on his mother's cottage are not yet open – and it is almost midday. He investigates, only to find that she had died peacefully in her sleep.

The funeral is only a small affair; close family and a handful of friends. All share the same sentiment; the relief that she no longer had to endure the trauma of unceasing pain that had undermined her enjoyment of life. Claude naturally reflects on the emotional pain that she must have also endured because of his family problems; no doubt, the wagging tongues would conclude that she had 'died of shame'. Claude takes the opportunity of talking with Caroline and Jean about the future of the cottage. They remain committed to their holding in Pouilly-le-Monial: for the time being the cottage that they have inherited would stand empty.

Claude now sets about arranging his return to Paris. He carefully arranges his papers; the *Report* neatly tied with a purple ribbon. His afternoon reading had largely consisted of delving into philosophical texts – of Comte, Tenneman and his favourite Descartes: so he had to pack these as well. As he goes about his domestic tasks, his mind dwells on his own philosophical 'position'. Colleagues had sometimes branded him as a philosopher. He might be flattered, but he could not see himself in this guise. There was only one philosophical principle that provided a platform for his research: the eminently practical *determinisme*. If the conditions of an experiment were identical, then the result had to be the same. Everything stemmed from this idea; whether it was the hypothesis, the design or the interpretation of the experiment. If his colleagues chose to label him as a philosopher within this or that school of thought, then they were welcome!

As he clears his desk, he again comes upon the letter that he had received from Fanny; her reply to his carefully but necessarily direct letter to her. It could only be described as vicious. She railed against him for his seven-month silence and suggested that he should consider dosing her with one of the poisons with which he was so familiar. There is now no way that he could consider returning even briefly to the family home in *rue de Luxembourg*; he writes to the Davaines accepting their earlier offer of lodging, until he can find another apartment.

It is accordingly there that the cab deposits him on one warm night in June.

CHAPTER 16

TO FACE REALITY

Claude returns to a Paris giddy with excitement and self-confidence. The *Exposition Universelle* had opened. In every part of the city, some new structure had been hurriedly completed; Haussmann had been busy ensuring that Paris would present its best face to the visiting international community. Claude is pleased to be living with the Davaines, in the same attic room in which he had taken refuge from his first major domestic crisis six years earlier. His friends had added a few new items of furniture; more appropriate for a longer stay.

"You are not looking at all well, you know. Perhaps you should have stayed away longer?" Offers Davaine.

"Thank you my friend, but no! My health has reached a plateau; I must restart my professional life."

"I didn't know that you had ever left it!"

Claude smiles. "There's still much that I want to do, and there are limits to what I can achieve in St Julien."

"Of course; I understand. By the way, I must tell you some serious news. Poor Pierre probably has not very much longer to live. Both his heart and his kidneys have come to the end of a long road; he cannot leave his house now and has resigned his post as Dean of the medical school."

"Yes, Marcel wrote to me about the decline in his health. I must see him very soon then. Since his wife died he must be feeling so very much alone."

"Certainly. On top of that I must tell you that Théo is also not well. It's probably tuberculosis, but he's been away from his laboratory now for three weeks."

Claude shakes his head in disbelief at the sad predicament of his colleagues.

"At least you look well, Casi."

"Thanks to God – and of course Georgina! She only complains that she would like to see a little more of me!"

"But you must be very pleased about the Bréant award."

"Of course the money is useful and it encourages me to continue with the research. By the way I must tell you about my last series of experiments on heating my *bactéridies*."

"And…"

"Well you were right of course. Heat did kill them – presumably as it does the germs that we presume to cause putrefaction; a temperature of 55 degrees was quite enough."

"Did you try desiccating them; to see whether you could suspend animation, like my little rotifers?"

"I've just finished the last series of experiments. I kept them dehydrated for six weeks, but what happened then was amazing. When I added water, they were still able to cause disease in guinea pigs – and just as virulent, too. While they were dehydrated, they also seemed more resistant to heat; I found that I could expose them to temperatures of 100 degrees without apparently harming them. They are hardy little creatures!"

"Rather frightening actually. I hope that you are taking adequate care not to infect yourself."

"Of course!"

On his way to Rayer's home, Claude decides to call on Pelouze. He is pathetically thin, and his eyes had lost the luminosity that was usually so evident. He was sitting upright in his bed, breathless. A trace of a smile creases his face as Claude arrives, but even talking is repeatedly interrupted by a racking cough. Claude stays for only a short time with an unrealistic promise to Pelouze and his wife that he will return on another day when his friend is a little more comfortable.

Now he is at Rayer's home and the maid takes Claude through to the salon, seemingly unchanged from his first memorable visit some twenty-five years earlier – his first exposure to the concept of *positivisme*. Rayer is sitting in a tall armchair propped up by pillows; a faded image of his former self. His badly swollen legs rest on a stool, his sparse hair is tousled and a sad smile creases his jowly face. The attractive young woman sitting beside him introduces herself as his daughter Josette and then quickly withdraws.

"So illness has ravaged us both, my friend." Rayer begins.

"....and poor Théo whom I have just visited. At least I am on the road to recovery."

"I fear that recovery for me is out of the question. Andral is doing his best, but that will not be good enough. Odd isn't it; with my medical interest in the kidneys..."

He looks ruefully down at his deformed legs;

"...and now their failure, which is causing me so much mischief? As if God is challenging me!"

"God and medicine hardly go together in my view, Pierre; otherwise we would have even more difficulty in our reasoning of illness."

"You may just be right. I am glad to see you back, although I would assume that you'll return to the Beaujolais for the harvest."

"Yes. But it was important for me to try and set up the laboratory again; I've also quite a bit of personal business to deal with."

"Do you mean about Fanny?"

"Yes, Casimir has probably told you that I am finally going to leave her."

"He did. Of course my emotions are rather mixed, but I want to speak quite frankly with you. If not now, it will never be."

Claude nods but remains silent at the ominous tone.

"Despite the undoubted professional success which your marriage made possible, I do of course feel deeply guilty about the sorrow that has accompanied it. I have recently had almost too much time to reflect on what is perhaps the only such calamity for which I hold myself alone responsible. All I can do is to apologize."

"You do not need to, Pierre. I was a willing partner and quite aware of what I was doing. You and Théo may have laid the path, but I agreed to walk down it – so I do not want you to give it another thought."

Rayer smiles.

"There is something else I need to tell you Claude. Before Fanny's father died, he managed to attend his last annual reunion. He told me that in no way did he hold you responsible for the crumbling marriage; apparently he had fallen out of favour with Fanny as well because he had taken your side in a number of arguments. He fully knew the defects in her personality too. By the way, when you want to see a *notaire*, you might consider Jean Marisot; he's a fine man. If you will allow me, I will write him a brief letter of introduction….while I have the energy….."

Rayer's voice suddenly breaks as he starts to cough; Claude passes him a mug of water. Indeed there is little more to say on the subject.

"I have much to thank you for, Pierre. You have helped me up the ladder in so many ways. But why?"

"You know Claude; I have recently done little but look back on my life. Some two thousand students have probably passed through my service at the *Charité* since I started working there. Why does one help some more than others?" He begins to cough again; now interspersed with deep wheezing breaths. "I have decided that success depends on only two personal characteristics: passion and curiosity. Without either of those, a person has little prospect of achieving anything in this world. You have both – as did the others whom I helped over the years. The result, dare I say is self-evident!"

"You were so kind to me Pierre; and now you are improving my morale as well."

"Well, you cannot be too surprised at what I have just said. It is widely known that you have helped others too – and I trust will continue to do so. Pasteur and Davaine have been enriched by your support, not to speak of your *préparateurs,* pupils and all those visitors to your laboratory." He pauses: "People might criticize me for my approach of helping the successful rather than the feeble. However, I suppose we all develop a sixth sense about who will, and who will not achieve in our profession. Since we have neither the time nor the ability to help everyone, I have always believed that with our limited resources it makes the best sense to help those people with the most promising attributes – those most likely to succeed. If you look carefully, you will see that every successful man has had one or more willing mentors to guide and support him: that's the way of the world."

Rayer is breathing more heavily than ever with the exertion of his last words and a film of sweat now covers his brow. Claude feels that it is time to leave.

"You're tired Pierre, and I must go too."

He clasps Rayer's right hand firmly between his own two, and their eyes meet momentarily with a deep understanding that does not call for further words.

Rayer and Pelouze die within three months of one another: two friends who had so generously guided him in his professional, even if less successfully in his personal life. It was such irony too, that having arranged his marriage to Fanny, they should both die just as he is initiating separation proceedings against her.

Another recent death would also impact on Claude's life. A brilliant Paris physiologist, Pierre Flourens had occupied chairs both at the *Collège* and at the Natural History Museum for many years. In his younger years, his work on the brain had revealed that each region controlled the function of a different part of the body. It was also he who had proved that the semicircular canals of the inner ear were involved with the control of balance. Davaine is now at the *Collège* to discuss with Claude and several other colleagues details of a memorial conference to honour Pierre Rayer's contributions to medical science. He had also raised the possibility of a similar conference to honour Flourens. The two friends are now alone in Claude's room above the laboratory. Davaine is looking at Claude; as always deep in thought:

"You seemed to be rather ill at ease when the subject switched to Flourens."

"I just hope that they don't expect me to provide a memorial lecture for him."

"There were others that knew him better Claude; I doubt that you will be involved."

"It's just that I am now getting many reproaches for omitting his work from my '*Report*'."

Claude had indeed been harshly criticized for omitting Flourens' discoveries from his otherwise highly regarded document. He had mentioned him only in one context; as having attributed to Charles Bell – rather than to Magendie – the discovery of the functions of the nerves that left the spinal cord – hardly a commendation!

"To be honest with you Claude, most people will have read between the lines. They will know that you worked with Magendie on those nerves – and that you supported the primacy of his work."

"But it *wasn't* Bell who discovered the sensory nerve roots: he just deduced it. That's not scientific proof. Anyhow, as you know, Flourens hardly performed any original research in his last thirty years. He was more of a medical historian and publicist than a researcher. He may well have written some fine articles in the past, but I simply could not view his work as a contribution to France's 'progress in physiology'".

"But he had been was permanent secretary of the *Académie des Sciences* for no less than thirty-three years – and his seat on the *Académie Française* was surely justified?"

Claude is tiring of a discussion that was unlikely to resolve anything.

"Alright Casi; the critics of my *Report* may have a point!"

Dreading the emptiness resulting from his mother's death, Claude does not stay in St Julien one day longer than the *vendange* itself. He contacts neither his friends nor his family. Even back in Paris, his mood hardly improves. Twice he visits the *Exposition Universelle*, mindlessly wandering through the labyrinthine galleries and the many pavilions and gardens. On his second visit, he drifts towards the painting galleries. Where was the work of Courbet? A helpful attendant directs him to the *avenue de l'Alma*, not too distant from the exhibition, where in adjacent buildings Courbet and Manet had mounted separate exhibitions of their work. Only a small handful of visitors are to be seen. Claude still feels attached to the Romantic style of painting although he likes the colour and ideas in the painting of both artists.

The *exposition* had also stimulated new theatre – and music too, if one had the passion for it. In a fit of loneliness, he visits the theatre that Jacques Offenbach had recently opened just opposite the exposition. Called the *Bouffes-Parisiennes* it was staging a new type of entertainment, a work by Offenbach himself appropriately named *la Vie Parisienne*. Out of curiosity, Claude goes to see it and later writes to Ronne that the plot had been even sillier than his own *Rose du Rhone*. Surprisingly however, its music had briefly lifted his spirits.

Claude wants no invitations to dinner; neither intelligent conversation nor idle chatter appeals to him at the moment. Furthermore, he is desperately scared lest some food or other upsets his still-sensitive intestinal tract. It is only with the Davaines that he feels comfortable; able there to share his innermost thoughts and concerns. Nevertheless, he knows that he has to find alternative accommodation. He spends hours vacillating about this or that apartment, none of which please him. Hanging over him is the need for an important decision. An unseen hand is propelling him towards finally dissolving his marriage, and with this in mind, he contacts the man whose services Rayer had previously recommended.

The office of the notary Jean Marisot smells very musty as Claude looks across the desk at the man who he hopes will help him. He has in front of him the documents that Claude had sent the previous week. Mumbling softly to himself, the gaunt notary now looks down at them, displaying his totally bald, almost spherical head. Finally, he issues a deep sigh and looks at his client:

"I have read all these documents; from which there are some obvious issues to address. As always, the most important is your reason for requesting the separation.

Claude does not hesitate:

"I can firstly assure you that there is no other liaison in question; my conscience is clear in that respect....."

Marisot nods; he had indeed been a very close friend of Pierre Rayer. He was certain that Rayer would have at least hinted at any such transgression when he had sent him the letter of introduction that lay on the desk in front of him.

"....but I would like you to picture how it has been for me to live with someone, whose every thought and action opposes that in which I believe."

"And what is that, may I ask?"

"Very simply; the use of animal experimentation to help understand the difference between the healthy and the diseased body."

"I see; but was your wife's concern about your methods not reasonable? After all there are many who would support her views – and quite firmly at that."

Marisot is looking at Claude with such a stern expression that he is in no doubt about how his interrogator feels about the matter.

"Undoubtedly. However, I never made any secret of my activities and they were fully evident at the time of our marriage. At no time did I make a commitment to her that I would discontinue what I considered to be essential methods for my work."

"Did she *ask* you to discontinue that type of experimentation though?"

"On many occasions after we were married, I am afraid, and that has been the major problem. My reputation was, and still is built upon what I have done experimentally and the conclusions that I have drawn from those studies. I can provide you with documentation of the recognition I have received for these – from many august bodies within and outside this country and even from the Emperor himself. I think that it would be difficult for anyone to claim that I could have reached those findings and conclusions – quite valuable ones I might add – by any other means."

"Yes, I understand, although you will appreciate that I am not here to judge your achievements."

Marisot is now smiling to himself as he begins to write hastily on a clear sheet of paper, during which the scratching of his pen seems to fill the room. Meanwhile Claude's mind is re-living the many conflicts that he has suffered during his marriage; and finding it difficult to suppress tears of frustration and despair. Marisot could hardly miss seeing his discomfiture, yet continues his intense interrogation:

"And how did Madame Bernard's disapproval of your activities show itself?"

"Firstly by being hostile towards me at the slightest provocation; and then denying me the privileges of hosting my friends – largely my professional colleagues. She has also turned my two daughters against me in such a way that I have no communication with them, despite my best intentions."

"Has she denied you sexual intercourse?"

"No, but her attitude towards me suppresses any sexual urges that I might have felt for her. For the last two years we have led quite separate lives – and slept in separate rooms."

Marisot continues to scratch his ideas onto two further sheets while Claude is looking around the room at the shelves of elegantly bound books.

"Monsieur Bernard, may I say that the concern which you have expressed in your letter about the sixty-thousand franc dowry is perhaps premature."

"Possibly so, but financial matters generally and that in particular have prompted much of our discord. I mentioned it in my letter only because I know that my wife will most certainly raise the matter as well."

"Oh yes; I accept that financial affairs are always pre-eminent in cases of separation. By all means tell me of her concerns – and of course yours."

"You now have my detailed records and naturally the bank has its own which they would surely make available to you. At issue are the seven thousand francs that I used to support my parents' needs at the time – and which I have now repaid from their estate. Then there were the ten thousand francs that I used to support my research. I maintain that it was that which eventually allowed me such professional advancement that I could raise the quality of our life to a very high level. To my way of thinking that is the purpose of a dowry, is it not?"

Marisot smiles and nods:

"...so you must understand that my wife's continuous complaint of my usage of her dowry has been a thorn in my side?"

"But nonetheless Monsieur, *that* is hardly a reason for you to leave her."

"Yes, I accept that."

"Well Monsieur Bernard, I have noted everything that you have said. If it comes to a settlement, I will consider all your points. As you present your points to me, you have made an understandable case for requesting separation. I suspect that Madame Bernard may not object to separation in principle – she cannot be happy as things stand. However...."

He glares meaningfully at Claude

"....do not for a moment underestimate her anger, even fury at being denied a future – dare I say, with a man of your standing. That will have a price. I will write to her shortly inviting her to make an appointment. May we leave it that I will contact you when I have something of relevance to tell you."

Claude shakes the rather limp hand that Marisot offers him, and meets the *notaire's* cold blue eyes that give absolutely nothing away. If he had expected sympathy, even understanding then he was to be disappointed. If anything, the dismay and guilt that he feels is even more oppressive than before.

Claude hesitates before finally accepting Pasteur's dinner invitation. When he arrives, he sees a simply furnished apartment with barely any decorative items; as if there only to provide lodging while its master and his wife explored science and nature. Three of their five children – together with Louis' father – had died within the last six years; anguish is still in the air. Out of consideration for Claude's health problem, Marie Pasteur had prepared a wonderfully light dinner of fish, for which their sixteen-year old son Jean-Baptiste and nine-year old daughter Marie-Louise had joined them. When introduced, mention of her name creates a sudden torrent of nostalgia and yearning in Claude: he decides that he will arrange to see his daughters again as soon as possible.

They are now sitting in the salon drinking some fine dessert wine that had came from their vineyard at Montigny. Pasteur is staring at Claude with his penetrating eyes:

"You are still not well Claude, are you? I just wonder which seed is at fault."

"Either that – or my *terrain* is just too welcoming to any seed that chooses to pass my way!"

"Oh please! I have enough of that in my continuous debates with Béchamp; and I expect that there will be more of the same at the *Académie* next month when I present my findings on those little silkworms."

"What did you find then?"

"Quite the opposite of what I expected. I have not yet found any evidence of any external agent. There are certainly spots on the affected cocoons but no form of corpuscule to indicate an external agent: it will probably turn out to be something like our bizarre weather that is causing it. Of course, Béchamp says just the opposite; claims it's a contagious disease caused by what he calls a *microzyma*. He even thinks that creosote is the answer!"

Marie decides to have her say:

"Louis, you seem to have a never-ending battle with Béchamp; in fact ever since you were both in Strasbourg together all those years ago."

"That's a story for another time Marie! To more important things! I am very worried about *phylloxera*. Where I was studying the silkworms – near Alès – they've already lost some vines from it"

Claude had only read about it in *le Moniteur:*

"Yes; I believe they're expecting it to move north."

"Well, let's hope that it doesn't affect our vines. I gather that the Agriculture Commission is asking Henri Marès to look into it.

Marie was looking worried:

"You are surely not going to get involved with him on that project as well Louis? You have far too much to do at the moment; you don't need any more projects!"

"Well it depends, Marie. I have the Emperor eating out of my hands now. I have virtually solved all his wine problems and I dare say I can deal with the silkworms as well – given better facilities. I want to give him all the best reasons for improving my laboratories – and of course yours as well, Claude. How are they coming on, by the way?"

"I was there earlier this week. They have pulled down one wall into a neighbouring cellar to increase space, but I really need new premises. Anyhow, I haven't the head for lecturing or research at the moment – no students or *préparateur* to help me either. I have told the council that I still need more time to recover. Casimir has given me a table for the room I use in his apartment and I still have most of my reference material in my room at the *Collège*. So I can still write!"

"By the way Claude, it might have taken a little time but the real value of your book is at last being acknowledged; you were just too impatient – far too hard on yourself! Did you see the reviews in *Annales Médicales* and *Annales de la Médecine Physiologique?*"

"Yes, Baillière's people send me all the reviews and of course I must admit that I am now happier about it. It's also selling very well: they recently wrote to me that they want to do an English translation, too."

"I am pleased for you Claude."

Much as he was enjoying the evening, Claude is keen to avoid late nights; he thanks his hosts most warmly – for what was his first social engagement for a whole year.

CHAPTER 17

TOWARDS THE HIGHEST HONOUR

The year 1868 is a special one for Claude. After a mild winter, his health was improving, no doubt helped by a remarkable series of letters and invitations. Rayer's death had necessitated a replacement on the committee of the *Société de Biologie* – and he is elected to be its life-President. Simultaneously the *Académie des Sciences* votes him its president for 1869, while not even two weeks later he is informed that he is to be advanced to the title of Commander of the Legion of Honour. Princess Mathilde (who always knew of such matters before anyone else) had written offering her congratulations – and an invitation to the *rue de Courcelles*.

It turns out to be a boring affair: he finds himself talking most of the time with the poet Théophile Gautier while the preponderance of women are drinking tea and chattering noisily at the other end of the room. Mathilde comments – none too flatteringly – that both men look like ghosts. Claude is surprised to hear from Gautier that he has heard about Claude's *Introduction*. He promises that he will not only read it, but also review it for *le Moniteur,* where he had his regular weekly column.

The most intriguing happening of the year is a letter that he receives from Sainte-Beuve. It begins with an enquiry after Claude's health, with a soft reproach that he had not been at 'the dinners' for some time. However, he goes on to urge Claude to apply for a seat at that most prestigious of societies, the *Académie Française* – in which he himself also occupied a seat – *un fauteuil*. Seat twenty-nine had just become vacant because of the death of Flourens. That most illustrious of all the *académies* was primarily dedicated to the French language: *literati* had overwhelmingly dominated the forty seats in its two hundred and thirty year history. Claude could only suppose that it was the success of his book that had placed him in such a fortunate position. Indeed Sainte-Beuve concludes his letter by congratulating him on his '...*masterly piece of writing*'. Claude would have to talk with Sainte-Beuve in more detail, but for the moment, the challenge of joining the pinnacle of French intellectual activity was one that he could not possibly refuse.

"*Laboratories are the tombs of scientists...*" Pasteur had written in his article, angered by the lack of progress with upgrading of laboratories. So aggressive were his words that the *le Moniteur* turned it down, although it had now been accepted by a scientific review journal that he well knew would catch the Emperor's attention. He described key laboratories in France (including Claude's), contrasting their poor facilities with the magnificence of their counterparts in Germany. "*...and how could France hope to retain its position of excellence in the scientific world, if it deprived its scientists of facilities and obliged them to move to Germany to pursue their profession.*"

The consequence of the article is that Duruy invites Claude to sit with some fellow scientists and senior government officials at a meeting dedicated to this topic. His particular predicament is singled out for attention. Pasteur, who is of course also present makes a proposal which the conference finally accepts: that Claude would transfer from the Sorbonne (where he has so little support) to the Museum of Natural History in the *Jardin des Plantes,* where Flourens previously had his main premises. They would also invite Paul Bert (who had a series of research successes in Bordeaux) to return to Paris and occupy the chair of comparative physiology at the Sorbonne.

It would be a strange person whose spirits would not have been lifted by this turn of events. Claude's health is improving too, and fewer people are making comments about his appearance. He walks with a spring in his step and he sleeps and eats well. His boost in self-confidence is of particular help with the forthcoming challenge for the election to the *Académie* – which he is now discussing with Charles Sainte-Beuve.

"It's not a simple process, *Monsieur*. You are going to have to work hard at it!"

"I still feel that I am hardly qualified to be an academician. The literary eminence of the other members is so extraordinary; and my own credentials seem so paltry by comparison."

Sainte-Beuve says nothing for a few moments:

"It's simply not true. Quite apart from your *Introduction*, which is a masterpiece in its own right, those of your scientific papers that I have read represent the very essence of clarity. And do not underestimate the literary value of the articles on curare and on the heart that you published in the *Revue des Deux Mondes*; amongst the people who matter there will be few who will *not* have read them. I accept that you do not consider yourself a philosopher, yet the reasoning that you employ puts you in a league well above some of the current members of the *Académie*. The mere fact that it is a scientist who has those 'credentials' – as you call them – is a revelation. It will be an example to others both inside and outside the *Académie*; it must surely have occurred to you that your ideas and principles are relevant to pursuits well beyond experimental medicine."

"Yes it has; and thank you for strengthening my confidence."

Sainte-Beuve smiles as he looked down at the table at his list of the current members – the forty *immortels*. Next to each name, he had scribbled personal details and the sphere of interest of each member.

"Of course, there is now not a single scientist on the *Académie* who can speak for you. I have my friends – the liberals, but some will be supporting our friend Théo Gautier who is after the other seat vacated by the death of Ponsard. I am not sure about the other nominations. Rousset is a historian – and we have plenty of those already! Foissac is a doctor, but whoever put him forward cannot believe that the *Académie* needs an expert in mesmerism!"

Claude laughs.

"Well Flourens got into the *Académie* just when he was pronouncing the wisdom of phrenology – which as far as science is concerned isn't much better!"

"You are rather cynical this morning, *Monsieur*! Let's be more positive and see if we can come up with a list of people whose goodwill you might canvass."

Sainte-Beuve looks again at his list:

"Now there's no point in seeing Montalembert or Gratry – as clerics they'll probably give you short shrift. The same goes for our esteemed Bishop of Orléans, Dupanloup."

Claude vividly recalls Dupanloup's vicious outburst against Littré at Pierre Rayer's salon those many years ago. Sainte-Beuve suddenly looks up:

"By the way, have you written your *lettre* yet?"

Sainte-Beuve was referring to the document – essentially a curriculum vitae and a letter of intention – which each prospective member had to submit to support their case for election.

"Of course I have a draft, but now that you've reminded me, I believe that it has to be submitted by the end of this week."

"I am of course well aware of your religious beliefs – or should I say absence of them? There is one question that you will undoubtedly be asked in your interrogation by the company of members: and it's a simple one. Are you for God – or for the Emperor?"

"Simple and difficult at the same time!"

"Exactly! You must surely know of my own anticlerical leanings, but it will not help your acceptance by our august society if you are too honest *before* your election! As I recall the only stance you have taken so far, and which could be interpreted as anti-religious is your condemnation of *vitalisme*. In your letter, do you think that you can possibly say something about God which is nevertheless consistent with your philosophical and scientific beliefs?"

Claude laughed. "It's a tall order. It will take me at least four pages to do that."

"Fine; do it if you can. However, let's get back to my colleagues. Do you know Merimée?"

"Yes; I met him in Compiègne a few years ago."

"Excellent: you must lobby him. Didn't you once tell me that you also knew Girardin?"

"Years ago. I thought that I had written a wonderful play. He convinced me that it would be a disaster – and that I should study medicine!"

Saint-Beuve laughed: "And you haven't seen him since then?"

"No; he wrote me a congratulatory note when my award of the *Legion d'Honneur* was announced. I seem to recall that I thanked him for that, but I suppose that I should have made efforts to keep in touch."

"It's not too late: he still carries a lot of influence, and he'll probably be pleased to hear what you have achieved with his guidance and advice! I would also suggest you see Villemain and de Falloux. They're both liberals, but their views are much respected by the others – even by the clericals!"

Claude passes the Sorbonne the next day, hoping to arrange an appointment with Girardin. In the event, the eminent critic is in his room. He is not at all surprised at Claude's visit and suggests that they might take that very opportunity of talking together. Claude cannot believe how little had changed: the room was exactly as he had remembered it. Girardin himself was grey and a little stooped, but his eyes were just as bright and intense. He seemed genuinely pleased with Claude's visit:

"You've come a long way since we last met – what was it, thirty years ago?"

"Exactly – and quite long ones at that!"

"And my advice then? You have no regrets?"

"None at all. I hope my passion for discovery will still sustain me for a while to come."

"A scientist with passion; now that's something: I always considered scientists to have rather measured emotions."

He points towards a pile of paper on the corner of his desk.

"At this very moment I'm writing a treatise on how different playrights explore the use of passion in drama. I am covering the entities of passion in the family, platonic and conjugal love, tenderness, honour – and of course jealousy, which is surely one of the strongest passions of all. However, I must admit that I cannot recall scientific passion being explored in a play!"

"Well, I can give you examples – even from my own life – about how all those individual passions that you mention can also play a part in the scientist's existence; in fact how they may result from or conversely affect his activities."

There is silence as Girardin digests Claude's words. He looks at Claude with his piercing eyes.

"How extraordinary: I've never considered that. Perhaps you should put your hand to writing a play again when you have some spare time: a scientific play perhaps!"

Claude laughs. There is more silence as Girardin looks up at the ceiling, his elbows on the table; fingers steepled.

"You know, when I heard about your candidacy for the *Académie*, I made it my business to learn about your activities. While you have been forging ahead on new ground, I seem to have been trudging along in the same tracks saying the same things in the same places – and more-or-less to the same people. Do not for a moment think that I am a melancholic, yet we might well spend more time together in the future if you will allow it; my ideas need refreshing!"

Claude is pleased at the direction of their conversation, but Girardin must have been reading his mind.

"But now it is *you* who need *my* help. We academicians are a wily and devious lot, don't you know?"

"So Sainte-Beuve tells me. I believe that above all I need to stand on the side of God."

"But of course; it is so obvious if you look at the composition of the *Académie*. Have no fear though, for once you are *in*, you can change your stand on any matter; academicians are supposed to be flexible thinkers. They won't stand for hypocrisy, but a well-reasoned change of position on any matter can be seen as a sign of strength rather than weakness, don't you think?"

He had to admire his daughters. At nineteen and twenty-two years of age, they stood tall and straight and were well-dressed: all-in-all a tribute to their mother. They had agreed eagerly enough to join him on this sunny afternoon in early summer; in fact, Claude had been quite surprised by the enthusiasm of their reply to his letter – the first that he had ever written directly to them.

Together they had walked the full length of the *Jardin des Tuileries* and were now sitting on one of the wooden benches not far from that on which he sat with Davaine – when the whole question of the impending marriage to Fanny was troubling him. Until now, the conversation had been both sparse and superficial. Claude feels that the time had come to speak frankly.

"I am sure that you are both as sad as I am about the way our family has fallen apart."

Silence.

"Of course I will admit that I haven't always made it easy either for your mother or for you...."

The girls shuffle their feet and draw their shawls more tightly around their shoulders as if to protect themselves from what was surely to come.

"...but at least I have been able to help your mother provide the best for you both – and a good education."

Claude pauses, realizing that he really does not really know how well their education had progressed.

"Papa, I know that you mean well enough otherwise those people wouldn't have heaped so many honours upon you. But there are certain things that cannot be changed."

Claude looks questioningly at Tony whose mouth is pressed into a firm line – just like her mother's.

"You see Papa; it is a matter of your single-minded commitment to science by your abuse of animals. Our life couldn't be more different. We are committed to God, through protecting those helpless creatures."

"I do understand your conflict Tony, but isn't there something beyond our differences. Cannot a father still have love for his daughters: a love which might even be reciprocated? And believe me, I do understand how you feel; you are certainly in the company of many people with similar views and beliefs."

There is silence for a full minute before Claude continues;

"And if I were to stop my experiments now, how would that alter things?"

Marie-Louise jumps to her feet and stands directly in front of her father as if to challenge him, the colour rising in her face.

"It's too late Papa! It would be hypocrisy because it would not be in your heart and soul to do that. It would not be your belief; only your gesture. And God says that one must be true to oneself as well as to others."

Tony decides to support her sister:

"Maman told us that you were reducing the number of your own experiments; but we know that your assistants are nevertheless continuing as usual – at your bidding. Nothing will change our beliefs and principles. In fact with the help of Maman, and some money from the SPA we are now establishing a home for stray dogs."

Claude sighs about the futility of it all. In the silence that follows, one could hear the distant 'clink' of teacups, and they walk in silence to the nearby tent. They refresh themselves in the shade of an enormous oak tree, the girls looking everywhere but at their father. Tea is being offered from a large shiny urn, and while satisfying their thirst they resume superficial and meaningless talk about Paris, the weather and the beauty of the flowers in the meticulously kept garden plots around them. Wordlessly, Claude accompanies his daughters back to the *rue de Luxembourg*, their empty farewells creating such despondency that he could hardly drag himself back to the Davaines.

The election interview for membership of the *Académie* takes place on a grey and solemn morning when Claude's nasal cavities seem obliterated by an infection; his head twice its normal size. Exactly as Sainte-Beuve had predicted, he is asked about 'God and the Emperor'. As he answers, he hopes that God is not listening: hypocrisy was not usually one of his failings. His letter to the *immortels* – all four pages of it – had exercised his skills at tortuous reasoning about how he placed himself between spiritualism and materialism – yet naturally more on the side of the former!

The combination of his impeccable credentials, reputation and performance – and the devious academic politics conducted behind closed doors, result in Claude winning twenty-one of the thirty-two votes cast. He is duly elected. What lies exactly one year ahead is the ceremony for his formal admission – and an acceptance speech which would traditionally involve his tribute to his predecessor – Pierre Flourens.

There are just two things to be done before he leaves for St Julien. Firstly, he had to let the *Collège* know that he would be recommencing his lectures with the coming winter term. He had prepared a list of topics that would embrace his approach – philosophically and practically – to 'experimental medicine'. He duly deposits it with the council for their approval. His second mission is to the Natural History Museum. Its director Eugène Chevreul is a chemist and naturalist of international fame. It was through the Barrals – father and son – that he had originally met Chevreul, and for some years, they had sometimes met on Sundays in his salon – just to talk. Claude had also spoken with him at meetings of the *Académie des Sciences* to which he still contributed; at the age of eighty-three still able to make a sharp comment when discussion got out of hand. Lectures were also held at the museum, and Claude had occasionally presented some of his research findings in the intimacy of its small auditorium. Chevreul had more than once congratulated him on his lectures; yet Claude knew that in general people appreciated their content more than his actual delivery.

"We are truly looking forward to having you join us here, Monsieur Claude."

Claude is surprised: "You know, I haven't been addressed that way for almost fifty years!"

"My apologies then, but I meant no offence."

"I know that. At the time, I was apprentice to a pharmacist and he meant it kindly too. It simply brings back memories."

"And memories sometimes hurt, don't they?" replies the octogenarian, nodding vigorously, his wild hair in even more disarray than usual. Claude decides not to be drawn out in this way:

"I must tell you that I too am looking forward enormously to having a laboratory here. As you know I am fascinated by the parallels between animal and vegetable life: there can hardly be a better place than this to pursue that idea."

"Certainly! More would come of science if we diversified our sources of inspiration. I have never regretted being a chemist with the Gobelin tapestry people: it helped me define my 'law of simultaneous colours' back in the thirties."

"Forgive my ignorance, but what was that?"

"Basically, if you place small dabs of contrasting colour next to one another on a canvas, the retina perceives a much more vibrant effect than if those same two colours are mixed together before applying them to the canvas."

"Ah yes; didn't Delacroix use that theory in his later paintings?"

"Indeed! I'm impressed that you know that. Of course, others are using the theory now." Chevreul looks pensive, "Delacroix often came here to discuss colour with me. Such a remarkable man, and he would have had so much to give us were it not for his untimely death."

Without speaking they continue to walk slowly through the *Jardin des Plantes* towards the small, dilapidated building that had been Flourens' base at the Museum.

"I think that I have been remiss in not congratulating you on your election to the *Académie...* er...Claude."

Claude laughs.

"Thank you. It was a surprise as you can imagine; but now rather daunting. I had seen myself purely as a scientist, but since my little book was published, it has prompted some people to mistakenly call me a philosopher. This election now appears to throw me squarely into the world of letters!"

"I think I know what you mean: the seemingly unavoidable need to live up to the expectation of others."

"Yes: I seem to spend my life trying to do just that. My first task in fact is to write my discourse for the *Académie*. I will apply myself to that during my autumn break in the Beaujolais; but I have already come up with a problem. I will have to begin with the traditional tribute to my predecessor. As you know, there have been very few academicians who were not men of letters – or of the church. Flourens was one of very few scientists to take a seat – as it were."

"Yes, he was a special man; in fact when I read your *report* on the progress of French physiology last year I was surprised that you hardly mentioned his research. I consider that to have been quite a serious omission – if you don't mind me saying so." Chevreul had stopped walking, and was now looking directly at Claude: "You know, we at the Natural History Museum are very proud of his contributions to the physiology of the brain and bone, most of which he made – right here!"

Chevreul gestures towards the building at which they had just arrived; the small rather squat edifice, overgrown with ivy would soon be Claude's second centre of research. Claude feels thoroughly embarrassed at Chevreul's comment, but there seems little point in offering an excuse.

"Others have made that point too, Monsieur. I will have to live with my mistake; that is certain."

They had walked around the building in which Flourens had worked for thirty-three years of his life. Now they were discussing the alterations: changes that would not be exactly those which Claude had hoped for. Some weeks after the meeting at which the sorry state of French laboratories had been discussed by Pasteur, Duruy had written to say that Claude would be receiving only half of the 400,000 francs which he had requested for renovations, equipment and staff. The Emperor had apparently decided that physiology was costing him almost as much as the artillery! Chevreul sees the grim look on Claude's face:

"Have no worries, Claude, work will start very soon here; you'll see big changes by the time you return in October."

Drafting the outline of his acceptance speech is occupying much of his time in St Julien. Never has he had such difficulty in phrasing what he wishes to say; and Chevreul's reproach about Flourens continues to haunt him. As has become the routine, Ronne visits him for the day, and when Claude rather hesitatingly asks him to read the latest draft of his speech Ronne pronounces it 'a fine piece of rhetoric'. That ceremony was still a few months off and Claude had more immediate lectures to prepare – his winter series at the *Collège*, the first of which would take place in January. Towards the end of his stay in the Beaujolais Claude receives a most upsetting letter from Pasteur:

> "...and imagine my distress when I woke up to find that I had lost the use of my left arm – completely. At first, I thought I had simply slept upon it as one does sometimes. It soon became clear that it was more serious; my left leg was weak too and I could not speak properly! My doctor has diagnosed what he calls a 'vessel obstruction' within the right brain hemisphere. Several weeks on and I can still barely walk; Marie must assist me even more than usual! What will this mean to my work, Claude? Can one recover from such a disability? The doctor tells me that I should be happy that the damage was not on the other side of the brain; else I would not even be able to write you this letter! I hope that your stay and the harvest have both been fruitful. If time permits, I would much value your reply – to Montigny if you will, where we have now come to recuperate for a few weeks.
>
> *Affectionately and respectfully yours, Louis*

Claude replies immediately:

> St Julien, October 27th 1868
> Dear Louis
>
> *I was immensely distressed to get your letter. My anatomical and physiological wheels have been turning ever since, and I must say that you are indeed fortunate that the lesion was not on the opposite side. I must admit my experience to be minimal in this area – at least from the clinical viewpoint. Yet I have sometimes seen such cases as yours notably returning to full activity within – admittedly – months. So, you must not lose your will. My work with curare leads me to advise full range passive movements and massage of both your affected arm and leg. I feel sure that Marie will oblige with this:*

I reason that this will minimize the spasm and contractures which might otherwise occur.

I look forward to your return to Paris, which will obviously be considerably later than mine. I leave next week after a stay that has been notable for all the writing I have done. May I also say that before coming here I met with that marvellous Chevreul who was as welcoming as he could possibly be. I must thank you again for your bold appeal for our laboratory needs; it was an extraordinary performance!

To you and Marie I send best wishes,   Claude

He is sweating with anxiety. It is more than three years since he last gave a lecture here. As he enters through the side door of the *Collège* amphitheatre, he feels the familiar spasm in his stomach. He remembers Magendie telling him once that if he ever stopped feeling anxious about speaking in public, he would cease to be a good lecturer! Claude notes the additional gas lamps that had been installed; attached by steel brackets to the newly painted white walls. The resulting brightness promptly lifts his spirits. People are everywhere – even sitting and standing in the aisles – and as he takes his place behind the lectern, the audience leaps to its feet and applauds enthusiastically. Emotion grips his throat as he realizes just how much he had missed this part of his life. His concerns, apprehension and uncertainties all melt away as he begins to speak:

"*Mesdames et Messieurs*, it was regrettable that illness compelled me to miss three years of winter lectures. Your warm welcome prompts me to reassure you that although my voice may not have been heard – because my body needed rest – at least my mind was kept active. Accordingly I wish now to challenge *your* minds with some ideas and results; those that put experimental medicine on to the scientific plane on which it belongs."

He pauses to take a sip of water, meanwhile glancing at the audience that seemed to consist of more women than usual, and quite young and attractive ones at that.

"Post-mortem examination of patients dying from disease is an important exercise which we do as often as we can. It may tell us why someone died, yet only rarely does it provide information on how the disease has arisen. My lecture series on experimental pathology explored the challenge of understanding how physiology undergoes its transition to pathology. I must emphasize again: this process is always a continuum and not the two disconnected processes in which most people still believe. So now we are at the point where, using experimental logic and procedures we can examine the mechanism of symptoms and the approach to treatment of disease."

Claude pauses to allow latecomers to find a niche for themselves in the overcrowded auditorium.

"Regrettably we cannot experiment on human illness. Why? Because that would mean either a medical or surgical intervention – and not necessarily for the benefit of the patient. Our ethical and moral principles make such experiments on man difficult, if not impossible. Of course, we can learn something just by observing what happens to the ill person without treatment – what is referred to as the natural history of an illness. Such observation has merit, if only because it provides us with a point of comparison. Furthermore, allowing an illness to run its natural course – the so-called *treatment expectante* of Pinel – may indeed be a prudent approach in many instances. Yet one may consider that unethical too; doctors always feel compelled under the Hippocratic Oath to try to cure illness. Therefore, in their wish to do *something* for their patients – dare I say in return for the fees they receive….."

He pauses to allow a ripple of laughter to pass through the audience;

"….doctors have mostly employed empirical – in other words, improperly evaluated – therapies. This empiricism has hindered understanding and progress for too long. It is no secret that that I do not involve myself in medical practice: there are simply too few treatments whose efficacy I can vouch for."

Claude realizes that he may be moving too rapidly – but continues the step by step development of his ideas:

"I will say however, that we may be deluded in thinking that a recovery from illness is a consequence of our action. Many conditions do improve without our intervention; we may simply be observing a naturally-improving illness for which any treatment which happens to be given at that time incorrectly gets the credit. Such faulty reasoning has given rise to the adoption of the most bizarre forms of treatment!"

"I also want to emphasize that anything we give to patients – even a totally inactive compound – may produce an improvement in symptoms; the so called placebo effect. We still have very few ways of judging the progress of an illness other than by its symptoms. Accordingly, we may think that it is our actions are benefiting a patient, when this is not the case. Going beyond this, my esteemed predecessor François Magendie always maintained that every effective medicine is – when used in larger doses – a poison! In that way, we may quite easily harm our patient – even fatally. Later in this series of lectures I will show you that the reverse also holds true: poisons when used in lesser quantities may prove to be useful drugs."

Now he was coming to the awkward part:

"In practice we need to turn to experiments on animals; to use vivisection in order to answer important questions. This again has ethical and moral aspects to it. Yet many people would surely agree that sacrificing a small number of animals in return for the saving of many human lives would be a fair exchange. Furthermore, we have for centuries used or sacrificed animals – for labour, for their fur and for food. We therefore need to put the vivisection of animals into a sensible perspective."

Again he takes a sip of water, and is aware of hushed conversation within the audience. He notices that only ten minutes of his lecture remain.

"I will conclude by informing you that in each of the next lectures in this winter series I will be dealing one by one with the systems of the body. I will describe how the experimental method which I use allows us to approach disease and its treatment. I appreciate that the complexity of today's subject may have proved confusing and as usual I welcome your questions."

There is an understandable reluctance of the audience to begin discussion, but suddenly there is a sea of hands.

"How can your approach lead us to understand the influence of *vitalisme* on the cause and the progress of disease?"

The question is from a middle-aged man whom Claude guesses might be a physician.

"*Vitalisme* is really a cloak under which we hide our ignorance. In subsequent lectures, I will provide evidence that if carefully investigated the admittedly fickle and unpredictable behaviour of disease – which has been traditionally attributed to *vitalisme* – can be explained by definable physical and chemical factors. My colleagues Davaine and Pasteur, amongst others, have also recently shown that minute organisms, variably called germs, viruses, *vibroniens* or *bactéridies* are also often responsible for illness. Over time, I believe that *vitalisme* will increasingly be seen to be a totally meaningless entity."

The questioner is not to be silenced however:

"...but some years ago I heard the late Professor Magendie – whom you referred to earlier – invoke *vitalisme* as the reason for the inconsistency of his experimental results. Surely you must still experience the same problem."

Claude wonders if he has time to deal with that question; it brings back vivid memories of Magendie's strange attitude when he could not repeat a previously successful experiment. He had to reply.

"Much as I respected my late master, I have shown that *vitalisme* can not be invoked in research either. If one looks carefully enough at two seemingly identical experiments but with different outcomes, it is always – and I must emphasize *always* – possible to find that the conditions of the two experiments were different. This is the concept of 'scientific determinism'. In brief then, if the conditions of two experiments are identical, then the outcome will also be identical. I will be giving numerous examples of this in my forthcoming lectures. I should add that I get extremely excited when I get a different result when I repeat an experiment. When I eventually identify the extra 'condition' responsible for the difference in outcome it often turns out to be both surprising and highly important."

The full hour of the lecture had already passed, but a woman in the audience is frantically waving her hand:

"My imminent return to America precludes me from attending your further lectures. Could you provide some examples of your statement concerning the poisons that have turned out to be useful medicaments?"

Claude uses a sip from his glass of water to marshal his thoughts:

"Perhaps the best known is the foxglove plant. The poisonous nature of its leaves was recognized in the sixteenth century, but the active component, *digitaline* was only found to have beneficial effects in heart failure two hundred years later – and it is still in use. Another example is the plant called Deadly Nightshade. A dose as little as one tenth of a grain is poisonous to man, yet in even more minute doses the extract of its leaves can be used to treat kidney and stomach disorders."

He pauses for breath.

"But I can think of no better example than curare, that powerful killer poison which South Americans use to tip their arrows. One of my previous students, Doctor Vella in Turin has shown that in much smaller doses, it can be used to relieve the spasms of tetanus and to treat the convulsions of epilepsy; I have shown the same using strychnine. One of my early teachers, Armand Velpeau, who died two years ago raised the possibility in one of my lectures that curare might be used during anesthesia – to achieve muscle relaxation and thereby facilitate surgery, especially on the chest and abdomen. To my knowledge this has not yet been attempted."

Many more hands are now trying to attract his attention, but Claude raises his own arms aloft, palms facing forward in a gesture that indicates that he cannot take further questions. With a smile on his face, he bows briefly and leaves the amphitheatre with loud applause ringing in his ears. He retrieves his overcoat, and is standing in the vestibule of the *Collège* preparing to brave the wintry wind.

"*Monsieur*, if you have a moment?"

"Madame, at your service."

The woman who had addressed him is elegantly dressed in a dark green coat in a strange brocade material fastened high in the neck. Her jet-black hair in bouffant style is topped by a 'sensible' hat of the same colour set off by a white ribbon that is echoed in a pair of white silk gloves that she clutches in one hand; a white umbrella in the other. Bright eyes look steadily into his, and a half-smile suggests that what she is going to say is not to be taken too seriously.

"I first wished to say how much I enjoyed being at your lecture. I am not a scientist, but your words have given me considerable cause for thought."

"Thank you, Madame."

"But I really wished to ask for your advice."

"If it is in my power to help you, then…"

"Only a minor matter really. I have a problem with my ear that a surgeon wishes to deal with by operation. As I listened to you – and particularly hearing of your comments on doubtful treatments, it seemed that you might help me find another opinion; so that I may be sure that I make the right decision."

She was speaking with a most unusual accent – and phrasing; certainly not French by birth or education, he thinks.

"Right now, I am somewhat pressed for time. Could you write me a brief note outlining your problem? I promise that I will reply to you quite soon. A letter sent here to the *Collège* will find me easily enough."

"You are most kind."

"Good evening, Madame!"

"And to you, Monsieur."

CHAPTER 18

SHINE ON THE HORIZON

Renovations were in full swing at the Museum: a new roof already in place, and windows that would better exclude draughts. Claude's room is small, but a large window would allow him to look out on to well-manicured shrubbery: south facing, too, so that on sunny days the room would be pleasantly warm. He would welcome that warmth, since a succession of colds accompanied by bad headaches had all but prevented him from working at times. He would use the long narrow room for experimental procedures. It communicated at one end with the new animal house; at the other with the chemical laboratory. There were so many projects that he wanted to get under way, yet his current priority was to prepare his lectures: a process that seemed to take him longer with each passing year.

Back at the *Collège,* he is sitting at his table perusing his correspondence: first a note from notary Marisot who had eventually persuaded Fanny to visit him. Having considered her future prospects she had indicated that she did not wish to remain at *rue de Luxembourg*; she and their daughters would move out of the apartment in the following spring. She assumed that Claude would support her and the children at the same level as he had done during the preceding year. Marisot mentions that he was due to see Fanny again during March and would write again thereafter. Claude is not sure whether he should be elated about this news. However, it does resolve his dilemma about finding an apartment.

Another letter was written on expensively embossed notepaper headed five, *rue des Bassins*. He knew the street well; two facing rows of distinguished mansions that he had often passed – enviously. It was from the woman who had approached him after his recent lecture – a certain Marie Raffalovich. Apparently, their mutual friend Ernest Renan had recommended that she attend the lecture, and speak with Claude afterwards. In her letter, she briefly describes her symptoms: some general malaise accompanied by an earache with a mild discharge. What concerned her most was some loss of hearing in that ear. She hoped that Claude could suggest someone who could advise treatment that would avoid surgery! Claude immediately thinks of his old student colleague, Alfred Richet, with whom he had dissected at the *école pratique* all those years ago. He was now the professor of surgery, and might well be attending one of Claude's forthcoming meetings.

The foyer is humming with excited voices of the scientists arriving for the first *séance* of the *Académie des Sciences* for 1869. Since Claude would be its president for the year, he is mingling with a number of members with this or that suggestion before the meeting begins.

"Well, Claude, here I am!"

Claude turns to see Pasteur leaning awkwardly on a cane; left arm hanging limply by his side.

"I did exactly as you said I should, and here I am!"

His face is lop-sided, left side drooping; speech as forceful as before yet lacking in clarity. They embrace each other unashamedly, attracting the attention of the few scientists still in the foyer.

"It is good to see you Louis. When did you get back to Paris?"

"Just before Christmas. We were obliged to leave the children with Marie's cousin during our stay in Montigny; but she refused to spend Christmas without them!"

"Of course, I understand. Are you at the *École* yet?"

"I've visited once, but it isn't easy. Have you ever tried using a microscope with just one hand?"

Even if Pasteur's brain functions were intact after his stroke, the physical disability would surely hinder everything he would try to do.

"I suppose you will have to delegate rather more of your responsibilities."

"We'll have to see whether the Emperor agrees with you. I may be stretching my luck to ask for even more help with all his projects. After this meeting, I am off to meet the dean of the faculty: perhaps he will be sympathetic to my needs."

Taking Pasteur by the arm, Claude helps him into the auditorium and eases him gently in a seat at one end of row of benches, noting at the same time that his old friend, Alfred Richet is indeed in the audience. He moves to the ornamental desk at the front of the auditorium from where he will be chairing the meeting, reflecting that it will be quite a special occasion, not only as his first chairmanship of such a *séance*, but because Berthelot and Davaine will each be presenting papers on their latest research.

Berthelot's presentation is on different forms of carbon in the chemical world. Claude is only vaguely interested and there are few comments or questions when it ends. Not so with Davaine's paper. He describes the serial transmission of anthrax from one animal to another and provides the proof that the skin condition of malignant pustule is the earliest stage of the usually fatal anthrax syndrome. It stimulates considerable discussion and argument.

Claude reflects that his weekly leadership of these meetings would be a heavy commitment. Yet it would expose him to discoveries not only in the medical sciences but also in geology, inorganic chemistry – even engineering design. It would do him no harm to appreciate the length and breadth of French discovery and innovation, even if they were outside his immediate spheres of interest. He is truly proud of his fellow scientists in France and would enjoy presenting the thirty or so prizes which the *Académie* awarded in the course of the year.

"Alfred; a moment please if you can spare it?"

The session has just concluded and Claude had pursued Richet out of the auditorium so that he would not lose him in the crowd.

"Claude, well done. I liked your chairmanship and your comments."

"Thank you but I didn't stop you to invite your compliments! Could I interest you in seeing an acquaintance with what sounds like a simple ear problem?"

"But of course!"

"If you can give me a date and time, we could perhaps go there together and I could introduce you to her."

Richet rummages in his pocket and produces a small diary.

"Would ten-thirty on Friday of next week be in order, do you suppose?"

"I will drop the lady a note today – her name by the way is Raffalovich; lives in the *rue des Bassins*. If you don't hear from me please assume it is indeed in order."

"In which case may I collect you from the *Collège* at ten o'clock?"

"With pleasure – and thanks, Alfred."

A number of men are jostling for Claude's attention. It is only a half hour later that he is able to leave the building. Pasteur had disappeared.

It had been some time since Claude had travelled in a carriage so well isolated – from both the cold and from the noise of wheel over cobble. The seats were upholstered in red velour, and had unusually large armrests that were holding him firmly despite the carriage's swaying motion.

"You have indeed become quite eminent, Claude; and my compliments on becoming an *immortel*; I should have dropped you a note earlier."

"Thank you Alfred. I'm quite looking forward to doing something a little different; it's not quite the *academia* that I have been used to."

"By the way I also heard about your unfortunate family affairs; and I am truly sorry."

They are crossing the Seine over which the dense morning mist still hung ominously.

"Yes; it's upsetting to say the least; such a long drawn-out process, too. What about your family Alfred? Do I recall correctly that one of your children studied medicine?

"Yes. In fact Charles is still at medical school – takes his doctorate this year all being well."

"....and into his father's footsteps?"

"Not necessarily. He is certainly a hard worker, but they still don't teach medical students how to think; it would probably do him some good to spend some time with you. Are you still teaching at the Sorbonne?"

"Fortunately I finish there at the end of this academic year. I would have been happy to continue had they at least provided a demonstrator and laboratory; but it is not to be. Anyhow Paul Bert is probably better at that type of teaching; he is due to start there quite soon; when I move to the Natural History Museum."

Meanwhile they had arrived at the Raffalovich residence and the maid shows them into a drawing room resplendent with colour, gilt and the softness of wood. The unusual design of the chairs immediately catches Claude's attention: and even more so, the glitteringly ornate way in which they had been decorated.

"Do you like those chairs?"

Madame Raffalovich had entered the room so quietly that both men look around, startled. Not wishing to display his ignorance of furniture design, Claude decides against continuing that line of conversation.

"Madame, may I present Professor Richet, whom I mentioned in my letter. I feel sure that he can help you."

"Without surgery I hope." She says, extending her hand. "I am such a coward."

"*Enchanté*, Madame. Perhaps we should talk about your symptoms first and not jump too soon into treatment."

"May I suggest that you come into the library then? We can leave Monsieur Bernard to admire the furniture – indeed, sit on it if he so wishes. Katrina, do offer the gentleman some tea. Do you also wish for some, Monsieur Richet?"

"Thank you, no. Perhaps afterwards...."

Some time later, they emerge from the library.

"It's a straightforward infection of the middle ear, Monsieur Bernard." Richet announces. "I have suggested a gargle, some ear drops and the avoidance of excessive heat in the apartment. Treatment may need to continue for two weeks or so."

He turns towards his new patient.

"It's most unlikely that you will need surgery Madame, but may I call again in two weeks?"

"With pleasure. And may I now offer you tea?"

"Thank you, but I have another appointment."

He turns expectantly to Claude whose tea had only just been poured. Madame Raffalovich helps resolve his dilemma:

"By all means stay and finish your tea, Monsieur Bernard – unless you also have urgent business to attend to?"

"Since I live so close by, Alfred, I believe I might accept Madame's offer; and thank you again for helping us. By the way, do please ask

Charles to call in and see me at the *Collège* if he has a spare moment; I'd really like to meet him."

The story of the Raffalovich family unfolded over a succession of cups of tea, served from a copper samovar whose intricate enamel and gilt decoration Claude was now closely examining.

"That one," she comments, "was made in the town of Tula, south of Moscow. That's where they also make our guns and even some wonderful steel furniture – like that chair."

She is pointing towards a contrastingly austere and surely uncomfortable chair standing in the corner of the room.

"Thankfully we could bring most of our belongings with us from Russia. It helps to remind the children of their roots."

She explains that she is Jewish and was born in Odessa, on the Black Sea.

"We were so young when we got married. Grisha was nineteen and I was only seventeen. He is actually my uncle, and our two families almost lived together in neighbouring houses. My mother always said that we were destined for one another – you know, that sort of arrangement was common enough in our part of the world!"

Claude cannot resist the rather impertinent question:

"And you are happy together?"

A moment's hesitation, then:

"I think I am lucky. He is a good husband, and an even better father: I hope that you will meet our children too, and you will soon see why I consider myself fortunate."

"What does your husband do here in Paris?"

"Now that's a long story. Are you sure you want to hear it?"

"Indeed I do."

Madame Raffalovich pours more tea, continues:

"Grisha worked for his father's business in Odessa. Enormously successful they were too, exporting our wheat and corn all over the world. Then life started to have its problems. First, we had to overcome the battering that our city received during the Crimean war. Then there were attacks on Jewish property."

"Why?"

"Envy; jealousy. The usual. Some Greeks whom the company employed burned down our warehouses; I suppose they had a grudge against us. More people joined in by damaging other Jewish property. You know, with our names it was not so difficult to know that we were

Jewish – and once the ball was rolling, matters got out of hand. It is part of our history. We were never very popular in Russia – unless we were needed; like the branch of our family who are bankers. The Tsars employed them as financial advisors!"

Claude shakes his head in disbelief; how remote he feels from such religious discrimination. Madame clearly wished to continue:

"Anyhow I developed a strange illness and Grisha took me to Vienna where they are supposed to have some of the best doctors; yet they couldn't find out what was wrong. Grisha had to go to Paris on business in '63, so he took us all along – Arthur and Sophie too. To cut a long story short the Emperor's physician, a certain Doctor Rayer got me better. Did you know him by any chance?"

Claude cannot believe the co-incidence.

"Not only did I know him but he was my mentor: I believe I owe him much of what could be called my success."

"Isn't it such a small world; we were all so sad when he died? Well, Grisha was so happy with my recovery that he decided that we should stay in Paris. He had always intended to establish a company office that would service the western European countries, and at the same time provide financial advice that would link French and Russian business interests. And so here we are: not Misha and Grisha anymore – but Marie and Hermann!"

"What an enormous upheaval it must have been for you all."

"Not really. Firstly we Jews are used to pulling up our roots and moving – when we have to! And then, I already spoke fluent French: did you know that it's the first language of educated Russians?"

"I had no idea. But you wouldn't have known a soul here?"

"Fortunately my sister was already living near Paris – married to the Comte de Chaptal, so that gave us a useful *entrée*. Soon afterwards, my parents came as well. You know, when you have so much family nearby and three children to keep you busy, you cannot feel lonely. We are really happy enough."

Her smile is so radiant that Claude does not know what to say next; but Madame Raffalovich is quite content to continue her story. With a healthy income and some capital, the couple had quickly established themselves. The appointment of a maid and a children's nurse had made it possible for her to continue her literary activities. These consisted largely of interviews and writing articles which she sent back to the *Journal of St Petersburg*, on topics ranging from politics and finance to music, art and even the sciences.

She had a particular aptitude for foreign languages, and it had not taken long for her to meet interesting people from all walks of life. She welcomed the unusual, the extreme and the exotic, either as entertainment or for their market value in the articles she wrote. Quite unashamedly, she tells Claude that based on the lecture she had heard him give at the *Collège*, he would fit into both categories!

"Hearing your life story makes me realize what a protected existence I have led." Claude comments, once she has finished.

"Then it is time for you to tell me about *your* life!"

Claude tells his story, not entirely chronologically but in a way that seems to hold her attention. She is obligingly silent throughout, and when he has to hesitate – which his deep emotions sometimes dictate – she does not attempt to prompt him.

"And so I now mainly lecture and write. Such experimental work as I do consists of filling in the gaps in my earlier work….."

He hesitates again; Madame Raffalovich must have thought that he was debating with himself about which project he should complete first – but his mind was already one step ahead:

"…and putting it into context with what is being done in other countries."

As an afterthought, he adds: "It would surprise you to learn that I have never travelled outside France."

"So how do you keep in touch with your colleagues' work?"

"Some of them visit me, and of course we also have access to their journals, but you will have surely discovered that French national pride dictates that foreign languages are not widely taught. On top of that, I am singularly inept at learning other languages: I have been trying for years to master the German language. Germany – and Russia as well – are our biggest scientific rivals, you know."

Claude is decidedly happy about the direction of their conversation: could he foresee the possibility that Mme Raffalovich might translate for him this or that document, an important letter or an article that he had read? Although tempted to now present his set piece about German and Russian laboratories, he decides that he had sufficiently unburdened himself. Indeed, he finds it quite difficult to tear himself away from the warmth of his meeting with this intelligent, charming and extremely attractive woman. He unashamedly suggests that they might keep in touch.

Paris, February 5th
Dear Madame

A recent encounter with Richet prompts me to write to you. As he will have told you himself, he affirms his view that your problem should not require surgery. Since infection seems the likely cause, I might put my own view that, one's general health – insofar as that can be defined – plays a role in the resistance or otherwise to such an assault. Given the demands placed upon you by your work and family, we both suggest that a brief stay in Enghien – even better St Germain – might help your recovery.

I truly enjoyed the discussion of our respective lives. It would give me great pleasure also to meet your husband and children although, as I explained, I am not currently in a position to offer hospitality. That will change by the summer. I trust by then that my own proneness to infections – simply a cold at present – will also have resolved.

I send you my very best wishes for a quick recovery.

Claude Bernard

The fabric of French life was beginning to shred. Rural cotton industries were being threatened by competition from the major centres as railway connections improved. Entire vineyards in the southern wine belt were being punished by phylloxera, and the disease was continuing its penetration northwards, creating terror in the wine industry. Silk production was threatened too, not this time by strikes or riots but by a spreading silkworm disease that was resisting all attempts to eradicate it. The people of France now saw that with the victory of Prussia over Austria, the balance of strength in Europe had changed; France was no longer the European military power that it had been in the fifties; there was much talk – and fear – of a future powerful German empire; re-armament therefore an expensive necessity. The peacetime expansion that had so pleased the Parisians had consumed much of the money that was now needed – and that ridiculous Mexican adventure had yet to be paid for!

So that he could re-vitalize Paris, Haussmann had been allowed to dig an enormous hole in the country's coffers. Now his golden image had tarnished because there was little credit to fill that hole. His fellow politicians were sharpening their knives – and Louis-Napoleon's illness was beginning to undermine the Bonaparte charisma. All this was creating extreme *angst* amongst the moneyed classes. As a result, they chose to leave their wealth lying dormant in the banks of France. Amongst others, the important investment bank, Crédit Mobilier had just gone to the wall. Nor would it be salvaged by such a weakened government.

However, life had to move on and the structure of government had to be maintained. In early May, Claude is invited – even summoned – to serve Louis-Napoleon on the Senate. It flatters his ego and will certainly provide new experiences. The blue livery that senators are expected to wear for Senate sittings is alone extravagant; undoubtedly also impressive to the public who for the first time that November are allowed to witness its sittings; but they will not hear Claude, who is consistently silent and acquiesces to all the Senate's resolutions. Yet he has the benefit of rubbing shoulders with the *élite* of Paris; Nieuwerkerke, Sainte-Beuve, Merimée, Duruy and Count Walewski, the son of Napoleon I – to name but a few. The additional 30,000 franc annual 'pension' was also more than welcome at this stage of his life.

Paris, March 21st
Dear Dr Bernard

Since you were so kind as to write to me, I thought that the least I could was to tell you my health has indeed improved: Professor Richet seemed pleased when he saw me at the end of last month. I much appreciate that you recommended him and will certainly take your advice about leaving the bad air of Paris for a week – which is as much as I can persuade my husband to take away from his business. I hope that the disorder that was afflicting you has by now fully resolved. Perhaps the demands which you make upon yourself are also weakening your resistance. May we discuss the intriguing matter of the physiology of leisure at some later date?

It also occurs to me that I might translate for you, from German or Russian scientific journals, one or more articles that may be of value to your researches. Please do let me know if this would be helpful to you. Meanwhile my husband and I would be pleased if you could join us here for dinner on April 10 at seven o'clock.

With my kind regards,

Marie Raffalovich

One evening Claude is sitting with the Davaine's after one of Georgina's finest dinners; a fine roast of lamb that she said always reminded her of visits to her paternal family in England. He decides to share his plans with them:

"After much thought I've decided to return to the apartment in *rue de Luxembourg;* Marisot told me that Fanny is indeed moving out in April – to a house in *rue de Cherche Midi*, it seems."

"But why so soon?"

"I'm not sure; even Marisot is puzzled. But her new place is just at the other side of the *Jardins de Luxembourg* from the *Collège*, at least it might prove convenient to meet Tony and Marie-Louise in the gardens from time to time."

"There's no harm in being optimistic Claude, but I suspect that there's a long way to go before that happens." Georgina comments. "Perhaps Fanny has a new friend?"

Claude shakes his head. "Not Fanny. More likely, something to do with her animal protection society. Unfortunately the apartment has the wrong sort of memories for me, but I don't have a mind to search for a new place at the moment."

"You'll have to find some help. Would your servants stay?" asks Georgina.

"I will really only need a maid when I leave here. I will offer that Jean-Paul remains with Fanny – if she can accommodate his horse and carriage. She and the children can make better use of them and I am quite happy to rely upon cabs to take me here and there. Anyhow, you have both been wonderful to me: I am sure that you appreciate how it has been for me to have your company at a difficult time."

Nothing is said for a few minutes, and Claude's mind returns naturally to his current concern: his acceptance speech to the *Académie*.

"May I ask a favour, Casi: it is about my reception speech at the *Académie Française* next month?"

"Of course. Do you wish me to read it?"

"No real need for that: there's one aspect that continues to bother me."

"And that is...?"

"Flourens!"

"I see. Is it that small problem you told me about before – his eulogy?"

"Exactly. But it's not a small problem, as you well know! I simply cannot bring myself to praise a man for whom I carry so little respect."

"I'm not used to hearing such harsh words from you, Claude."

"You don't think that they are justified?"

"I'm not sure that justification is the point. From what you told me previously, you believe that Flourens supported Bell's originality over Magendie's; not because of his scientific conviction but because of a difference he had with Magendie on another matter."

"Exactly."

"But the rest of the scientific world acknowledges Magendie as the one who truly discovered the function of both the anterior and posterior nerve roots?"

"Also correct!"

"Then why bother? Why can't you find something else pleasant to say about him? After all, he was obviously very literate: both a good historian and a good lecturer by all accounts. In such a discourse you are surely not obliged to describe his research in detail or refer to anything personal in his attitude."

Claude is silent; his friend is right. There was indeed no advantage in antagonizing a scientific community whose support he might later need.

He had never before experienced such warmth and intimacy as on that Friday evening in April. For the Raffalovich family, celebration of the Sabbath was of course a routine observance. For Claude it was an expression of family unity of a depth that he had rarely felt with his parents, and certainly never with his own children.

Before he sits at the table, he is obliged to put on the little embroidered skullcap; it keeps falling off, much to the delight of the children! Once Monsieur Raffalovich had pronounced the blessing on both the sweet wine and the traditionally platted loaf of sweet bread with its covering of poppy-seed, there was even more joking and hilarity. The two older children, Arthur and Sophie tease each other mercilessly, while young André (who had been born the year after the Raffalovich family arrived in Paris) scurries around the room uttering squeaks of delight as he discovers little felt animals that his sister has hidden away in remote corners.

"Marie tells me that you are at the *Collège*."

"Yes; I spend most of my time there. I'm also at the Sorbonne for the moment until they arrange my new laboratory at the Museum; I will have proper research facilities there."

"I was at your *Collège* last week listening to a debate." Raffalovich comments. "Those remarkable economists, Chevalier and Levasseur were speaking. Wonderful minds, but I doubt that they have the answer to this country's problem."

"Which is…?"

"Basically there's not enough money – and what there is in circulation seems to be in the wrong pockets! Look at Haussman's indulgences! Now Duruy is moving towards free state education throughout France. That's not cheap either."

Madame had her ideas on that subject.

"But it's such a wonderful concept, Grisha. The church has had far too large a hold on education – and on young people's minds, too. It's about time too that girls had the option of being educated outside the church system; then we wouldn't have to spend our money on a governess either!"

Raffalovich realises that he might be on a better footing with the country's finances:

"I'm also not sure that the free trade arrangements that Chevalier worked out with Cobden a few years ago is in our interest either. It is far too concessionary to our rivals. Our government needs to be stronger, and in lots of ways. We are rapidly becoming weak, even if not quite yet the poor man of Europe."

Claude is wondering whether the Senate will be discussing these matters. He realizes that his ignorance of economics will again prevent him from making a meaningful contribution to any discussion on the matter. He is glad when Raffalovich changes the subject.

"I must thank you for arranging a medical opinion for Marie: she is so much better now. By the way, she tells me that she is going to do some translations for you."

"Yes, I am most grateful for that: knowledge of languages is not one of my attributes I am afraid."

"In Russia you can't get very far without them. Marie has such talent with words!"

Raffalovich looks at his wife with admiration as the children are dispatched to their rooms. Their discussion about the world and their past lives continues well into the night. Claude is quite sad when his visit ends and he is transported home by the Raffalovich's carriage.

Claude is obliged to visit Fanny in the *rue de Luxembourg* to discuss the division of their goods; a painful necessity. She had insisted on having the fine furniture from the salon and bedroom, and the contents of the children's room. He asks her to allow him to keep a few mementoes of their earlier life together and some photographs of the children. Of course, all his books and his study furniture would remain, as well as its extra bed in which he had slept for much of the time.

There is little personal talk, and Claude's questions concerning the activities of the children are met by monosyllabic answers. Agnès had decided that she would not work any longer for Fanny. Claude is tempted to ask her to remain with him; the memory of her concern for him, the allure of her soft smile and her still trim figure stirring an urgent sexual longing that he had thought would have long since passed him by. Common sense dictated that he should not pursue this approach.

The maid whom he eventually employed on his return to the apartment was a stark contrast. Mariette Rey stemmed from the Auvergne, and it was Lesage who had arranged the initial interview. She was the epitome of a rough diamond, and it rapidly became evident that her only desire was to protect and nurture him – but in her own rather dominant way. To keep the peace he soon learns to give in gracefully to her notions of how the apartment should be re-equipped and organized; even what and when he should eat. Any discussion seems pointless. He wisely decides that he would reap the benefits of her benevolent authority, which would then allow him to concentrate on his academic needs. Was there anything at the moment more important to him than his discourse?

Paris on May 27, 1869 is fair and warm. Claude feels that it augurs well for the ceremony in which he is about to participate; a noble and a festive affair. He is brilliantly elegant in green livery, three-cornered hat and the ceremonial sword, which seems to him so inappropriate for a man of letters! It is time for his discourse to begin and for almost the first time in his life his heart is beating uncontrollably. How foolish, he thinks; it would surely not be a catastrophe if he failed to entertain the members and their guests!

What he presents in his talk is the outcome of innumerable changes over the course of a whole year. In the event it is also a tired presentation, probably because of its long and tortuous journey! Its lack of spontaneity, warmth and wit disappoint the critics from both *le Figaro* and the *Journal des Débats*: "The new immortel...' they later wrote, '...*was singularly ill at ease*'.

Indeed he had been on edge. He had begun by relegating the soul into the realm of poetry; it was simply not a subject for scientific study, he had insisted. But why (he asked himself afterwards) had he interpreted conscience, reason and will in such a materialistic manner? It was simply not convincing. He had also not hit the right note when it came to fitting the concept of intelligence into Flourens' research on neurophysiology. Nor had he dealt well with Flourens' clear separation of psychology from physiology – probably because of his own conviction that the two were so closely integrated!

Later in his speech he had stated that the world of letters was the '... elder sister of the world of sciences'. Yet the *cogniscenti* would have recognized that this idea had its origins with Auguste Comte, whose theme he had borrowed: Comte had maintained that during civilization 'letters' had evolved first; therefore they were *inferior* to the 'sciences'! It was just as well that the *Académiciens* were not aware of one of Claude's many notebook entries:

> '...*a man of letters is one who talks pleasantly about nothing. The scientist who writes well can never be a man of letters because he does not write just for the sake of writing, but to say something. The man of letters must, in terms of his profession sacrifice substance for style.....*'

When he arrived at the subject of Flourens himself, he had emphasized his qualities as a historian and publicist. Remembering Chevreul's comments, he had referred to Flourens' research – but again so broadly and vaguely that it did him no justice – in every sense damning him with faint praise. Observers who knew of Claude's prejudice had later argued that it was asking too much for the death of Flourens to have dulled Claude's animosity towards him.

Towards the end of his discourse, he had referred to the 'wonderful support' that Flourens had received from his wife. Thanks to the wagging tongues of the press, the news of Claude's marital collapse was now in the public domain. There would have been many in the audience who would have readily understood the envy attached to those words. Finally, he could not bring himself to make any mention of God! Therefore, the spiritualists were dismayed and the materialists branded him as a lukewarm partisan. It was only his friends in the audience who appreciated that Claude had spoken largely according to his beliefs, with no hypocrisy or false sentiment. At the end, he had received only polite applause, as the critics later emphasized in their respective newspapers. Claude must have realized that he could not have expected otherwise.

There were surprisingly few repercussions. Claude's first meeting as Senator and his first official presence at the *Académie* follow soon after one another. He receives an occasional sharp comment, yet in neither gathering does he sense that he has done serious damage to his image.

Claude is now at the Raffalovich household every Thursday evening. Tired after chairing the meetings of the *Académie des Sciences*, his contact with the family has become a high point of each week. Mostly he stays for a meal – and brings gifts: a book on mathematics for Arthur, a pair of recently hatched chickens for Sophie or a toy for André. His flowers thrill Marie, while a bottle of wine always appeals to Hermann. Of the three children, it is with Sophie that he establishes the warmest friendship.

Marie's translations begin to appear – of an article about the action of the heart from the Cyon brothers in Russia; and of another article from Wilhelm His in Switzerland. When he leaves Paris for St Julien, he takes them with him.

From the edge of the terrace, the full moon is clearly illuminating vines now denuded of their fruit. The familiar smell of recently crushed grapes fills Claude's nostrils. He takes a deep breath of gratitude; that providence had allowed him this luxury of space and freedom. The harvest had taken less of his time than ever before. Morel and his family had done well: with luck, there would be at least 150 barrels of wine to send off to the bottlers. He reminds himself to take a few bottles back to Paris with him. He reasons that he should not have a problem with the *octroi* – the Paris customs officers – since his own label would be on them!

He had spent much time reading; and with such pleasure. Within her translations, Marie Raffalovich had placed question marks and even an occasional phrase in the margins – as if trying to understand as well as translate. He wonders if he could also ask her to translate letters to the scientists who had written those articles. At times, he swears that he can smell her perfume emanating from the pages in front of him. Now, a disturbing thrill passes like a wave through his body as he recollects her beauty; the darkness of her eyes, her full breasts and her deep voice. What would he sacrifice for such an attractive and smart woman to be by his side – with his work – in his bed?

Disturbed and unsettled, he returns to his study to try and finish revising his report on French physiology. Already overdue, Hachette had asked for it as a matter of urgency. As he sets his mind to the task, it dawns on him how little had been achieved in that domain in the three years since its first edition. What a contrast with the explosion of new discoveries from Germany and Russia – and even England! He feels the blood rising in his cheeks as he realizes how much time and energy he – and Pasteur – had expended in their fight for French research laboratories; and with so little success. To calm his anger he sets aside the manuscript, and begins a letter to the woman who had created such a new dimension in his life; calming him, yet stimulating and sustaining his daily momentum.

Almost within the week, he receives her reply:

> ...*and you will be sad to hear that Sainte-Beuve died suddenly last week. Ernest and Cornélie Renan were here for dinner last night and told us that his demise was blissfully swift and painless. Did you read that Hector Berlioz has also died?*
>
> *Please do not anger yourself about laboratories and such. You give of your best always and no one can ask for more; and you must not feel concern about people calling you a materialist. Such statements imply systems that you tell me you always disregard. As I remember it, your goal is only 'truth'; and as far as I can see that has no system attached to it.*
>
> *We do miss your company on Thursdays, and the children are looking forward to your return – at the end of next week, I suppose. I was pleased to hear that your health has improved; there really must be something special about the vines that surround you! Grisha and I were only remarking yesterday how much illness you seem to suffer here in Paris. We also benefited from our stay in Trouville in the summer. Were it not for Grisha's need to be here, I suppose we would be better off living in the country – like my sister. By the way, Grisha*

is off to Odessa again tomorrow – he needs to spend some time on further expansion of the business there! If your work permits, will you call in to see me and absolve me of my loneliness?

Yours truly,

Marie

PS I have just today completed a translation of that article by Justus von Liebig. Do you think that animals can change inorganic into organic substances, as he has shown to be the case in plants?

Claude could hardly wait to visit the Natural History Museum, yet when he arrives it seems to him that little progress had been made with his new laboratory. Chevreul is nevertheless in high spirits:

"You know, I was very pleased to substitute for you at the *Académie des Sciences* during your absence."

"I can well imagine. It didn't tire you too much?"

"Please; I'm only eighty-four!"

They both laugh heartily.

"Eugène, I want to be quite sure that we get first-class help for my courses here – whenever they start. Working with both plant and human physiology calls for someone with more skills than those of my usual *préparateurs*."

"I'll keep my eyes and ears alert for someone, but I imagine it won't be until spring now that everything will be ready for you here."

Winter and spring pass seamlessly into one another. His new *préparateur* at the *Collège* is proving very helpful with the practical aspects of his course on experimental medicine. Unfortunately, the young Louis Ranvier does not fully share Claude's passion for vivisection, but he does have an interest in learning about the microscopic anatomy of nerves. Thanks to a letter sent off by Marie Raffalovich, Claude had been able to purchase, through von Liebig in Germany, a microtome of unique precision. It meant that particularly thin sections of any sample of tissue, such as a nerve could be prepared for microscopic examination – thus allowing more detail to be revealed. Ranvier is a contented young man!

The knowledge that he would soon be moving into his new laboratory at the Museum makes Claude agonize less about his facilities at the

Collège; for a change, he feels very positive about the direction his life is taking. His health had also never been better. Marie had observed the change too; whereas he had eaten little food on his previous visits, Claude had just enjoyed a wonderful meal with her family – excepting Marie's husband, who was still in Odessa. Claude finishes the evening by playing a card game with Sophie that he had discovered in a nearby market on his way to their house. The children had now all been sent to their rooms for the night.

"I'm not sure that it wouldn't be better for you to spend the night here, Claude."

Marie Raffalovich had pulled aside the heavy curtains and was now staring into the street; awash with a succession of heavy downpours of rain that had started earlier in the day.

"I can't see any cabs out there – and I surely don't blame them in this weather..." She hesitates. "...and you know, we do have a spare room that you are welcome to use – would you care to see it?"

Claude does not miss the coquettish smile as she issues an invitation that is quite impossible for him to refuse.

In the month of May, 1870, Claude finally moves into his new laboratories at the Museum: so wonderfully spacious – and for the first time not in a cellar! Chevreul had come up with a possible candidate for the post of *préparateur:* a young man by the name of Lemaistre. He had some grounding in plant biology but little experience of animal experimentation.

For the lecture he had just concluded on the principles of research in experimental medicine, Claude had persuaded Ranvier to come from the *Collège* to help him. It had not been one of his best. The audience was restless and yet another cold and the usual accompanying headache had made it difficult for Claude to concentrate. He had not been happy that Marie Raffalovich had decided to witness his first lecture at the museum. The very next evening, a Thursday as usual, she broaches the subject of his talk:

"As a journalist, Claude, may I make a comment about your presentation a few days ago?"

"Please; I would be delighted."

"The ideas and facts which you share with your audience are fascinating, and you take great pains to explain everything, even – dare I say – quite often repeating yourself. Yet you do not always seem to give yourself time to develop your ideas and reach a final conclusion."

"You know, that's the first time I have hear that shortcoming so well described. I've been aware of it, but if you can help me devise a solution, I would be most grateful."

There is silence as they both think about the challenge. Marie speaks first:

"I appreciate the value of your approach: your listeners are allowed to draw their own conclusion from a set of observations, which of course challenges their intellect."

"Correct; I have also considered that this process allows my 'message' to become more firmly etched in their mind…"

"…and yet, if some of your audience is not used to such an approach…."

"Yes; I see what you mean. Perhaps it would be better if I try to present fewer concepts in the course of a single lecture; less tiring for the intellect, would you say?"

"Yes, that might be the way forward."

"In that case, would you do me the honour of attending next week's lecture?"

"With great pleasure! And shall we have some tea now?"

CHAPTER 19

A Storm Brewing

Queen Isabella of Spain had been deposed. For its new head of state, the generous King Wilhelm of Prussia offers the Spanish a distinguished member of the Höhenzellern family, who would become its King Leopold. Louis Napoleon is furious; even scared. He is already fearful of Prussia to his northeast expanding in size and strength: adding a Höhenzellern to the south would be a further threat to France – in fact, totally unacceptable. Obligingly, Leopold withdraws and Benedetti, the French ambassador in Berlin is given the task of exacting a promise from Wilhelm that no further attempt will be made along these lines.

Perhaps Benedetti does not speak as diplomatically as he should have done; or perhaps Bismarck, King Wilhelm's chancellor is jostling for European supremacy. In any event, the King refuses to make such a promise. Bismarck then presents to the press such a powerful rebuttal that it produces fury in hearts of their Imperial majesties, the French government and the people of France – as was surely intended! Accordingly on July 19th, 1870, the French nation responds by declaring war on Prussia. More accurately it is the Empress Eugénie who does so, since Louis is at end of his tether with illness, and quite incapable of issuing such an authoritative statement!

Claude now decides to attend the Senate hearings more regularly. There is barely room in that stiflingly hot chamber, where possibly for the first time the entire complement of senators is jostling for places; a bizarre eagerness to hear what could only be bad news. The gallery is also overflowing with an inquisitive and frightened public wishing to make full use of its recently acquired rights. They chatter loudly and anxiously despite Rouher, president of the senate repeatedly calling the house to order. Senators, especially from the border regions of Alsace and Lorraine are given ample chance to speak; it is there that the conflict will surely erupt.

Claude goes directly to the Raffalovich household to share his news. The door is opened personally by a very pale Marie; anxiety etched on her face:

"Marie, you and the family must leave Paris! At the *senat* today they decided to make an official recommendation that whoever can leave should do so, and as soon as possible."

"Yes; so I heard. But where to?"

"Hermann will have his own thoughts; but perhaps your usual summer retreat in Brittany. If the Prussians should get the upper hand, the battle front will move south towards Paris; the north-west should be safer."

"Hermann has just left for the *préfecture*; he wants to make a decision before the children get back from school. What about you, Claude?"

"I have time to decide: it's easier if one is alone. I was due to go to St Julien anyhow – but I will probably leave earlier in view of the circumstances. You must not fret about me; it is the children's safety which we must consider first."

"...and *your* family?"

Claude suddenly feels guilty: he had not given given Fanny or his daughters a moment's thought over the last few days.

"I will write to Fanny this evening. The only thing that I can offer them is the safe haven of St Julien; but they probably won't accept it. Pride will take priority over common-sense."

They are standing side by side, silent, looking beyond the deep window towards the wonderful garden, rich in spring colour. Claude's arm suddenly encircles her waist and she turns to face him; eyes meeting.

"I feel so confused, Claude. You are a remarkable man....and that night when it rained..."

Their embrace is urgent and tender, obliterating all thoughts and concerns; yet each seeking protection and reassurance in a world of uncertainty. The sound of the entrance door opening drives them instantly apart, Marie dabbing swiftly at moist eyes. Seconds later, Hermann walks into the salon; face grey with concern. If he is aware of anything unusual, it certainly does not show, although Claude senses that his greeting is perhaps more perfunctory than usual:

"I have just seen Bélin at the *préfecture*, Misha. I think we should leave very soon, even though he assures me that there is no immediate risk. There seems to be little confidence either in our armaments or in the men who will have to use them."

"The *senat's* conclusion today was that we have absolutely no allies on whom we can rely." adds Claude.

"Absolutely, Claude. Louis might have hoped that after the help he gave Italy against Austria, it would now come to his assistance; but it won't. He's alone in this world!"

"So why did he declare war?"

"It's simple; Prussia's annexing of the south German states has given it the confidence to threaten France's presumed supremacy; that was what the Höhenzellern affair was all about. This war is nothing but a question of stupid pride!"

He turns to his wife:

"Misha, I am sorry, but I do want to be away from here by the end of the month."

"Of course, but I was just talking with Claude about where we should go; he was thinking of Brittany."

"I would have preferred the neutrality of Switzerland, but getting there would probably mean travelling through the area of conflict. Trouville might be safe, but I think that Nice would be even better; they are unlikely to invade that far south."

Claude feels that he is in the way and makes his apologies:

"Do please let me know of your plans; so we may keep in touch by letter."

"Certainly Claude, and please don't delay your own departure."

Claude feels his abdomen tightening as he leaves *rue des Bassins*; desperate fear mixed with heartache and frustration with his passion for Marie. He must distract himself with his work: there was a lecture to give at the Museum, one at the *Collège* and a paper to present to the *Académie des Sciences*. Nor will he desert his *préparateurs* before it is absolutely necessary.

They had all assembled in his room – to hear and to be heard. Claude feels that it is his responsibility to share with them his knowledge of the political situation. He had just returned from a further meeting of the *Senat* and tells them that French forces have taken Saarbrücken. News of that success had spread like wildfire and there was so much rejoicing in the streets that Claude had to fight his way to the *Collège* through the rejoicing crowds. 'On to Berlin!' they were shouting, the call echoing along the narrow alleyways.

There is much debate that afternoon and the tone of his young colleagues' discussion is impressive: an atmosphere of bonhomie and spirit, perhaps because they were under a common threat. Claude realizes that he had never spoken with them collectively in this way and wonders if such regular meetings might prove just as valuable for scientific discussion? They easily reach a unanimous and simple decision: they would all work together until either conscription or an official announcement called for termination of their experiments.

As he leaves the *Collège* that evening, he encounters a grim-faced Renan. How it plays havoc with the emotions, he comments sadly. For Renan it was the German philosophers and theologists: for Claude the likes of Ludwig, von Liebig, Voit and the many other German scientists. Until now they had all been on the same side of progress and understanding; their German counterparts revered for their thoroughness and brilliance. And now, Prussia was using those same qualities against France.

Within two weeks, the German invaders occupy three important towns in the north-east of the country: Froeschwiller, Wissembourg and Spicheren. Louis had played the opening game very poorly; or more accurately, he had interfered with the 'game' of his most senior soldiers. Recovering briefly from his illness he had charged north, interfering with generals whose own plans might just have borne fruit in those early stages of the conflict. His forces had armaments, but the big muzzle-loading guns often misfired hopelessly, while the *mitrailleuses* were so new that the soldiers had not been properly instructed in their use!

Fearing the worst, the fortification of Paris was now proceeding at a great pace, creating *angst* in the hearts of all Parisians. Nor were they reassured by the eighty kilometers of nine-metre high walls that encircled Paris; neither the wide moat beyond it, nor the peripheral railway within its walls which could readily redistribute troops to where they were needed.

News of the fall of Sedan, accompanied by the capture of Louis spreads instantly to Paris. Bonapartism had failed the French and the public becomes a seething mass of angry disappointed republicans, breathing fire. They rapidly occupy the legislature. The Empress Eugénie and the Prince-Impérial escape to England under the cloak of her dentist Thomas Evans. Princess Mathilde and her entourage flee north to Belgium. Meanwhile and almost overnight, the third Republic is born.

'*Leave Paris immediately*' is the order of the day. By mid-September, Claude is on his way to St Julien, on the very last train that will leave Paris for some time to come. Some of his fellow passengers have no idea where they are going; but anywhere is preferable to a Paris that they are certain will be overrun by Prussians. It is a circuitous voyage for Claude; priority has rightly been given to troop movements. He realizes that his train will be stopping at Bourges, where he presents himself, unannounced at the house of a most-surprised colleague from his medical school days. He only reaches St Julien at the end of the month, missing the harvest that is so dear to his heart.

The first thing that greets him in St Julien is a letter, rich with the scent of Marie's perfume:

Nice, September 20th 1870

Dear Claude

You will be pleased to hear that we are now safe and comfortable enough with our old friends her in Nice. The Gurevich family moved here some years ago and can accommodate us well. Grisha immediately travelled onwards to Odessa via Genoa and Milano and heaven knows where else. I feel so blissfully remote from danger that I feel guilty at having left Paris so far behind. I am assuming that likewise you are now settled amongst your happy vines.

We are not alone in our southern retreat. Merimée is in Cannes, though very ill, and others too have found a hopefully safe haven here. I hear that Renan has sent his children to Brittany for safekeeping.

He and Cornélie have decided on principle to stay in Paris as moral support. Such a fine man! Our three young ones seem happy enough here and begin their schooling again quite soon. I had often heard about this southern climate, but it is hard to describe adequately the gentle warmth of the sun – and the softness of the sea. Perhaps if it becomes dangerous there, you might join us – and we can then reassure one another. There is surely sufficient space in this sprawling mansion that overlooks the ocean.

So very affectionately,

Marie

Josephine had received advance notice of Claude's arrival, the telegraph lines out of Paris having been cut by the invaders only on the day following his departure. Accordingly, she has had time to make the house warm and fill the larder. The perfume of late summer roses is permeating the downstairs rooms and particularly Claude's study. How long would he have to stay? Moreover, would he indeed need to move further south if the war threatened?

"What do you think of all this, Josephine?"

"Bad, Monsieur! Christophe has been called up and left for Lyon yesterday. They say we are safe here, but who knows?"

"And Jean-Pierre?"

"He wanted to go too, but he's apparently too old. He would be happy to take you about in the carriage when you need him."

News of the Prussians' encirclement of Paris comes only a few days later: subsequent bulletins telling of the impact of the siege are in all the Lyon newspapers. Claude receives several letters from Paris by means of the carrier pigeons which ferry mail *via* Tours. Each produces in him the most wretched feelings of sorrow and guilt. He should have acted like a Goncourt, Renan and Gautier (whose writings on the siege were now being distributed to provincial newspapers) and stayed in Paris to at least provide moral strength where it was much needed. Claude also sends some messages inbound to Paris using the balloons travelling inwards from Tours.

Autumn merges inconspicuously into winter, and his walks amongst the vines and in the woods become fewer and shorter, until heavy snowfalls and drifts render him housebound. His mood slips even further towards the melancholy as news of the ongoing siege and its consequences reach him:

> *Nice, November 18th 1870*
>
> *Dear Claude*
>
> *I hear that 23,000 brave Frenchmen have already died. Where will it end? You should know that Merimée too is dead, while in Paris no doubt many more will die in weeks to come. We hear little except through the newspapers. The surrender at Metz means that all the pressure will now be on poor Paris. The siege is into its second month and I feel guilty when I eat chicken and fresh tomatoes, for in Paris it is apparently horses, rats and cats and then only for the fortunate few. Grisha is now with us again, which I find re-assuring since there is disorder in Marseilles, which he feels could move east.*
>
> *Thank you for your letter. I enclose a translation of Voit's article on nutrition, which seems so irrelevant in the face of what I mention above. I trust that your body and mind remain active and that the other parts of your anatomy (which you mention in your last letter as causing you such distress) are being kind and considerate to you.*
>
> *I laughed when I read your comments about novels: how you are bored by them having the same sort of ending! I am sure that exploratory science brings with it much more exciting endings – by now, you have surely gone back to reading Diderot, Descartes, Ludwig and von Liebig!*
>
> *Right now, I miss your company so very much.*
>
> *Affectionately,*
>
> *Marie*

The Prussian forces had reached Lyon; its fortresses now under occupation. Anxiety is mounting in the Beaujolais, and Josephine is concerned that she had not heard from her son for some time. It is not just war injury that is weakening the French forces – but disease. Smallpox had gradually made its way through France, adding to the disability from dysentery and typhus. Some soldiers were so weak and ill that they had deserted to the Prussian lines, only to be turned mercilessly back.

Presuming that the Prussians would not penetrate beyond the immediate surroundings of Lyon, Ronne writes that if circumstances permit he would visit Claude soon. The small occupation force in Villefranche should not interfere with his plan.

Meanwhile time is hanging heavily on Claude's shoulders and the early, sharp winter makes it impossible for him to find animals for the experiments that he would like to perform. A recurrence of his abdominal pain and headache is also making it difficult to concentrate on writing. The snow is already knee-deep; even his wanderings unappealing now. As Marie had predicted, he consoles himself with books on science; with a myriad of articles that feed his imagination on parallels between animal and plant biology. During the day, he makes a few notes that he hopes will eventually allow him to perform crucial experiments for his book on that subject.

Ronne can only spend one day in St Julien, since pharmacists were now drafted 'on duty' at the hospital in Villefranche, a staging post for the war-injured. He arrives quite late in the morning, since his carriage had become stuck in a snowdrift at the foot of the hill. Two burly farmers had to lend a hand to free the heavy wheels. After one of Josephine's excellent lunches, they decide that they should simply enjoy the fire that she had prepared in the salon. Claude observes that Ronne had suddenly aged: his face is grey and deeply lined, while his previously prolific hair had receded to hardly more than two bushy sideburns. A slight spinal curvature gives him a dismal and introverted aspect; not at all consistent with the Ronne he had known.

"Where is this all going to lead, Claude? Our Henri is under Bazaine with his Army of the Rhine, and we have heard nothing since he left. You should be glad that you have no sons!"

"I might as well have no daughters either. I have sent three notes into Paris now – via Tours of course – asking about their well-being. No reply! Perhaps the pigeons have headed south to the sun! For the moment, I assume that at least within the walls of Paris all is well – except perhaps for food shortages."

"But such unnecessary suffering and disorder! How did we get ourselves in such a mess?"

"I maintain that it is all a question of education."

Ronne looks at him curiously.

"I'm serious, my friend! Of course I am talking about higher education: willingness to use some basic psychology and philosophy – not just history!"

"They will have you training the army soon!"

"No Ronne, I am serious. There is absolutely no reason why one cannot view politics – and war strategy – in a systematic and scientific manner, instead of employing deviousness and impulsiveness, and the assumption that exactly what worked before will work again. I was only thinking yesterday that the *determinisme* which I apply to science can be equally applied to war."

Ronne laughed. "You'll have to convince me!"

"I will try!" Claude leans back in his chair; eyes fixed on the ceiling.

"Will you grant me that no two battles are the same, and that one can regard each war as an experiment? After all, victory is never assured in advance?"

Ronne nods.

"So then if one carefully studies the successful wars that have been waged in the past, one should be able to identify exactly those conditions which made it so. Historians have done that rather well now for centuries. The next step involves recreating those conditions."

"Yes but that step is so crucial, Claude; you are oversimplifying war? What about geographic conditions, climate, enemy attitudes and troop morale? They are all beyond a general's control."

"They might not be under his control, but to some degree he can time his initiative with optimal political conditions, and launch the offensive on favourable terrain, with appropriate visibility – good or bad according to requirement – and at a time when morale is higher rather than lower. I am not suggesting that it would be easy, but I would like to be present when those famous generals who decide our fate make their plans, just to see how much real intelligence they bring to bear on the problem."

They both laugh.

"It is good that you can make light of war, Claude. However, tell me about yourself. Are you not lonely?"

"Certainly not! Of course I would rather not be shut off from civilization."

"That's not quite what I meant; I am referring to Fanny and the children."

Claude hesitates – as always when challenged about personal matters.

"If I said that I have put all that behind me Ronne, you would call me callous and heartless. Yet I have to survive. Fanny is a lost cause; as far a Tony and Marie are concerned, I consider it wiser simply to wait. I have tried my best, so far with no reward for my effort. I can do no more, and therefore my life must move forward. As you well remember, years ago I told you that love was not for me."

"How can you be certain? Have you given yourself the chance?"

"Perhaps not Ronne, but my life has been and still is – almost entirely – committed to science now. I am not prepared to give that up."

Claude had at first been reluctant to speak about Marie Raffalovich, but decides that it would be sad if he could not confide in his best friend.

"There's a wonderful woman who now helps me with translating articles; she and her family have taken me under their wing, too; almost a second home, you could say."

"Is she attractive?" Says Ronne, with a knowing smile.

"Er...very!"

"And happily married?"

"I have my doubts. She and her husband – she's a journalist and he is in the finance and export business – each have their own professions and separate interests. Certainly they make fine parents for their three children."

"...and you're fond of her Claude; I can see that!"

"I think that any man would give his right arm to have a wife with her warmth and intelligence."

Nothing is said for a full minute. Ronne is staring at the fire – now reduced to glowing embers. Claude looks self-consciously at his boots, then at his friend and finally into the fire too, as if it held the answers to hidden questions. One corner erupts momentarily into a bright flame.

"How often do you see her?"

"At least once a week; I have a regular invitation to dine with the family on Thursday evenings after the sessions at the *Académie des Sciences*. You know Ronne, she never fails to ask about what new research was presented; and then she interrogates me about its significance. If it is on a physiological topic, she even wants to know how it relates to my own work and what...."

He halts in mid-sentence; his eyes glistening with tears. He shakes his head, hopelessly. Ronne puts a hand on his knee:

"Have you heard from her since you arrived in the Beaujolais?"

"Several times – the family has taken refuge in Nice – and we send letters to each other almost weekly."

Ronne sighs; gets up from his chair to fill his glass from the decanter on the sideboard:

"May I...?"

"Of course; perhaps mine as well....I need it."

Ronne is sipping from his glass, thoughtfully:

"So there is a woman who is capable of turning your head, Claude – even if only for a moment."

A crooked smile and an uncharacteristic blush momentarily displace sadness from Claude's face.

"Yes; I suppose so...but what a wonderful moment it was."

They are both silent for a full minute.

"And where does this lead you."

"Nowhere, Ronne: I tell you! I have been given the privilege of sharing in the life of her family in a manner I never thought possible. Her children are also very affectionate towards me; obviously no replacement for my own family, but at the same time so very heart-warming. I am not going to spoil all that for some nebulous excitement that has no future."

"And what does she say about it?"

"Oh! We talk about it when we get the chance. She certainly returns my affection; we are physically very attracted to one another. She agrees though that we would risk destroying our lives – and the lives of those around us. It's a decidedly unsettling *modus vivendi!*"

"Claude, how I wish I could help you."

Ronne gets up, warmly hugs his friend. Their conversation switches to the vineyards and the activities of their mutual friends; and not much later he leaves for Villefranche.

Back in Paris, academic life continues miraculously – even the *Académie des Sciences* maintains its Thursday meetings with the ageing Chevreul in the 'chair'; yet another of Claude's colleagues who had felt the call of loyalty. In St Julien, Christmas passes quietly. In its little church, prayers are said for the safety of those exposed to danger, all thoughts with the suffering of Paris and the uncertainties in the provinces.

The New Year ushers in the next terrible phase of the war: the shelling of the capital. Far from being directed at military targets, the shells tear up trees, shatter tombs, and char churches, several hospitals, schools and a prison. Many die and thousands are injured. In the second week of January, the Museum receives a number of hits which shatter the glasshouses and a few other buildings – while sparing Claude's new laboratories. Fortunately, there is no loss of life, but it prompts Chevreul to announce to the *Académie des Sciences* on the following Thursday that he holds King Wilhelm of Prussia and his chancellor personally responsible for the atrocity!

Despite that violence, Claude is now considering a return to Paris. He is bored and frustrated – '...*like a caged lion*' as he says in one of his letters to Marie. What even more agitates him is a letter he receives notifying him that professors at the Sorbonne and at the *Collège* would have their salaries terminated unless they reappeared for duty. Crazy, he thinks; many of the students would have been drafted into the army and the rest could not possibly have a mind to absorb information. If *he* had difficulty marshalling his thoughts, one could not expect better from students. There is also talk that unoccupied apartments in Paris might be requisitioned for the use of the army and for those dispossessed because of the siege. Claude had frightful images of his one thousand books being used to stoke a fire in his salon!

News of the humiliating armistice comes at the end of January; '...*a shameful and disastrous outcome*', Claude calls it in another letter to Marie. The indemnity that Bismarck later demands in return for peace is five billion francs and the annexing of Lorraine and Alsace to Prussia – plus a triumphal parade with all his troops down the *Champs Elysées*. It is the end of February when the treaty of peace is finally signed at the Prussian headquarters in Versailles.

During that month, Claude had managed to bring himself to sketch the outlines of his new book – and with it the list of experiments that he wished to do on his return to the Museum. He could do no more until he returned to Paris. He is therefore delighted when he receives a letter from Pasteur who had been in the Jura during the war together with his family – except for his son Jean-Baptiste who had been called up to serve his country. In his letter, Pasteur mentions that he had lost touch with his son after the fall of Metz but had eventually located him – starving and ill – but fortunately not seriously injured. Pasteur was now staying with his brother-in-law in Lyon. Being so close, he was keen to spend Saturday visiting Claude before he returned to Paris.

Pasteur takes the train to Villefranche and then the coach to St Julien. Having noted his disability, the coachman had made a special detour, and deposited the incapacitated Pasteur right at the gates of Claude's house. They were now sitting together in his study.

"Excellent dinner, Claude – and the wine of course!"

"Thank you for the compliment. As you can see, I am not badly off here, although I am most anxious to return to Paris. Do you suppose it is safe yet?"

"There's still no gas lighting in the streets and of course no cabs; it can't be very safe. There is such anger that the government has capitulated to the Prussians. People are threatening reprisal against Thiers' government for capitulating to the Prussians. When Frenchmen threaten other Frenchmen in that way, things have got to a sorry state. I'm not sure whether I am more fed up with this country or with those Prussian bullies!"

"I understand your sentiments, Louis. Have you heard whether your laboratories have been damaged?"

"Shells have apparently demolished one whole wing of the *École* and soldiers are bedded down in my laboratory; that is why I must go there. By the way, I've decided to send back that honorary degree I got from the University of Bonn: I realized that it has Wilhelm's signature on it – as the university's chancellor!"

"I sympathize with you; I must look at my degrees from Leipzig and Berlin to see whether they bear his signature! My laboratories both at the Museum and the *Collège* are apparently unharmed, but I suppose that it now depends on what happens when the Prussians fully withdraw."

The Prussians only withdraw to the east of France, holding on to Alsace and Lorraine while they wait for their five billion francs of indemnity. Angry at French capitulation to German demands, self-branded leftist *communards* take over the *Hotel de Ville* and assassinate two generals to show how they would deal with any opposition. A new Paris government composed of the untrained and the inexperienced is put into power. It is supported by angry lower classes now relegated by Haussman to scruffy outer suburbia, and by the National Guard and a handful of professionals and artists including Gustave Courbet, who initiates the destruction of the column of the Vendome, symbol of the Third Empire. Then the 'second siege' begins. Government troops storm the barricades of the *Commune* firing recklessly, indiscriminately; wholesale senseless slaughter. In one bloody week – the *semaine sanglante* – the communards retreat, setting fire to hundreds of innocent buildings. The raging conflict claims 30,000 lives – more than had been lost in the Franco-Prussian war itself.

In June, Claude returns to the catastrophe that is Paris. Hundreds of trees had been uprooted as if some angry giant's hand had plucked them from the ground. Buildings are in ruins, paving stones scattered and dirt and disorder are everywhere. The magnificence of *his* Paris was a thing of the past. He swears that he can still smell burning flesh and wood. Around him, the demoralized and the dispossessed wander aimlessly with hollow hopeless eyes. He heads for his apartment. A few neighbouring buildings had been damaged, but the only injuries to his possessions are one broken window and thick layers of dust covering every horizontal surface. His precious books are safe. Where is his life; where are his friends and colleagues? He pays a call on the Raffalovich household. Marie and he embrace with relief, and he hears heart-rending stories of their experiences during the evil weeks of May.

"It's hard to realize from what a nightmare we have now awoken, Claude. I am grateful indeed that we were away from Paris."

"And your sister and her family?"

"They are all well: de Chaptal went to Bordeaux when the new Republican government left Paris. They gave him a small administrative job since his bad arm didn't allow active service; he was back in Versailles when they signed the treaty a couple of weeks ago."

"I'm relieved to to hear that they are well. And what of your other friends?"

"No tragedies that I have heard about, except poor Henri Regnault who got killed at Buzenval, as you may have heard."

Claude is shocked; his face pales. The young man in question was the son of Victor Regnault, the talented engineer and physicist whom he had only known vaguely at the *Collège*. Later, through being invited to dinner with him at the Raffalovich family they had become very close friends. Young Henri had more recently won the *Prix de Rome* for his superb painting, which was of a style that had immediately endeared itself to Claude's romantic spirit; he had made it his business to see as many of his works as he could in various galleries around Paris and in the artist's studio. The critics had anticipated a remarkable career for the young man. What a tragedy!

"That is awful; how did Victor take it?"

"He is beside himself as you can imagine. Not only that, but down in Sèvres where he was spending so much of his time, the Prussians broke into his study, burned all his notes and books and destroyed his instruments."

Claude is speechless.

"I think that you have been lucky Claude; and probably wise to have stayed in the Beaujolais."

"Yes. However I am really sorry that you didn't visit me on your way back from Nice."

"In the end, I decided to travel back alone; to put things in readiness for the arrival of the rest of the family. I thought it best not to delay..." The look that she gives Claude is full of warmth and intimacy. "...and it was probably better that way. I must tell you that we have decided to move. Grisha wants to be closer to his office and has found a house in *avenue de Reine Hortense*. We will be moving next month, so if you have any translations for me it would be better to let me have them in the next few days."

"I do have one or two articles. Have you heard from the Renans?"

"Oh yes, they're here; perhaps you can join us all for dinner next week? Ernest mentioned in passing that the Davaines are also back."

Claude had only received one letter from his friend while he was in the Beaujolais, to say that he had deposited Georgina and Jules with his extended family in St Amand-les-Eaux near Lille. Casimir was then about to join a field medical team to service the immediate needs of wounded soldiers in the north of the country. Claude is relieved that his friend is safe, makes his farewells and sets out for the *Collège*. On the way he posts a letter that he had written to his daughters.

A Prussian shell had only damaged one part of the *Collège* building, and he finds the auditorium, his room and the laboratory intact, but filthy. Lesage had spent the entire war in Paris, and was already in the process of cleaning up. He had many stories to tell; about the collapsing wall that had injured his elder sister, and his experiences of providing first aid and other help to the injured and needy. He and Claude now embrace each other like the old friends that they were, and discuss how they would begin the massive task of restarting research.

His next port of call is the Museum. Chevreul is as sprightly as ever, still viciously abusive of the Prussians' damage to his gardens, where exploding shells had destroyed priceless collections of plants as well as shattering many glasshouses. Claude's laboratory was ready for occupation, and he leaves the Museum with a strange feeling of buoyancy and optimism.

Davaine is in similarly high spirits when they meet later in the week at a *café* near the *Collège*. He bombards Claude with many tales of his experiences in the field and the variety of injuries he had been treating. Because of his interest in infectious disease, he had been asked for his opinion about the many cases of smallpox that had stricken the French troops. Regrettably, there had been little that he could do for them; there were few recoveries – and those despite, rather than because of treatment. The awful nutrition of the troops had made for devastatingly severe disease and rapid death.

"You know Claude, I believe that having taken so many French prisoners – 700,000 I believe – their Prussian captors will be at considerable risk from catching smallpox themselves, and then civilians as well will be affected; people who would have wished for nothing else but peace and harmony."

"Yes, but that's war. Show me a country in which the people were asked for their opinion before their leader declared war!"

"Well, both the government and the people of France certainly urged Napoleon to engage with Prussia. If only they had known how it was all going to end...but tell me; how did you fare in the Beaujolais?"

"I am ashamed to say that I hardly knew there was a war on. Of course, St Julien sent off its men into battle; and there were many casualties. Many families suffered by not knowing what was happening to their loved ones. I suppose I'll hear plenty of stories when I go back in September. I've already had a note to say that Lemaistre, my *préparateur* at the museum was killed in action: he was in the ambulance section, poor chap!"

"...and your own health?"

"Oh, some pain, my usual colds and a lot of headache. I have also had some pain when I pass urine but that may be my diet."

"I should really examine you Claude; it doesn't sound right."

"Perhaps later Casi. I would like to get back to the *Collège* now and arrange matters for myself there – and at the Museum."

"Is there that much for you to do?"

"It will certainly take time to put both laboratories in motion; pairs of hands, equipment, chemicals, animals – they all have to be organized. It almost seems as if I am starting research for the first time!"

"Who is looking after you now, Claude?"

Claude looks at his friend; surprised at the change of subject.

"Do you mean as a maid?"

"Yes, of course."

"Still the wonderful Mariette Rey. She spent the war in the Auvergne with her family, but she is back again now, running the household – and me; but she thinks that our apartment is too big. They haven't finished rebuilding the ones opposite the *Collège*. That's where I would like to live – like my German counterparts – on the doorstep of my laboratory!"

The months pass quickly. The summer is mild and kind to the people of France, who deserve some joy in return for the hardship, worry and the pain that war had imposed on them. The rebuilding of Paris had begun remarkably quickly. Shops had re-opened: modernized and redecorated. Most important for the science of France, the Academies had restarted their regular meetings. Claude finds himself in the 'chair' again at the *Académie des Sciences*, amazed at the speed with which researchers in so many fields had regained their momentum.

His visit back to St Julien in '71 was special in a number of ways. He had reasoned that leaving Mariette in Paris would make little sense since the apartment would be unoccupied for the better part of six weeks. It would surely be better if she accompanied him to St Julien, to provide the continuity he so valued. She would certainly enjoy the change of scene and benefit from some country air. He writes a short letter to Josephine to explain the situation; perhaps she might nevertheless be kind enough to prepare the house for their arrival. He also writes a note to his sister in Pouilly-le-Monial inviting the Cantin family to stay for a weekend. On recent visits, he had only fleetingly seen his niece Jeanne (whom he preferred to call Jenny) and had even less contact with her husband, Joseph Devay; it would be a fine opportunity for him to become better acquainted with the young couple and their one-year-old son, Jean-Antoine. Certainly he had lectures to prepare but there would be ample time left for that.

It is a magnificent Sunday in early October. Joseph had helped Mariette to move the heavy table and the dining chairs on to the terrace for them to be able to enjoy lunch *al fresco*. Earlier in the morning, they had all walked through the vineyards, down the hill and in to the village in order to visit his parents' graves, on which they had placed a bunch of Claude's finest roses. A similar arrangement in a vase now graced the centre of the lunch table around which everyone is sitting, replete after an excellent meal prepared by Mariette and served by Josephine.

"It's all so peaceful!" comments Caroline looking around her. "It's hard to believe what we've all been through in the last year or so."

Claude nods: "It is probably best if we put that behind us and ...."

"That's so easy for you to say." Joseph interjects. "Two of my best friends were killed alongside me; that's not so easy to forget! At least I only have this to show for it."

He pulls up his trouser-leg to reveal an ugly scar extending from knee to ankle.

"I am sorry Joseph; I did not wish to be disrespectful to you or those who lost their lives, but it was such a pointless war; ill-conceived, badly timed and irresponsibly led. We have to put the blame on the Emperor for his presumptuous incapacity; but he has now left the scene."

"Where is the bastard now?"

"In England, and probably leading quite a comfortable life with Eugénie and the Prince-Impérial. I have to say however that one has to give him some credit for what he did for Paris and the support he gave to both the arts and the sciences."

Joseph looks at Claude angrily.

"And what did he do for those of us in the provinces, the people who helped create the wealth that made such a beautiful Paris possible – and who live too far away to enjoy it?"

"You do have a point Joseph. That's precisely why there was so much bloodshed in the first part of this year."

Fortunately, the line of conversation is broken by the arrival of Mariette with a large bowl of strawberries.

"I was just thinking," Claude announces as he finishes his last strawberry, "that Louis actually did quite a lot for our wine industry. He directly financed the research that led to the heating process that stopped wine and beer from spoiling. On top of that he put extra money into finding the cause of the silkworm disease."

"But that problem hasn't yet been solved, has it?" asks Jeanne.

"No. But it is only a matter of time until they find the right chemical."

"What about phylloxera; there's no answer to that yet, is there?"

Claude cannot provide Joseph with an immediate answer. Just before the war, Planchon, from the eminent agricultural *École de Gaillard* in Montpellier had identified masses of yellowish insects in the roots of vines dying in the lower regions of the Rhône Valley. That evil disease was now gradually creeping up the Rhône towards the Beaujolais. Planchon was convinced that the insects were the cause of the problem. However, there was vitriolic argument between him and the Paris establishment about whether they were indeed the cause or the result of the disease.

"Actually, Joseph it's yet another aspect of what you were complaining about earlier; no-one in Paris trusts the the *Montpellierains*, despite their eminence in the agricultural world; in the same way that Parisians turn up their nose at the quality of the southern wines!"

"Exactly! It's Paris against the rest of the France. We can never win!"

"Let me tell you Joseph that if I could, I would live here permanently. After just a couple of weeks in Paris, I can assure you that you would appreciate your way of life in Pouilly rather more."

"You don't understand me *Monsieur*! It's not that I wish to live in Paris – or that I don't appreciate our life in Pouilly, but we should have more of the country's money invested here in the provinces."

"That will surely happen, if only because otherwise the vines will die and literally hundreds of millions of francs will evaporate. Just before I left Paris to come here, I heard a scientist at the *Académie* reporting that the yellow insects in diseased vines are only in the bushes we imported from America. They are trying different chemicals there; France will have to do the same – once the people who matter can convince the Paris sceptics that the little beasts are indeed the cause of phylloxera!"

It seems as if everyone had become tired of exploring the topic. Caroline, Jean and Joseph decide to read the newspapers while little Jean-Antoine had his afternoon sleep. Claude invites Jeanne to join him for a walk through the vines. He himself follows this routine every day, silently hoping that he would not come across any bushes diseased by phylloxera.

"I would very much like to help you – financially." he says, as they approach the house again. "I thought of establishing an account in the name of Jean-Antoine. I can deposit a regular amount each month; it's amazing how capital grows over time."

"That's wonderfully generous of you: it would be nice to have some extra security. The war has been so unsettling, particularly for Joseph. You probably noticed that his personality has changed since he came back from the war."

"In what way?"

"Not seriously. He is still so very kind to me, but just a bit over-sensitive and reactive – like he was with you earlier. I hope you weren't offended."

"Not at all. I don't mind his forthright manner; at least one knows where one stands. Be happy that you have a sensitive person with whom to share your life; I have to tell you that Fanny rather lacked that quality."

"Yes. I only met her once but it was not difficult to appreciate that. Are you very lonely now?"

Claude laughs. "Fanny never really contributed much to my well-being, Jenny. Of course Tony and Marie-Louise do not wish to see me either, which pains me more. I think that my good fortune will have to come from other directions."

He is glad when they reach the house again.

The rest of the weekend passes quietly and uneventfully. Before they all leave, Claude has an opportunity to speak privately with Caroline; able to assure himself that she too is content and well cared for. Mariette had made a fire in the salon, and once the carriage had moved off, Claude settles down in his most comfortable chair to read the translations – with its wonderful accompanying letter – that he had received from Marie Raffalovich in the mail just before the arrival of his family.

Lesage had done wonders while he was away. Once more Claude has a healthy supply of guinea pigs, rabbits and rats. All the necessary chemicals, tubes, supports and equipment were back in position on the shelves; even blindfolded, Claude could readily lay his hands upon any item. A young man called Armand Moreau had come forward as a researcher; keen to get experience in animal experimentation. Claude had yet another assistant by the name of Mathias Duval, one of whose attributes – the neatness of his writing – soon became apparent.

His first visitor is Paul Bert. Always committed to local politics he had decided that he could provide effective republican support in the Yonne, of which Auxerre, town of his birth was the centre. He had offered his services to Gambetta early in the war and had been appointed 'Prefect of the North'.

"So you honesty believe that you can fulfil both functions, Paul?"

"I don't see why not. University vacations allow me ample opportunity to visit Auxerre; to be honest, my lecture programme at the Sorbonne is not so demanding that I cannot allow myself time both for my experiments and to meet with my political masters here in Paris."

He adds with a smile:

"...and I have you as my model of what can be fitted into a working day!"

"You flatter me! How did you manage to squeeze a laboratory out of the University?"

"I didn't: I am using part of the medical physics department, but don't tell anyone!"

Claude smiles; he had always liked Bert's energy, enthusiasm and initiative.

"And where were you during the war?"

"All over France: but mainly between Auxerre and Paris. As you can imagine, I had the chance to try out skin grafting on all those horrible injuries; I have to say that they worked quite well. Do you remember that Swiss surgeon Reverdin who commented on my presentation at the *Académie de Médecine* in '65?"

Claude nods.

"I used his 'pinch graft' variation of my method on some of the casualties; it worked well. I am inclined to agree with him that the skin areas are less likely to become infected if one takes smaller pieces and allows the skin between the grafts to granulate."

"Did you ever try grafting under increased atmospheric pressure?"

"I did, but I still couldn't graft from one animal species to another; but then again no-one else seems to have been able to duplicate Baronio's results! However, you started me in an interesting direction: I am now looking at the effect of varying atmospheric pressure on different biological functions. For example, the altitude sickness in balloon flight needs a better explanation than just a shortage of oxygen. I think it might also help to understand exactly what happens with the diving problems that we keep on seeing. I suppose that you will be in the 'chair' when I present some more results later in the year at the *Académie des Sciences*."

"Hopefully! I think I was ill last time you presented something on grafts."

"Are you completely well again?"

"Not really. Those headaches and abdominal problems keep returning. Now that I am back in Paris, I will see if Casimir Davaine has any new ideas."

Paul Bert glances at his watch, grimaces, springs to his feet and within a few seconds he had left the room with an apology and a wave of his arm. Claude also realizes how long he had been talking. Marie would be outside the *Collège* at any moment. Together they had been invited to the *Jardin des Plantes* for the official ceremony marking the installation of new glass in the *serres*, so damaged by Prussian bombs. Chevreul would be a happy man!

At the Museum, Claude had gradually amassed the resources and facilities of which he had previously only dreamed. At one end of the laboratory, the animal house was equipped with deep tanks for the crayfish; there were also appropriate cages for marmots, rats, dogs, larger and smaller cages for birds and indeed for any animal upon which he wished to experiment. There was also a small glass-roofed annexe – on the advice of one of the Jardin's horticulturalists.

Because of Lemaistre's death in the war, Claude had asked Albert Dastre to transfer to the Museum; he had arranged for shelves to be built on which he could arrange trays of seeds and shallow water-containing tanks. Watercress was one of the plants on which Claude would be working: interested in the environmental factors that controlled germination. He also wanted to extend his observations on those smallest of animals – rotifers and tardigrades. For that purpose, he needed a different type of tank whose content would be supplied by water from various stagnant ponds in the gardens.

Chapter 20

Soft Awakening, Hard Decisions

Claude and Mariette Rey were standing at the window, looking out towards the *Collège* immediately opposite.

"It couldn't be more convenient for you, Monsieur. However, I think that you would spend more time than ever in your laboratory. This is certainly a better size place for us both though…and I suppose that I could always bring you some lunch if you were busy!"

Claude looks fondly at the woman on whom he had become so reliant. She was certainly a tyrant, but he had long ago realized that in her brusque manner there was only concern for his well-being. Now she was smiling broadly, and he makes the instant decision to take the apartment that they had just inspected – and to move in as soon as possible.

He had never been more content in a Paris that was recovering, albeit slowly. The venerable Thiers and his National Assembly had managed to find the money to pay the price demanded by the Prussians – with the help of the Rothschild Bank. Within a few months, the country could be completely rid of its German occupation. Claude is happy that he no longer has to sit on the *Senat*. In its place, he had accepted the presidency of the newly formed French Association for the Advancement of Science. It would be an interesting – and more appropriate – responsibility, although he would need to travel more: each meeting was to be held in a different city.

He also decides to attend more regularly his dining club at the *Brébant*: Renan and Berthelot had apparently dined there throughout the war, mainly in the company of Gautier, Flaubert, Goncourt and the journalist Nefftzer. Claude had seen Berthelot a few times since his return: he had been made senator-for-life under the new Republic, and was gaining much public respect for his aggressive support for changes to higher education.

"Isn't it rather too close to your laboratory Claude?" says Davaine, predictably.

"Mariette said that, too, Casi. No, it's perfect actually! You know, our research colleagues in Germany and in Russia are given apartments directly above their laboratories. Of course, it's partly as a reward for their services; yet I am sure that their masters recognize so much better than ours that good research involves a level of commitment that only such an arrangement allows."

"I'm not so sure. I enjoy working as much as anyone, but getting away afterwards to be with Georgina – in what I would call the normal world – carries a high priority with me. Perhaps you would feel differently if you had a 'Georgina' of your own!"

Claude looks down at his feet in silence; then takes a sip of the wine that Mariette had poured for them both. Davaine is puzzled:

"Have I said anything wrong?"

"Sorry, Casi. You are a good friend, and so I should have told you earlier – about Marie."

"I think I know already, you villain! I didn't want to say anything, but there are already rumours flying about."

"Oh! My God!"

"Don't worry: Paris loves to conjecture about their prominent citizens, as you well know, and your *Madame R* is surely well-placed on the social register!"

"What should I do?"

SOFT AWAKENING, HARD DECISIONS

"Nothing, of course: I am sure that you are the very soul of discretion. Unless I misunderstand you completely, you are not going to let your little digression get out hand. She's a fine woman and you deserve a little romance after what you've been through!"

"Possibly. Anyhow, getting back to our research, would you mind if I quote the result of our joint enterprise in my next lecture at the Museum? It's quite exciting."

Davaine shakes his head at his friend's sudden change of topic; smiles:

"Of course; it will be interesting to hear how the audience reacts."

The result referred to by Claude was a repeat of some of Davaine's earlier research. It had involved injecting a minute portion of blood from a patient with anthrax into the superficial layer of the trunk of a cactus. Within a couple of days, an unusual area of 'rot' had appeared; similar to the so-called 'malignant pustule' seen in early human anthrax disease. If they exposed the plant to a temperature of 52 degrees for thirty minutes, the rot would dry up and fall away – while the plant lived on normally. Of course, the important question is whether the technique is applicable to animals – even man – particularly with more widespread disease. Probably not, he thinks, since his early work had shown that a blood temperature of only 45 degrees was lethal to most mammals. For Claude, the interest lies simply in the similarity of plant and animal life!

They are sitting in his room after completing a set of experiments:

"By the way Claude, you won't believe it but I had a letter from Fanny yesterday."

"I am surprised. Did she ask about me?"

"I'm afraid not. She has asked me to see Tony and Marie-Louise about protection against smallpox and cholera. They have quite an ambitious plan for a dog refuge, which the girls will manage. Fanny wants to ensure that they have all possible protection against diseases that they might pick up from the dogs...."

"...like rabies?"

"Certainly, although there isn't a vaccine yet that I have heard of; perhaps Chauveau is working on that."

The man in question occupied the post of director at the now-famous veterinary school in Lyon; the same one that Claude and Ronne had so often visited during their apprenticeship in pharmacy. Over the years, Claude had been in touch with him quite regularly, because Chauveau had copied one of his early techniques of placing tubes into the heart:

he wanted to understand the pressure changes that occurred within its chambers.

"How would you feel about coming to St Julien again, Mariette?"
"Aha! Is it because you will miss my little basket lunches?"
"That in any case, but I see little point in you staying here alone while I am away for those six weeks."
"I do believe that you are concerned that I would be bored during your absence!"
"Certainly not: but I expect to have more guests this time and Josephine would surely welcome your help again. I would really appreciate if you could keep things running in St Julien as smoothly as you do here."
"Ah! Such flattery! And she won't resent my presence?"
"Most unlikely! She is not so young any more: she would certainly appreciate someone to reduce her burden. I feel sure that you could share the responsibilities without getting in each other's way."
Mariette is silent for a few seconds; her forehead deeply creased with concentration.
"Might it then perhaps be possible to spend the last week with my family in Tallende? I believe that there is a train from Lyon to Clermont-Ferrand, from where I can get to our village quite easily."
"Of course; it would be a fine opportunity for you to see them."

A late but warm spring and an early start to summer had prompted Morel to write to Claude. The *vignerons* were expecting an early harvest. Perhaps Claude would consider coming to St Julien rather earlier then usual. Morel is also concerned about the vines, and wants to discuss protection against phylloxera. There is no sign of a problem in St Julien, but a few diseased vines had been discovered in a vineyard situated some kilometers to the south. Accompanied by an enthusiastic Mariette, Claude accordingly leaves Paris at the end of August. On the train, he is obliged to listen to a catalogue of events relating to her impossibly large family in the Auvergne.

Already on the day following their arrival, Morel and Claude are sitting together in the salon.
"I wonder what you would think about trying water submersion in our vineyards."
"Has anyone else in our area done it yet?"

"Not as far as I know, but everyone is discussing it. Faucon's experiences near Avignon seem now to be accepted by everyone; most particularly by Planchon in Montpellier."

"Is it worth inviting Faucon to visit us?"

"I doubt it. His principle is simple enough: one just has to avoid overdoing the flooding stage and decide on the correct timing. The main problem is cost. We would have to build tanks to collect the winter rains and make appropriate dams at the lower end of each row of vines. I have estimated a cost of at least two thousand francs."

"I suppose that one has to set that against the financial risk of losing some of the vines…"

"…or all of them!"

"Are there any alternatives?"

"Only sand, perhaps. I suppose that you heard that the vines growing in the sand-hills of Aigues-Mortes in the Camargue are quite free of disease."

"But is there any evidence that if we dig sand into the roots it will prevent phylloxera?"

"I don't think so."

They sit for a while sipping wine from the previous year's harvest. Morel looks serious and indeed quite tired – and the harvest has not even begun.

It is all too much for Claude on the day after a tiring trip.

"It will need careful thought; let's discuss it again after the harvest."

Claude distracts himself by spending some time re-arranging his laboratory. The German company Leitz had just marketed a new travelling microscope. He had initially resisted the idea of buying one: memories of war still too recent. However, its newer optics were considered superlative and it had a rotating turret which carried the three objective lenses. Neither Nachet nor Duboscq had produced similar models, and so he had finally bought the Leitz and had now taken it with him to St Julien to help with some new studies on fermentation that had been occupying his mind.

He also had some letters to write: the first to Marie, who with her family was again spending the summer in Nice: he was hoping that they might interrupt their return visit to Paris with a short stay in the Beaujolais. He would also write to Chauveau in Lyon to see if he would like to spend a few days in St Julien to discuss a joint research project that he had in mind.

The harvest is successful and a good yield of wine seems likely. Claude is deliriously happy when he receives a letter from Marie Raffalovich accepting his invitation to visit St Julien on their way back from Nice. However, Arthur and André would go directly to Paris with their governess since Arthur had to commence the new school year. Marie writes that they would be obliged if he would arrange the booking at a hotel in Villefranche, again concluding that "...*it might be better that way!*" Their visit would be prior to Mariette's departure, and Claude spends a considerable time discussing with her how they would arrange the day, and the minutest detail of the lunch that they would provide for their guests.

"It's a large house for one man – even of your greatness..." Marie says to him with a smile, as they proudly complete the tour of the important rooms, including his study, "....and I think that many a woman would be happy and proud to share it with you."

She looks at him sideways to observe his reaction.

"I won't even comment on that observation, Madame!"

In silence, they both stare for a few moments through the window of the study towards the endless vista of vines:

"Would it be presumptuous of me to ask what Fanny felt about this place?"

"She only visited this house once – you know, I only bought it in '60. I suspect that even if it were a palace, she would have objected to life in the country. Above all she could not come to terms with my family who lived in the cottage behind the house – they were too rustic for her!"

"I would like to see the cottage if there is time. Did the children like it here?"

"I think that they *would* have liked it, but they were always influenced by their mother. That was my fault too: with the amount of time I spent on my work I could hardly have expected otherwise."

They had come back to the salon where Hermann Raffalovich was leafing through a scientific journal that Claude had left on a small side-table.

"Complicated stuff, Monsieur! Do you write much now?"

"Too much, I suppose. There is little point in doing research unless one shares one's results with the scientific world. I much prefer writing to lecturing. Marie can verify that I don't lecture particularly well."

"Nonsense! Your lectures are always fully attended." Marie interjects.

"Could I come and listen to one of your lectures?

They all laugh: it is Sophie, who until then had been trailing behind them. At age twelve, already quite tall.

"Of course, Mademoiselle Sophie; and if I did an experiment during a lecture, would you assist me?"

They all laugh again, while Sophie blushes.

"Who comes to your lectures, Claude?" asks Hermann.

"When I was still at the Sorbonne it was mainly medical and veterinary students. As you know, at the *Collège* anyone can come and listen. It is like that at the Museum too, now that I have my other home there. I suppose it is that which can make it difficult to lecture. I am sure that many in my audience have no scientific background; simplification has never been my strong point. Of course when I write or present papers to the *Académies* or to the *Société de Biologie*, I can assume that most of the audience is able to follow what I am trying to say."

That was a touch of false modesty: he knows that people are coming from everywhere to hear him and from all trades and professions. Emperor Dom Pedro of Brazil is often in the audience. He is well known for his love of France and everything French; widely travelled and equally well read. The Prince of Wales had attended twice, and the Comte de Paris had also been on a few occasions. Then there were the scientists from Europe and America who flocked to a Paris that was still the centre of the scientific world; even if that honour was in the process of being passed on to Germany.

Claude suddenly claps his hands together. "That is enough about me! Let's explore the world of wine!"

He takes them through one of the vineyards, along one of the firmer paths that would not abuse his visitors' shoes. They visit the sheds where all the tools and equipment were kept; meticulously arranged on shelves or suspended from hooks and brackets along an entire wall; then the pressing and bottling rooms and the large vats where the wine was undergoing fermentation. Sophie wrinkles her nose at the insistently musty smell and they all laugh.

The lunch that Mariette and Josephine had prepared was excellent. The conversation was light-hearted and Hermann and Claude exchange a few jokes, which Sophie does not understand. Later Mariette takes Marie and Sophie on a tour of the upper storey while Claude and Hermann enjoy a little more wine in the comfort of deep armchairs.

"Apart from my few contacts in the realm of physiology, I know so little of what I might call your parent country, Hermann."

Raffalovich looks at Claude, not quite knowing where to begin.

"It is both strange and wonderful. Being Jewish rather distorts one's views; but despite the ever-present anti-Semitism, I still hold Russia dear to my heart."

"There seem to be connections between our two countries at so many levels."

"That's certainly true and politically the links could become stronger: France is naturally trying to make Russia their friend against the mounting strength of the expanding Germany. Yet Bismarck is rather smart: you may have heard that he is now trying to create a tri-partite alliance with Russia and the Austro-Hungarians, just to prevent them from forging links with France! For the moment though, there are at least Franco-Russian connections on the educational front; France was involved with the establishment of Russia's higher technical schools – and they were indeed badly needed."

"What about in your area – trade and so on."

"Each country works in its own interests of course; and money dominates politics – as always. We can still sell our corn and wheat to the highest bidder, and since Europe needs both, at least for the moment my business is reasonably secure. At the moment, I am trying to look beyond my own trading interests towards cementing financial links between France and Russia: as always, it is all about information and communication."

They sit without speaking for some moments, until Raffalovich asks:

"Perhaps you would be interested in visiting Russia?"

"It's strange. I have close contacts – by letter – with my colleagues there; and as you know, Marie helps me with that correspondence. It would be logical and even useful for me to visit them. I even have an honorary degree from the University of St Petersburg: courtesy alone would dictate that I pay them a visit. Yet I have a peculiar dislike – not actually a real fear – of travelling. You must have thought it odd, even rude that I have not accepted your kind invitations to visit you in Nice."

Raffalovich nods; he had indeed wondered, but says nothing. Claude continues:

"I like to move forward with my ideas, research, lectures and writing; and I find that travel interrupts that."

"That is indeed a pity, because our world is full of wonders and surprises. I know that it sounds rather trite, but travel really does broaden the mind; even one already as expansive as yours!"

"I can see what I am missing out on. Unfortunately, I also have an awkward habit of pandering to the expectations of others, and so I find myself accepting to be on this or that committee, with all that it entails. I find it ridiculously difficult to say 'no'!" "Then you should take a lesson from Arthur and Sophie; they are experts at it!"

They are still laughing as Madame Raffalovich returns from her guided tour.

"Well Claude, I have learned quite a bit about you from your wonderful Mariette. You have always said that she is somewhat of a tyrant; but she says the same about you! I am really surprised that you get on so well together."

Now they all laugh. Unfortunately, it is time for them to leave. It is with real sadness that Claude finally helps them into his carriage, which Jean-Pierre had polished to perfection, just for the occasion.

"He is an unusual man, Misha."

"Unusual and also quite sad. What a catastrophe that he had such an unfortunate marriage. I often wonder if his immense dedication to work is a way for him to bury his sadness."

"...but to the benefit of science!"

"That is certainly true!"

They are silent for a while, each buried in their own thoughts as the countryside changes from dense woods to open fields. Sophie's nose is pressed against the carriage window. Marie Raffalovich shakes her head – puzzled.

"It is tempting to think that the right woman in his life could even now make a difference; he does need someone, you know."

Perhaps it is the tone of her voice that prompts Raffalovich to glance at his wife:

"What do you mean, Misha?"

"Well, when we ask him to one of our evenings, it is always with serious people like Barral and Renan. Why don't we invite him next time with a theatre crowd? We could ask Jacques Offenbach to come, and Sarah is still in Paris – in that Beaumarchais play: she would certainly put a bit of spirit into him!"

"She's much too young for him, if that is what you have in mind; and hardly his type!" Raffalovich replies. "Anyhow, Claude would probably cancel at the last moment; he always seems to have one illness or another."

"Yes that is strange; perhaps he just works too much!"

"Even so much that he does not want to travel?" He shakes his head:"All those lame excuses! I think that beneath that calm exterior he is quite an anxious person; just driving himself to achieve and succeed."

Sophie turns away from the window:

"Can't we invite him to Nice one summer? He would like that."

"I have tried that Sophie; twice in fact. When he is not working in Paris, the only other place he wants is St Julien; and of course, he works there as well. Did he show you his laboratory?"

"Yes Maman; and all those animals…." She hesitates: "…and I think I can sort of understand why his daughters don't want to see him."

Back in St Julien time speeds by and Claude manages to complete a couple of experiments on the effect of heat on the activity of some snails which he had collected from the garden. A few days after the Raffalovich visit he makes a trip to Pouilly-le-Monial. He takes with him a present for Jenny who had just given birth to her second child. It had been an uneventful delivery and he was pleased to see his ever-expanding family looking so well and happy. Caroline and Jean seem content with their life, and to his relief Joseph seemed to have shed his anger and was more joyous. His bitterness about the war had clearly receded and his crops were doing so well that he had bought some more land in nearby St Laurent. Claude and Jenny were now sitting together in the shade of a large chestnut tree, the baby cradled in his niece's lap fast asleep.

"What are you doing now in your new laboratory?"

Jenny had always been interested in Claude's activities; probably the only one of his family to show genuine interest.

"I'm trying to show that there really is not much difference between animal and plant life."

She laughs, but kindly.

"I know it sounds strange Jenny, but you can find the same chemical reactions in the body of your little Emilie as you would find in one of those vines."

"How is that possible? They are so incredibly different."

"Aha! It was on purpose that I did not say it the other way around. Of course, Emilie's body has a greater variety of reactions than a plant's, but they still have much in common. The similarities with plants are even greater in lower forms of animal life – like the tiny creatures in that pond over there."

"Why is that so important then?"

Claude hesitates; that was not an easy question to answer.

"I believe that if we understand how lower forms of life behave – in other words their physiology – we may be able to understand human disease rather better; even perhaps life and death. You have heard of anaesthetics, of course?"

"Naturally!"

"Well, you will really laugh now, because in my laboratory at the moment, I am putting some plants to sleep with chloroform and ether; the same anaesthetics that we use on humans."

There is silence as she is obviously trying to imagine the process of induced sleep in a plant!

"And do they recover afterwards – like we do?"

"Good question! They seem to, although at the moment, I am not sure if any of their chemical processes have been harmed by the experiment."

"I would really like to see that. Perhaps I can come over to St Julien one day and watch you experiment. In fact, if you ever need some help in your big mansion I would be happy to stay for a while. Maman says that we must make more use of the little cottage too, and Joseph can always find something to do; I noticed last time we were there that the walls downstairs badly need a coat of paint!"

Just before his return to Paris, and on the day before Mariette was due to leave St Julien for the Auvergne, Claude suffers a recurrence of his long-standing abdominal illness. The pain is excruciating, but the vomiting is over in a couple of days. It is only the first such episode that he had suffered since employing Mariette. She tries to insist that he gets immediate medical advice, but Claude re-assures her that it would pass quickly enough without intervention. She is quite disturbed about the whole affair, naturally fearing that it had been due to her food; it needs much persuasion to convince her that this was not the case and that it was safe to leave him with Josephine. The episode does prompt him to cancel both his visit to Bordeaux and the visit of his colleague Chauveau from Lyon. It was not that urgent; his friend would probably come to Paris anyhow for one of the meetings of the *Académie des Sciences*.

The winter of '72 is mild, and Claude disciplines himself to getting as much fresh air and exercise as possible. Twice he had written to Tony and Marie-Louise, suggesting that they might meet him for a walk in the

Jardin de Luxembourg. To neither letter does he receive a reply. Perhaps they had moved house; he wonders whether Casimir Davaine might know of their whereabouts. He also allows himself to accept an invitation to the theatre on two occasions, and thoroughly enjoys it, even imagining that his concentration on the next day has improved. That was important to him, because he needed to write.

The *Revue de Deux Mondes* was a general interest magazine dedicated to an educated public. It is there that one finds a historian's analysis of the war, a critique of current English literature or an assessment of French educational system: and it was there that a few years earlier Claude had published his major article explaining the mysteries of the heart. The editor had been so pleased with the public's reaction that he had asked Claude to provide a similar review on the brain; and that had gone to press earlier in the year with similar success. Claude was now thinking of writing one on the broad phenomenon of 'life'.

Although she is finding it increasingly difficult, Marie tries to ensure that Claude keeps his work in perspective with the rest of his life. She invites Claude and George Barral to an exhibition of the paintings of Henri Regnault, who had been killed so tragically in the latter stages of the war. In the same gallery were paintings of Pissarro; also Manet, who had tried to depict the horror of the assassination of the *Communards* in the Pére Lachaise cemetery. Claude finds it moving but still indicates his preference for Regnault's more romantic style; he is convinced that he would have risen to extraordinary heights of achievement had tragedy not struck.

The Raffalovich family also had their own box at the Opera. They naturally invited Claude from time to time, including in the party this or that elegant woman whom they considered eligible for his attention. Afterwards they would go to supper in a nearby brasserie, where he could barely disguise his boredom with the banal conversation. He accepted these invitations more out of politeness than genuine interest and increasingly excused himself after the first act of an opera, on the pretext of having a headache or other indisposition. He would then head quickly back to his apartment, where Mariette had long since retired to bed. He would light a fire in his study and resume his writing until the early hours. The next morning his hunched shoulders and bleary eyes would be evidence enough for Mariette, who would scold him as if he were a little child.

As usual, people are occupying every seat in the Museum auditorium. Some medical students are obviously keen to discover facts that lie beyond their curriculum; typically, they had arrived late and so were unable to find a place. They are very young and mostly shabbily dressed, standing at the back or squatting on the hard, cold steps. The front row had been reserved for the staff of the museum and their guests. According to long-established tradition, Chevreul is occupying its centre, flanked by Claude's 'disciples': Gréhant, Moreau, Duval and Ranvier and staff from other departments. Marie Raffalovich, Pasteur and Davaine sit together at one end of the row. How Claude had aged in the last year, they whisper.

He had been speaking for the best part of an hour and was now exhausted: standing at the bench supporting himself with outstretched arms, as if he might otherwise fall. Albert Dastre is at his side, casting nervous glances at the pale, tired face of his master. Claude's 'tools' – the glass chambers containing plants, the cages with frogs and bizarrely arranged tubes and flasks litter the bench which spans the room.

There are also scrawled formulae and lists on the blackboard behind him; long curved arrows joining words and phrases so that the audience is not left in any doubt about how one idea, theory or fact had led to the next. He had specified the exact conditions under which he had performed every experiment; conditions so precise that each could be infinitely repeated with similar results – his fundamental concept of *determinisme expérimentale* yet again restated.

"….and so *Mesdames et Messieurs*, I will summarize my talk. I first showed you how plants use starch as a store of energy to provide glucose as and when needed – for their fruits, flowers and leaves. Then I spoke of animals of every class, and how they store their equivalent of starch, namely *glycogène*. The glucose that is generated when *glycogène* is broken down then provides the energy for movement, thought and probably every chemical process in the body. Glucose is the very fuel of life – whether we speak of plants or animals."

"In passing, you will have seen that Bichat was incorrect in his notion of 'one-organ, one function'; that the liver does not simply excrete bile, but is also the organ which contains the body's largest store of *glycogène*. This fact must alone lead us to re-examine every organ; to discover just how blind we may have been and how many additional functions might lie hidden from view."

"You now know that the chlorophyll of leaves may also be found in the smallest members of the animal kingdom, and that the chemistry of the bark of trees is similar in its composition to the chitin which clothes certain terrestrial and aquatic animals. Just as plant seeds lie dormant, awaiting the correct humidity and temperature to begin germination, so certain animals may do likewise. The rotifers and tardigrades, admittedly the most primitive of the animal kingdom may survive drying for a century, to be re-awoken by a drop of water, and I ask you; is the hibernating field mouse only a modest extension of this principle?"

"I have also shown you that anesthesia, that great contributor to surgical safety and patient comfort can also be applied to plants, from which we may understand the way in which anesthetics work. You have also seen from the work of my colleague Doctor Davaine, that we can infect plants with anthrax, and that the resulting lesions are similar to those in man. Now we can explore different methods of treatment; using plants rather than animals. Those of you who have been critical of my vivisection may even take heart from this revelation!"

A ripple of laughter passes through the audience.

"Above all, earlier scientists were quite wrong in attributing uniquely to plants the capacity for chemical synthesis and creation, while allowing animals only the infinitely more humble role of combustion and utilization. In this great world of ours, plants and animals are now seen to be truly alike. The lessons that we may learn from the parallels and interactions between the two kingdoms are limitless. In future lectures of this series, I will be comparing in more detail the various biological processes that I mentioned; I shall look forward to seeing you then. "

He takes a deep breath.

"I thank you for your attention."

The enthusiastic applause that follows Claude's talk had never previously been heard in that venerable institution. In response, Claude should normally have invited questions, but his pale and drawn face testified to the enormous effort that he had already expended in preparing and presenting his lecture. Davaine rapidly reaches his side and assists him from the auditorium and into the waiting carriage.

When they finally reach the apartment, Claude collapses into the armchair while Mariette busies herself with setting a fire in the broad hearth.

"Claude, why do you insist on driving yourself so?"

"It is like that Casi – and at my age I cannot change."

"We can all change if we have to – and want to!"

"Do you think that my lecture was well received?"

"You could hardly be in doubt about that!"

"Well then, I should continue, shouldn't I?"

Nothing is said for a full minute; there was no future in that conversation.

"I have been meaning to ask you if you know of Tony and Marie-Louise's whereabouts. I assume you are still seeing them – medically."

"They are still in *rue du Cherche-Midi* as far as I know. Why do you ask?"

"I wrote to them twice from St Julien, and again last week from here; and with no reply. Obviously I am keen to know if they are well; I rather hoped that we might meet after all this time."

Davaine bites on his lower lip. It would be a bitter pill for his friend to swallow, but when he had last seen Claude's two daughters – in the company of their mother – they had hardly uttered a word, and certainly not enquired after Claude's health or welfare. He could only be frank with his friend:

"They are well Claude, but I think you should stop pressing them to see you. Perhaps it would be best if you let them take the initiative, whenever that might be."

Claude looks crestfallen.

"I expect that you are right; and probably about my lectures as well. Yet that is what I am paid for, both by the *Collège* and the Museum."

"Yes, but not necessarily at that level. The way you lecture must be so demanding, despite the help of your *préparateur*. You deliver much more than what an audience – or your employers – can reasonably expect of you."

Claude nods, shrugging his shoulders as if it is all too much for him. He allows his head to lie back against the tall, softly upholstered back of his armchair. The fire is now radiating comforting heat and within a minute he is fast asleep. Davaine walks quietly out of the room, pays his respects to Mariette and leaves the apartment.

Before he leaves Paris for St Julien, Claude sets down carefully for each of his junior colleagues the experiments that he wishes them to complete before he returns at the end of October. The major emphasis was on the connection between glucose and the generation of body heat. Duval would study the effect of curare on body temperature, to see if there was any relationship to changes in blood glucose levels. Moreau would study the effect of temperature on the formation of glucose in the liver. Ranvier would sever the nerve supplying the muscles of one leg of a rabbit, and compare the changes in blood glucose in the veins of the two legs. Dastre and Gréhant would work together to see if intense glucose feeding raised body temperature in rats. Since Berthelot had come up with a suggestion on how they might improve the accuracy of the copper reduction method for measuring glucose levels in body fluids, he had also asked them to do some comparisons between the new and the old method.

Well satisfied with his research plan, he is sitting back in his chair when there is a knock at the door. It opens abruptly to reveal an even more heavily bearded Louis Pasteur than usual: *"....and I just thought I would see if you could spare me a few minutes!"*

Claude leaps to his feet to welcome his friend.

"Of course; come in. It is wonderful to see you."

"Mind you, I can't stay long; I am leaving Paris again tonight; on my way to Holland."

"Selling beer again?"

They both laugh. France had for some time been battling against the problem of poor beer – or more accurately, its inconsistent quality. By contrast, Germany had long since discovered the 'lagering' technique whereby at necessarily low temperatures, a particular yeast would initiate alcoholic fermentation, yet itself settle at the bottom of the fermentation vat leaving a deliciously-golden clear supernatant. However, at such low temperatures the process was slow and therefore costly.

"Yes, as you obviously have read, I have declared my own war on Germany with my 'Beer of Revenge'! My new and wonderful little yeast does the same as theirs, but at a higher temperature. So the process becomes four times faster too. My beer-tasting colleague Bertin swears that it also tastes better than the German stuff! I am off to see Gerard Heineken at his new brewery in Rotterdam; with my yeast, they can quite smartly put Bismarck's lot out of business. I have just been to England and they are considering using it, too."

"It is quite change from silkworms, isn't it Louis?"

Pasteur smiles:

"I'm still keeping an eye on that problem. The trouble is that my selective breeding technique necessarily results in lower silk production; it is still only a quarter of what it was in '60."

"Did you ever get around to testing Béchamp's creosote method for controlling Pébrine?"

"No; but it obviously can't work as well as selective breeding. Besides, chemicals are such a crude way of dealing with a problem, don't you think?"

"His results looked impressive enough when he presented them to the *Académie des Sciences*."

"Maybe, but I don't trust his figures."

Claude feels that there is no point in discussing the matter further. Pasteur and Béchamp had also competed with one another on the matter of 'spontaneous generation'. Pasteur had insisted – perhaps incorrectly – that it was he who had destroyed the concept, long before Béchamp.

"How is Jean-Baptiste now?"

"Fully recovered, thank goodness. Typhoid is a devilish disease, isn't it; it took him the best part of a year to get well again. When I get the time, I want to get back to my work with those epidemic diseases: I am sure that I can work out a way of preventing them – based on the smallpox vaccination principle."

"Yes. Chauveau and Davaine both think that such an approach is possible."

"Really. They must have read one of my articles."

Claude smiles to himself. Pasteur had not changed his stripes!

"And are you well again, my friend?"

Claude was not sure how to answer that.

"I have the feeling that I'll never be truly well again, Louis. If it is not my abdomen, then it is my head and my recurring colds. I'm looking forward to getting back to the Beaujolais next week; I am always better off there."

"Are you doing any research in your little laboratory there?"

"Some – when I am not writing. I have one or two new ideas on fermentation, if only I can get my equipment to work properly."

"Do you still have that strange idea about soluble ferments Claude?"

"Yes, I do. I was reading von Liebig's article again recently: the one he published back in '39. I agree with his logic."

Pasteur shakes his head in disbelief.

"My logic runs differently to von Liebig's – and thus I suppose yours. I have just submitted an article on fermentation to the *Revue Scientifique*. I will be interested to hear your reaction to it when it is published."

He looks at his watch and gets up from his chair.

"I really must go Claude. I trust you will feel better after your country stay."

They shake hands warmly and Pasteur leaves, his left arm hanging awkwardly by his side.

Chapter 21

More Problems - But More Solutions

That year, Claude is particularly glad to escape to St Julien. He is weary of his lectures and had taken note of Davaine's warnings. He would try and reduce the number he gave both at the *Collège* and at the Museum, and concentrate on the writing that he preferred. He had written to his niece to ask whether indeed she might indeed install her family in the cottage for the last week of October: Mariette had so enjoyed the week with her family in the Auvergne that Claude wanted her to have the same pleasure again.

However, that arrangement was not to be. By return mail, he receives a hastily scribbled note to say that Joseph had developed catastrophic diarrhea; typhoid fever had been diagnosed and within four days he had died. Claude is devastated; Jenny had become so much closer to him during the last couple of years and his mind hums with the implications of her husband's death. At the same time, he knows that Caroline and his brother-in-law will give her all the emotional support that she needs. Claude feels that he will now also be able to help – financially.

On his way from Paris he spends a few days in Lyon, for his first chairmanship of the French Association of the Advancement of Science. He soon appreciates the fact that this society meets in a different city each year; it enables him to meet a large number of scientists who until then had been faceless names to him. Even the Montpellier school is well represented, amongst them Planchon, the expert on phylloxera. Neither of the two papers on this problem gave much hope for an early resolution of the threat.

As usual, Jean-Pierre is at the station in Villefranche to pick him up. Before leaving town, they pay a brief call on Ronne's pharmacy on the *rue Nationale* so that Claude can issue an invitation to the Blancs for a weekend stay in St Julien. Claude is pleased to see how busy he is; four assistants fully occupied in the pharmacy.

Claude is particularly anxious to see the new water tanks on his property. They had cost more than Morel had anticipated, and the *vignerons* had carried out the preventive submersion technique in the early spring. Claude had asked him to withhold 'treatment' from one hectare of vines: they would act as a control to determine the effectiveness of submersion on the other eight hectares.

"I think we did the right thing, although there is no evidence of disease yet in the untreated vines. Up in Montmelas, Brocard has found some affected vines, and regrets that he didn't follow our example."

"In any case Morel, it was a good investment. Have the tanks filled up again?"

"I would guess they are half full; the rains we had in late spring were quite heavy."

"Excellent; it is a good feeling to have some reserves in case we need them."

The harvest proceeds smoothly; Claude can never concentrate on anything else during those crucial weeks. He forever pokes his nose into this or that corner of the sheds, and above all enjoys chatting with the men both during their midday break and at the end of the day's work. As soon as it is over, he visits Pouilly-le-Monial to see his sister and niece, and the two delightful children who seem miraculously unaffected by their recent bereavement. He decides to spend the night with them and the next morning arranges with the bank for a regular monthly transfer into his niece's account.

No sooner had he set foot in Paris again, than he catches one of his perennial colds. He has a fever for a week and Mariette forbids him to go outside, let alone to his laboratory. However, he has a steady stream of visitors and one by one, his young colleagues bring to his apartment the results of their research. Everything they had found fits nicely into his hypotheses; he resolves that 1874 will be the year in which he will reveal his theories and findings in the domaine of *la chaleur animal* – body heat.

The *Collège* notice board had listed his first lecture in February as 'Regional Aspects of Body Heat'. The full amphitheatre is now very attentive as Claude explains the procedure that he would follow, and what he and the audience might expect to gain from his demonstration.

It starts well enough. He had just anesthetized a dog, and by means of straps attached to his legs it was now on its back on the operating platform that Claude had designed. Moreau had set up equipment consisting of a length of fine rubber tubing through which a pair of thin wires was connected at one end to a thermocouple and at the other to a galvanometer (which would register the temperature to which the thermocouple was exposed).

Accessing the circulation from incisions in a major vein or artery, Claude explains, he would be threading the tube through the heart and into the limb circulation, the liver and the lungs. He wished to show the difference that existed between arterial and venous blood temperature in different locations, and relate these to corresponding glucose levels in the blood (which he would obtain by withdrawing samples through the rubber tube. From that, he explains, he would deduce the intensity of chemical activity, otherwise known as metabolism, in different regions of the body.

He had just manoeuvered the tip of his tube into the main pulmonary vein when the galvanometer suddenly refuses to work. Moreau checks all the connections and finds them to be in order. Meanwhile the audience is getting restless – a few are even getting up to leave – when a young man approaches Claude from the rear of the audience.

"May I help? I have some interest in electromagnetic equipment."

"With pleasure; if you can do something I would be most grateful."

Taking a small screwdriver and fine pliers out of his pocket the young man, who Claude presumes is a student, soon has the galvanometer disassembled into its components. He points out that two wires are in fact in contact with one another, creating a short circuit. Five minutes later, the galvanometer is re-assembled and re-calibrated, and the experiment resumes.

Everything goes according to plan. With much applause, the audience shows its appreciation, both of the demonstration as well as the intervention of the young man, who then introduces himself to Claude as Jacques-Arsène d'Arsonval, a student *interne*. Claude immediately invites him back to his apartment for an aperitif.

"Where did you acquire those marvellous skills?"

"It's just a hobby, Monsieur. When I was still at school, nothing would give me more pleasure than taking apart a piece of machinery and then re-assembling it. Later, my father found that he could keep me out of mischief by providing me with various broken down clocks. I even managed to get one or two of them working again! I never go anywhere now without my two little tools; the screwdriver and the pliers which were given to me by a retired watchmaker in my home town."

"And where is that?"

"Oh, a tiny village called St Germain-les-Belles; just south of Limoges, where I started my medical course."

"When do you expect to qualify?"

"In '77, all being well; I have quite some way to go."

Mariette interrupts their conversation, reminding Claude that it is time for his supper.

"I don't suppose that we have enough so that we can invite this young man to join us?"

"There is more than enough; I'll lay an extra place."

D'Arsonval looks pleased:

"That is most kind of you. Is that lady your wife, Monsieur?" he asks as Mariette leaves the room.

Claude laughs. "Indeed no; although given her unceasing concern over what I do and eat, she may as well be. No, I have separated from my wife, and it seems also from my daughters – but that is another story. Let us have some supper."

They continue talking over a wonderful omelette embellished with a rich variety of vegetables. D'Arsonval peppers Claude with questions about his research, expressing particular interest in body temperature and its control.

"My mother died some years ago. If she was in a temperature below five or six degrees Celsius for more than hour or so, she always became sleepy and weak: it was as much as my father and I could do to keep her awake. What do you imagine could have been the physiological explanation for that? In summer, she never had the problem."

"I shall give it serious thought, young man! In the meantime, if you feel that you would like to join my little scientific family to help with our research, I would be happy to accommodate you. I fully realize the demands on your academic life, but the offer is open to you whenever you want."

"That is most kind. Would it be at the *Collège* or at the Museum?"

"Wherever you wish, but perhaps at the *Collège* to begin with: it is there that we are currently doing most of work in which you appear to be interested."

D'Arsonval leaves soon afterwards, clearly delighted with what Claude had offered him. For Claude it had been a marvellous co-incidence. For some time he had wished to develop better measuring equipment; with d'Arsonval's combination of medical knowledge and technical skill, it was just possible that the young man could contribute in a major way to Claude's research. Claude cannot dispel the still-vivid memory of his first contact with the illustrious Magendie: it had been in that very same auditorium almost forty years ago that Magendie had demonstrated the mechanism of vomiting – with Claude's help!

He is suddenly awake. It is as if all his pains from the preceding years had combined into one massive assault on his abdomen; he vomits several times without easing his pain. Claude sends Mariette to Davaine's home and they return an hour later. Davaine examines Claude carefully; but finds nothing but extreme abdominal tenderness.

"Have you had any urinary symptoms, Claude?"

"No more than usual; passing urine has been painful at times, but not at the moment."

Davaine shakes his head.

"I don't know what is going on inside there, Claude; I can't think of offering you anything but alkalinization of your urine – as we have done before. Please stay in bed and let Mariette spoil you for a few days. If it doesn't settle I think I will ask Gosselin to see you."

"And what can he do?"

"He has been given one of those new optical cystoscopes by his colleague in Vienna; he can now get an excellent view into the bladder; perhaps you have a stone like our recently departed Emperor."

"...and if so?"

"Don't press me Claude; one step at a time!"

"I am sorry Casi; it is just that I am getting tired of feeling so unwell all the time."

Davaine slumps into the chair next to the bed.

"I'm sorry too Claude; I shouldn't be so abrupt with you. I have to admit that I am getting rather fatigued myself. My practice is getting ever busier, and this continuous battle against the critics of my research sometimes makes me wonder if it's worth all the effort. Now it is Colin at the veterinary college who is disputing my research findings, just because he cannot duplicate them. Perhaps I should just try and get rich on my private practice – like your late father-in-law!"

Claude smiles: "That would be no good: I would lose my partner in research."

"Tell me Claude; how does Pasteur manage it? He never seems to be put off by criticism."

"Ah. That is because self-doubt has no place in his life; it is not part of his character. If you are really convinced that what you do is correct, then you can deal with all manner of insults and criticisms. However, I suspect that he is indeed quite human; he needs his persuasive rhetoric to convince himself – as well as his audience!"

They both laugh.

"You do me a lot of good Claude. We really should spend more time together – and not just in the laboratory. You know, I am seriously thinking of leaving all this in a few years. I can then give Georgina the attention she deserves. I was in Garches recently visiting the d'Eichtals so that I could collect a few rabbits for my next series of experiments. I think they are getting a bit tired of accommodating my menagerie. While I was there, Adolphe made a point of showing me a vacant plot of land nearby with an old *pavilion* on it. I could renovate that little house and set up the rose gardens about which I have always dreamed. Then I can start boring you with stories about my roses, as you do to me with your vines and minor periwinkles!"

Davaine leaves, and Claude tries to distract himself from the pains by reading. Marie's driver has delivered yet more translations for him, two of which are by von Liebig on the subject of fermentation; an article which might help him to confirm the existence of any soluble ferment capable of converting sugar into alcohol.

News of Claude's most recent illness reaches George Barral who visits him in his apartment a few days later. He had intended to brighten up Claude's day with a recent article that he had found on the life of Delacroix, as well as an interesting collection of Daumier's caricatures that he knew would entertain him. However, he makes the mistake of asking Claude about progress with his research.

"I am obsessed with alcohol at the moment, Georges!"

Unaware that Claude was referring to alcohol in the context of his research, Barral initially mistakes his comment for an admission that Claude had been tippling in secret.

"No Georges, it has not come to that yet, I am pleased to say! However alcohol is an area of chemistry still shrouded in mystery, which is why I am exploring it."

"Well, you know that I am always interested in mysteries!"

"Alright; here are the facts! I am sure that you already know that living yeast cells act on variety of different sugars – grape sugar, sugar beet or any other fruit – to form alcohol. Fermentation is the most important reaction in the production of wine and beer."

"That much I know."

"There is fermentation in animals too. For example, the digestive juices from the salivary and pancreas glands contain ferments that carry out similar chemical reactions to those of yeasts, in the intestinal tract. But they do not make alcohol!"

"That's a pity!" replies Barral with a smile.

"The next fact is that the ferments in digestive juices work independently of the cells that produce them; in the intestinal tract they are delivered by ducts to where they act; and quite far from where they are produced. The liver too contains a ferment that can convert the *glycogène* molecule into glucose – that was Berthelot's discovery. He can extract it from liver tissue and show that it works without the needing the cells that created it. My theory is that there is consistency across the biological spectrum; quite simply, one should not *need* the presence of living cells for the process of alcohol fermentation to occur. On that matter I disagree with my colleague Louis Pasteur, whom I think you have met."

"Yes; I remember him quite well; his name is also often in the newspapers these days."

"There has also been a long-running disagreement; almost hostility between Pasteur and my good friend Berthelot. Pasteur has added fuel to the fire by now claiming – without proof I might add – that fermentation to alcohol occurs only in the absence of air. He reasons that it is only 'asphyxia' of the yeast cells that causes them to break down sugars: you see, the fermentation process yields not only alcohol but also oxygen – which he believes keeps the yeast cells alive!"

"That combination would keep me alive too – very happily!"

"Now you are making fun of me, Georges!" Claude is wagging his finger at him playfully. "The ridiculous thing is that Pasteur's 'life without air' theory is so contrived. There is no biological precedent; neither has it been proven by his experiments."

Barral's face becomes quite serious.

"Monsieur, am I allowed to enquire whether part of what you refer to as your 'obsession' with this subject rests in your relationship with Pasteur?"

Claude looks at the intelligent, thoughtful face of Barral steadily for a minute, without speaking.

"I have to admit that there is somewhat of a conflict there. I am quite fond of him as a person, but then mainly outside the realms of science. He has the annoying habit of creating a theory that rapidly acquires the dimensions of a belief. He then hammers away at the facts until they finally agree with his belief. I find that irritating – indeed totally unscientific. If I have a theory, I examine the facts that result from the relevant experiment; but I am quite prepared to discard or amend the theory if the facts don't support it."

"I am surprised that those differences have not come between you and Pasteur before this."

"Therein lies the problem, I suppose. He has always been most kind to me. He is also what you might call well-connected; after all, he almost single-handedly saved the country's wine, beer and silk problems! A quiet word in the appropriate ear can do wonders, and those words have helped me enormously over the years. Challenging him openly would be like biting the hand that feeds me!"

"Will not your own research on the subject *bite* him anyhow – if it shows that he was wrong?"

"He may not need to know. I suppose that I am doing this particular research for my own satisfaction."

Just then Mariette enters the room.

"Monsieur, it is time for you to take the bicarbonate that Monsieur Davaine prescribed for you."

"You see Georges, it is time for us to end our discussion!"

Claude's recovery is slow and punctuated by many visits from his colleagues: since the *Collège* is so close, it is a simple matter for them to see him at the end of their working day. Berthelot and Renan are frequent visitors, relaying snippets of academic gossip and bringing him the occasional interesting article that they have come across. Paul Bert spends a whole afternoon describing his latest underwater pressure studies, and wisely avoids any reference to his political activities, while Marie comes for tea one afternoon together with Sophie – and an armful of translations.

Two weeks later Claude returns to his usual duties. True to his words and with the agreement of both Chevreul and the committee of the *Collège*, he limits his lectures and soon realizes that he is indeed benefitting from his reduced commitment. With Dastre and Moreau he spends his time carefully editing his lecture notes on the course in general physiology that he had given at the Museum, as well as those on experimental medicine that he had given at the *Collège*. In due course, he would submit them for publication to the *Revue Scientifique*.

He is particularly pleased that his young team had received d'Arsonval with such great warmth. If they had to scratch their heads over a technical issue or if there was an item of equipment missing or malfunctioning, they discover that he would come to their rescue either with an interesting idea – or with his watchmaker's tools. One way or the other he had made himself indispensable. His cheerful disposition had also helped. Claude immediately approaches the medical school for their permission to appoint him as an additional *préparateur*.

D'Arsonval was from a noble family and already had a little money in his own name; this had enabled him, at the young age of twenty to set up home with a widow and her infant daughter. Now they lived together in a tiny apartment near the *Collège*, yet he was now spending so much time in the laboratory that Claude became concerned that he might be neglecting both his clinical work at the *Hôpital de l'Infant Jésus* as well as his little family.

One Sunday afternoon he invites them to have supper with him. During the excellent meal that Mariette had prepared, the conversation is superficial, much of it dealing with the antics of their daughter, Émilie.

Now the larger story of their life emerges. Marie was a few years older than Arsène. It had been necessary for her to cut short her education, first with the unexpected birth of her child and then with the protracted illness of her deceased husband. Claude soon realizes that she is very well informed and quite unafraid of airing her views on many topics.

"I must tell you Madame, that Arsène has wrought miracles since he started working with us."

"It seems to work both ways. I have never seen him so content; I truly believe that he has found his niche."

"That's true." D'Arsonval interjects. "I can think of nothing more enjoyable than spending the rest of my life in laboratories such as yours, Monsieur – and in such stimulating company."

They talk freely about their earlier lives, while Émilie plays with a basketful of dolls of different sizes that they had brought with them. Claude hears that d'Arsonval's father is a doctor in St Germain-les-Belles, having followed the tradition set by his own father in the same village.

"I suppose that I will eventually take over his practice – according to tradition, of course."

He looks so dejected that Claude thinks that it might be useful to reminisce about his own past.

"I was in a somewhat similar situation when I qualified; it was everyone's expectation that I would become a village doctor in the Beaujolais; especially when I failed my *agrégation*!"

D'Arsonval is sitting forward on his chair:

"*You* failed your *agrégation*? What happened?"

"I guess that I was already too involved with research: I didn't tell the examiners what they wanted to hear! Anyhow, some very well-meaning colleagues came to the rescue with an arranged marriage. You may remember thinking, on the occasion of your first visit here, that Mariette was my wife!"

Arsène nods – smiles at the recollection.

"Well my estranged wife is the daughter of the late Doctor Henri Martin whom you may have heard of – and we have two daughters of about your age. Sadly, all three women have come to resent my research – particularly the aspect of vivisection on which so much is based. Living together became impossible and we separated – and that includes the children who wish to have nothing more to do with me. It is some years since I have been able to speak with them."

"You must be terribly sad. Was there no way of reaching a compromise?"

It was Marie who had asked the question. Claude's sister, his mother, Madame Raffalovich, the notaire Morisot, Georgina Davaine and many others had asked him that same question over the years. He was never happy that he had provided an adequate response to it.

"It is a horrible thing to say, but I suppose that I was not prepared to give up what I enjoyed most in life."

There is complete silence as they all digest this observation. Eventually d'Arsonval speaks; his face serious:

"I am honouring my father's wishes, even to the point of studying medicine; my own choices would have been otherwise, as you may have gathered. I am even less pleased about the prospect of working in our village; my enjoyment from life – perhaps much as yours, Monsieur – will, I am certain come from rubbing shoulders with like minds. I know that my father will be most disappointed if I do not go back as soon as my studies have been completed. Neither his health nor my mother's is very good either; they could probably do with my support."

"How do you feel about that, Madame?"

"Arsène asked me to live with him despite all my problems: I was a melancholic, unable to work and had a rather badly behaved daughter – probably the product of several years of domestic turmoil. If he was prepared to do that out of his love for me, then the least I can do is to stand by his side, whatever *his* choice. If he is happy, then we will be too…"

She scoops up Émilie in her arms and kisses her,

"…and wherever we are."

There are tears in her eyes as d'Arsonval puts his arm around her shoulders. After the young couple leaves, Claude sits for some time gazing out of his window. He has to wonder, yet again what his professional life would have yielded, had he been lucky enough to have a supportive wife. He reflects on the Pasteurs; even Flourens who had been so fortunate in that regard. The great Lavoisier, whose theories Claude had recently overturned also had such a marriage – to a thirteen-year-old bride who soon became his closest ally. She had been fluent in English and Latin and had translated extensively for her husband. His work as a regional tax-administrator occupied his days, and his great discoveries were all made at night, when his wife would roll up her sleeves and assist him. It was tragic that he had to lose his life by the guillotine in the days of the Revolution – just when his research was at its most prolific.

The following day, Claude and d'Arsonval are sitting in his room at the *Collège,* planning his new *préparateur's* involvement in various projects. Claude is reminiscing about his earlier work with mercury thermometers:
"It was extraordinary back in the forties; we were always scared that the thermometers would break inside the arteries and veins!"
"When did you start using thermocouples?"
"Only in the early sixties, but I think that there is still room for improvement."
"Certainly, and probably at both ends of your rubber tubes! We could start by experimenting with different metals for the thermocouple tips; Fourier's model allows one to predict what electric current can be generated. We could also try to reduce their size so that you could get into smaller blood vessels."
"If you can do that Arsène, it would open up an entirely new chapter in research."
"Of course, the critical part would be the measurement aspect; devising a galvanometer sensitive enough to measure the small currents that would be generated from such a small thermocouple. That is another aspect upon which I could work."
"Aside from those technical challenges Arsène, I wonder if you might help with documentation?"
"In what way?"
"Last year I gave no less than forty lectures and demonstrations on body heat. Moreau's recorded notes need to be re-written in a form that Baillière can publish them – with all the necessary diagrams and tables. I think that doing this would also help you to understand the biological factors involved in temperature control; you might even find an explanation for your mother's problem!"
"I would be more than happy to do all that."
"Thank you. I have asked Duval to follow a particular style with annotating my lectures on anesthesia and asphyxia; perhaps you could use the same type of presentation in your compilation of the new book. I have already written the sections dealing with its history: you know, the old *vitalisme* theory and Lavoisier's outdated idea that the lungs were the seat of body heat. Reading those will give you some idea of the style that I would like you to follow."

"Are you going mention the dispute that you had with Bouillaud?"

"I am surprised that you know about that."

"I do read the proceedings of the *Académie* quite regularly, Monsieur. You must have been tearing your hair out with those arguments!"

Claude indeed had a hard time the previous year. Bouillaud was the man on whom Balzac had modelled his character of the medical student Bianchon. In real life, he was considered by very many of his colleagues to be a difficult person. Very reactionary, he had once said that effort and expenditure on scientific research was unnecessary: there was nothing wrong with the old and well-tried principles! Despite overwhelming evidence that it was ineffective and even dangerous, he was also one of the very few physicians who still practiced bloodletting as a 'cure' – and for almost every ailment. At the *Académie*, he had announced quite viciously (as an ardent admirer of the late Lavoisier) that he disbelieved Claude's experimental results and conclusions. He could not accept that all body tissues generated body heat. He was convinced that the situation was as Lavoisier had indicated eighty years earlier: that it was only the lungs that converted oxygen to carbon dioxide, resulting in heat production. On another occasion at the *Académie*, Bouillaud had also come to blows with Pasteur on the matter of spontaneous generation, which he believed in – and quite passionately.

"That type of debate is all part of our academic life, Arsène. It demands infinite patience and persistence. When you tread new ground, you will surely have to deal with that type of challenge too! Anyhow, there is much to be done. Do talk with Mathias Duval. Perhaps we should speak again once you have dealt with the first two lectures. Do come and see me at any time."

Claude was tired, and his stay in St Julien did nothing to improve his wellbeing. He could not get enough sleep; waking during the night dripping with sweat, his mouth as dry as a bone. He had one cold after another and what he assumed to be neuralgic pains in his legs that made it impossible for him to find a comfortable position in his bed. He could not find a medicament capable of dealing with them; reluctant as always to use opium compounds. On top of that, his mind was continuously active and restless, and he had lost his appetite for writing letters. He owed one to Marie, who had again invited him to spend time with the family in Trouville. The harvest had also been rather lean; it annoyed him that neither he nor the *vignerons* could find an explanation. Above all, he had a feeling – shared with Ronne in a recent letter – that his time was running out; his overall health was definitely declining.

Several days later Ronne pays a visit, unannounced, concern written all over his face.

"What is all that nonsense, Claude?"

"I am sorry Ronne. It was not my intention to drag you out here, but it's not my imagination. I know my body and it's gradually failing me. The frightening thing is that my mind seems as sharp as ever."

"Perhaps you just need a holiday; I never see your weeks here as anything other than an extension of your work: you expect so much of yourself. You tell me that the Raffalovich family is pressing you to visit them in Trouville or Nice. Why not accept for once?"

"You know how I feel about travelling – or holidays, come to that!"

"It's about time that you became a little more flexible – for the sake of your health – and being in the villa of your attractive assistant shouldn't be such an ordeal!" He adds with a wink and a crooked smile.

Claude's stubborness is familiar and irritating and Ronne decides to change the subject; interested now in how Paris is rebuilding in the wake of the war, as well as the details of Claude's complex life. Looking at his friend's grey, lined face however, Ronne sees how he is paying the price for single-minded commitment to science.

Claude does take note of Ronne's advice; writes a reply to Marie Raffalovich assuring her that he will be delighted to visit them in Trouville during the following spring.

Chapter 22

A Slow Decline

Claude is indeed enjoying Trouville. He is surprised at the size of the Raffalovich summer residence: two resident staff, plus two from their Paris apartment, including Sophie's governess. He is the only guest for the five days of his visit, giving him the chance to talk with each member of the family in peace and quiet. Arthur had just finished his economics course at the Sorbonne; not yet employed, but overflowing with ideas on how he might improve the world: particularly for the poor. Claude is struck by his close affinity with Russia, even though he had left it when so young.

The family are marvellous hosts, leaving him to his own devices earlier in the day while entertaining him lavishly in the late afternoons and evening. They had an excellent library, but none of the books capture his attention. He had brought with him notes and research articles that he wanted to read, and was determined that he would not impose his professional needs on Marie during his stay. On the day before his departure, the family decides on a walk along the beach, but Claude elects to stay at the house with his books and papers. There is a knock on his door and Marie enters.

"...just to see if you need anything, Claude!"

"I thought that you would surely be with the others, Marie."

"I have a headache...better to take it easy: a little peace and quiet suits me."

She draws up a chair next to the table at which he is working, a smile playing on her lips; familiar perfume erasing any idea of further work.

"It's such a pity that you cannot stay longer, Claude."

"...yet better this way, don't you think?"

She smiles at his choice of phrase, and they sit in silence for several seconds. Claude slowly turns to the woman who had so enriched his life, his eyes moist. Taking her head in his hands as if it was the most fragile and valuable work of art, he kisses her tenderly on the lips. Some minutes later, both dabbing at moist cheeks, it is Claude who speaks:

"I do mean what I say, Marie. Nothing in the world must allow me to upset your equilibrium – or that of your family."

"But my equilibrium – as you seem to want to call it – is already upset!"

"Perhaps so, but the more we allow this to continue, the more pain we will bring upon ourselves and to those around us. I just cannot live with that!"

Confused, torn by unrequited passion, Marie slowly gets to her feet, walks slowly to the door and leaves the room. Claude watches her; then turns to stare out of the window at a seascape as disturbed as his thoughts. Later that evening, the others return; hair and faces showing evidence of the brisk wind and sea spray against which they had to fight on their way back. It is Sophie who finds Claude in a deep armchair, head supported on a soft cushion.

"Are you not well?" She asks.

"Why do you ask, Sophie?"

"You do look rather pale and tired."

"Everyone says that these days; but I am not so young any more."

"Everyone says that you have more energy than they have, though."

"Let us say that I have set myself goals and I have to get them finished."

"...like my homework perhaps?"

"Exactly!"

The activity of his laboratory is declining. Claude had managed to persuade the *Collège* to create a histology laboratory with Louis Ranvier at its head; an excellent platform for him to pursue his ideas on nerve structure and function, while at the same time servicing the interests of other *Collège* research groups. Duval had decided to move to a teaching post in biology, and when Claude returns from Trouville, Dastre informs him that he too had been successful in gaining a chair at the Sorbonne.

Claude had become aware that his repeated illnesses and numerous absences were discouraging other would-be *prèparateurs*; by the end of the year, there would be only d'Arsonval and himself, with the trusty Lesage maintaining the laboratory. D'Arsonval had been busy in Claude's absence; now in the last stages of assembling for publication Claude's lessons on body heat. It comes as a shock to learn that d'Arsonval's father had written; disturbed by his son's decision to stay on in Paris once he was qualified. Claude immediately writes to the senior d'Arsonval to emphasize that in fact Arsène had all the attributes necessary to achieve great success in research.

A week later, d'Arsonval comes to his room brandishing a letter:

"He has agreed *Monsieur*, my father approves of my plan to stay on and do research."

"Wonderful. Let's get moving straight away on preparing you for your *doctorat*....and don't worry; I will make sure that you have a place here to continue with our research."

"Do you mind if I use the laboratory for the project I need for my thesis?"

"Not at all. What do you have in mind?"

"Just some studies on the elasticity of the lungs and how this relates to the way that blood pressure changes during breathing. I have found a way of improving the accuracy of our blood pressure measuring equipment. You might also find that equipment useful one day."

"It is a nice thought, but I think I will be content to tie up the loose ends in all our other projects. That reminds me that I must speak with you at some length about alcohol fermentation, on which I'll probably do some work while I am in St Julien later this year."

"Is that a new project?"

"Not really. I have been interested in it for many years."

D'Arsonval is frowning.

"I was cataloguing all your articles and books during your absence. You have generated more than 250 articles, and as many notes and reports; but unless I have missed something I do not believe that you have ever written about alcohol fermentation."

"Correct Arsène, and a million thanks for all your effort with the cataloguing; I'm ashamed that you had to do that for me. You know of course that I have always been interested in ferments; both the ones secreted into the bowel as well as the ones involved in breaking down *glycogène* in the liver."

"Certainly; I consider those to be your most important discoveries, Monsieur."

"Well, fermentation leading to alcohol formation is a special interest, perhaps because I fancy myself as a *vigneron*! I might discuss the subject briefly in one of my Museum lectures later this year, but first I want to complete my talk on the *milieu intérieur*."

It is indeed an important lecture; one about which Claude was somewhat anxious. His usual lectures and conclusions depended heavily on reliable and repeatable research results. For once – and possibly against his better judgment – he had to develop theory and hypothesis in public. It was the concept of the *milieu intérieur* that he wanted to promote, in the full knowledge that he would have to leave his successors to complete the proof of the concept. Once again he reflects on the image of bridges – that he had built by his research – for others to cross, explore and discover, further and deeper into medical science.

"Yes Arsène, I am going to base my talk on one of my earliest discoveries: that the blood glucose level normally fluctuates between remarkably narrow limits – except of course in the patient with diabetes. That constancy must be so important to animal survival; and not restricted to glucose, either! I want to explore the idea that the kidney is not just an overflow organ for unwanted substances: it must surely be helping to keep constant a dozen or more other chemicals in the fluids that bathe the body's cells."

Claude receives a standing ovation for his lecture: and so many questions that he finds it almost impossible to call a halt to the flood of suggestions and ideas that flow from his audience. As had become his routine, Georges Barral attends that lecture at the Museum, and afterwards invites Claude to supper at the *Café de la Paix*. They are given a quiet corner, comparatively free of cigarette and cigar fumes. Georges draws Claude's attention to Sarah Bernhardt who is sitting with a group of noisy young men and rather outlandishly dressed women.

"Did you know that she is taking the role of Doña Sol in Hugo's *Hernani* next year? Wasn't it that which inspired you to write your own play?"

"It was; what is more I have never seen it performed although I must have read it more than a dozen times! It reminds me that I would like to ask a favour of you – I want to have *Arthur de Bretagne* published – but not just yet."

"I don't think I quite understand."

"I don't want it published until at least five years after my death."

"But why, Monsieur?"

"It is quite awkward to explain, but in principle if I publish it now, it would seem out of place with my scientific publications."

Barral nods, unconvinced. Claude continues:

"Five years after my death, any image of my science is likely to have dimmed considerably...."

"Surely unlikely!"

"....and the play can be viewed more objectively. I did put an enormous amount of work – and hope – into writing it. You can't imagine how disappointed I was when Girardin and Ligier turned it down. It still pains me. It may sound arrogant, but having reached the public eye with my scientific writing, I hope that one of my publishers might eventually be interested in my play. Having it performed is yet another matter; I can't put that challenge on to your shoulders!"

"Of course, I will do what you ask. It may help – if you agree – if I write a short preface to it when it comes to it."

"I was coming to that; in fact I would hope that you mention in that preface that the play was damned by Girardin; he died three years ago as you know."

"I will certainly do that. Perhaps you can also give some thought to the matter of royalties, and to whom they should be paid. Anyhow it will surely be a long time yet before I have to do all that; I fancy that you are looking much better since you spent those days in Trouville."

Before leaving Paris, Claude spends some time in Berthelot's laboratory. His friend had developed a new sensitive method for measuring small quantities of alcohol that required reagents, glassware and measuring equipment that Claude didn't have in St Julien. Later Berthelot comes to the apartment to help Claude to pack these items carefully in rather awkward size packages, leaving Mariette to deal with the clothes and other paraphernalia that they needed.

It is unbearably hot in Claude's laboratory in St Julien. He has one immediate task; to discover if – as Pasteur had repeatedly claimed – yeast fermentation of sugars only resulted in alcohol formation if air was absent; his special concept of 'life without air'. He decides that he would first try different methods of excluding air from the vessels in which the yeast reactions would take place. It does not take long for him to realize how difficult it is to be sure that he has achieved that 'simple' objective.

Over the next three weeks, he tries the experiments several times, using the must from the recent vintage. He measures the alcohol production; annoyed that the agreement between duplicate experiments is so poor; he can therefore not rely upon them. He almost tears his hair out with frustration, and eventually decides that the high temperature in the laboratory is the problem. He would have to defer the experiments until his return to Paris; perhaps d'Arsonval would help him.

He had other projects to consider, too. In thinking about how disease arose, he had always spoken of secondary or immediate causes – in other words, *how* they arose. He had equally made the point that identifying the primary causes – *why* diseases occured – was not amenable to research. His views had not changed but he wanted to develop other terms to describe his ideas and that would mean reading a couple of books on philosophy that he had also brought with him.

Claude is determined to fulfill his functions in the Association of the Advancement of Science, which in October of that year would hold its meeting in Clermont-Ferrand in the Auvergne. Accordingly, at the end of their stay in St Julien he travels with Mariette to Clermont-Ferrand. At the station, she introduces him to her rather obese brother who had come from Tallende to welcome her for her annual visit.

He is well looked after during the scientific meeting, at which he gives the keynote speech on sensitivity in the animal and vegetable kingdoms. He includes his fascinating experiments on anesthetizing plants. The highlight of his visit is an excursion to Vichy and another to the Puy de Dome, where he inaugurates a new meteorological observatory on behalf of the Association. It is an impressive ceremony, not least because of the extraordinary panorama of extinct craters and the celebratory picnic. Unfortunately, he gets caught in the rain on his return from the event and is quite ill by the time he arrives back in Paris. Another three weeks of lectures have to be cancelled before he can return to his usual routine.

"You know Arsène, while I was giving my speech in the Auvergne, it occurred to me that we could try anesthetizing yeast cells; that might be one way of determining how much fermentation is due to the living cell and how much is strictly chemical."

"How could you be sure that anesthetized cells were not still capable of fermenting? After all, countless biochemical processes must continue in animals while they are anesthetized."

"A good point, young man!"

D'Arsonval seemed bothered.

"I still do not understand why you are pursuing this line of research so vigorously. It doesn't seem relevant to your other important work on anesthetics, nerve function, the heart and nutrition; not to speak of *glycogène* and diabetes."

"I honestly believe that we have already done our best work in those areas, Arsène. It is in the laboratories of Germany and Russia that our kind of research will now flourish; that is where the support is to be found; the money and the organization that one needs to run a proper laboratory. France is neglecting those of us in the biological sciences; virtually everyone at the Association meeting in Clermont-Ferrand was agreed on that point."

D'Arsonval is looking at Claude in disbelief.

"And then look at me, young man! You can see that I am gradually running out of steam. Each of those damned infections that I pick up seems to drag me down even further. Fermentation has always fascinated me, and of course, I admit that it is a sort of scientific indulgence. However, if it is ultimately possible to isolate the relevant yeast ferments chemically, they could be of immense value to science, even to industry. It is only a few months until you are qualified; then I really would appreciate your help with that project. I promise you that you will still have plenty of time to pursue your own ideas."

"Of course; you can count on me."

During that winter and the early part of '77, Claude is intent on committing to paper some of his more general ideas on experimentation; a sort of extension of the *'Introduction'* that he had published in '65 – and which was now selling quite well. He had always thought – and spoken – in terms of an eventual three-volume treatise on the principles of experimental medicine, but his energy is waning rapidly and he now has serious doubts whether he can ever achieve his aim. Dastre had suggested politely that he should now more regularly come over from the Sorbonne so that they could assemble the material for the book about which Claude is more excited than any other: his *Phenomena of Life Common to Animals and Plants*. Duval also now re-appeared from time to time. Claude had previously given him the task of putting together for publication his lectures on diabetes and *glycogène*. That task too had to be completed.

Spring is turning into summer; normally his brightest period. Yet he now needs every ounce of his will to get himself moving in the mornings. Everything is laced with a melancholy that he cannot recall ever having experienced before. Much to the disappointment of Georges Barral, he cannot bring himself to go to theatre to see *Hernani* and he cancels a dinner invitation at the *rue de Berry*; the last that Princesse Mathilde would be arranging before going to St Gratien for the summer. One evening he is with the Raffalovich family, so fatigued that he had to ask them to arrange a cab home even before the last course had been served. The next day he had a further recurrence of sharp abdominal pain.

Davaine is concluding a careful examination of his abdomen.

"I suspect that it's that stone again, Claude, and probably obstructing your urinary system."

"...about which you can't really do anything, Casi. Isn't that true?"

"It's a matter of whether the kidneys have been damaged by the obstruction. I'll get Gosselin to bring his cystoscope, and then we can talk again."

Twice Claude is subjected to the painful cystoscopy with the new magical machine from Vienna; first by Gosselin – the next by his assistant: on neither occasion is a stone visible. Pasteur calls in to see him soon after the second procedure:

"It hurts me to see you like this Claude; I surely hope that something can be done."

"I don't think so, Louis. I fear that the end of the road is looming. I'm sure that Davaine is right: my kidneys are failing me, as they did Pierre Rayer; and there is not much that one can do about it. You will be amused, though. The first time the cystoscopy was done by my colleague Gosselin, and after he completed the procedure, he carefully washed his hands over there in the corner. Unfortunately, the illumination on his instrument had failed."

"He saw nothing then?"

"He didn't get the chance of course. However, he sent his assistant with another cystoscope the next day, a young chap called Guyot. He washed his hands *before* he did the procedure. I just thought that you would like to know that your ideas about preventing infection are beginning to take hold – at least in the younger generation!"

"Yes. I am now in regular correspondence with Lister in Edinburgh. He seems to have persuaded the surgical fraternity on that side of the channel about the need for antisepsis. It is a shame that our country didn't accept the idea during the war – like the bloody Germans did; we might have had far fewer problems from all those horrible wounds."

"I didn't know that the Germans had used that approach."

"Of course! They are always just one step ahead; damn them! How is your work progressing?"

"I am gradually doing less, Louis; just no energy, although I am desperately keen to get everything written up and published. Dastre, Moreau and Duval are all hard at it, compiling the papers and getting them ready for the publishers. The only person I have in the *Collège* laboratory now is that bright young man, d'Arsonval. At the museum, everything's come to a halt, I am afraid."

"That's a great shame."

Pasteur gets up to leave.

"You are going to be well enough to chair the *Académie* next Thursday, I hope?"

"Yes, I am determined to be there, Louis…" He smiles."…if only to hear your paper!"

By the end of the summer, Claude is only just well enough to take the trip to St Julien. Nevertheless, he is intent on spending as much time as possible in his small laboratory. From Pasteur's paper at the *Académie* he had picked up a new and very simple technique for detecting tiny amounts of alcohol, and had brought the necessary glassware and chemicals with him in the train.

Every day finds him experimenting and making copious notes; convinced that air was indeed necessary for alcohol to be produced during the fermentation process. When Mariette comments that he is spending far too much time in such unhealthy conditions of his laboratory he tells her – with some excitement – that it is all worthwhile. He soon realizes that he needs better equipment to quantify accurately the alcohol that his experiments generate. Using wax, he seals the many small tubes containing the products of his experiments: d'Arsonval will help him with the actual measurements once he is back in Paris.

There is strange sadness in the air that autumn. Claude cannot blame the harvest, which had been even more successful than usual – and still no sign of phylloxera. Ominously, Josephine is also feeling her age and comments to Claude that she can no longer continue to provide his needs at the house. Mariette summons all her resources and does a wonderful job of providing hospitality for his many visitors. Ronne comes for a weekend, and a few old friends from the village join him for the occasional meal. He had the deep and dismal feeling that this would be his last visit to his beloved Beaujolais.

"I haven't got much longer, have I, Casi?"

Now back in the *rue des Écoles,* Davaine had just completed the most detailed examination of Claude, who had lost considerable weight; his skin of a deep sallow complexion; eyes sunken. He shakes his head.

"I wish that I could come up with something, Claude. Drink plenty: just plain water is the best, but cold tea if you need the variety. Try and manage at least three litres a day."

Claude is gazing thoughtfully out of his bedroom window at the buildings of the *Collège.*

"I have almost finished tying up the loose ends of my research. D'Arsonval knows where everything is – and of course there is the writing up and collation of my unpublished papers, some of which I might still be able to do. The rest I will have leave to Dastre. He's a good chap."

"Do you need any help with – other matters, Claude?"

"Thanks, Casi, but no. I have seen all of this coming. Marisot knows the situation, and I have made appropriate arrangements for Tony and Marie-Louise. Have you seen them recently?"

"I'm afraid not. Shouldn't they be told about your illness now?"

"I'll think about it, Casi."

Claude asks Mariette to re-organize his furniture – with the help of d'Arsonval. He now wants his bed in the salon where there is more air and space – and a better fire. He wants his table just alongside the bed where he can spread out his books and papers more conveniently. The room is brighter too; through its two windows, he can see the comings and goings at the *Collège.* Very occasionally he crosses the street to his laboratory, helped by Mariette. He and d'Arsonval work leisurely on some experiments, after which his young *protégé* would escort him back to his apartment, where they could pore over the results together. Sometimes Berthelot would join them after finishing his lectures at the *Collège.*

The winter is harsh, and Claude no longer leaves his apartment. During the day he sits huddled in his chair. With a comforting blanket over his shoulders, Mariette now brings his food to his bedside. Georges Barral often visits, offers to read him an item from the newspaper or an interesting short story that he has recently come across. However, Claude always asks him, ever so politely, to read instead from one of the many scientific journals that the librarian regularly brings over from the *Collège*.

On New Year's Day, nothing gives him as much pleasure as the visit from Marie, who had recently returned from a few weeks in the country with her sister.

"I am sorry that I didn't write to you while you were away: I'm so lazy these days; but as you can imagine, there isn't much to report." He hesitates: "By the way, you know that I've kept all your letters: there must be at least two hundred of them?"

Marie leaves her chair to kiss Claude tenderly on the cheek.

"I have all of yours, too – and they're even more numerous! Anyhow, all that is not so important now; fortunately we may see each other easily again now that I'm back in Paris. You haven't any more translations for me, have you?"

They both laugh, and a few tears appear on Marie's cheeks:

"You are being well looked after?"

"I can't ask for more; one simply wishes to feel comfortable, and Mariette sees to that admirably. Talk to me about the family."

"Grisha is well; back in Odessa again on business which seems to go well for him. Arthur has just got a job with a department of the Russian State Bank and seems happy enough. I think he will want his own apartment soon. Monsieur Bébé is as naughty as ever; hates his school even more and has started to write poetry. He asked me to give this to you..."

She passes him an envelope, which he places on the table next to the bed.

"Sophie says that she will come and see you soon. I am just going to speak with Mariette though; I have brought a little something for us to enjoy together!"

Marie leaves the room with an enormous handbag and finds Mariette in the pantry. A few minutes later they return. Mariette is carrying a tray bearing a dish piled high with his favourite *bugnes*, three glasses and a bottle of wine from his own cellars. Marie is smiling broadly:

"Mariette tells me that you have no special diet to follow – and that wine is allowed, too; so I will not accept excuses!"

Claude had completely lost his appetite, but is touched to the point of tears. He enjoys every mouthful of a delicacy that always helped him revisit the days of his youth. While Mariette returns to the kitchen, he and Marie continue to talk – of his life, of hers and of the good fortune of their meeting ten years earlier. It is probably his second glass of wine that allows him to fall into peaceful sleep in his high-backed chair. Marie adjusts his rug around his painfully thin shoulders and plants a soft kiss on his forehead.

In the adjoining study she has no difficulty in locating the countless letters that she had written to him: all on blue paper, filling two drawers of his desk and neatly tied by red ribbons. Passing the kitchen, she waves a casual farewell to Mariette – who would certainly not notice that her bag was now even more bulging than when she had arrived.

January brings snow to the streets; more visitors to his bedside. Marie, Davaine and d'Arsonval come almost daily and Paul Bert, Dastre and Duval come regularly enough with items of news for which Claude tries to show interest. Ernest Renan often visits in the evenings; just to talk. In early February, Mariette finds Claude restless and feverish after what has been a totally sleepless night. Bert had sent a letter to Claude's sister a few days earlier indicating that the situation was serious enough to justify a trip to Paris, and it is on this morning that she arrives in his apartment. Davaine had not been for some days, having himself come down with a devastating attack of double pneumonia.

To relieve the burden on Mariette, Claude's four 'disciples' take it in turns to stay the night, using a sofa in his bedroom, while Caroline is found a place to sleep with Mariette's sister who lives nearby. Bert has notified Claude's daughters of his serious condition and Tony appears one day in the apartment, yet seems unable to face her father.

Claude wakes up that morning complaining of feeling extraordinarily cold. D'Arsonval is 'on duty' and Claude asks him to place around his feet the old travelling rug that he normally wraps around his so-emaciated shoulders. He turns to his young *protegé*: "This time it will serve me for the voyage from which there is no return: the voyage of eternity."

CHAPTER 23

DISCLOSURE

How would Paris farewell a scientist who had almost become a household name, thanks to his public lectures at the *Collège*, his articles in the *revue des Deux Mondes* and the journalists' pens – forever busy publicizing the advance of French science. Recently re-appointed to the French Assembly, Paul Bert proposes – and with the full support of his fellow members – that for the first time a scientist should be awarded a state funeral. It is a remarkable event - leaving St Sulpice with a *cortège* of 4000 (and some estimate as many as 8000) mourners. On a typically dreary February morning, Bernard's body is laid to rest at the Père Lachaise cemetery amongst the similarly famous and revered – and not so far from the grave of his late mentor, Magendie. There are three funeral orations – including one by Paul Bert himself.

Later that evening they are sitting, cramped together around the table in Bernard's old room at the *Collège*: Bert, Berthelot, Dastre, d'Arsonval, Moreau, Tripier and the trusty Père Lesage. Davaine is not with them, still suffering from the ferocious attack of pneumonia that had prevented him being at his friend's side during his last hours. The atmosphere is sombre, thoughtful – each man reflecting on the man and his achievements, his moments of joy, his personal and professional disappointments, but above all the contributions Bernard had made to their individual lives. Words were sparse.

"We are going to have to tackle the loose ends, you know" observed Dastre. "Last week, he asked me to finish and submit his *Phenomena of Life* to Baillière for publication; but what about the rest?"

"There's not so much, as far as I know" commented Bert, "His *Science Expérimentale* is still with the publishers: I think that I will ask them to put Dumas' and my funeral speech in as a preface." He turns to d'Arsonval. "If am not mistaken, Arsène, the master's *Pensées* are still with you?"

"Certainly; I now have the proofs, which I will get around to checking next week. But there's also a mountain of papers on his desk in his apartment, and the drawers are still full of files. What do we do with those?"

Bert spreads his hands wide. "Well, you were his loyal assistant Arsène, so I suggest you spend a few days going through his desk. Barral is apparently dealing with the master's book collection next week, so it would be helpful if you could also clear up the academic elements quite soon."

D'Arsonval shrugs his shoulders in resignation at the task ahead when there is a knock at the door, and Pasteur's bearded face appears around the corner.

"Ah! I thought I would find you all here." He said.

"Do come and join us, Louis." Bert offers, immediately pouring a glass of wine for their visitor from a dusty bottle with an illegible label, and then topping up the glasses of his friends. Pasteur shuffles into the room awkwardly, prompting Bert to wonder if his stroke had somehow progressed since he last saw him – where was it – at the *Académie des Sciences*? He pulls up the only remaining chair for his visitor, into which he subsides with a groan.

"A sad day." Pasteur observes. They all nod.

"We've just been discussing how to deal with the master's last projects." offers Bert. "He has left us a few issues to deal with."

"I'm not surprised." said Pasteur, "when I last saw him last week, he was still full of ideas...." He hesitates, sips some wine, looks down at his boots, and without looking up, he asks "...I don't suppose that he said anything to any of you about his last series of experiments in the Beaujolais."

Bert scans the faces of the others, and is met either by a shaking head or a quizzical look. Berthelot though looks rather amused. "He often left us in the dark about his activities in St Julien. Were you interested in anything in particular, Louis?"

Pasteur looks uncomfortable. "No, nothing special, but we had a few interests in common, as you know....anyhow, I had better be off." He drains his glass, slowly gets to his feet and ambles to the door. Turning to the others he manages a vague gesture of despondency with his partly paralyzed left arm and leaves the room.

"Such an odd chap." said Berthelot, "I always felt that he used the master for his own benefit, although Claude never seemed to mind. Arsène, when you deal with the papers, keep an eye out for anything that might shed light on the fermentation experiments – that's what Louis was after, you know!"

"I wonder when your feud over alcoholic fermentation will ever be put to rest." said Dastre. "It must be at least twenty years since you and Pasteur first crossed swords."

"Something like that!" Berthelot utters with a sad smile.

There is little more discussion, and one by one they leave the *Collège*.

An array of obituaries and tributes to Bernard appear in the newspapers over the next week or so. *'All Paris weeps for him'* is only one of the many deep sentiments uttered by the press. The writer Gustave Flaubert approves of the majesty of the funeral; commenting that Bernard is more deserving of such public attention than Pope Pius IX, who had died just three days earlier! Behind closed doors, there is much discussion about Bernard's religion? Perhaps he had a vague belief in God, but even whether he received the last rites is in doubt. Certainly, during his last days he was visited by the Abbé Castelnau, curé of Saint-Séverin and Père Didon, a Dominican priest. With two other priests, Didon had been a regular attender of Bernard's lectures at the *Collège de France* and was known to have befriended him.

There would be other questions concerning the destiny of the master's ideas, such as the trail left by his philosophy in the wake of his death? Would one or other leader of a philosophical doctrine claim Claude Bernard as one of their own? If anything, it is the reverse! The man who had first inspired him, Émile Littré writes in the *Revue de Philosophie Positive* about Bernard's shortcomings as a *positiviste*. The *materialistes* disown him formally in their journal, *Pensée Nouvelle*. All this would please

Bernard in his after-life, never having wished to be classified as anything but a good scientist. Although he would never have denied borrowing parts of his personal scientific philosophy from both these schools, the consensus was that his *déterminisme* which was the most meaningful principle underlying his search for scientific truth.

Arsène d'Arsonval is standing at the window of Bernard's apartment, looking across at the steps of the *Collège*, as his master must have so often done in his last weeks. Mariette Rey enters the room.
 "Surely Monsieur, you will have something to eat or drink before you begin."
 D'Arsonval turns, smiles, unused to such concern. "Thanks, but no. Tell me, what do you plan to do now?"
 "Nothing for the moment. There is quite some wrangling over the master's various possessions, as you can imagine." She grimaces. "In fact, that solicitor Marisot is coming here this evening. My salary is paid until the end of March, so I'll stay here to keep an eye on matters, and move back to Tallende for Easter. Life is going to be pretty empty for me, you know."
 Tears begin to course down her cheeks, and d'Arsonval embraces her comfortingly; sharing, understanding only too well the depths of her distress. Leaving her sitting in Bernard's favourite chair, he walks through to the room which had served as Bernard's study and closes the door quietly behind him. Mariette had lit a fire, and deeply moved by the familiar atmosphere, he sits motionless behind the desk reminiscing, before reluctantly beginning the onerous task of sorting his late mentor's academic affairs.
 By the end of the morning, he had only managed to put in cartons the hundred or so notebooks taken from the shelf behind the desk, some of which he cannot resist leafing through – particularly fascinated by those dealing with the origin of glucose. He now starts leafing through a pile of papers which he had taken from the top drawer of the desk, and notices a single sheet of blue paper lying awkwardly between two thin cardboard files. It is a letter written in an immaculately neat feminine script and signed 'Marie'. He is unable to resist reading it.
 The first part was a response to Bernard's query about her translation of an article received from a colleague in Russia. The rest however is a warm recollection of an evening that she had obviously spent alone with Bernard. The terms of endearment were touching, and d'Arsonval

feels himself blushing at their frankness. For a while he sits motionless, wondering. His master's relationship with Marie Raffalovich had often been the subject of benevolent gossip amongst his colleagues, but discretion had been observed and many questions remained unanswered – until now. He rises from his chair, walks to the fire, and drops the letter ceremoniously into it, watching thoughtfully as the flames consume the evidence of an appropriately silent chapter in Bernard's life. D'Arsonval smiles to himself; a strange contentment diffusing through his body as he returns to the desk to continue his chores.

Hardly had he returned to his pile of assorted papers and files, when several sheets pinned together catch his eye. More correctly, it is the encircled word *OUI !* written in bold letters on the corner of the top sheet which gains his attention. Patiently, but with considerable excitement, he reads the immaculately neat and dated records of his late master's final experiments on fermentation performed in St Julien during the previous October. Pasteur's theory and Bernard's dedication to proving it incorrect is clearly the sole motive behind the entire batch of experiments as he re-reads the report. On the sheet detailing the last of the twenty experiments – dated 20th October 1877 – he sees the triumphant conclusion "...the theory is destroyed!" A broad smile stretches across his sensitive face. Roughly pushing the remaining documents into a pile on the desk, he places the sheets that he has discovered into his satchel and abruptly leaves the apartment.

"Back tomorrow!" he shouts to Mariette, "It's a bit much to deal with in one day."

He finds Berthelot alone in his laboratory, in the process of clearing up after the day's experiments.

"You must see this, Marcellin. Your suspicions were entirely correct: it's all there! Oxygen is necessary for alcoholic fermentation, but more importantly, it definitely does not need living yeasts for the process to occur."

Berthelot begins to carefully peruse the notes, d'Arsonval taking the sheets again one-by-one as he discards them – to read them yet again. When they are both finished, there is silence for a full ten minutes. "Remarkable Arsène – but puzzling, because it raises two questions. Why didn't he mention his results to us, or indeed tell Louis himself....and then, what do we do with them now?"

Again there is silence, while Berthelot makes bizarre scribbles on a piece of paper. "One thing is clear," he continues, "They can't be ignored...." he hesitates, "...in fact, I think that we are obliged to submit them for publication. Forget for a moment that he has shown Pasteur's theory to be wrong: that's a minor matter compared with the implications of his discovery. If ferments – or enzymes, as that chap Kühne now suggests we call them – can be extracted from yeasts and used completely independent of living cells, they can be almost certainly used to achieve other important chemical reactions. We should be able to make entirely new compounds. This is the beginning of a completely new branch of chemistry!"

"And his secrecy...."

There is silence again for a minute or so. "Oh! You could argue that he was unsure of the accuracy of his results, but his conclusions are so definite, and he was not a man to mislead anyone – least of all himself. Perhaps he couldn't bring himself to embarrass – to publicly show up Pasteur as being wrong – especially since he was using Pasteur's own analytical method for alcohol to provide the proof."

It was not to be easy. Berthelot had a hostile reception from the *Académie* since they had never encountered such a situation before. Bernard was no longer, so how could his results be legitimately promulgated by another scientist: the author would not be there to defend their integrity? Furthermore, considering the twenty years of public squabble, the French scientific world would know only too well that Berthelot himself was vehemently opposed to Pasteur's theory. Would publication of Bernard's results be seen as his way of getting back at his old rival? Debate and discussion continues for many weeks in the highest circles of that hallowed scientific institution, as spring gives way to one of the hottest summers in the history of Paris.

It is indeed a spectacularly hot, but clear morning in July as Armand Moreau emerges from the *Académie des Sciences*. Blinded by the sun, he collides with Pasteur on the steps. Helping him to his feet apologetically, Moreau leads him to a table at the adjoining *café* and offers him a coffee.

"I'm so sorry, Monsieur: so careless of me."

"I'm quite alright, young man – but tell me, how are things at the *Collège* now?"

"Still in some disarray, I gather. The master's old rival, Brown-Séquard has been appointed as the new prof, but he is still to arrive from America."

Pasteur shakes his head unbelievingly. "...and my old friend then – long since forgotten, I suppose?"

"Not by any means! Haven't you seen the *Revue Scientifique* this week: there's an article in it about some of his unpublished research."

Pasteur is stunned, but continues drinking his coffee, accompanied by some idle chatter concerning Brown-Séquard and his earlier relationships with Bernard. Quite abruptly he terminates the conversation, thanks Moreau for his kindness, stands up from the table and limps off towards the entrance of the *Académie*. At that time of day, the library is empty and he quickly locates the latest issue of the *Revue Scientifique*. Sure enough, no less than seven pages are devoted to experiments performed by Bernard during his final visit to his laboratory in the Beaujolais. Blood rises to his cheeks, his heart hammers insistently in his chest as he reads – and then re-reads – the article.

It is July 22nd. The president of the *Académie des Sciences* for the year 1878, the eminent optical physicist Hippolyte Fizeau has just explained the background to the last-minute addition of Pasteur's paper to the list of communications for the day. The meeting room is full to capacity, and a murmur of anticipation passes through the audience. Pasteur approaches the lectern ponderously and begins a lengthy diatribe: first against Berthelot – for daring to submit notes for publication without the authorizing hand of its author. Then he attacks Bernard himself – for having pretended to work together with him, yet preparing a report separate from him. Finally, Bernard had surely misinterpreted his results and made incorrect statements! With the permission of Fizeau, Berthelot springs to his feet to confirm that the notes as published were in Bernard's own hand and therefore '....as good as signed by him'. He also supports his own actions by emphasizing the importance to the scientific domain of Bernard's results and conclusions.

Exactly a week later, Pasteur is again at the lectern at the *Académie*, attacking Bernard's well-known attitude, that "...one had a responsibility to destroy theories" – and so uncomprehending that in December, they could have sat side by side in that very room without Bernard mentioning to him, colleague and friend, a single word about his findings? Then he attacks the editors of the *Revue* for not having published Bernard's notes intact: indeed for 'suppressing' parts of the original notes (which he, Pasteur has now had the privilege of reading). Berthelot is again on his feet. He defends his actions, and accepts an offer from Pasteur to repeat the experiments of Bernard, exactly in the way he had described them.

Two months later, Pasteur indeed performs an experiment in public intending to show that it is indeed *his* theory which is correct. Unfortunately, the result is equivocal. He then resorts to the desperate; referring to the fact that Bernard had been ill at the time and that perhaps his 'critical powers' had been impaired. Correspondence on the matter continues for some time until the autumn of 1879, when Pasteur publishes an unsupported but vigorous rejection both of Bernard's findings and his conclusions – and turns his full attention to the vaccination studies that he had begun earlier in the year.

More than a year after Davaine's severe attack of pneumonia, he is still painfully thin but his mind is as sharp as ever. The decision to retire, to move permanently to Garches to tend his immense collection of roses had been a difficult one. As guest of honour at a ceremony in the *Société d'Agriculture*, its members have just conferred on him the 1879 Béhague Prize, for Davaine is a biologist extraordinary. Of course, he had he identified the causative germ of the human and animal disease anthrax, and so laid the foundation stone for the germ theory of disease. However, his broader interest in plant biology and his concern for diseased crops had meanwhile also identified a series of responsible organisms and a resulting solution for the farmers. It was that for which he had again been honoured.

Leaving the building with his wife Georgina proudly at his side, they walk slowly down *rue de Bellechasse* and then briefly along the Seine, which they cross by the *Pont Royal*. The *Jardins des Tuileries* in early autumn had a special atmosphere, and although the roses were no longer at their best, there was plenty to observe for lovers of the plant world. Passing the octagonal *Grand Bassin* surrounded by its massive sculptures, his eyes suddenly fall on the stone bench on which Claude and he had sat in deep discussion more than thirty years earlier.

"I'm tired, Georgina: can we sit here for a moment…" he hesitates, pointing at the bench, "…you know, this is where it all started?"

Davaine removes his coat and lays it across the bench so that they could sit more comfortably. Immediately in front of them birds are pecking for elusive worms amongst the earliest fall of autumn leaves – just as they were doing, so many years earlier. A strange shiver passes down Davaine's spine.

Georgina looks at him, puzzled; "I'm not sure what you mean."

"This is exactly the spot where Claude first told me about his proposed arranged marriage to Fanny."

"Ah yes, I remember you telling me about the talk you had with him. He really did lead a strange life, didn't he Casi?"

"Well, he was certainly wedded to his work, first and foremost – and he did achieve a lot. It was so fitting that Paul managed to arrange that extraordinary funeral in his honour: how I wish I could have been there."

"What was all that fuss about his last experiments, though?"

There was silence as they both focused on a particularly persistent Robin trying to extract a worm from deep beneath the leaves.

"Quite simply, it exemplified Claude's character..."

"...meaning?"

"You know, Georgina, I loved him dearly; but he had an awkward character. Truth and proof mattered so much more to him than emotions and feelings. He and I never fell out over academic matters – and that was just as well."

Georgina patted him on the knee fondly:

"I can't imagine anyone falling out with you, Casi!"

He smiles: "...but that was Claude's problem. He simply couldn't give his family any priority – it was simply a marriage of convenience. Since Descartes was his real love, it would always remain so – and probably with enough passion to make even Marie jealous!"

They both laugh.

"Of course, Louis is just as awkward, but in a different way. He is a real self-publicist and must always be seen to be right, even if it means sailing away from the truth. I really think that those two would eventually have had a truly serious and divisive argument – had Claude indeed told him about his last fermentation results."

"Do you mean that Claude kept back his results in order to preserve peace and friendship during his last moments?"

"Well, as you know, there wasn't too much peace at the *Académie* last year! But then again, what *were* his alternatives?"

Epilogue

Eduard Büchner, a young German biochemist performs some experiments in which he extracts the contents of yeast cells under great physical pressure. He shows that the extract – totally devoid of any living tissue – is indeed able to ferment sugar to alcohol. The year of Büchner's definitive proof is 1897, two years *after* Pasteur's death! In 1907, Büchner is awarded the Nobel Prize in chemistry for this important work on enzymes, which continue to benefit human welfare through science, medicine and nutrition. In his Nobel address, he is generous enough to acknowledge Bernard's contribution as an important 'precursor' to his own discovery.

And what happened to the key people in Bernard's life?

Fanny and her two daughters moved several times before settling in Bézons, Seine-et-Oise in 1893. They established a rescue home for dogs while their house served the same function for countless cats. After Fanny's death in 1901, Tony and Marie-Louise continued to live there. They shared the inheritance of the manor house in St Julien, although they never lived there permanently. Somewhat later they surprisingly became friendly with the family of Claude's sister Caroline at Pouilly-le-Monial.

Bernard's daughters died soon after one another in 1922 and 1923, following which their house was found to be teeming with cats and in disgusting condition. His niece Jeanne (Jenny) stayed in Pouilly-le-Monial near the home of her parents. Her son Jean-Antoine Devay moved to the cottage in St Julien, married, and later died there.

Marie Raffalovich continued to interview and write articles for the *Journal of St Petersburg*, while cultivating an even bigger circle of the rich, the gifted and the famous of Paris; her husband meanwhile mainly concerned himself with business matters. Their elder son Arthur became a highly respected economist, because of his models of care for the poor and the links that he created between France and Russia. Sophie, who had been the closest of the children to Bernard, married the Irish writer and politician, William O'Brien and moved to County Cork in Ireland. When her husband died, she moved back to rural France. There she wrote memoirs which helped the author of this book discover Bernard's character in a little more depth. Marc-André (Monsieur Bébé) settled in London and became a successful poet and society figure in the exotic circle of author and playwright Oscar Wilde.

Casimir Davaine died of abdominal cancer in 1882. Louis Pasteur meanwhile devoted a considerable effort to research into anthrax, noting that chickens were immune to the disease – and that they ran body temperatures of around 44 degrees. Recalling that Davaine had shown intolerance of the anthrax *bactéridies* to high temperatures, Pasteur artificially lowered the chickens' temperature and showed that they then became susceptible to the disease. Using Jenner's concept of attenuating the cowpox 'germ' to prevent animal cowpox, he did the same with anthrax and devised a successful vaccine against the disorder – estimated to save the French economy some 20 million francs annually. His last major project was the development of a successful vaccine against rabies. Pasteur maintained his stance on fermentation until his death in 1895.

Auguste Tripier became an electrotherapist extraordinary, and achieved notoriety by using electrical stimulation to induce orgasm in women for the treatment of their hysteria! Paul Bert continued his research into deep-water physiology and decompression sickness. His studies in high altitude biology led to his later title as 'father of aerospace medicine'. He eventually gave up science for politics and was responsible for the introduction of universal free education throughout France. He was appointed Minister of Education (Public Instruction) in 1881: a post that he held only for one year until the end of Gambetta's government. Nevertheless, during that time he ensured that the *Collège de France* established a laboratory of biophysics – to be directed by d'Arsonval. Bert later supported the greater colonial France as governor of Tonkin in

Indochina, where he eventually died. 'Père' Lesage at age seventy continued his laboratory responsibilities under Brown-Séquard. He never tired of pointing out to his new master how Bernard would have done this or that procedure.

After Bernard's death, d'Arsonval published much of Bernard's hitherto unpublished material. He remained at the *Collège de France* as assistant to Édouard Brown-Séquard, and inherited the chair in 1894 on Brown-Séquard's death. After 1882 however, his main occupation was as director of the newly established biophysics laboratory at Nogent-sur-Marne. He perfected a high-sensitivity galvanometer that is still in use. He developed the first telephone for the French government; then a cordless model. He worked on the principle of the thermos flask and the technology behind liquefied gas. He eventually married his companion, Marie in 1885 (once his father was no longer alive!). She died in 1902, whereupon d'Arsonval married his stepdaughter Émilie, then age 37. His major contribution to medical science was the development of high-frequency current apparatus for use in physiotherapy, of which paramedical practice he is considered to be the founder.

The manor house in St Julien, preserved and renovated, now functions as the *Musée Claude Bernard*. It holds many relics of Bernard's life: pictures, documents, instruments and furniture. Until recently, its top floor acted as a small conference centre, attracting international participants and lively discussion on ideas and principles originally formulated by Bernard himself. Behind it lies the cottage, rather less well maintained but still providing some of the atmosphere of its original owners. Bernard's vineyards have been replanted many times over and still produce – in his name, but in small quantities – the light but fine Beaujolais wine that remains in demand throughout the world.

Vivisection continues to be practised in the course of medical research, although many sophisticated analytical methods are progressively rendering it a less-important tool for the modern investigator. Looking back 150 years, Bernard might today justifiably comment on his use of animals: "…but what *were* my alternatives?"

Interested in knowing more?

The facts forming the framework of this book come from a wide variety of resources, which are listed in the bibliography section of my academic website www.claude-bernard.co.uk. Here, you can also find (in both English and French) Bernard's detailed biography, comprehensive references to his published work, together with hypertext links to the actual manuscripts of most of his articles, lectures and books. Also included are quotations and many images relating to his life.

I have tried to remain true to the situations and relationships obtained from existing literature, in accord with the general concept of the biographical novel. The book raises many issues however, and I welcome feedback from readers on http://tinyurl.com/BernardBlog. You may also leave your reactions to this book on wisepeter3@gmail.com. *A Matter of Doubt* can also be downloaded as an e-book from Amazon/Kindle at http://tinyurl.com/matterofdoubt. This book is also available in French translation as *Un defi sans fin*, published by the Societe des Ecrivains, Paris.

Made in the USA
Charleston, SC
29 December 2011